Praise for *First Grave on the Right*

"Sexy, sassy . . . Jones's characters, both living and dead, are colorful and endearing. . . . Cheeky charm . . . sarcastic wit."　　—The Associated Press

"Jones's wickedly witty debut will delight aficionados of such humorous paranormals as Casey Daniels's Pepper Martin Mysteries and Dakota Cassidy's Accidental Friends series."　　—*Booklist* (starred review)

"Jones skillfully establishes the novel's setting and keeps up the pace with plenty of action. And let's be honest—the sex is pretty hot, too. Fans of Sherrilyn Kenyon and other authors of paranormal romance will love this series debut."　　—*Library Journal* (starred review)

"Fast-talking Charley's wicked exuberance and lust for life will appeal to fans of MaryJanice Davidson and Janet Evanovich and maybe fill a hole for those mourning the recently canceled *Ghost Whisperer*."
　　　　　　　　　　　　　　　　　　　—*Publishers Weekly*

"Jones makes a truly memorable debut with her unique tale that is sexy, mysterious, and sarcastically fun!"　　—*RT Book Reviews*

"It's a fun, sexy, exciting read."　　—*Suspense Magazine*

"A true paranormal princess has been proclaimed. Bravo Ms. Jones, you have just hit the big time. . . . A brilliant novel . . . Do not walk; run to get your copy of *First Grave on the Right* when it debuts."　　—*Night Owl Reviews*

"This book is full of surprises and fun to be had for all. I barely finished this book and already can't wait to visit with Charley Davidson again in the next novel, *Second Grave on the Left*. *First Grave on the Right* deserves nothing less than a Five Angel, Recommend Read status."　　—*Fallen Angel Reviews*

"Hold on to your hats and get comfortable, you won't want to get up for a long, long time as Charley Davidson sweeps you in and holds on tight."
　　　　　　　　　　　　　　　　　　　—*The Romance Reviews*

"A smashing, award-winning debut novel."　　—*Goodreads*

"In the currently crowded paranormal world, *First Grave on the Right* is a bright beacon of originality. Jones writes with a sharp, addictively acerbic sense of humor, and she combines genres with the carefully controlled precision of a master literary mixologist." —*Reader to Reader . . .*

"A fast and fun read [that] will leave you begging for more. *Second Grave on the Left* is due out in August, and I can't wait." —*Fresh Fiction*

"This book takes a humorous view on the old Grim Reaper cliché. Charley is a smart, enjoyable character with enough snark to keep one laughing even as the plot darkens." —*Affaire de Coeur*

"The best debut novel I've read in years! Hilarious and heartfelt, sexy and surprising . . . I'm begging for the next one!!"
—J. R. Ward, *New York Times* bestselling author of *Lover Avenged*

"I am furiously envious of Darynda Jones and rue the day she came up with this concept, damn her eyes. *First Grave on the Right* . . . kidnapped me from the first paragraph, and didn't let go until the exceedingly yummy conclusion."
—MaryJanice Davidson, *New York Times* bestselling author of *Undead and Unwelcome* and *Me, Myself and Why?*

"*First Grave on the Right* is smart, sharp, and wickedly entertaining. Grab this one."
—Jayne Ann Krentz, *New York Times* bestselling author of *Fired Up*

"*First Grave on the Right* is witty, darkly thrilling, and oh, so sexy!"
—Gena Showalter, *New York Times* bestselling author of *The Darkest Whisper*

"*First Grave on the Right* is a phenomenal debut! This series opener has it all— rollicking humor, sizzling sexual tension, and a spine-tingling mystery. I'm eagerly awaiting the next Charley Davidson tale!"
—Kresley Cole, *New York Times* bestselling author of *Pleasure of a Dark Prince*

First Grave on the Right

Darynda Jones

ST. MARTIN'S GRIFFIN
NEW YORK

For Annette.

My beautiful sister.

You are like sunshine:

bright,

incandescent,

and oddly irritating at times.

But what else are sisters for?

FIRST GRAVE ON THE RIGHT. Copyright © 2011 by Darynda Jones. All rights reserved. Printed in the United States of America. For information, address St. Martin's Press, 175 Fifth Avenue, New York, N.Y. 10010.

www.stmartins.com

The Library of Congress has cataloged the hardcover edition as follows:

Jones, Darynda.
    First grave on the right / Darynda Jones.—1st ed.
        p. cm.
    ISBN 978-0-312-66275-2
    1. Women private investigators—Fiction.   2. Women mediums—Fiction.   I. Title.
    PS3610.O6236F57 2011
    813'.6—dc22

                                                                                    2010039154

ISBN 978-0-312-57742-1 (trade paperback)

First St. Martin's Griffin Edition: July 2011

10 9 8 7 6 5 4 3 2 1

Acknowledgments

A huge, heartfelt thank-you to:

My amazing agent, Alexandra Machinist. Thank you for believing in this book and for putting up with me. Your energy is infectious. If you could bottle it, you'd make a fortune.

My brilliant editor, Jennifer Enderlin. Your enthusiasm is humbling. Your hard work, inspiring. Your incredible savvy, priceless.

Every member of my family, even the unstable ones. Where would I be without such extraordinary kin? The Eakins Clans, the Duartes, the Joneses, the Campbells, the Scotts, the Swopeses, Dooley and Snick, and last but never, ever least, the Mighty, Mighty Jones Boys: Danny, Jerrdan, Casey, and our newest addition, Konner Mason. You all have my heart and undying gratitude.

The goddesses of LERA, each and every one, especially my critique goddess, Tammy Baumann.

My Ruby-Slippered Sisters, the 2009 RWA Golden Heart finalists. Your warmth and support have been invaluable. Thank you for your friendship and sisterhood.

A special thanks to those who have read my work and have lived to tell the tale. I am especially grateful for the feedback from: Annette, Dan Dan, DD, Ashlee, Tammy, Sherri, Bria, Kiki, Emily, Klisty, Gabi, Carol, Melvin, Cathy, Michael, Kit, Danielle Tanner (aka D2), and to my pimp, Quentin. I cherish all your input. And so do my books. And I have to thank Mike Davidson for his unending patience.

Speaking of those who have lived to tell the tale, a gargantuan thank-you to J.R. Ward, MaryJanice Davidson, Jayne Ann Krentz, Gena Showalter, and Kresley Cole. I cannot thank you enough. I considered sending fruit baskets, but even produce falls short when trying to express the depth of my gratitude. Thank you from the nethermost regions of my heart.

And to Mom. Hope your trip up was magical. May your hips always sway to Tom Jones. Say hey to Dad for us.

Chapter One

Better to see dead than be dead.
—CHARLOTTE JEAN DAVIDSON, GRIM REAPER

I'd been having the same dream for the past month—the one where a dark stranger materialized out of smoke and shadows to play doctor with me. I was starting to wonder if repetitive exposure to nightly hallucinations resulting in earth-shattering climaxes could have any long-term side effects. Death via extreme pleasure was a serious concern. The prospect led to the following dilemma: Do I seek help or buy drinks all around?

This night was no exception. I was having a killer dream that featured a set of capable hands, a hot mouth, and a creative employment of lederhosen when two external forces tried to lure me out of it. I did my darnedest to resist, but they were fairly persistent external forces. First, a frosty chill crept up my ankle, the icy caress jolting me out of my red-hot dream. I shivered and kicked out, unwilling to acknowledge the summons, then tucked my leg into the thick folds of my Bugs Bunny comforter.

Second, a soft but persistent melody played in the periphery of my consciousness like a familiar song I couldn't quite place. After a moment, I realized it was the cricketlike chime of my new phone.

With a heavy sigh, I pried open my eyes just enough to focus on the numbers glowing atop my nightstand. It was 4:34 A.M. What kind of sadist called another human being at 4:34 in the morning?

A throat cleared at the foot of my bed. I turned my attention to the dead guy standing there, then lowered my lids and asked in a gravelly voice, "Can you get that?"

He hesitated. "Um, the phone?"

"Mmm."

"Well, I'm kind of—"

"Never mind." I reached for the phone and grimaced as a jolt of pain ripped through me, reminding me I'd been beaten senseless the night before.

Dead Guy cleared his throat again.

"Hello," I croaked.

It was my uncle Bob. He bombarded me with words, of all things, apparently clueless to the fact that predawn hours rendered me incapable of coherent thought. I concentrated super duper hard on concentrating and made out three salient phrases: *busy night, two homicides, ass down here.* I even managed a reply, something resembling, "What twirly nugget are you from?"

He sighed, clearly annoyed, then hung up.

I hung up back, pressing a button on my new phone that either disconnected the call or speed-dialed the Chinese takeout around the corner. Then I tried to sit up. Similar to the coherent-thought problem, this was easier said than done. While I normally weighed around

125 . . . ish, for some unexplainable reason, between the hours of partially awake and fully awake, I weighed a solid 470.

After a brief, beached whale–like struggle, I gave up. The quart
of Chunky Monkey I ate after getting my ass kicked had probably
been a bad idea.

In too much pain to stretch, I let a lengthy yawn overtake me instead, winced at the soreness shooting through my jaw, then looked
back at Dead Guy. He was blurry. Not because he was dead, but because it was 4:34 A.M. And I'd recently had my ass kicked.

"Hi," he said nervously. He had a wrinkled suit, round-rimmed
glasses, and mussed hair that made him look part young-wizard-we-
all-know-and-love and part mad scientist. He also had two bullet holes
on the side of his head with blood streaking down his right temple and
cheek. None of these details were a problem. The problem resided in
the fact that he was in my bedroom. In the wee hours of dawn. Standing over me like a dead Peeping Tom.

I eyed him with my infamous death stare, second only to my infamous fluster stare, and got a response immediately.

"Sorry, sorry," he said, stumbling over his words, "didn't mean to
frighten you."

Did I look frightened? Clearly my death stare needed work.

Ignoring him, I inched out of bed. I had on a Scorpions hockey jersey I'd snatched off a goalie and a pair of plaid boxers—same team, different position. Chihuahuas, tequila, and strip poker. A night that is
forever etched at the top of my Things I'll Never Do Again list.

With teeth clenched in agony, I dragged all 470 throbbing pounds
toward the kitchen and, more important, the coffeepot. Caffeine would
chisel the pounds off, and I'd be back to my normal weight in no time.

Because my apartment was roughly the size of a Cheez-It, it didn't
take me long to feel my way to the kitchen in the dark. Dead Guy

followed me. They always follow me. I could only pray this one would keep his mouth shut long enough for the caffeine to kick in, but alas, no such luck.

I'd barely pressed the ON button when he started in.

"Um, yeah," he said from the doorway, "it's just that I was murdered yesterday, and I was told you were the one to see."

"You were told that, huh?" Maybe if I hovered over the pot, it would develop an inferiority complex and brew faster just to prove it could.

"This kid told me you solve crimes."

"He did, huh?"

"You're Charley Davidson, right?"

"That's me."

"Are you a cop?"

"Not especially."

"A sheriff's deputy?"

"Uh-uh."

"A meter maid?"

"Look," I said, turning to him at last, "no offense, but you could have died thirty years ago, for all I know. Dead people have no sense of time. Zero. Zip. *Nada.*"

"Yesterday, October eighteenth, five thirty-two P.M., double gunshot wound to the head, resulting in traumatic brain injury and death."

"Oh," I said, reining in my skepticism. "Well, I'm not a cop." I turned back to the pot, determined to break its iron will with my infamous death stare, second only to—

"So, then, what are you?"

I wondered if *your worst nightmare* would sound silly. "I'm a private investigator. I hunt down adulterers and lost dogs. I do not solve murder cases." I did, actually, but he didn't need to know that. I'd just come off a big case. I was hoping for a few days' respite.

"But this kid—"

"Angel," I said, disappointed that I didn't exorcise that little devil when I had the chance.

"He was an angel?"

"No, his name is Angel."

"His name is Angel?"

"Yes. Why?" I asked, becoming disenchanted with the Angel game.

"I just thought it might have been his occupation."

"It's his name. And believe you me, he is anything but."

After a geological epoch passed in which single-celled organisms evolved into talk show hosts, Mr. Coffee was still holding out on me. I gave up and decided to pee instead.

Dead Guy followed me. They always—

"You're very . . . bright," he said.

"Um, thanks."

"And . . . sparkly."

"Uh-huh." This was nothing new. From what I'd been told, the departed see me as something of a beacon, a brilliant entity—emphasis on the *brilliant*—they can see from continents away. The closer they get, the sparklier I become. If *sparklier* is a word. I've always considered the sparkles a plus of being the only grim reaper this side of Mars. And as such, my job was to lead people into the light. Aka, the portal. Aka, me. But it didn't always go smoothly. Kind of like leading a horse to water and whatnot. "By the way," I said, glancing over my shoulder, "if you do see an angel, a real one, run. Quickly. In the opposite direction." Not really, but freaking people out was fun.

"Seriously?"

"Seriously. Hey—" I stopped and twirled to face him. "—did you touch me?" Somebody practically molested my right ankle, somebody cold, and since he'd been the only dead guy in the room . . .

"What?" he said, indignant.

"Earlier, when I was in bed."

"Pffft, no."

I narrowed my eyes, let my gaze linger menacingly, then resumed my hobble to the bathroom.

I needed a shower. Bad. And I couldn't dillydally all day. Uncle Bob would stroke.

But as I stepped toward the bathroom, I realized the worst part of my morning—the *let there be light* part—was fast approaching. I groaned and considered dillydallying despite the state of Uncle Bob's arteries.

Just suck it up, I told myself. It had to be done.

I placed a shaky hand on the wall, held my breath, and flipped the switch.

"I'm blind!" I yelled, shielding my eyes with my arms. I tried to focus on the floor, the sink, the Clorox ToiletWand. Nothing but a bright white blur.

I totally needed to lower my wattage.

I stumbled back, caught myself, then forced one foot in front of the other, refusing to back down. I would not be stopped by a lightbulb. I had a job to do, dammit.

"Did you know you have a dead guy in your living room?" he asked.

I turned back to the dead guy, then glanced across the room to where Mr. Wong stood, his back to us, his nose buried in the corner. Looking back at dead guy number one, I asked, "Isn't that a bit like the pot calling the kettle African-American?"

Mr. Wong was a dead guy, too. A teeny-tiny one. He couldn't have been more than five feet tall, and he was gray—all of him, almost monochrome in his translucence, with a gray uniform of some sort and ash gray hair and skin. He looked like a Chinese prisoner of war. And he stood in my corner day after day, year after year. Never moving, never speaking. Though I could hardly blame him for not getting out more with his coloring and all, even I thought Mr. Wong was a nut job.

Of course, the mere fact that I had a ghost in the corner wasn't the creepiest part, and the moment Dead Guy realized Mr. Wong wasn't actually *standing* in the corner, but was hovering, toes several inches from the floor, he'd freak.

I lived for such moments.

"Good morning, Mr. Wong!" I semi-shouted. I wasn't sure if Mr. Wong could hear. Probably a good thing, since I had no idea what his real name was. I just named him Mr. Wong in the interim between creepy dead guy in the corner and normal walking-around dead guy he would someday become if I had anything to say about it. Even dead people needed a healthy sense of well-being.

"Is he in time-out?"

Good question. "I have no idea why he's in that corner. Been there since I rented the apartment."

"You rented the apartment with a dead guy in the corner?"

I shrugged. "I wanted the apartment, and I figured I could cover him up with a bookcase or something. But the thought of having a dead guy hovering behind my copy of *Sweet Savage Love* gnawed at me. I couldn't just leave him there. I don't even know if he likes romance."

I looked back at the newest incorporeal being to grace me with his presence. "What's your name, anyway?"

"Oh, how rude of me," he said, straightening and walking forward for a handshake. "I'm Patrick. Patrick Sussman. The Third." He stopped short and eyed his hand, then glanced back up sheepishly. "I don't guess we can actually—"

I took his hand in a firm shake. "Actually, Patrick, Patrick Sussman the Third, we can."

His brows drew together. "I don't understand."

"Yeah, well," I said, going into the bathroom, "join the club."

As I closed the door, I heard Patrick Sussman III freak out at last.

"Oh, my god. He's just . . . hovering."

It's the simple things in life, and all that crap.

The shower felt like heaven covered in warm chocolate syrup. Steam and water rushed over me as I inventoried each muscle, adding a mental asterisk if it ached.

My left biceps definitely needed an asterisk, which made sense. The asshole in the bar last night wrenched my arm with the apparent intention of ripping it off. Sometimes being a private investigator meant dealing with society's less-than-savory characters, like a client's abusive husband.

Next, I checked my entire right side. Yep, it ached. Asterisk. Probably happened when I fell against the jukebox. Stealth and grace, I ain't.

Left hip, asterisk. No idea.

Left forearm, double asterisks. Most likely when I blocked asshole's punch.

And then, of course, my left cheek and jaw, quadruple asterisks, where my block proved utterly useless. Asshole was simply too strong and too fast, and the punch had been too unexpected. I went down like a drunken cowgirl trying to line dance to Metallica.

Embarrassing? Yes. But strangely enlightening as well. I'd never been KO'd before. I thought it would hurt more. Somehow, when you're knocked senseless, the pain doesn't show up till later. Then it's a cold, heartless bitch.

Still, I'd made it through the night with no permanent damage. Always a good thing.

As I tried to work some of the soreness out of my neck, my thoughts turned to the dream I'd had, the same dream I'd been having every night for a month. And it was proving harder and harder to vanquish the remnants after I woke, the lingering touches, the fog of hunger. Every night in my dreams, a man appeared from the darkest recesses of my mind, as if he'd been waiting for me to fall asleep. His mouth, full, masculine, would sear my flesh. His tongue, like flames across my skin, would send tiny sparks quaking through my body. Then he would dip south, and the heavens would open and a chorus singing hallelujah would ring out in perfect harmony.

At first the dreams started small. A touch. A kiss light as air. A smile I could see only in the periphery of negative space, finding beauty where I'd never expected. Then the dreams developed, became stronger and frighteningly intense. For the first time in my life, I'd actually climaxed in my sleep. And not just once. In the last month, I'd come often, on more nights than not, in fact. All at the hands—and other body parts—of a dream lover I couldn't see, not fully. Yet I knew he was the epitome of sensuality, of male magnetism and allure. And I knew also that he reminded me of someone.

I figured my dreams were being invaded, but by whom? I've had the ability to see the departed all my life. I had been born a grim reaper, after all. *The* grim reaper, though I didn't discover *that* little jewel until I was in high school. Even so, the departed have never been able to enter my dreams, to make me quake and quiver and, I admit, beg.

As far as my ability goes, there's nothing particularly special about it. The departed exist on one plane, and the human race exists on another, and somehow—whether by freak accident, divine intervention, or psychological disorder—I exist on both. A perk, I suppose, of grim reaperism. But it's all quite simple. No trances. No crystal balls. No channel surfing the dead from one plane to the next. Just a girl, a few ghosts, and the entire human race. What could be easier?

And yet, he was something more, something . . . not dead. At least he seemed that way. The person in my dreams radiated heat. Dead people are cold, just like in the movies. Their presence will fog your breath, make you shiver, stand your hair on end. But the man in my dreams, the dark, seductive stranger I'd become addicted to, was a furnace. He was like the scalding water rushing over me, sensual and painful and everywhere at once.

And the dreams were so real, the feelings and responses his touch evoked so vivid. I could almost feel him now, his hands sliding up my thighs, as if he were in the shower with me at that very moment. I could feel his palms rest on my hips and the length of his hard body press against my backside. I reached behind me, ran my fingers along his steel buttocks as he pulled me onto him. His muscles contracted and released underneath my touch, like the tide's flow and ebb under the sway of the moon. When I forced a hand between us, slid it down his abdomen to encircle his erection, he hissed in a breath of pleasure and hugged me to him.

I felt his mouth at my ear, his breath fan over my cheek. We had never spoken. The heat and intensity of the dreams left little room for conversation.

But for the first time, I heard a whispered utterance, faint and almost imperceptible. "Dutch."

My heartbeats skyrocketed, and I jerked to attention, glancing around the shower, searching for ghosts in cracks and crevices. Nothing. Had I fallen asleep? In the shower? I couldn't have. I was still standing. Barely. I clutched the shower valves to keep myself upright, wondering what in the crazy afterlife had just happened.

After steadying myself, I turned off the water and grabbed a towel. *Dutch*. I'd distinctly heard the word *Dutch*.

Only one person on Earth had ever called me Dutch, once, a very long time ago.

Chapter Two

So many dead people, so little time.
—CHARLOTTE JEAN DAVIDSON

Still reeling from the potential identity of Dream Guy, I wrapped myself in the towel and slid open the shower curtain. Sussman poked his head through the door, and my heart took a belly dive into the shallow end of shock, cutting itself on the jagged nerve endings there.

I jumped, then placed a calming hand over my heart, annoyed that I was still so easily surprised. As many times as I've seen dead people appear out of nowhere, you'd think I'd be used to it.

"Holy crap, Sussman. I wish you guys would learn to knock."

"Incorporeal being," he said, giving attitude.

I stepped out of the shower and grabbed a squirt bottle from my vanity. "You set one foot in this bathroom, and I will melt your face with my transcendental pest repellent."

His eyes widened. "Seriously?"

"No," I said, my shoulders deflating. I had a really hard time lying to the departed. "It's just water. But don't tell Mr. Habersham, the dead guy in 2B. This bottle is the only thing that keeps that dirty old man out of my bathroom."

Sussman's brows arched as he scanned my lack of attire. "Can't say that I blame him."

I glowered and swung open the door, pulling it through his face and disorienting him. He put one hand on his forehead and one on the doorjamb to ride out the dizzy spell. Newbies were so easy. After giving him a second to get his bearings, I pointed to the sign tacked on the outside of my bathroom door.

"Memorize it," I ordered, then slammed the door shut again.

" 'No dead people beyond this door,' " he read aloud from beyond the door. " 'And, yes, if you suddenly have the ability to walk through walls, you're dead. You're not lying somewhere in a drainage ditch waiting to wake up. Get over it, and stay the hell out of my bathroom.' " He stuck his head through the door again. "That's a bit harsh, don't you think?"

My sign may have seemed a tad brutal to the untrained eye, but it usually got my message across. Unless it was Mr. Habersham. Him I had to threaten. Often.

Even with the sign, I tended to wash my hair as if the apartment were on fire. Dead people standing in the shower with me after the rinse cycle was a bit much. You're never quite the same after a shotgun-blast-to-the-head pops in for tea and a sauna.

I pointed a sharp index finger. "Out!" I ordered, then turned back to the quandary that was my bruised and swollen face.

Applying foundation after you've been knocked on your ass was more of an art than a science. It required patience. And layers. But after the third layer, I ran out of patience and washed my face of the whole matter. Seriously, who was going to see me this early in the morning? By the time I pulled my chocolate brown hair into a ponytail, I almost had myself convinced that bruises and black eyes added a certain je ne sais quoi to my appearance. A little concealer, a little lipstick, and voilà, I was ready for the world. The question remained, however, Was the world ready for me?

I stepped out of the bathroom in a plain white button-down and jeans, hoping the generous expanse of bosom I carried would help me achieve a solid 9.2 on a scale of 10. I had breasts aplenty. Just in case, I undid the top button to show more cleavage. Maybe no one would notice the fact that my face resembled a topographical map of North America.

"Wow," Sussman said, "you look hot even with the slight disfigurement."

I stopped and turned toward him. "What did you say?"

"Um, you look hot?"

"Let me ask you something," I said, easing closer. He took a wary step back. "When you were alive, like, five minutes ago, would you have told some chick you'd just met that she looked hot?"

He thought about that a moment, then answered, "No. My wife would divorce me."

"Then why is it the moment you guys die, you think you can say whatever you want to whomever you want?"

He thought about that a moment, too. "Because my wife can't hear me?" he offered.

I stabbed him with the full power of my death stare, likely blinding him for all eternity. Then I grabbed my handbag and keys. Just before I shut off the lights, I turned back and said with a wink, "Thanks for the compliment."

He smiled and followed me out the door.

Apparently, I wasn't as hot as Sussman thought. I was freezing, in fact. And, naturally, I'd forgotten my jacket. Too lazy to go back for it,

I hurried into my cherry red Jeep Wrangler. Her name was Misery, in homage to the master of horror and all things creepy. Sussman oozed into the passenger's seat.

"The grim reaper, huh?" he asked as I clicked my seat belt.

"Yep." I hadn't realized he knew my job title. He and Angel must have had quite the talk. I turned the key, and Misery purred to life around me. Thirty-seven more payments, and this baby was all mine.

"You don't look like the grim reaper."

"You've met him, have you?"

"Well, no, not really," he said.

"My robe's at the cleaners."

That got a sheepish chuckle. "And your scythe?"

I shot him an evil grin and turned on the heater. "Speaking of crimes," I said, changing the subject, "did you happen to see the shooter?"

"Neither hide nor hair."

"So . . . no."

He slid his glasses up with an index finger. "No. I didn't see anyone."

"Darn. That doesn't help." I turned left onto Central. "Do you know where you are? Where your body is? We're headed downtown. This might be you."

"No, I had just pulled into my drive. My wife and I live in the Heights."

"So, you're married?"

"Five years," he said, a sadness permeating his voice. "Two kids. Girls. Four and eighteen months."

I hated that part. The people-left-behind part. "I'm so sorry."

He looked at me with *that* expression, that you-can-see-dead-people-so-you-must-have-all-the-answers expression of so many who'd come before him. He was about to be very disappointed.

"It's going to be hard on them, isn't it?" he asked, surprising me with the direction of his thoughts.

"Yes, it will be," I answered honestly. "And your wife will scream and cry and go through a depression from hell. Then she'll find a strength she never knew she had." I looked directly at him. "And she'll live. For the girls, she'll live."

That seemed to satisfy him for the moment. He nodded and stared out the window. We drove the rest of the way downtown in silence, which gave me unwanted time to think about dream lover. If I was right, his name was Reyes. I had no idea if Reyes was his last name or his first, or where he was from, or where he was now, or any other thing about him, for that matter. But I knew his name was Reyes, and I knew he was beautiful. Unfortunately, he was also dangerous. The one and only time I'd met him was years ago, when we were both in our teens. Our one encounter was full of threats and tension and skin and his lips so close to mine, I could almost taste him. I never saw him again.

"There it is," Sussman said, dragging me from my thoughts.

He'd spotted the crime scene several blocks away. Red and blue lights undulated along buildings, pulsing through the pitch black morning. As we drove closer, the bright spotlights set up for the investigators lit up half a city block. It looked like the sun had risen in that one spot alone. I saw Uncle Bob's SUV and pulled into a hotel parking lot nearby.

Before we got out, I turned to Sussman. "Hey, you didn't happen to see anyone in my apartment, did you?"

"You mean, besides Mr. Wong?"

"Yeah. You know, like, a guy?"

"No. Was somebody else there?"

"Nah, forget it."

I had yet to figure out how Reyes did the magic shower trick. Unless I had the uncanny ability to sleep standing up, he could do more than just enter my dreams.

After I got out—and Sussman more or less fell out—I looked for Uncle Bob. He stood about forty yards away, a spotlight casting an eerie glow around him as he gave me the evil eye. He's not even Italian. I'm not sure that's legal.

Uncle Bob, or Ubie as I liked to call him—though rarely to his face—is my dad's brother and a detective for the Albuquerque Police Department. I guess he got a life sentence, because my dad was a cop, too, but he retired years ago and bought a bar on Central. My apartment building sits directly behind it. I make a little extra cash occasionally tending bar for him, which brings my current job count to 3.7. I'm a private investigator when I have clients, a bartender when my dad needs me, and technically, I'm on the APD payroll as well. On paper, I'm a consultant. Probably because it sounds important. In real life, I'm the secret to Uncle Bob's success, just as I was for my dad when he worked APD. My ability rocketed them through promotion after promotion until they both became detectives. It's amazing how easy it is to solve crimes when you can ask the victims who did it.

The .7 stemmed from my illustrious career as the grim reaper. While it does take up a significant amount of my time, I never profit from that part of my life. So, I'm still undecided as to whether or not I should call it a job.

We walked under the police tape at exactly five thirtyish. Uncle Bob was livid but surprisingly stroke-free.

"It's almost six," he said, tapping his watch.

That'd teach me.

He wore the same brown suit as the day before, but his jaw was clean shaved, his mustache neatly combed, and he smelled like medium-priced cologne. He pinched my chin and maneuvered my face to get a good look at the bruises.

"It's much closer to five thirty," I argued.

"I called you over an hour ago. And you need to learn to duck."

"You called me at four thirty-four," I said, swiping at his hand. "I hate four thirty-four. I think four thirty-four should be banned and replaced with something more reasonable, like, say, nine twelve."

Uncle Bob released a long breath and popped the rubber band at his wrist. He'd told me it was part of his anger management program, but how the infliction of pain could possibly help control anger was beyond me. Still, I was always willing to help a surly relative in need.

I leaned into him. "I could Taser you if you think it'll help."

He slid me the evil eye again, but he did it with a grin, and that made me happy.

Apparently, the supervisor for the Office of the Medical Investigator had already done his part, so we could walk onto the crime scene. As we did, I ignored the plethora of sideways glances directed my way. The other officers have never understood how I do what I do, how I solve cases so fast, and they look at me with wary suspicion. I guess I can't blame them. Wait a minute. Yes, I can.

Just then I noticed Garrett Swopes, aka pain-in-the-ass skiptracer, standing over the body. I rolled my eyes so far back into my head, I almost seized. Not that Garrett wasn't good at his job. He'd studied under the legendary Frank M. Ahearn, probably the most famous skiptracer in the world. From what I'd heard, thanks to Mr. Ahearn, Garrett could find Hoffa if he put his mind to it.

He was also easy on the retinas. He had short black hair, wide shoulders, skin like Mayan chocolate, and smoky gray eyes that could capture a girl's soul if she stared into them long enough.

Thank God I had the attention span of a gnat.

If I had to guess, I would say he was only half African-American. The lighter skin tone and gray eyes screamed hybrid. I just didn't know if his other half was Latino or Anglo. Either way, he had a confident walk and easy smile that turned heads wherever we went. So, looks were certainly not an area he needed to work on.

No, Garrett was a consummate pain in the ass for other reasons. As I stepped into the light, he looked at the bruises on my jaw and smirked. "Blind date?"

I did that thing where you scratch your eyebrow and flip someone off at the same time. I'm good at multitasking like that. Garrett just smirked. Again.

Okay, it wasn't his fault he was an ass. He used to like me until Uncle Bob, in a drunken stupor, told him *our little secret*. Naturally, he didn't believe a word of it. Who would? That was about a month ago, and our friendship took a nosedive from barely there to nonexistent. He's pretty much slotted me for the loony bin. And Uncle Bob, too, for believing I can actually see the departed. Some people have no imagination.

"What are you doing here, Swopes?" I asked, a little more than annoyed that I had to deal with him.

"I thought this might be one of my skips."

"Is it?"

"Not unless meth heads wear three-piece suits and fifteen-hundred-dollar Crisci loafers."

"That's too bad. I'm sure it's much easier to collect your fee when the skip is dead."

Garrett shrugged, semi-agreeing.

"Actually," Uncle Bob said, "I asked him to stick around, you know, for an extra set of eyes."

I was doing my darnedest to keep my own eyes off the body—dead people I could handle, dead bodies not so much—but a movement in my periphery had me zeroing in on that very thing.

"So, are you getting anything?" Uncle Bob asked—he still thinks I'm psychic—but I was too busy staring at the dead guy in the dead body to answer.

I inched over and nudged the body with my foot. "Dude, what are you still doing in there?"

The dead guy looked at me with wide eyes. "I can't move my legs."

I snorted. "You can't move your arms either, or your feet or your freaking eyelids. You're dead."

"Jesus H.," Garrett said through clenched teeth.

"Look." I turned to face him head-on. "You play on your side of the sandbox, and I'll play on mine. *Comprende?*"

"I'm not dead."

I turned back. "Hon, you're as dead as my great-aunt Lillian, and trust me, that woman is now in a perpetual state of decomposition."

"No, I'm not. I'm not dead. Why isn't anyone trying to revive me?"

"Um, because you're dead?"

I heard Garrett mutter something under his breath, then stalk off. Nonbelievers were such drama queens.

"Okay, fine, if I'm dead, how am I talking to you? And why are you so sparkly?"

"It's a long story. Just trust me, mister, you're dead."

Just then, Sergeant Dwight walked up, all crisp and formal looking in his APD uniform and military buzz. "Ms. Davidson, did you just kick that dead body?"

"For heaven's sake, I'm not dead!"

"No."

Sergeant Dwight tried his hand at a death stare. I tried not to giggle.

"I got this, Sergeant," Uncle Bob said.

The sarge turned to him, and they eyed each other a full minute before he spoke. "Would you mind not contaminating my crime scene with your relatives?"

"*Your* crime scene?" Uncle Bob asked. A vein in his temple started pulsing.

I considered popping the rubber band at his wrist, but I still had doubts as to its efficacy. "Hey, Uncle Bob," I said, patting his arm, "let's go over here and talk, shall we?"

I turned and left without waiting, hoping Uncle Bob would follow. He did. We strolled past the spotlights to a tree and assumed innocuous conversational positions. I tossed a smile to Sergeant Dwight Yokel that leaned heavily toward smart-ass. I think he growled. Good thing I wasn't into people-pleasing.

"Well?" Uncle Bob asked as Garrett reluctantly rejoined us.

"I don't know. He won't get out of his body."

"He what?" Garrett raked a hand through his hair. "This is classic."

I ignored him and watched as Sussman walked over to a third dead person on the scene, a striking woman with blond hair and a fire engine red skirt suit. She screamed femininity and power. I liked her instantly. Sussman shook her hand. Then they both turned to look at the only dead person present lying in a pool of his own blood.

"I think they know each other," I said.

"Who?" Uncle Bob asked, glancing around as if he could see them.

"You got an ID on this guy?"

"Yeah." He fished out his notebook, reminding me I needed to dash into Staples. All my little notebooks were filled to maximum capacity. As a result, I kept writing pertinent information on my hand, then accidentally washing it off. "Jason Barber. A lawyer at—"

"Sussman, Ellery, and Barber," Sussman said in unison with Uncle Bob.

"You're a lawyer?" I asked him.

"Sure am. And this is my partner, Elizabeth Ellery."

"Hey, Elizabeth," I said, reaching out to shake her hand. Garrett pinched the rim of his nose.

"Ms. Davidson, Patrick told me you can see us."

"Yep."

"How—?"

"Long story. But first," I said, heading off the barrage of questions, "let me get this straight: You are all three partners at the same law firm, and you all three died last night?"

"Who else died last night?" Uncle Bob asked, tearing through his notebook.

"We were all three *murdered* last night," Sussman corrected. "All nine-millimeter double taps to the head."

Elizabeth raised her perfectly arched brows at him. "Double taps?"

He smiled sheepishly and tried to kick the dirt at his feet. "I heard the cops talking."

"I only got two homicides."

I looked up at Uncle Bob. "You have only two homicides from last night? There were three."

Garrett went still, probably wondering what I was up to, how I could know any such thing since I couldn't possibly see dead people, so dead people couldn't possibly tell me they were dead. It just wasn't possible.

Uncle Bob studied his notebook. "We got a Patrick Sussman found outside his home in the Mountain Run area, and this guy, a Jason Barber."

"Okay, here with us now is Patrick Sussman . . . *the Third*," I said, tossing Sussman a grin, "and Jason Barber. But he's in denial right now." I looked over as the coroner zipped the body bag.

"Help!" Barber yelled, squirming like a worm in a frying pan, "I can't breathe!"

"Oh, for heaven's sake," I whispered loudly. "Would you just get up?"

"And?" Uncle Bob asked.

"Elizabeth Ellery was killed, too," I said, hating to do it with her standing right there. It just felt awkward.

Garrett was now eyeing me with open hostility. Anger was a common emotion when faced with something impossible to believe. But quite honestly, fuck him.

"Elizabeth Ellery? We don't have an Elizabeth Ellery."

Elizabeth was studying Garrett. "This guy seems a little upset."

I nodded my head. "He doesn't believe I can see you guys. It's upsetting him that I'm talking to you."

"That's too bad. He's—" She inclined her head to study his backside. "—nice looking."

I chuckled, and we did a discreet high five, making Garrett even more uncomfortable. "Do you know where your body is?" I asked her.

"Yes. I was going to visit my sister near Indian School and Chelwood. I had a present for my nephew. I missed his birthday party," she added sadly, as if realizing at that moment that she would miss all the rest as well. "I heard the kids playing in the backyard and decided to sneak up to surprise them. That's the last thing I remember."

"So you didn't see the shooter either?" I asked.

She shook her head.

"Did you hear anything? If you were shot, surely—"

"I don't remember."

"He used a silencer," Sussman said. "It sounded weird, muffled, like a door slamming."

"The shooter used a suppressor," I relayed to Uncle Bob. "And neither of these two saw who did it. Where is your body, exactly?" I asked Elizabeth. As she told me, I repeated the address to Uncle Bob. "She's around the side of the house. There are lots of bushes, which could explain why no one has found her."

"What does she look like?" Uncle Bob asked.

"Um, Caucasian, about five-ten," I said, calculating her height minus the three-inch heels.

"Hey, you're good," she said.

I grinned appreciatively. "Blond hair, blue eyes, a light birthmark on her right temple."

She wiped at her temple self-consciously. "I think that's blood."

"Oh, sorry. The coloring is sometimes a bit hazy." I pointed helpfully to Uncle Bob's notebook. "Scratch that birthmark." Then I looked up at him. "She should pretty much be the only dead person there in a red designer skirt suit and stilettos."

Garrett almost snarled at me. "Get in my truck," he ordered through his teeth, "and bring the dead chick with you." He said the last bit sarcastically.

I turned back to Uncle Bob. "Are you going to let him talk to me that way?"

Uncle Bob shrugged. "He does have a mean apprehension record."

"Fine," I said in a huff. Not that I couldn't handle Garrett. I just wanted to complain. Before leaving, however, I had to deal with Barber. Elizabeth, Sussman, and I strolled over to the ambulance as the coroner was talking to Sergeant Dwight. Barber's nose was peeking out of the body bag. "Dude, I'm not kidding—you have to get out of your body. It's freaking me out."

He leaned up just enough for me to see his face. "It's my body, dammit. I know the law, and possession is nine-tenths of it. And as for you," he said, pointing a finger out of the bag, "aren't you supposed to be here for us? To aid us in our time of need? Isn't that what you do?"

"Not if I can help it."

"Well, I have two words for you: compassion fatigue," he said, his voice accusatory.

I turned to Sussman and sighed. "Nobody appreciates my inability to appreciate their situation. Could you please talk some sense into him?"

Garrett stood by his truck, stewing over the fact that I hadn't followed him to it like a groveling puppy.

"Davidson!" he yelled over the hood.

"Swopes!" I volleyed, mocking the long-standing tradition of referring to comrades by their last names. I looked back at my lawyers.
"Meet us at my office later."

Sussman nodded, then glared at Mr. I'm Not Dead as a Doornail in
August.

Elizabeth walked beside me to Garrett's truck. "Can I sit beside the
hunk?"

I graced her with the biggest smile I could conjure. "He's all yours."

Chapter Three

Never knock on death's door.
Ring the doorbell then run. He totally hates that.

—T-SHIRT

Garrett broke a cold pack, shook it, then tossed it to me as he swerved onto Central. "Your face is lopsided."

"I was hoping nobody would notice." I winked at Elizabeth, who sat between us, a fact I neglected to mention to Garrett. Some things were better left unsaid.

Garrett turned an irritated gaze on me. "You thought nobody would notice? You pretty much live in your own little fucked-up reality, don't you?"

"Damn," Elizabeth said, "he doesn't pull any punches."

"You pretty much annoy me and thus can kiss my ass," I said. To Garrett, not Elizabeth.

There's a certain responsibility that comes with having a name like Charley Davidson. It brooks no opposition. It takes shit from no one. And it lends a sense of familiarity when I meet clients. They feel like they know me already. Sort of like if my name were Martha Washington or Ted Bundy.

I looked in the side mirror at the black-and-white following us to the address where Detective Robert Davidson, from an anonymous tip, believed there might be another victim. Uncle Bob got lots of anonymous tips. Garrett was starting to put it all together.

"So, you're his omnipotent anonymous source?"

I gasped. "Do you kiss your mother with that mouth? Though I do like the *omnipotent* part." When Garrett just glowered, I answered, "Yes. I'm his anonymous source. Have been since I was five."

His expression turned incredulous. "Your uncle took you to crime scenes when you were five years old?"

"Don't be ridiculous. Uncle Bob would never have done that. He didn't have to. My dad did." When Garrett's jaw fell open, I chuckled. "Just kidding. I didn't have to go to crime scenes. The victims always found their way to me without my help. Apparently, I'm bright."

He turned away and watched the pinks and oranges of the New Mexico sunrise ribbon across the horizon. "You'll have to forgive me if I don't fall for it."

"Um, no, I don't."

"Okay," he said in an exasperated voice, "if this is so real, tell me what my mom was wearing at her funeral."

Great. One of those. "Look, most likely your mom went elsewhere. You know, into the light," I said, wiggling my fingers to demonstrate. "Most everyone does. And I don't have the secret decoder ring for that plane of existence. My all-access pass expired years ago."

He snorted. "That's convenient."

"Swopes," I said, finally gathering the courage to press the cold pack to my cheek. Pain shot through my jaw as I reclined my head against the rest and closed my eyes. "It's okay. It's not your fault you're an asshole. I learned a long time ago not to tell people the truth. Uncle Bob shouldn't have said anything." I paused for a response. Receiving none, I continued. "We all have a certain knowledge about how the universe works. And when someone comes along and challenges that knowledge, we don't know how to deal with it. We aren't hardwired that way. It's difficult to question everything you've ever thought to be true. So, like I said, it's not your fault. You can believe me or not, but whichever you choose, you're the one who has to deal with the consequences. So make your decision wisely, grasshopper," I added, the nonswollen side of my mouth curving into a grin.

When I didn't get one of his trademark comebacks, I opened my eyes to see him staring at me. It was through Elizabeth, but still . . . We sat idling at a stoplight, and he was using the time to analyze me with his super skiptracer senses. His gray eyes, striking against his dark skin, sparkled in curiosity.

"Green light," I said to break his spell.

He blinked and pressed the gas pedal.

"I think he likes you," Elizabeth said.

Since I hadn't told Garrett she was sitting there, I tossed her an abbreviated version of my death stare. She chuckled.

We drove a few more blocks before Garrett asked the ten-thousand-dollar question: "So who hit you?"

"Told ya," Elizabeth said.

I ground my teeth and winced as I maneuvered the cold pack lower. "I was working on a case."

"A case hit you?"

I heard an inkling of the old, non-asshole Garrett. "No, the case's husband hit me. I was keeping him busy while *the case* boarded a plane to Mexico City."

"Don't tell me you got involved in a domestic abuse situation."

"Okay."

"You did, didn't you?"

"Yep."

"Damn, Davidson, have you learned nothing from me?"

Now it was my turn to stare incredulously. "Dude, you're the one who taught me what Frank Ahearn taught you on how to teach people how to disappear. Why did you think I needed that information?"

"Not for you to get involved in domestics."

"My entire client base is domestics. What do you think private investigators do?"

Of course, he was a licensed PI as well and could private investigate circles around me, but he focused his business on skips. Bond recovery pays well when you're as good as he is. And, actually, I had to agree with him on this one. I'd gotten in way over my head. But it all turned out okay in the end.

The case, otherwise known as Rosie Herschel, got my number from a friend of a friend and called me up one night, asking me to come to a Sack-N-Save on the Westside. It was all fairly cloak-and-dagger. To get out of the house, she told her husband they needed milk, and we met in a dark corner of the Sack-N-Save parking lot. The fact that she had to make up an excuse just to leave the house set my nerves on edge. I should have turned tail then, but she was so desperate and so scared and so tired of her husband taking out the fact that he was a certifiable loser on her that I couldn't turn her down. My jaw doesn't compare to the horrific shiner she was sporting the first time I met her. She knew, and I believed it, too, that if she'd tried to leave her husband without help, she would never have seen another birthday.

Since she was originally from Mexico and had relatives there, we cooked up a plan for her to meet her aunt in Mexico City. The two of them would then travel south with a deed and just enough cash to open a small inn, or posada, on a beach not far from her grandparents' village.

From what Rosie told me, her husband had never met any of her relatives from Mexico. The chances of him finding the right Gutierrez family in Mexico City were slim to none. But just in case, we had new identities drawn up for them both. An adventure in itself.

In the meantime, I sent an anonymous text to Mr. Herschel, pretending to be an admirer and inviting him for drinks at a bar on the Westside. Though I longed for the security of my dad's bar, no way could I risk someone blurting out my real name. So I dropped Rosie at the airport and took off across the Rio Grande. Rosie would have to be there a few hours before her plane departed, but I had a plan to keep Herschel busy for the entire night. I goaded him into hitting me and pressed charges. Not that it was easy. Flirting like a vixen in heat then pulling the emergency brake in such a way that the mark felt like I'd just slapped him took skill. And naturally, a man like Herschel would take great offense to being led on. Throw in a few insults about small penises and a degrading giggle or two, and the fists start flying.

While I could have just gotten him drunk-off-his-ass wasted, then dumped him in an alley somewhere, I couldn't risk him finding Rosie gone until the morning. One night in jail was all we needed. And now she was well on her way to an esteemed career as a *posadera*.

"This is it," Elizabeth said.

"Oh, here," I said, relaying the info to Garrett. "This house on the corner?"

She nodded.

And she was right where she said she'd be. I saw her shoes first, red and sharp and expensive; then I glanced at departed Elizabeth's. Perfect match. That was good enough for me. I strolled back to the porch and plopped down while Garrett and the officer called it in.

While I was busy scolding myself for not examining the body and scouring the crime scene for clues like a real PI would, a blur in my peripheral vision captured my attention. It wasn't like a normal blur, the kind that everyone sees. This was darker, more . . . solid.

I'd glanced to the side as fast as I could, but I'd missed it. Again. That'd been happening a lot lately. Dark blurs in my periphery. I figured either Superman died and was swooshing around the country at the speed of light—because dead people don't move that fast; they appear out of nowhere and disappear the same way—or I was having lots of those little ministrokes that would someday lead to massive and devastating cerebral hemorrhaging.

I totally needed to have my cholesterol checked.

Of course, there was another possibility. One I hadn't really wanted to consider. But it would explain a lot.

I'd never been afraid of the unknown, like other people. Things like the dark or monsters or the bogeyman. I suppose if I had been, I wouldn't have made a proper grim reaper. But something or someone was stalking me. I'd tried for weeks to convince myself that I was imagining it. But I've seen only one thing in my life move that fast. And it was the only thing on Earth, or the hereafter, that terrified me.

I'd never quite worked out the reasoning behind my unnatural fear, because the being had never hurt me. Truth be known, it had saved my life on several occasions. When I was almost kidnapped as a child by a paroled sex offender, it saved me. When Owen Vaughn tried to run me down with his dad's Suburban in high school, it saved me. When I was being stalked in college and eventually attacked, it saved me. At the time, I hadn't taken the stalking thing that seriously until it showed up. Only then did I realize, almost too late, that my life had been in danger.

So, you'd think I'd be more grateful. But it wasn't just that it had saved my life. It was the way it had saved my life. The ability to sever a man's spinal cord in half without leaving any visible evidence as to what happened was a tad disconcerting.

And in high school, when other teens were trying desperately to figure out who they were, where they fit in the world, it told me what

I was. It whispered the role I would play in life into my ear as I was applying lip gloss in the girls' bathroom, words I never heard, words that
lay thick in the air, waiting for me to breathe them in, to accept who I
was, what I would become. As girls fluttered around me for glimpses in
the mirror, I could see only him, standing over me, a huge cloaked
figure bearing down on me like a suffocating vacuum.

I'd stood there for a solid fifteen minutes after the other girls left,
after he left, barely breathing, unable to move until Mrs. Worthy busted
me for skipping and sent me to the office.

He was basically dark and creepy and just sort of showed up in my
life every so often to impart some juicy tidbit of afterlife wisdom—
and scare the bejesus out of me—only to leave me quaking in the wake
of his visit. At least I was a bright and shiny grim reaper. He was dark
and dangerous, and death seemed to waft off him like smoke off dry
ice. When I was a child, I decided to name him something ordinary,
something nonthreatening, but Fluffy just didn't fit. Eventually, he was
christened the Big Bad.

"Ms. Davidson," Elizabeth said, sitting beside me.

I blinked and glanced around. "Did you just see someone?"

She scanned the area as well. "I don't think so."

"A blur? Kind of dark and . . . blurry?"

"Um, nope."

"Oh, okay, sorry. What's up?"

"I can't have my nieces and nephew wake up to my body. I'm right
under their windows."

I'd thought of that, too. "You're right," I said. "Maybe we should
break the news to your sister."

She nodded sadly. I called Garrett over, and we agreed for me and
the cop to ring the doorbell and give Elizabeth's sister the news. Maybe
Elizabeth could help me with what to say. Her presence might make
the whole thing easier on us all. At least I'd thought so.

An hour later, I was in my uncle's SUV, breathing into a paper bag. "You should have waited for me," he said really helpfully.

Never again. Obviously there were siblings out there who actually liked each other. Who knew? The woman had an emotional breakdown in my arms. What seemed to upset her most was the fact that Elizabeth had been outside her house all night and she hadn't known. I might should've left that part out. The woman grabbed my shoulders, her fingernails digging into my skin, her morning hair, a cross between disco and crack addict, shaking in denial; then she crumpled to the floor and sobbed. Most definitely an emotional breakdown.

The bad part came when I crumpled to the floor and sobbed with her. Dead people I could handle. They were usually beyond hysteria. This was the people-left-behind part. The hard part. We hugged each other a long time until Uncle Bob arrived on-scene and dragged me off her. Elizabeth's brother-in-law got the kids ready, and they all went out a side door and loaded up the car for a trip to Grandma's house. All in all, they were a very loving family.

"Slow down," Uncle Bob said as I panted into the bag. "If you hyperventilate and pass out, I'm not catching you. I injured my shoulder playing golf the other day."

My family was so caring. I tried to slow my breathing, but I just kept thinking about that poor woman losing her sister, her best friend, her *comadre*. What would she do now? How would she go on? Where would she find the will to survive? I started crying again, and Uncle Bob gave up and left me alone in his SUV.

"She'll be okay, hon."

I looked in the rearview mirror at Elizabeth and sniffed.

"She's tough," she added.

I could tell she was shaken up, and I probably wasn't helping.

I sniffed again. "I'm sorry. I should never have gone in there."

"No, I appreciate you being there for my sister instead of a bunch of male cops. Sometimes guys just don't get it."

I glanced over at Garrett as he talked to Uncle Bob, shook his head, then leveled an expressionless gaze directly on me. "No, I guess they don't."

I needed to get the heck outta Dodge—and how—but Elizabeth wanted to go to her mother's to check on things. We made plans to meet up at my office later; then I asked another officer to drive me back to my Jeep.

The ride was calming. People were just getting out, heading to work. The sun, still looming over the horizon, cast a soft glow on the crisp morning, suffusing Albuquerque with the prospect of a fresh start. Pueblo-style houses with neat lawns slid past us and broke away to a business district with new and old buildings covering every available inch.

"So, are you feeling better, Ms. Davidson?"

I peered at Officer Taft. He was one of those young cops trying to get in good with my uncle, so he agreed to give me a ride, thinking it might boost his career. I wondered if he knew he had a dead child in his backseat. Probably not.

"Much better, thank you."

He smiled. Having asked the requisite question of concern, he could now ignore me.

While I normally don't mind being ignored, I did want to ask him about the tiny blonde, who looked to be about nine years old, gazing starry-eyed like he'd just saved the earth from total destruction. But this line of questioning took tact. Skill. Subtlety.

"So, are you the officer who had a young girl die in his squad car recently?"

"Me?" he asked in surprise. "No. At least I hope not." He chuckled.

"Oh, well, that's good."

He shifted uncomfortably in his seat as he thought about what I'd said. "I haven't heard that. Did someone—?"

"Oh, just a rumor, you know." Officer Taft had probably heard all about me from the other kids on the playground. Recess could be such a gossip den. Clearly he wanted to keep the conversation to a minimum. But my curiosity got the better of me. "So, did you have a young girl close to you die recently? Something in a blond?"

He was now eyeing me as if I were drooling and cross-eyed. I wiped the swollen side of my mouth just in case.

"No." Then he thought about it. "But there was a young blond girl who died at the scene about a month ago. I gave her CPR, but we were too late. That was tough."

"I bet. I'm sorry, too."

The girl sighed. "Isn't he the greatest?"

I snorted.

"What?" he asked.

"Oh, nothing. I just think that would be really hard."

"Look, bitch."

I concentrated with every fiber of my being not to let my eyes widen in reaction. It just looks odd to the living when you react to something they can't see or hear. I eased around to the girl, pretending to take a special interest in the scenery behind us, and raised my brows in question.

"You can't have him, okay," she said from behind the wire barrier.

"Mm-hmm," I whispered.

Officer Taft looked at me.

"This is certainly a beautiful neighborhood."

"Yeah, I guess."

"I will scratch those eyes out of your ugly head."

Ugly? That was it. Time to play cell phone. "Oh," I said, digging through my bag. "I think my phone vibrated." I flipped it open. "Hello?"

"I'd cut back on the glitter makeup if I were you. It's not helping."

"I don't wear glitter—"

"And you'd best quit looking at him. He deserves someone much prettier."

"Look, sweetheart," I said, easing around to admire the scenery behind us again, hoping I didn't look like I was talking to a dead person in the backseat and just pretending to talk on the phone. "I have my own impossible relationship with a guy I can't really have. *Comprende?*"

She jammed her fists onto her pajama-clad hips and glared at me. "I'm just saying, bitch."

"Would you stop calling me that, you little . . ."

I noticed Officer Taft's brows slide together in concern.

"Relationships," I said with a shrug. Of course, the cell phone trick worked best in silent mode. As I pretended to explain to my third party that sometimes there is a really bright light nearby and she should go into it, my phone rang out in Beethoven's Fifth Symphony, which meant Uncle Bob was calling. I almost dropped the phone, then smiled at Taft. "My previous call must have been disconnected." I dared not comment on the fact that it had supposedly been on vibrate mere seconds ago.

The poltergeist in the backseat howled out an evil laugh. Where the hell did this kid come from? Then it hit me. Maybe that was the problem. Maybe she was actually from hell.

"Hell-o," I said.

"You just want me to go into the light so you can make your move," Demon Child said.

"That's not what I want!"

"Okay," Uncle Bob replied, a wary hesitance in his voice. "No more 'hey, kiddos' for you."

"Sorry, Uncle Bob, I thought you were someone else."

"I'm often mistaken for Tom Selleck."

Taft perked up. "Does your uncle need anything? A coffee? A latte?"

Sucking up was so unmanly. "He needs someone to bear his illegitimate child if you're interested."

Taft's mouth thinned into a solid line as he turned back to the road.

Okay, I admit it. That was rude. The demon in the backseat thought so, too. She took a swing at me.

I laughed when I dodged her fist by accidently-on-purpose dropping my cherry lip balm to the floorboard.

"I'll take that as a can-do," Uncle Bob said.

"Oh, right. My office, nine o'clock. Got it. I'm just going to run by my apartment and grab a bite, then I'll be there."

"Thanks, kiddo. And, are you okay?"

"Me? Always," I said, just as the golden-haired demon dive-bombed for my eyes. She fell out of the car somewhere between Carlisle and San Mateo. "But I have to say, Uncle Bob, I've recently uncovered irrefutable evidence of why some species eat their young."

Chapter Four

*I love children, but I don't think
I can eat a whole one.*

—BUMPER STICKER

I was worried Demon Child would follow me to my apartment and get
her freak on, so I made sure she was nowhere in sight before I climbed
into Misery and hightailed it home. Just in case, though, I stormed into
my apartment, tossed a quick hello to Mr. Wong, then rummaged
through my entertainment center to lay out all my exorcism equipment.
I kept it in my entertainment center because exorcisms were nothing if
not entertaining.

   And, no, I can't actually perform one, even with my auspicious
status as the grim reaper. I can only help the departed figure out why
they're still on Earth, then lure them across planes afterwards. I can't
force them to go against their will. At least I don't think I can. I've
never actually tried. I can, however, trick them. A few candles, a quick
chant, and—voilà—exorcism du jour. The departed fall for it all the

time and end up crossing despite themselves. Except Mr. Habersham down the hall. He just giggled when I tried to exorcise him. Old
fart.

Despite Mr. Habersham—and, come to think of it, Mr. Wong—I
loved living here. Not only does my apartment building, the Causeway, sit right behind my dad's bar and, thus, my office, it's also something of a local landmark.

I've lived here a little over three years, but when I was young—too
young to know that evil existed—this old building became fused into
my memory, through no fault of its own. Later, when my dad bought
the bar, I stepped into the back parking lot and saw the building again
for the first time in over a decade. Looking up at the intricate medieval
carvings along the entrance, a rarity in Albuquerque, I stood transfixed
as a montage of memories, dark and painful, rushed through me. They
made my chest hurt and stole my breath, and I became obsessed with
the building from that moment on.

We had a history together, a horrible, nightmarish history that
involved a paroled sex offender scoping for a fix. And maybe by living here, I felt I was somehow conquering my demons. Naturally, this
worked best when demons didn't actually come to visit.

I put on a pot of coffee and headed to the bathroom to see if my eyes
were as swollen as my jaw. Sobbing like a movie star in rehab was not
the best beauty regimen. But I soon realized the red swelling brought
out the gold in my eyes. Cool. I turned on the hot water full blast, then
waited the requisite ten minutes for it to actually get hot.

And they say New Mexico has a water shortage. Not according to
my landlord.

Just then, I heard Cookie, my neighbor-slash-best-friend-slash-
receptionist, burst through the door, coffee cup in hand. Cookie was a
lot like Kramer from *Seinfeld,* only not so nervous, like Kramer might
have been on Prozac. And I knew she had her coffee cup in hand be-

cause she always had her coffee cup in hand. I think she had difficulties forming complete sentences without it.

"Honey, I'm home!" she yelled from the kitchen.

Yep, she had it.

"Me, too!" came another voice, soft and giggly.

I met Cookie when I moved into the Causeway. She had just moved here as well, following an ugly-ass divorce—her words—and we became instant friends. But she had a daughter, Amber, and they came as a package deal. While Cookie and I hit it off immediately, I was a little worried about the kid. I'd never taken to four-foot creatures who had the uncanny ability to point out all my flaws in thirty seconds flat. And just for the record, I can too read without moving my lips. But I was determined to win Amber over, no matter the cost. And after just one game of miniature golf, I was putty in her hands.

"I'll be right out," I said from the bathroom. Mrs. Lowenstein down the hall must be doing laundry, because it didn't take long for the water to reach its usual two thousand degrees. Steam rose up around me as I splashed my face. Then I looked in the mirror and gave up once again. Thank God Dream Guy didn't have to see me like this. I patted a towel over my eyes, then stepped back as a name glittered and formed in the condensation.

DUTCH.

My breath caught. Dutch. I hadn't imagined it. Dream Guy, aka Reyes, aka God of Fantasies and All Things Sensual, had really said *Dutch* to me in the shower. Who else could it be?

I glanced around the bathroom. Nothing. I stopped and listened, but the only thing I heard was Cookie clanking around in the kitchen.

"Reyes?" I peeked behind the shower curtain. "Reyes, are you here?"

"You need a new coffeepot," Cookie called to me. "It's taking forever."

I gave up the search with a sigh and ran my fingers along the path of each letter on the mirror. My hand shook. I snatched it back and, after one last sweep of the area, stepped out of the bathroom, bracing myself for the *oohs* and *aahs* my face would elicit.

"What the bloody heck in Hades for crying out . . ." Cookie had put the coffee cup down. She picked it up and started over. "What happened?"

"Ooh!" Amber crooned, skipping over to me for a better look. Her huge blue eyes widened as she studied my cheek and jaw. She looked like a wingless fairy, the promise of grace evident in every stride she took. She had long dark hair that fell in tangles down her back, and her lips formed a perfect bow.

I chuckled as her curiosity drew her brows together in deep concentration.

"Aren't you supposed to be in school?" I asked.

"Fiona's mom is picking me up this morning. We're going on a field trip to the zoo and Fiona's mom is a chaperone so she told Mr. Gonzalez we'd just meet the class there. Does that hurt?"

"Yep."

"Did you hit back?"

"Nope. I was unconscious."

"No way!"

"Way."

Cookie pushed past her daughter and studied my jaw for herself. "Did you get checked out?"

"Yeah, by a hot blond who sat in the corner of the bar and made googly eyes at me."

Amber giggled.

Cookie pursed her lips. "I meant by a doctor."

"No, but a balding yet bizarrely hot paramedic said I'd be fine."

"Oh, and he's an expert?"

"At flirting," I said. Amber giggled again. I loved the sound, like a tinkling wind chime in a soft breeze.

Cookie leveled a chastising motherly glare on her, then turned back to me. She was one of those women too big for the one-size-fits-all category, and resented the commie makers of such clothing wear. I once had to talk her out of bombing a one-size-fits-all manufacturing company. Other than that, she was pretty down to earth. She had black wiry hair that hung past her shoulders and lent itself nicely to her reputation as a witch. She wasn't one, but the furtive glances were fun.

"Any coffee yet?"

Cookie gave up and checked the pot. "Seriously, this is beyond torment. This is like Chinese water torture, only less humane."

"Mom's going through withdrawal. We ran out of coffee last night."

"Uh-oh," I said, grinning at Cookie.

She sat at the counter with me as Amber rummaged through my cabinets for Pop-Tarts. "Oh, I forgot to tell you," Cookie said, "Amber wants your dad to get a teriyaki machine so she can sing for all the lonely barflies."

"I'm a good singer, Mom." Only a twelve-year-old could make the word *mom* sound blasphemous.

I leaned into Cookie. "Does she know it's not called—?"

"No," she whispered.

"Are you gonna tell her?"

"No. It's much funnier this way."

I chuckled, then remembered Cookie's doctor's appointment the day before. "How'd your visit go? Any new debilitating diseases I should know about?"

"No, but I have reaffirmed my respect for lubricating jelly."

"Fiona's here!" Amber said, flipping her cell phone closed and rushing out the door. She rushed back in, kissed her mom on the cheek, kissed me on the cheek—the good one—then rushed back out again.

Cookie watched her go. "She's like a hurricane on crystal meth."

"Have you considered Valium?" I asked.

"For her or me?" She laughed and headed for the coffeepot. "I get the first cup."

"When do you not get the first cup? So, what'd the doc say?" Cookie didn't like talking about it, but she'd once fought breast cancer, and the breast cancer almost won.

"I don't know," she said with a shrug. "He's sending me to this other doctor, some kind of guru in the medical community."

"Really? What's his name?"

"Dr.— Hell, I don't know."

"Oh, him." I grinned. "So he's good?"

"Supposedly. I think he invented internal organs or something."

"Well, that's a plus."

She poured two cups, then plopped down beside me again. "No, I'm fine." She stirred sugar and cream into her coffee. "I think my doc just wants to make sure history doesn't repeat itself."

"He's cautious," I said, stirring my own cup. "I like that in a person, especially one with the power of life and death at his fingertips."

"Well, I don't want you to worry is all. I haven't felt this good in years. I think you keep me young." She winked from behind her cup.

After a long sip, I asked, "Isn't that Amber's job?"

She snorted. "Amber takes every opportunity possible to tell me how old and uninteresting I am. 'You're nothing like Charley,' she says. Repeatedly. She's about ninety percent positive you hung the moon."

"At least someone thinks so," I said with a shrug of my brows.

"Uh-oh," she said, putting her cup down. "Did you have another run-in with that hot skiptracer?"

I slumped back into my chair, annoyed that he'd even been mentioned. And in my own apartment, no less. "He's such a jerk."

"You did," she said, her face brightening. She had quite the thing for Garrett. It was . . . disturbing. "So, spill." She scooted closer. "What did he say? Did you two have words? A fistfight? Angry sex?"

"Ew," I said, crinkling my nose. "Not even if he was the last hot skiptracer on Earth."

"Then what? You have to tell me." She grabbed my shirt collar with her free hand. I tried not to giggle. "When will you realize I live vicariously through you?"

"You do?"

"Duh." She smoothed my collar and went back to her coffee. "I have a teenage daughter. I have no social life. No agenda that doesn't involve the Disney Channel. And sex," she said with a dramatic wave of her hand. "Don't even get me started. I haven't had sex with anything non-battery-powered in years. I need details, Charley."

After I recovered from the *non-battery-powered* comment, I said, "I tried to set you up with Delivery Dave."

"The bread guy?" She thought about it, her mouth a grim line. "I guess I could do worse."

A chuckle escaped me, and she smiled.

"So, are you gonna tell me what happened last night?" she asked.

"Ah, yes. Last night." I went into the whole evening with Rosie's asshole husband, assuring her I'd gotten Rosie on the plane and safely out of the country. Then I told her about my morning with the other asshole, Garrett the skeptic skiptracer. Then I told her about my disastrous time with Elizabeth's sister. Then I told her the best part. The Reyes part.

"So, Reyes, huh?"

"Yeah."

She laughed. "Could you say that with a little more sigh?"

I grinned and scooped a layer of strawberry cream cheese onto a blueberry bagel, getting a serving of grains, dairy, and fruit in one shot. "The first and only time I've ever seen him was that night in the South Valley with Gemma."

"What night?" Then Cookie's eyes widened. "You mean?"

"I mean. If I'm not mistaken, it's him."

She knew the story. I'd only told her a dozen times. At least. As Cookie sat speechless, I thought back to what I knew about Reyes. Unfortunately, I didn't know much.

I was a freshman in high school the one and only time I'd seen him, and my psycho sister Gemma was a senior. Ever true to form, she was trying to graduate high school a semester early so she could start college full-time, but graduating early involved a class project she was too chicken to pull off by herself. Enter Charlotte Davidson, supersister, saint, and project getter-doner.

Not, however, without complaint. Oddly, I could remember our conversation like it was moments ago. But twelve years had passed since that terrible and beautiful night. A night I would never forget.

"If you ask me," I'd said, mumbling through the red scarf wrapped around my nose and mouth, "no class project is worth dying for, even with that whole ten-points-extra-credit thing going for it."

Gemma turned to me and lowered Dad's camera to push back a blond curl. The cold of December at midnight added a metallic luster to her blue eyes. "If I don't get this credit," she said, her breath fogging in the icy air, "I don't graduate early."

"I know," I said, trying not to sound annoyed. "But seriously, if I die two weeks before Christmas, I'm totally coming back to haunt you. Forever. And trust me, I know how."

Gemma shrugged, unconcerned, then turned back to the autofocused images of Albuquerque. Luminarias lined sidewalks and buildings, casting eerie shadows over the deserted streets. For a final on community awareness, Gemma opted to make a video. She wanted to capture life on the streets of Southside. Troubled kids in search of acceptance. Drug addicts in search of their next high. Homeless people in search of sustenance and shelter.

So far, all she'd managed to get on tape was a skateboarder wiping out on Central and a prostitute ordering a soft drink at Macho Taco.

Our curfew had come and gone and still we waited, huddled together in the shadows of an abandoned school, shivering and doing our
best to be invisible. We kept getting hassled by gang members who
wanted to know what we were doing there. We had a couple of close
calls, and I got a couple of phone numbers, but all in all, the evening
had been pretty quiet. Probably because it was thirty below out.

Just then I noticed a kid huddled under the steps of the school. He
wore a semi-white T-shirt and dirty jeans. Even though he wasn't wearing a jacket, he wasn't shivering. The departed weren't affected by the
weather.

"Hey, there," I said, easing closer.

He glanced up, shock plain on his young face. "You can see me?"

"Sure can."

"No one can see me."

"Well, I can. My name is Charley Davidson."

"Like the motorcycle?"

"Something like that," I said with a grin.

"Why are you so bright?" he asked, squinting.

"I'm a grim reaper. But don't worry, it's not as bad as it sounds."

Fear crept into his eyes anyway. "I don't want to go to hell."

"Hell?" I said, sitting beside him and ignoring Gemma's sighs of annoyance that I was once again talking to air. "Trust me, hon, if you'd
been penciled in for a personal interview with evil incarnate, you
wouldn't be here now."

Relief softened his expressive eyes.

"So, you just hanging?" I asked.

It didn't take long to find out that the kid was a recently departed
thirteen-year-old gangbanger named Angel who took a nine millimeter to the chest during a drive-by. He was the driver. His redemption,
in my eyes, came when I learned that he had no idea his friend was going to try to kill the *puta* bitch *vatos* trespassing on their turf until the

bullets were flying. In an attempt to stop his friend, Angel actually wrecked his mother's car, then wrestled his friend for the gun. In the end, only one person died that night.

While I was busy lecturing Angel on the benefits of bulletproof vests, a scene in a distant window caught my attention. I stepped out of the shadows for a closer look. A harsh yellow glare illuminated the kitchen of a small apartment, but that wasn't what got my attention. At first I wondered if my eyes were playing tricks on me. I blinked, refocused, then sucked in a deep breath as shock crept up my spine.

"Gemma," I whispered.

Gemma's saucy "What?" was quickly followed by a gasp. She saw it, too.

A man in a filthy T-shirt and boxers had a teenage boy pinned against a wall. The boy clawed at the man's hand clenched around his throat as a meaty fist shot forward. It slammed into the boy's jaw with such violent force, his head whipped back and hit the wall. He went limp, but only for a moment. His hands drifted up blindly to fend off the attack. In the span of a heartbeat, the boy's disoriented gaze seemed to lock on to mine. Then the man hit him again.

"Oh, my god, Gemma, we have to do something!" I screamed. I ran for an opening in the chain-link fence that surrounded the school. "We have to do something!"

"Charley, wait!"

But I was already through the fence and running toward the apartment. I glanced up in time to see the man wrestle the boy onto the kitchen table.

The steps to the apartment building weren't lit. I stumbled up them and pounded on the locked entrance door to no avail. A postage stamp window revealed a dark, deserted hallway.

"Charley!" Gemma was standing in the street outside the apartment. Because the window was set high, she had to stand back to be able to see in. "Charley, hurry! He's killing him!"

I ran back to her, but I couldn't see the boy.

"He's killing him," she repeated.

"Where did they go?"

"There. Nowhere. They didn't go anywhere," she said in a rush of emotion. "He fell. The boy fell, and the man—"

I did the only thing I could think of. I sprinted back to the abandoned school and grabbed a brick.

"What are you doing?" she asked as I scrambled through the fence and rushed back to her.

"Probably getting us killed," I said as I took aim. "Or worse, grounded."

Gemma stood back as I hurtled the brick through the kitchen window. The huge plate glass splintered but held steady for a breathless moment, as if shocked at what we'd done. Then it shattered the quiet night air with a roaring crash as shards of glass cascaded onto the sidewalk. The man appeared instantly.

"I'm calling the police, you bastard!" I tried to sound convincing enough to scare him.

His glared down at us, anger twisting his features. "You little bitch. You'll pay for that."

"Run!" Instinct took hold. I grabbed Gemma's arm. "Run!"

While Gemma tried to head down the street, I dragged her toward the very apartment building we were trying to get away from.

"What are you doing?" she screeched, fear raising her voice several notes. "We need to get to the car."

I ran for the cover of shadows. Pulling Gemma between the apartment building and a dry cleaning business, I dragged her down the narrow opening. "We can go across the arroyo. It'll be faster."

"It's too dark."

My heart pounded in my ears as I negotiated around boxes and weathered crates. The cold was no longer an issue. I felt nothing but the need to get help. To save him.

"We have to get to a phone," I said. "There's a convenience store across the arroyo."

When we emerged from the passageway, another chain-link fence blocked our path.

"What now?" Gemma whined helpfully.

The dry arroyo lay on the other side, and the convenience store beyond that. I pulled her along the fence, searching for an opening. Even with a security light behind the dry cleaning shop, we slipped and stumbled along the frozen, uneven ground.

"Charley, wait."

"We have to get help." That single thought blinded me to all others. I had to help that boy. I had never seen anything so violent in my life. Adrenaline and fear pushed bile up to sting the back of my throat. I swallowed hard and breathed in the crisp air to calm myself.

"Wait. Wait." Gemma's breathless plea finally slowed my progress. "I think it's him."

I stopped and whirled around. The boy was on his knees beside a Dumpster, holding his stomach, his body convulsing with dry heaves. I started back. This time Gemma grabbed my arm and struggled to keep her footing as she trudged behind.

When we got to him, the boy tried to stand, but he had taken a harsh beating. Weak and shaking, he fell back onto his knees and braced a hand against the Dumpster for support. The long fingers of his other hand dug into the gravelly earth as he tried to catch his breath, gulping huge rations of cold air. He wore only a thin T-shirt and a gray pair of sweats. He must have been freezing.

With empathy tightening my chest, I knelt beside him. I didn't know what to say. His breaths were shallow and quick. His muscles, constricted with pain, corded around his arms, and I saw the smooth, crisp lines of a tattoo. A little higher, thick dark hair curled over an ear.

Gemma raised the camera from around her neck to illuminate our surroundings. He looked up. Squinting against the light, he lifted a dirty hand to shade his eyes.

And his eyes were amazing. A magnificent brown, deep and rich, with flecks of gold and green glistening in the light. Dark red blood streaked down one side of his face. He looked like a warrior from a late-night movie, a hero who'd charged into battle despite ridiculous odds. For a moment, I wondered if I'd made a mistake and he was actually dead; then I remembered Gemma had seen him, too.

I blinked and asked, "Are you okay?" It was a stupid question, but it was the only one I could think of.

He fixed his gaze on me a long moment, then turned his head and spit blood into the darkness before looking back. He was older than I had originally thought. Perhaps even seventeen or eighteen.

He tried to stand again. I jumped up to help, but he backed away from my touch. Despite an overwhelming, almost desperate, need to assist him, I stepped aside and watched as he struggled to his feet.

"We have to get you to a hospital," I said once he was standing.

It seemed like a perfectly logical next step to me, but he eyed me with a mixture of hostility and distrust. It would be my first real lesson on the illogic of the male population. He spit again, then started down the narrow opening we'd just come through, hugging the brick wall for support.

"Look," I said, following him down the passageway. Gemma had a death grip on my jacket and jerked on it occasionally, clearly not wanting to follow. I pulled her along regardless. "We saw what happened. We need to get you to a hospital. Our car isn't far."

"Get out of here," he finally said, his voice deep and edged with pain. With effort, he climbed onto a crate and grabbed a high window ledge. His lean, muscular body shook visibly as he tried to peer into the apartment.

"You're going back in there?" I asked, appalled. "Are you crazy?"

"Charley," Gemma whispered at my back, "maybe we should just leave."

Naturally, I ignored her. "That man tried to kill you."

He cast an angry glare at me before turning back to the window. "What part of *get out of here* don't you understand?"

I admit, I wavered. But I couldn't imagine what would happen if he went back into that apartment. "I'm calling the police."

His head whipped around. A beautiful agility took hold of him, as if he was suddenly unfazed by the beating, and he leapt from the crates to land solidly before me.

With just enough force to let me know it was there, he placed a hand around my throat and pushed me back against the brick building. For a long moment, he only stared. A plethora of emotions flashed across his face. Anger. Frustration. Fear.

"That would be a very bad idea," he said at last. It was a warning. A cutting desperation laced his smooth voice.

"My uncle's a cop, and my dad's an ex-cop. I can help you." Heat drifted off him, and I realized he must have had a fever. Standing out in the frigid cold with only a T-shirt could not be good.

My audacity seemed to astonish him. He almost laughed. "The minute I need the help of a sniveling brat from the Heights, I'll let you know."

The hostility in his tone threw my determination askew, but only for a moment. I recovered and charged forward. "If you go back in there, I'm calling the police. I mean it."

He clenched his jaw in frustration. "You'll do more harm than good."

I shook my head. "I doubt it."

"You don't know anything about me. Or him."

"Is he your father?"

He hesitated, stared impatiently as if trying to decide how best to get rid of me. Then he made a decision. I could see it on his face.

His features darkened. He stepped closer, pressed the length of his body against mine, leaned into me, and whispered in my ear. "What's your name?"

"Charley," I said, suddenly afraid, too afraid not to answer. Then I tried to say *Davidson,* but he pulled the scarf down to see my face better, and *Davidson* came out as one mangled syllable that sounded more like—

"Dutch?" he asked, scrunching his brows together.

He was the most beautiful thing I'd ever seen. He was solid and strong and fierce. And vulnerable. "No," I said in a whisper as his fingers drifted down and brushed intrusively over my breast. "Davidson."

"Have you ever been raped, Dutch?"

The knowledge that he was aiming for pure, no-holds-barred shock value didn't lessen the question's impact. I was stunned and thoroughly terrified. I tried to resist the urge to run, tried to stand my ground, but self-preservation was a difficult thing to squelch. A quick glance at Gemma for support did little to help. My sister stood wide-eyed with mouth agape, absently holding the camera as if it still mattered, and somehow managing not to get a single moment on tape.

"No," I answered breathlessly.

His cheek brushed across mine as his hand eased back up to lock on to my throat. To an ordinary passerby, we would look like lovers playing flirtatiously in the dark.

He forced a hard knee between mine and spread them, gaining access to my most private area. I gasped at the intimate contact as his free hand dipped between my legs, and knew instinctively I was in way over my head. I grabbed his wrist with both hands.

"Please, stop."

He paused but kept his fingers cupped at my crotch. I put a hand on his chest and pushed gently, coaxing him off me. "Please."

He eased back and looked into my eyes. "You'll leave?"

"I'll leave."

His gaze remained locked with mine a long moment; then he raised both arms and braced them on the brick wall above my head. "Go," he said harshly.

It wasn't a suggestion. I ducked under his arm and ran before he changed his mind, grabbing Gemma along the way.

As we rounded the building, I turned back and stopped. He'd climbed onto a crate and was sitting atop it, staring up at the window. With a forlorn sigh, he rested his head against the wall, and I realized he wasn't going back into the apartment. He just wanted to keep an eye on that window.

At the time, I had wondered whom he'd left inside. I found out two days later when I spoke to an angry landlady. The family in 2C had moved out in the middle of the night and stiffed her for two months' rent and the costly replacement of a plate glass window. That whole self-preservation thing kept me from mentioning the particulars of the window. When I finally got her to stop harping about lost revenue, she told me she'd heard the old man call the boy Reyes, so Reyes it was. But the burning question was whom he'd left inside. Then the landlady told me.

A sister. He'd left a sister inside. And she had been alone. With a monster.

"I can't believe it," Cookie said, pulling me back to the present. "Is he, you know, dead?"

Cookie found out long ago that I could see the departed. She's never held it against me.

"That's what's weird," I said. "I just don't know. This is so different from anything I've ever experienced." I checked my watch. "Crap, I have to get to the office."

"Oh! That's probably a good idea." She chuckled. "I'll be there in a jiff."

"Okey dokey," I said, rushing out the door with a wave. "See you in a few. Hold down the fort, Mr. Wong!"

Chapter Five

Jenius.

—T-SHIRT

As I trudged the fifty or so feet across the alley and into the rear entrance of my dad's bar, I contemplated possibilities for why all three lawyers might have stayed behind instead of crossing over. My calculations—allowing for a 12 percent margin of error, based on the radius of the corresponding confidence interval and the surgeon general's warning—concluded that they probably didn't stay behind for the tacos.

I took a sec to put my sunglasses in my leather bag and allow my eyes to adjust to the dim lights inside the bar. To put it mildly, my dad's bar was gorgeous. The main room had a cathedral ceiling with dark woods covering every available surface, and framed pictures, medals, and banners from various law enforcement events covering most of that. From the back entrance, the bar stood on my right, round tables and chairs perched in the middle, and tall bistro tables lined the outer edges. But the reigning glory of the speakeasy was the elaborate, hundred-year-old ironwork that circled the main room like ancient crown molding. It spiraled around and lured the eye to the west wall, where a glorious wrought-iron elevator loomed tall and proud. The kind you see only in movies and very old hotels. The kind with all its mechanisms and pulleys open for its audience to enjoy. The kind that took forever and a day to get to the second floor.

My PI business took up most of the top floor, and had its own entrance on the side of the building, a picturesque New England–style staircase. But I doubted my ability to manage the stairs without undue pain. Since I categorized all pain as undue, I decided to take the elevator inside the bar instead, despite its limitations.

My dad's voice wafted to me, and I smiled. Dad was like rain on a scorched desert. During my childhood, he kept me from drying up and crumbling into myself. Which would just be gross.

I strolled inside and spotted his tall, slim form sitting at a table with my wicked stepmother and older, non-stepsister. While Dad was the rain, they were the scorpions, and I'd learned long ago to steer clear of them. My real mom died when I was born—hemorrhaged to death while giving birth to me, which has never been one of my favorite memories—and Dad married Denise before I'd turned a year. Without even asking my opinion on the matter. Denise and I never really clicked.

"Hey, hon," Dad said as I put my sunglasses back on and tried to ease past without being noticed, not really sure why I thought the sunglasses would help.

I was almost annoyed at being spotted before realizing I'd never have gotten away with it anyway. The danged elevator was louder than a Chevy big block and crept up like an injured snail. I was certain Denise would have noticed when a dark-haired girl in sunglasses started elevating beside her.

I strolled toward their table.

"Come have some breakfast," Dad said. "I'll share."

Denise and Gemma had brought Dad sustenance to break the fast. Apparently, I was not invited—big surprise—despite the fact that I live about two inches south of the back door.

Gemma didn't bother glancing up from her breakfast burrito. The movement might have displaced a hair. Denise only sighed at Dad's offer and started cutting into his burrito to give me some.

"That's okay," I said. "I already ate."

She glanced up at me then, overtly annoyed. I tended to do that to her. "What did you have?" she asked, a razor's edge to her voice.

I hesitated. This was a trick; I could feel it. She was feigning concern over the nutritional content of my breakfast to make me think she cared. I stood with my lips sealed shut, refusing to be taken in by such an obvious setup.

But she turned her powerful, laserlike glare on me, and I caved. "A blueberry bagel."

Her eyes rolled in irritation before refocusing on her burrito.

Phew. That was close. Who knew the mention of a blueberry bagel could irritate my stepmother so? Maybe I should have thrown in the strawberry cream cheese for backup. It was hard being such an utter disappointment to the woman who'd raised me, but gosh darn it, I gave it my all. I could have invented the wheel and she would have been disappointed. Or Post-it notes. Or bone marrow.

My dad unfolded from his chair for a kiss and gasped softly when he noticed my jaw. I was fairly certain Denise had noticed, too—I saw her lids widen a fraction of an inch before she caught herself—but since she chose to ignore it, I chose to ignore it as well.

I lowered my glasses quickly and shook my head at Dad. He paused, drew his brows together in displeasure that I didn't want to explain anything in front of my wicked stepmother, then kissed my forehead.

"I'll be upstairs in a bit." He was letting me know he expected an explanation nonetheless.

"That's where I'll be," I said, opening the cage to the elevator, "if you're lucky."

He chuckled.

Denise sighed.

My stepmother was never big on the whole nurturing thing. I think she used up all the good stuff on my older sister, and by the time she got to me, she was fresh out of nurture. She did, however, give me one pertinent bit of 411. She was the one who informed me that I had the attention span of a gnat; only, she said I had the attention span of a gnat with selective listening. At least I think that's what she said. I wasn't listening. Oh, and she told me that men want only one thing.

And on that note, I must give praise and thanks to the powers that be. I don't want much else from them either.

But truly, in my stepmom's defense, who could blame her? I mean, she had Gemma. Gemma Vi Davidson. *The* Gemma Vi Davidson.

It was hard to compete. Especially since Gemma and I were total opposites. Gemma had blond hair and blue eyes. I did not.

Gemma was always an A student. I was more of a B-all-you-can-be kind of gal.

When Gemma was into science, I was into skipping.

When Gemma was into foreign languages, I was into the hot Italian guy down the street.

And when Gemma went to college and graduated magna cum laude in three and a half years with a bachelor's in psychology, I went to college and graduated in three and a half years with a bachelor's in sociology, only I did it summa cum laude.

Gemma's never forgiven me for showing her up. But it did push her to continue her education as part of our never-ending struggle of one-upmanship, which is kind of like the struggle for survival, only not so noble. And she didn't stop at her master's either. She went all the way with a Ph.D. A married professor named Dr. Roland. Then she got her own Ph.D. and did it by the time she was thirty.

Clearly she needed to hit it with the professor more.

Denise has never forgiven me either. When Gemma graduated, Denise's eyes shimmered with tears of joy. When I graduated, Denise's eyes rolled more often than a heroin addict with a trust fund. I think she was annoyed that she had to miss her Saturday garden club to attend the ceremony. Or it could have been the T-shirt I was wearing underneath my shiny graduation gown that said JENIUS.

Dad was proud of me, though. For a long time, I pretended that was enough. I kept thinking that someday Denise would realize she had the superhuman ability to be proud of more than one person at the same time.

That day never came. So, in an act of utter defiance, I did exactly what Denise would expect me to do: I disappointed her. Again. Because Denise felt like a woman's place was in front of a classroom, I trotted down to a recruiting event on the university's campus and joined the Peace Corps. Disappointing her was so much easier than working my ass off trying not to. And those little sideways glances and sighs of dismay didn't hurt so much when they were clearly deserved. Not to mention the fact that I got to work with the military on several projects, and surprisingly, the military is chock-full of men in uniform. Truly, its cup runneth over. Hoo-yah!

The elevator finally reached the second floor, and I waved down to Dad before stepping into the hall that led to the back entrance of my office. The front outside entrance, the one I usually took, led directly to my reception area, with my office past that.

Then there was a third entrance that was a little trickier to maneuver and involved the fire escape out back. So when I saw Garrett in the hall, leaning against my office door, waiting for me, I realized he must have jumped to the fire escape and climbed in through the window.

Show-off.

"Do you remember the part about my dad being an ex-cop? What are you doing here?" I asked, annoyance hardening my voice. He was wearing a white T-shirt, dark jacket, and a nice-fitting pair of jeans.

He straightened and raised a questioning brow. "Any reason you took an elevator that travels at the speed of molasses in January instead of the stairs?"

Garrett was a looker, damn him, with his dark skin and smoldering gray eyes, but that was as far as it went for me. Any minute amount of attraction I may previously have harbored was now buried beneath a thick layer of resentment and animosity. And as far as I was concerned, that was exactly where it would stay.

I let my irritated facial expression answer for me, unlocked the heavy wooden door to my office, then looked past Garrett to the three departed visitors who'd also been waiting for me.

"Glad you could join us," I said to Barber. "You're much taller vertically."

Sussman elbowed him in a teasing gesture while Garrett strode into my office, apparently refusing to watch me talk to wallpaper.

"Sorry about my earlier behavior," Barber said. "I guess I kind of lost it."

His apology left me feeling guilty for not being more . . . I don't know, supportive. Maybe I needed sensitivity training. I once signed up for an anger management class, but the instructor pissed me off.

"I have no room to judge you," I said, patting Barber on the shoulder. "I've never died. Not officially."

"Officially?" Sussman asked.

"Long story."

"Yeah, yeah," Elizabeth said. "Can we get inside? I figure I don't have much time left, and I want to get in all the ogling at tall, dark, and skeptic that I can. Why couldn't I have met him yesterday? I could've died happy."

I knew how she felt. I had similar feelings about Reyes.

We stepped inside my office, which doubled as an art gallery for a friend of mine named Pari. Dark abstract paintings of life on Central lined my walls. One was a disturbing rendition of a Goth girl doing laundry, washing blood off her sleeves. The girl looked like me, a little joke, since I loathed laundry day. Thankfully, my image was difficult to make out in the frenzy of grays swirling around the scene.

Pari was also a tattoo artist and had a shop nearby. She designed the tattoo I had on my left shoulder blade. The one of a little grim reaper enshrouded in a flowing cloak with large, innocent eyes peeping out of it. Pari was chock-full of inside jokes.

Garrett turned toward me. I refused to acknowledge him with eye contact. Instead, I hung up my bag and started a pot of coffee just as Cookie came in the front door.

"You in here, sweetheart?"

"Back here," I called to her. "I've started the coffee." I kept the coffeepot in my office on the pretense of monitoring Cookie's caffeine intake. Actually, it was my answer to potpourri.

"Coffee. Thank the gods," Cookie said as she opened the door between her office and mine. "Oh." She saw Garrett. "Mr. Swopes, I didn't realize—"

"He was just leaving," I told her.

Garrett smiled at me, then placed the full power of his lopsided grin on Cookie.

The bastard.

"My, my, my," Elizabeth said a tad too breathlessly. "That's what I'm talking about."

Suppressing a helpless sigh, I watched as Cookie started to speak, stuttered something about paperwork, then waved and closed the door to give us our privacy.

"I know exactly how she feels," Elizabeth purred.

I plopped into the chair behind my desk as Garrett folded himself into the seat across from me.

"Well?" I asked.

"Well?" he mimicked.

"You're not here for a social call, Swopes. What do you want? I have three murders to solve."

My confidence seemed to amuse him. "I was just thinking we might go out for coffee sometime."

"Damn," Elizabeth said. "You guys are going out for coffee? Can I watch?"

I frowned at her. "We are not going out for coffee."

Garrett lowered his head, seeming to force himself to be patient.

"Look," I said, getting fed up with his 'tude. "I've already told you. You can either deal with my ability or not. Preferably not. There's the door. Have a nice day and kiss my ass."

He raised his head, his expression serious but not angry like I felt it should have been, considering the "ass" comment. "First of all," he said, his voice infused with exasperation, "I'm still getting used to all this, Miss Piss and Vinegar. Give me a little time."

"No."

"Second," he continued without missing a beat, "I just want to talk to you about it."

"No."

"I mean, how does it work?"

"Well."

"Do you see dead people all the time?"

"Every other weekend and holidays."

"Are they, you know, everywhere?"

"Is a frog's ass watertight?" I asked, leaning back in my chair and lifting my feet to rest them, dusty hiking boots and all, on the desk.

I crossed my ankles and steepled my fingers and glared to emphasize my impatience while I waited, impatiently, for Garrett to make a decision. To believe or not to believe.

I called this part "the dawning"—the part where people begin to wonder if I really can see the departed. Oh, they still have doubts. Most people rack their brains, trying to come up with an explanation, any explanation, of how I do what I do.

And as I lived and breathed, Garrett Swopes was struggling to come up with that very thing. After all, dead people don't walk around trying to solve their own murders. Ghosts don't exist. None of what I claimed was possible.

The dawning was like a relish fork in the road, and the proverbial traveler had to take one prong or the other. Unfortunately, the prong that led to Charley-sees-dead-people was much sharper than the safer, more travel-worn Charley-is-psychotic prong. Nobody wants to look like a fool. Nine times out of ten, that reason alone keeps people from allowing themselves to believe.

Garrett stared back at me a few seconds, then refocused on my fingers. I could almost see the wheels spinning in his head. After several moments more, I began to think those wheels needed a good oiling.

"But how did you know where to find Ms. Ellery's body?" he asked at last.

"I'm not explaining it again, Swopes."

"Seriously—"

"No."

After another long pause, he asked, "You've been doing this since you were five?"

I snorted. "I've been able to see the departed since I was born. It just took my dad five years to really believe me. But when I told him where to find a missing girl's body, he realized what an asset I'd be."

"The Johnson girl," he said.

I tried not to wince. The memory was not one of my favorites. In fact, if someone were to ask, I'd have a hard time choosing a lesser favorite. On the day of the Johnson Girl Fiasco, as I called it, Denise veered right onto the travel-worn prong, choosing not to believe me and vowing never to talk about it again. It was also the day that I recognized the abnormality of what I do. And that some people—people very close to me—would despise me for it. Of course, my stepmother slapping me senseless in front of dozens of onlookers didn't ingratiate me to the incident either.

"Are you okay?" Sussman asked.

I'd almost forgotten they were there. I nodded discreetly.

"You know," Elizabeth said, "I think he's really trying to be open-minded."

My expression turned into a dubious scowl. It was mean. She was only trying to help.

"Are they here now?" Garrett asked.

I sighed, not particularly craving his antagonism. But he'd asked. "Yes."

He took out his notebook. "Can you ask Ms. Ellery when her birthday is?"

"No."

Elizabeth walked forward. "It's June twentieth."

I looked at her. "He knows when your birthday is. He just wants to see if I do."

"No?" he asked. He seemed disappointed, like he wanted me to tell him, wanted to believe. For about five minutes, anyway. It was the fair-weather believers I had to watch out for. They had a nasty habit of sucker-punching me in the gut when I least expected it.

"Just tell him," Elizabeth said.

"You don't understand," I told her. "People like him never believe, not fully. He'll always have doubts. He'll always quiz me, drill me for information he already has just to see if I fuck up." I looked back at Garrett. "So fuck him."

"Elizabeth," Sussman said, "maybe we should just—"

"No!" she yelled, and I jumped, catching Garrett's full attention. "Just tell him." She rushed toward my desk, leaned over it. "He needs to get over himself and just believe you. He doesn't know what he'll be missing. He'll go through life with this one-dimensional view of the world he lives in. He'll have no sense of direction, no hope that the people he's loved and lost will go to a better place. That they'll be okay."

I realized Elizabeth was no longer talking about Garrett. She was talking about herself.

I stood and walked around to her. "Elizabeth, what's wrong?"

She almost cried. I could see tears shimmering in her pale eyes. "There's so much I want to tell my sister, but she's just like him . . . just like me. I would never have believed you either." Her shoulders deflated, and she leveled a guilty gaze on me. "I'm sorry, Charlotte, I wouldn't have. Not in a million years. And neither will she."

A relieved smile spread across my face. Was that all? I'd come across this problem countless times. "Elizabeth," I said, "of all the problems we have right now, that is the only one with a simple fix."

Garrett watched our exchange—or rather my exchange—but to his credit, his expression remained passive. I'd often considered how ridiculous I must look to the living, talking to myself, gesturing wildly, hugging air. But I didn't always have a choice. If Garrett refused to leave, he'd just have to deal with my world. I would not modify my behavior to appease his delicate sense of propriety in my own office.

Elizabeth sniffed. "What do you mean? What fix?"

"You leave a note."

"A note?"

"Sure. I do it all the time. It saves me so much explaining," I said with an encompassing wave of my hand. "You dictate a note to me, I type it—and predate it to before your death, naturally—and then it's miraculously found among your possessions. Kind of like an if-anything-should-happen-to-me note. You tell her everything you want her to know, and we just pretend you'd typed it before you died. I even have a guy who can forge your signature to seal the deal, if you'd like."

"Who?" Garrett asked.

I glowered at him in warning. What I did with the departed was none of his business.

A pretty look of astonishment came over Elizabeth's face. "That's brilliant. I'm a lawyer. I'm more organized than the Dewey decimal system. She'd totally fall for it."

"Of course she'll fall for it," I said, patting her back.

"Can I write one to my wife?" Sussman asked.

"Sure."

Then we all looked at Barber, expecting him to have someone to write to as well. "I only have my mom. She knows how I feel about her," he said, and I wondered if I should be happy about that or sad because his mother was all he had.

"I'm glad," I told him. "I wish more people took the time to make their feelings known."

"Yeah. I've hated her guts since I was ten. There's really not much else to put in a letter."

I tried to hide the shock I felt.

He noticed anyway. "Oh, trust me, the feeling's mutual."

"Okay, two notes, then."

"Hey," Elizabeth said, suddenly thoughtful, "what day is the first day of summer?"

"Planning on sticking around that long?" I asked.

She lifted her shoulders, referenced Garrett with a nod of her head, then wriggled her perfectly arched brows.

"Ah." I tried not to laugh. "It's June twentieth, or sometimes—"

Garrett gasped, and Elizabeth crossed her arms and smiled, smugness radiating off her in waves.

"You're right," Garrett said. "Elizabeth Ellery's birthday is June twentieth."

I leveled a mortified glare on her. "You tricked me."

"Lawyer," she volleyed, as if that explained it all.

Yeah, I liked her a lot. I strolled back to my chair and plopped down with my usual fanfare.

"She tricked me," I said to Garrett.

He grinned. But his grin was different. It had changed, and I realized why.

"Oh, no. No, no, no, no, no," I said, wagging a finger at him. "Don't even start with that crap."

"What crap?" he asked, all innocence and awe.

"The crap where you look at me like I have all the answers to every question in the known universe. I don't. I can't see into the future. I can't read your past. I damn sure can't read your palm, whatever the hell that's about. I can't—"

"But you're psychic, right?"

"Dude," I said, leaning over the desk, "I'm about as psychic as a carrot."

"But—"

"No *buts*!" I had serious issues with the *p-s* word. We'd never really bonded. I threw my hands over my ears and started humming to myself.

"That's mature."

He was right. I stuck out my tongue anyway, then put my hands down. "Listen, even I have more questions than answers. I'm fairly certain my abilities are more closely related to schizophrenia than to anything supernatural. Ask anyone. If I were edible, I'd be a fruitcake."

"Schizophrenia," he said doubtfully.

"I hear voices in my head. How much more schizophrenic does it get?"

"But you just said—"

I held up an index finger to stop him. Though a middle one would have been more to the point, I had to explain before I lost the ground I'd just gained. "Look, when people are in the position you're in now, when they're almost to the point of believing in what I can do, they pull out all the stops. They quiz me, ask me stupid questions, want to know where the next earthquake will hit or what the winning lottery numbers will be. Seriously, have you ever read the headline 'Psychic Wins Lottery'? I'm not psychic. I don't even know if such a thing exists."

"Tell him what you are," Elizabeth chimed in excitedly while Garrett flipped through his notepad.

I flashed her a desperate shut-up-or-die look. It didn't work. Probably because she was already dead.

"Seriously," she said, "just tell him. He's starting to believe you now. He'll think it's cool."

"No, he won't," I whispered through my teeth, forgetting that I was the only living person in the room who could hear her.

"A person sensitive to things beyond the natural range of perception." Garrett looked up at me. "The definition of psychic."

"Oh, well, okay. Maybe," I said. "But I still hate the word. And its implications."

"Fair enough," he said with a shrug. "And I won't what?"

"Think it's cool."

"What? Your abilities?"

"Not exactly."

"Then what?"

Then what? I guess if he really wanted to know, I'd hit him with the whole enchilada dinner. I was on a roll, after all. Why stop now? Not even my dad or Uncle Bob really knew the extent of what I was. I'd never needed to tell them. They believed me, and that was good enough. But since I really didn't care what Garrett thought of me . . .

"Fine," I said with a challenging edge to my voice. "I'll tell you everything. If I do, will you leave?"

After a pause, he agreed with an almost imperceptible nod.

"I'm a . . . I'm kind of a . . . I'm sort of like a . . . well, damn." I gritted my teeth and just blurted it out: "I'm a grim reaper. Well, *the* grim reaper, actually."

There. I'd said it. I laid it all out on the table, cleared the air, bared my soul, all the while vowing that no cliché be left unturned. But he didn't flinch. He didn't laugh. He didn't shoot out of his chair or stalk out the door. In fact, he didn't move at all. Not an inch. I wondered if he was still breathing; then it dawned on me. This was his poker face. His gray eyes stayed locked on mine as I waited for his reaction, but he wasn't going to give me one. I had to admit, his poker face was pretty good. I had no idea what he was thinking.

"I think he believes you," Elizabeth said as she bent over and looked at him before glancing back at me.

So she would have no choice but to see the doubt in every line of my face, I formed my expression carefully.

"How does that work?" Garrett asked at last.

I refocused my attention on him. "You said you would leave."

"If," he countered, "you told me everything."

Dammit. "Okay, how does it work? Hell, I don't know. It just does."

"I mean, what do you do?"

"Oh. I help people cross."

"Cross?"

"Um, to the other side?" I said, wondering just how clueless he was. "How?"

Geez, he was persistent. "Excuse me." I jumped up, scooted the office-furniture version of a love seat forward, then sat back down. The lawyers had eased closer, wanting to hear every word of the story as well. "Can you guys sit down? You're making me nervous hovering like that."

"Oh, sure," they said, and all three squeezed into the seat. I fought back a chuckle.

"How?" Garrett repeated.

Back to the third degree. A long breath slipped through my lips as I considered everything I'd been telling him. This stuff could be used as ammunition against me. It had happened before, by people I'd trusted much more than Garrett. Still, we'd come this far.

"Basically," I said, exaggerating my reluctance in the tone of my voice, "I try to help them figure out why they didn't cross. Then I lead them to the light."

"What light?"

"*The* light. The only light I know of," I replied, using the escape and evasion tactics I'd learned from a first lieutenant I dated in college.

"Uh-huh," he said, not falling for it. "What light?"

I hesitated. Some bits of information were just more sacred than others. Some were reserved for the departed only. It wasn't like the truth of what I do would help him believe me. More likely, it would send him running for the door. Come to think of it . . .

"Me," I said with a hint of self-righteous arrogance lifting my chin. I felt like I was back in middle school, begging the bully to challenge me.

After a thoughtful moment, he asked, "You?"

"Me," I repeated, with just as much arrogance. *Go ahead, Mr. Skeptic, make my day. Challenge me. Prove me wrong. As if.* "Apparently, I'm very bright."

I suddenly realized what I'd done. I'd said too much. I'd let my pride go to the party, and it ended up auditioning for Girls Gone Wild. It was so grounded.

Garrett sat back in his chair and let his gaze travel over every inch of me that he could see before relocking with mine. "So you help them figure out why they didn't cross."

No way to weasel out of the damned conversation now. No wonder pride was one of the seven deadlies. "Yes," I answered.

"And then you lead them to the light."

"Yes."

"Which is you."

"Yes."

"So when we cross," Sussman said, "it'll be *through you*?"

I glanced at him. I figured he was creeped out by the concept—one that could be considered sacrilegious on a thousand different planets—but he seemed fascinated. "Yes, you'll cross through me. Grim reaper," I said by way of explanation.

"Wow," Barber said. "That's about the coolest thing I've heard all day."

"You're a portal," Garrett said.

I shrugged. "I guess that's one way of looking at it."

An intrigued smile spread across his face as he studied me, making my nerve endings prickly with suspicion.

"He is so into you," Elizabeth said.

I ignored her and glanced at my watch. "Gosh, look at the time." Where the heck was Uncle Bob?

"So the spirits that don't cross are just hanging out on earth, walking through us without a care in the world?" Garrett asked, not ready to give up his quest.

I sighed. This could go on for days.

"No. They exist in the same time and space but on a different plane. Like a double-exposed picture. I'm just able to be on both planes simultaneously."

"Then that makes you pretty amazing," he said, appreciation shimmering in his eyes.

This was too much. I was still prying my jaw off the floor, metaphorically, that he believed anything I said.

"So, how about it? Let's go get some coffee," he suggested again.

"But I just explained everything."

"Sweetheart, I doubt you've even scratched the surface." When I hesitated, he said, "We can go as friends."

I scowled, just a little, then reminded him, "We're not friends, remember? You've made that painfully clear over the last month. We're not pals or buds or anything else even remotely resembling friends."

"Weekend lovers?" he offered.

That was it. I didn't know what game he was playing—though I was fairly certain it wasn't Monopoly . . . or checkers—but I refused to play along. I stood and walked around the desk so I could stand over him. Menacingly. Like Darth Vader, only with better lung capacity. After a meaningful stare-down, I pointed to the exit. "I have work to do."

He glanced at the door I was pointing at, the one through which I was suggesting he leave. "You have work to do? On that door?" he asked, all teasing and smart-assy.

"What?"

"Are you going to paint it?"

"No."

"I suggest a deep, rich brown to go with your hair." He stood, reversing the situation to tower over me. After another stare-down, one with a different meaning entirely, he leaned in and said softly, "Or gold . . . to go with your eyes."

"I think I just came," Elizabeth said.

The other two lawyers, after clearing their throats, had the decency to step out of the room. Elizabeth reluctantly followed them into the reception area, otherwise known as Cookie's-god-danged-space-and-don't-you-forget-it.

As Garrett waited for me to agree to have *coffee* with him, I saw it from the corner of my eye. The blurry Superman thing. It moved so fast that by the time I turned my head, it was gone. It had moved to my other side, brushed my arm, feathered across my mouth, then dived inside me, pooling in my abdomen, oozing warmth throughout my entire body.

My insides quaked, and I threw back my head with a startled gasp. Garrett stepped forward and grabbed hold of my arms to keep me from falling. Only then did I see the bewildered expression on his face. He pulled me closer. Then the feeling left me and Garrett shot backwards, as if a violent force had shoved him.

He stumbled, caught himself, then looked at me. We both stood stunned and wide-eyed. I toppled toward my desk, leaned against it to keep my knees from buckling.

"Was that . . . one of them?" he asked, absently rubbing his chest where he'd apparently been shoved. He glanced around wildly before placing a disconcerted scowl on me.

"No," I said, trying to slow my breathing, "that was something very different."

What, I didn't know. But I could guess, and I didn't like the direction my guesses were heading. Could it be the Big Bad? If so, why here? Why now? My life didn't seem to be in any immediate danger.

Fear was difficult for me to hide. I rarely felt it. But surely Garrett sensed it in me now. The thought of him seeing me afraid grated more than a little.

Then another scenario came to mind. Of all the times I'd seen Bad, he'd never *brushed against me*. He'd never even touched me, and he certainly hadn't dived in for a swim in my nether regions. Maybe it wasn't Bad at all.

I scanned the room, probably looking a little desperate. Was it Reyes? Could it have been him? Could he have been . . . jealous? Of Swopes? Was he serious?

I rushed to the door and asked everyone, "Did you see anything? Did he come this way?"

Elizabeth, who had been sitting on our sage green reception sofa, jumped up and said, "You lost him? How could you lose him?"

"Not Garrett," I said, possibly a little too impatiently. "The dark, blurry guy."

Cookie was slowly beginning to realize we had company. She eased up out of her seat as if a cobra were perched on her desk. "Charley, sweetheart, do we have clients?"

"Oh, yeah. I forgot to mention that. Everyone, this is Cookie. Cookie, we have the three lawyers who *left* us last night. The ones I told you about. We're working on their case with Uncle Bob. Okay, now, did anyone see him?"

The lawyers questioned each other with sideways glances and shrugs. I let a hapless sigh slip through my lips and slumped against the doorjamb.

You'd think, me being a grim reaper and all, I'd have connections, ways of obtaining Blurry Guy's identity. But since the only *connection* from the other side I'd ever made was that of Bad, aka death incarnate, inquiries proved difficult.

Then I noticed an odd shadow in the corner, one that undulated and shifted under the morning light. It was him. It had to be. I straightened, pried my fingers off the doorjamb, and eased into the room, trying not to scare him away.

"May I see you?" I asked, my voice too shaky.

Everyone looked toward the corner, but only the lawyers saw him, too. All three took a wary step back, so in synch, the movement looked choreographed, while I stepped forward pleadingly.

"Please, let me see you."

The shadow moved, disintegrated, disappeared, and reappeared before me in the same instant. Then it was my turn to retreat. I stumbled back as a long tendril of smoke raised, and suddenly an arm was braced against the wall beside my head. A long arm that angled up to a tall shoulder.

The lawyers gasped as the entity materialized before them, as smoke became flesh, as molecules meshed and fused to form one solid muscle after another. My gaze had yet to linger past his arm, sliding from the hand steadied against the wall—a hand that, even with the wear of hard labor, was beautiful—to the long, sinewy curve of a steel-like forearm. A rolled cuff, an oddly bright color, encircled the arm below the elbow, but above that, a biceps strained against the thick material, attesting to the strength it encapsulated. Then my gaze slipped farther up to a shoulder, wide and powerful and unyielding.

The entity leaned in before I could see its face, pressed the warmth of its body into mine, and bent forward to whisper in my ear. It was so close, I could only make out its jaw, strong and shadowed with at least two days' growth, and dark hair in need of a trim.

His mouth brushed my ear, sending shivers down my spine. "Dutch," he whispered, and I melted into him.

This was my chance, my opportunity to ask if he was who I thought he was—who I hoped he was. But I'd spiraled back into my dream world, where nothing worked right. My hands had a will of their own as they lifted to his chest. The bones in my legs dissolved. My mouth wanted only one thing. Him. His taste. His texture. He smelled like rain during a lightning storm, earthy and electric.

I curled his shirt into my fists—whether to push him away or pull him closer, I wasn't sure. Why couldn't I see him? Why couldn't I just convince myself to step to the side and look at him?

Then his mouth covered mine and I lost all sense of reality. My world took his form, became his body, his mouth, his hands, skimming over me, surveying the hills and valleys of all that was me, his moon. His very own satellite seduced into his orbit by the sheer will of his gravity.

The kiss deepened, grew more urgent, and my body responded with a quiver of desire. He groaned and pushed farther into me, his tongue delving between my lips, not just tasting, but drinking every part of me, melding my soul with his.

He pried one of my hands off his shirt and led it down his pants to cover his erection. I sucked in a sharp breath, inhaling the heat that drifted off him. I felt a hand squeeze between my legs, and liquid fire pooled in my abdomen. I wanted him on me, around me, and in me. I could think of nothing else but the utter sensuality of this perfect being.

My hunger seemed impenetrable until I heard my name from a distance and the fog began to evaporate.

"Charley?"

I tumbled out of the dream and snapped to attention. Everyone in the room stared at me openmouthed. Uncle Bob stood halfway in the door with a quizzical expression drawing his brows together. Garrett looked on as well. Agitation flashed in his eyes. He turned and strode out the door, nodding brusquely to Uncle Bob as he walked past.

And then I realized it was gone. He was gone. No longer able to bear my own weight, I sank to the floor and stewed in my own astonishment.

"Were you just possessed?" Cookie asked after a long moment, awe softening her voice. "'Cause let me tell you, sweetheart, if that was possession, I'm selling my soul."

Chapter Six

A.D.D. A lifetime of distractions.
——T-SHIRT

While I wanted nothing more than to quiz the dearly departed about Reyes—Did they get a good look at him? What color were his eyes? Did he seem, I don't know, dead?—Uncle Bob insisted on discussing the case. In the meantime, my sanity hung in the balance. My fragile sense of well-being. My ability to cope with the everyday realities of reality. Not to mention my sex life.

Was nothing sacred?

"Did you get an ID on the shooter?" Uncle Bob asked as we headed back into my office, currently dubbed the Dead Zone.

"No." The room seemed cold now, probably because I'd just had a near-sex experience with a blazing inferno. I cranked up the heat and poured a cup of coffee before sitting down.

Uncle Bob sat across from me. "No? Well, are they, you know, here?"

"Yes." How was this happening? Clearly Reyes wasn't your every-day, run-of-the-mill corpse. If it *was* Reyes. If he *was* a corpse.

"So, you haven't talked to them about it?"

"No." If he was dead, how was he so . . . hot? Like literally hot? Then again, if he was alive, how was he incorporeal? How did he move so fast? How did he switch from one molecular state to another? I'd never seen anything like it.

Uncle Bob snapped his fingers in front of my face. I blinked to attention, then glared at him.

"Don't get mad." He showed his palms in a gesture of peace. "You keep going elsewhere, and I need you here. We had another homicide last night. Though they don't appear to be related, I need to know for certain."

"Another one?" I asked as he lifted an autopsy photo from the file jacket he carried. "Why didn't you call me?"

"I did. Your phone's off."

"Oops."

"I've got the mayor breathing down my neck on this one. Three dead lawyers in one night looks bad on the evening news."

I checked my cell. "Sorry, my battery bit the dirt." I guess nothing was safe in the Dead Zone.

After I plugged my phone into its charger, Uncle Bob slid the photo across the desk. A bloated face, blue and purple, appeared before me. It had crusts of blood around several puffy wounds, as if the man had been in an accident. Considering the circumstances, I doubted any of his wounds were accidental. Whoever he was, death had not come easily.

"What happened to him?" I asked.

"He was tortured, then killed. But they weren't after information." He pointed to the guy's mouth and throat. "They taped his mouth and kept pressure on his windpipe to keep him from screaming. So he'd either already given them the info they needed, or they knew what he'd done."

I let my gaze stray, trying not to seem squeamish.

"The assailants wanted to inflict as much pain as possible before he died. If I had to take a street-educated guess, I'd say he snitched on the wrong guy. This kind of torture is usually reserved for traitors, either to a higher-up in a gang or to an entire group or organization. These days, crime syndicates are more hierarchical than English nobility."

The lawyers gathered around my desk, so I held up the photo, angling it away from my line of sight. Sussman made a face and stepped back. I was right there with him. But Elizabeth and Barber studied it more closely.

"It's hard to say for sure," Elizabeth said. "Maybe if he wasn't so blotchy . . ."

"It would help if we had a mug shot instead of an autopsy photo."

"No ID yet," Uncle Bob said to me before answering his ringing cell.

Sussman stared at Barber through his round-rimmed glasses. "Do you recognize this man, Jason?"

I glanced toward him. Barber looked stunned, struck speechless, pale despite the physiological impossibility. Since they lacked blood and all.

"That's him," Barber said. "That's the guy who asked me to meet him."

Elizabeth glanced back at the photo. "That's your mystery man?" she asked.

"I nearly know it is," he replied.

Sussman stepped forward and studied the photo again. "Are you sure?"

Barber gave a shaky affirmation. "I wouldn't bet my life or anything."

"Too late for that anyway," Elizabeth said, still gazing at the photo, her face morphing into varying degrees of revulsion.

Uncle Bob shut his phone. "Carlos Rivera. He has an arrest record as long as my legendary and much-envied memory."

"So, no priors," I said, holding back a chuckle.

He squinted his eyes and tapped an index finger on his temple. "Like a steel trap."

"Yeah, you seem to be forgetting that time you were supposed to get me out of Dad's car and put me to bed while he whipped up some margaritas. I woke up at two in the morning almost frozen solid in the backseat while you were making whoopie with Mrs. Dunlop next door."

He adjusted his tie. "I believe that was an alcohol-related incident," he grumbled. A strangely flattering crimson spread over his face, making the whole account worthwhile.

Just to add icing to the cake, I shook my head in mock disappointment. "Whatever helps you sleep at night, Uncle Near Negligent Homicide."

Elizabeth chuckled.

Uncle Bob didn't. "How 'bout we leave the filing of criminal charges to the DA." Before I could argue, he said, "We found Mr. Rivera floating in the Rio Grande."

"Maybe he was thirsty," I offered.

"Have you ever tasted the Rio Grande?"

"Not lately," I said, wondering when he had. And why. And if he carried any parasites because of it. "Barber thinks this might be the same guy who asked him for a cloak-and-dagger meeting."

Uncle Bob leaned forward, intrigued. "Oh yeah?"

"Yeah." As Barber explained the incident to me, I relayed the info to Uncle Bob, who, naturally, recorded everything in his notepad.

"This guy calls me," Barber said, easing onto the seat I'd pulled up earlier. Elizabeth followed suit, but Sussman walked to the window and gazed out at the university campus across the street while we talked. "He wanted to meet in an alley, which I thought was pretty odd. But he sounded, I don't know, almost desperate."

"Can he describe his behavior?" Uncle Bob asked me.

"He was nervous," Barber said, "jumpy. He kept looking over his shoulder, checking his watch. I just figured he was high on the latest jagged little pill."

"But you listened to him anyway?" I asked, butting into Uncle B's interview.

"He said he had information on one of our clients," Elizabeth said. "Jason had no choice but to listen."

"What information?" I asked, taking note of her knee-jerk leap to his defense. Interesting.

By the time Barber had finished his tale, we'd learned that, according to the deceased Carlos Rivera, there was a man going to prison for a very long time whose worst crime involved the smoking of a little pot in college. Admittedly, he inhaled.

But forensic evidence pointed to a more severe crime. Police found a murdered teen in his backyard and his own sneakers with the kid's blood on them inside his house. The sneakers were like the final nail in his coffin. Pile on a corroborating witness—an eighty-year-old woman with Coke-bottle glasses and bunions—and the poor guy went down for murder. The woman stated under oath that she saw the defendant stashing the kid in his backyard. Behind a storage shed. On a dark and stormy night. Clearly, she'd read too many mysteries.

"But it was dark," I said. "And stormy. She could have seen my great-aunt Lillian stash the body there and assumed it was your client."

"Exactly," Barber agreed. "Nonetheless, he was convicted of second-degree murder."

"Did your client know the kid?" Uncle Bob asked. That was totally my next question.

Barber shook his head. "Said he'd never seen him before in his life."

"What's your client's name?" I asked. Before Uncle Bob could.

"Weir. Mark Weir. He gave me a USB flash drive," Barber said.

"Who did? Your client?"

"Who did what?" Uncle Bob asked without looking up from his writing.

"Someone gave Barber a flash drive."

"Who did?" he repeated. For heaven's sake, didn't I just ask that?

"No, that guy." Barber nodded toward the photo. "Rivera. Though he never gave me his name, he did give me a location. He told me I could find the evidence I needed to clear Mr. Weir at a warehouse on the Westside. He said to be there Wednesday night."

"Time?" Uncle Bob asked. Apparently really good interviewers didn't need to use complete sentences. I made a mental note.

"He never gave me a time. I think he saw someone following him. He pulled up the hood on his sweatshirt and ducked inside a pizza place before I could ask him anything else." Barber glanced back at the photo. "I guess they busted him anyway, figured out what he was up to."

"Today is Wednesday," I said. "When did all this happen?"

Sussman turned back, and all three lawyers eyed each other. Then Elizabeth answered, a sadness softening her voice. "The day we died." She glanced at Barber. "It seems so long ago."

Barber covered her hands with his. Her tough bravado, her powerful don't-fuck-with-me demeanor, seemed to fade a little.

"This happened yesterday," I said to Uncle Bob.

"Okay," he said, launching into Nazi interrogator mode. He asked dozens upon dozens of questions, scribbling wildly in his notebook as I relayed the answers. I wondered if he'd ever heard of a digital recorder.

"The flash drive is on his desk at his office," I said, answering yet another question. "No, the guy didn't say what was on it, but Barber got the impression it was a video of some sort. Yes, this Wednesday, today. No, he didn't see who was following Rivera. They've already

filed an appeal, but it'll take months to get it before a judge. Yes. No. The client hasn't been transferred yet. Maybe. Not on your life. When hell freezes over. Um, okay. No, his *other* left testicle."

By the time Uncle Bob had run out of questions—a good thing, since they were veering way off subject—I had run out of energy. Not enough, however, to allay the niggling suspicions I had about this whole situation. This was more important than one innocent man, and I had a feeling it centered on the murdered teen. I needed more information on both.

We headed downstairs to grab a bite. Dad made the best Monte Cristos this side of the Eiffel Tower, and my mouth watered just thinking about them. When I finally had a moment to breathe, my thoughts strayed back to Reyes. It was difficult not to dwell on a man whose mere presence evoked images of the devil hell-bent on sinning.

"I love the name of your dad's bar," Elizabeth said as we trod downstairs.

I forced myself back to the present. Elizabeth's attitude toward me had changed since I'd almost had sex with an incorporeal being in her presence. But I didn't think she was angry. Or offended. Maybe it was something about Garrett. Maybe she felt as though I were cheating on him, since he seemed to have feelings for me. He had feelings for me, all right, but they weren't the warm and fuzzy kind.

"Thanks," I said. "He named it after me, to the utter chagrin of my sister," I added with a snort.

Sussman chuckled. "He named it after you? I thought it was called Calamity's."

"Yeah. Uncle Bob called me Calamity for years, as in Calamity Jane? And when my dad bought the bar, he just figured it fit."

"I like it," Elizabeth said. "I had a dog named after me once."

I tried not to laugh. "What kind?"

"A pit bull." A mischievous grin spread across her mouth.

"I can totally see that," I said with a chuckle.

We took a secluded table in a dark corner so I could hopefully talk to my clients without anyone staring. After a quick intro—and an abbreviated version of my night with domestic-abuse husband in the bar to explain the state of my face—I asked my dad if I had any messages.

"Here?" he asked. "Are you expecting one?"

"Well, yes and no." Rosie Herschel, my first assisted-disappearing case, was supposed to call only if she ran into trouble, so no news was good news. We didn't want to risk any communication otherwise, any connection to me and my job, thus spilling the fact that she'd hightailed it out of her asshole husband's pathetic life, not that the man lived anywhere near close enough to the town of Intelligence to figure out what had really happened.

" 'Yes and no' doesn't answer my question," Dad said, waiting for me to elaborate.

"Sure it does."

"Ah," he said, understanding my point. "Official business. Got it. I'll let you know if anything comes in."

"Thanks, Dad."

He smiled, held it for a moment, then leaned down to whisper in my ear. "But if you ever come into my bar with a bruised and swollen face again, we're going to have a serious talk about your *official business* and everything it entails."

Damn. I thought I'd gotten away with it. I thought I'd convinced him that my ass-kicking was more of an educational experience than a scarred-for-life one.

My shoulders deflated. "Fine," I said, adding a slight whine to my normally nonalcoholic voice.

He kissed my cheek and took off to cover the bar. Apparently, Donnie hadn't come in yet. Donnie was a quiet Native American with long black hair and killer pecs. He didn't care enough about me to give me the time of day, but I pretty much had the time-of-day thing covered anyway. And Donnie was nice to look at.

Uncle Bob closed his cell phone and placed his full attention on me. It was unsettling. "So," he said, "you want to tell me what was happening when I walked into your office this morning?"

Oh, that. I shifted in my chair uncomfortably. Making out with air must look ridiculous to the ordinary passerby.

"How bad was it?" I asked him.

"Not bad, I guess. I thought you were having a panic attack or something. But then I realized Cookie and Swopes were just staring at you, so I figured whatever it was couldn't have been life-threatening."

"Right, because Swopes would have been right there, giving me mouth-to-mouth or something else heroic."

Uncle Bob tilted his head as he thought back. "Actually, it was more the look of utter longing on Cookie's face."

A bubble of laughter rose from my throat. I could totally see the euphoria in Cookie's expression. Uncle Bob sat patiently, his furry brows raised in question as he waited for an explanation.

Well, he wasn't getting one. "You know, Uncle Bob, we might want to steer clear of this particular subject, you being my uncle and all."

"Okay," he said with a nonchalant shrug, pretending to drop the subject. He sipped from his iced tea, then added, "Swopes seemed pretty upset, though. Figured you might know why."

"I do. He's an asshole."

"He's a little moody sometimes, I'll give you that."

"So was Josef Mengele."

"But in his defense," he continued, doing his best to placate me, "this whole rift between you two is my fault. If I'd just kept my mouth shut. Darn those lagers."

"Well, lagers didn't turn Swopes into an asshole. I'm pretty sure he was born that way."

Uncle Bob sucked in a long, deep breath, then dropped the subject for real. "I can see where this is *not* going. But dammit, Charley, I have a job to do." I blinked in surprise, and he grinned. "I have to go harass your dad." He rose from the table and patted my shoulder, which was his way of saying we were good.

I slipped my hand onto his. "Harass him some for me, will you?"

After a soft squeeze, Uncle Bob strolled over to the bar, claiming— loudly—to be an investigator from the CDC. I cringed. Dad found few things less humorous than the thought of the Centers for Disease Control and Prevention paying him a visit. It lay somewhere between an IRS audit and a class action lawsuit.

I glanced back at the lawyers. They were sitting around the table— Uncle Bob had pulled out chairs for them—and talking amongst themselves.

"Do you know when your funeral is?" Elizabeth asked Sussman, her voice tainted with sadness.

He lowered his head. "They're meeting with the funeral director this afternoon."

She put her hand on his. "How is Michelle doing?"

"Not well. I need to get back to her."

Uh-oh. He was going to be one of those departed who stays behind to *take care* of his family. Similar to the idea that Barber could pale in shock, a ghost taking care of his family was physiologically impossible. I'd have to try to dissuade him from that path when all was said and done.

"What about you?" Barber asked Elizabeth. "Do you know when your funeral is?"

"I haven't heard either." She hedged closer to him. "So, are you going to yours?"

Barber shrugged. "I don't know. Are you going to yours?"

"I figured I might."

"Oh yeah?"

Elizabeth smiled and scooted closer. "I'll make a deal with you."

"Uh-oh."

"If you'll go with me to my funeral, I'll go with you to yours."

Barber thought about that for a moment, then gave a reluctant shrug. I tried not to crack up. They were like junior high kids trying to convince themselves they didn't really want to go to the school dance.

"I guess we could do that," Barber said. "You in, Patrick?"

"What?" Sussman seemed a thousand solar systems away. He forced his attention back to his colleagues. "I don't know. Seems kind of morbid."

"Come on," Elizabeth said. "We can listen to all the wonderful comments about us from the relatives who hated us most."

Sussman sighed. "Maybe you're right."

"Of course we are." Elizabeth patted his hand, then glanced at me. "Don't you think he should go to his funeral, Charlotte?"

"His funeral?" I asked, caught off guard. "Oh, well, sure. Who wouldn't kill to go to their own funeral?"

"See," she said, patting his hand again.

"I hope we're not buried in the same cemetery," Barber said. "I don't know if I could handle an eternity with you two as my neighbors."

Sussman snorted and Elizabeth socked him on the arm.

"I'm just saying," he said, a wide grin spreading across his face as Elizabeth glowered playfully at him. He turned to me then. "So, Reaper, what's next?"

I had to think about that one. "First of all," I said, poking him with an index finger, "that's Ms. Reaper to you, bub."

He chuckled.

"And second, I should probably take a look-see at your files on this case."

"Sure," Elizabeth said. "We have an emergency key hidden at the offices."

"Oh!" I said, raising my hand and squirming in my seat like a third grader with a UTI. "Is it in one of those fake rocks that looks like a real rock but it isn't because it's fake?"

"No," they said simultaneously.

"Oh, sorry. Go ahead," I said to Elizabeth, since I'd interrupted her.

"And we'll have to give you the security code in case Nora isn't there. If she is, you might have a difficult time getting anything without a warrant."

"Right. I didn't think of that. I'm sure Uncle Bob could get me one."

"If not," Sussman said, "you might want to consider breaking in tonight and getting the files then."

We all turned to him. He didn't seem like a B and E kind of guy.

"What? It's not illegal if we give her permission."

True enough. "Though I'm not sure the authorities would agree with you, I like it."

Sussman grinned. "I had a feeling you might."

"Can I ask you guys a couple of questions," I said, realizing it might be a good time to bring up Reyes, "about this morning?"

"Of course," Barber said. Elizabeth dropped her gaze, seemed to withdraw. Not overtly, but I read people well enough to know when the atmosphere changed. I was curious to know what happened, and what could make her so reluctant to speak with me about it.

Shifting back to Reyes, I decided to get the embarrassing part out of the way. "I've decided to get the embarrassing part out of the way," I said. Best to get these things out in the open. "I'm hoping, since you guys could see him, I didn't look ridiculous like I probably did to Cookie and Swopes. I mean, you saw him, right? It didn't look like I was fondling air?"

When they glanced at each other, seemingly confused, I asked, "You did see him?"

"Sure we did," Elizabeth said. "But you weren't fondling anything. You didn't move, if that's what you think. Not much anyway."

I leaned forward. "What do you mean?"

"You just stood there," Sussman said, sliding his glasses up with an index finger, "with your back against the wall and your palms plastered to it at your sides. Your head was thrown back, and you were panting like you'd just run the Duke City Marathon, but you didn't move."

His description sidetracked me for a moment. My arms were at my sides? My head was thrown back? "But he was there. You saw him. We were . . ."

"On each other like green on guacamole?" Barber asked.

"Well, yeah, I guess."

"I'm not complaining," he said with a negating wave of his hands. "Far from it. That shit was hot."

Somehow, trying not to blush makes me blush brighter. I felt heat travel over my face and could only hope it wasn't clashing with the blues and purples already there.

"But you didn't move," Elizabeth said. "Not physically."

"I'm sorry, I still don't understand."

"Your soul, your spirit, whatever you want to call it. That moved. You looked like us only with better coloring."

"Yeah," Barber said, "you separated from your body to . . . be with him. It was amazing."

I sat stunned. No wonder it'd felt like a dream. Did I do some kind of astral projection thing? I hoped not. I didn't believe in astral projection. But maybe, just maybe, astral projection believed in me.

"How on Earth did I manage to leave my body?" I asked, dazed and confused, though not from anything illegal.

"You're the grim reaper," Barber said with a shrug. "You tell us."

"I don't know." I looked at my palms as if they held the answers. "I didn't know such a thing was possible."

"Don't feel bad. I had no idea *any* of this was possible."

"I'm so floored," I said. I was supposed to be the knowledgeable one. How was being a grim reaper advantageous if all the good stuff was on a need-to-know basis? I was a portal, dammit. I needed to know.

"But he was superhot."

That brought me rocketing back. I looked at Elizabeth. "Seriously? Did you guys get a good look at him? I mean, I have to be totally honest here: I'm not sure what he is."

"You mean besides superhot?" Elizabeth asked.

"Actually, that part I got."

She laughed softly. We stopped talking while Dad brought over my sandwich, offered me ten thousand dollars to off Uncle Bob, then left with my butter knife tucked into his pants, apparently planning to shank the man himself. I thought about warning Uncle Bob, but where was the fun in that?

"Elizabeth, I have to ask you something," I said, pushing my sandwich aside for a moment.

"Sure, what's up?"

"I just feel like . . . well, ever since this morning, you've seemed a little distant."

"I'm sorry," she said, accepting responsibility without offering an explanation. In other words, trying to get out of one.

"Oh, don't apologize," I added quickly. "I was just worried. Did something happen?"

She sucked in a long, deep breath—another physiological superfluity—and said, "It's just, that guy who was able to materialize out of thin air, your guy, he was . . . he was so beautiful."

"Tell me about it," I said, nodding my head in agreement.

"And amazing."

"Still with you."

"And sexy."

I leaned in. "I like where this is headed."

"But . . ."

"Uh-oh."

"I just thought it odd."

"Odd?"

"Yes." She leaned in as well. "Charlotte, he was wearing . . . a prison uniform."

Chapter Seven

Genius has its limitations.
Insanity . . . not so much.

—BUMPER STICKER

A prison uniform? What did that mean? Had he gone to prison? Then died there?

The muscles around my heart clenched at the thought. He'd had such a hard life; that much had been painfully clear from the moment I first saw him. Then for him to end up in prison. I couldn't imagine the horrors he'd had to endure.

While I wanted nothing more than to rush off to the prison, I had no idea which prison he'd been in. He could have been in Sing Sing, for all I knew. I needed to cool my jets and focus on the case. Uncle Bob went to work on the warrant and court transcripts, and the lawyers went to check on their families, so I drove to the Metropolitan Detention Center to talk to Mark Weir, the man Carlos Rivera said was innocent.

The female corrections officer at the sign-in desk studied my APD laminate. "Charlotte Davidson?" she asked, her brows furrowing as if I'd done something wrong.

"That's me," I said with an inane giggle.

She didn't smile back. Not even a little. I totally needed to read that book on how to win friends and influence people. But that would involve an innate desire to win friends and influence people. My desires were a tad more visceral at the moment.

The officer directed me to a waiting area while she called back for Mr. Weir. As I sat pondering my visceral desires, specifically the ones earmarked for Reyes, I heard someone sit down beside me.

"Hey, Grim, what are you doing in my neck of the correctional system?"

I looked over and smiled before fetching my partially charged cell phone. Flipping it open, I made sure it was on silent before I spoke. "Dang, Billy," I said into the phone, "you're looking good. Are you losing weight?"

Billy was a Native American inmate who'd committed suicide in the detention center about seven years prior. I tried to convince him to cross, but he insisted on staying behind to help dissuade others from following his asinine example. His words. I often wondered how he might manage such a thing.

A bashful grin spread over his face at my compliment. Despite the fact that the departed couldn't lose weight, he did look a little slimmer. Maybe there was something I didn't know. Either way, he was a good-looking man.

He elbowed me playfully. "You and your phones."

"I gotta do this or they'll lock me up for talking to myself, Mr. Invisible."

A deep chuckle rose from his chest. "You here to get in my pants?"

"Is it that obvious?"

"Figures," he said, disappointed. "I always attract the crazy ones."

Sucking in a sharp breath, I was smack-dab in the middle of an Oscar-worthy performance—feigning offense with such emotion, such realism—when my name was called.

"Oops, that's me, big guy. When you coming to see me?"

"See you?" he asked as I jumped up to follow the officer toward the visitors' room. "How can I *not* see you? You're as bright as the damned searchlights outside."

When I turned back, he was gone. I really liked that man.

I sat down at booth seven as a gangly man in his forties sat across from me. He had sandy blond hair and kind blue eyes and looked like a cross between a beach bum and a college professor. A plate glass window separated us, one with thin wire latticed throughout to make it even more inescapable. Sure, I wondered how they got that wire in there, the rows so evenly spaced, but now was not the time for such musings. I had a job to do, dammit. I would not be sidetracked by latticework.

Mr. Weir studied me from the other side—not *the* other side, but the other side of the glass—his expression curious. I picked up the speaker phone and wondered how many people had used that same phone and how sanitary those people had been.

"Hello, Mr. Weir. My name is Charlotte Davidson." His face remained blank. Clearly my name did not impress him.

Another inmate strolled in to sit at the next booth, and he cast a wary glance over his shoulder, already eyeing others as if they were the enemy, already on constant guard, ready to defend himself at a moment's notice. This man didn't deserve to be in jail. He hadn't killed anyone. I could sense his clear conscience as easily as I could sense the guilty one of the guy next to him.

"I'm here with some pretty bad news." I waited as he turned his attention back to me. "Your lawyers were killed last night."

"My lawyers?" he asked, speaking at last. Then he realized what

I was saying, and his eyes widened in surprise. "What, all three of them?"

"Yes, sir. I'm terribly sorry."

He stared at me as if I'd reached through the glass and bitch-slapped him. Clearly he hadn't noticed the impossibility of such a feat, considering the latticework and all. After a long moment, he asked, "What happened?"

"They were shot. We believe their deaths are somehow related to your case."

That stunned him even more. "They were killed because of me?"

I shook my head. "This is not your fault, Mr. Weir. You know that, right?" When he didn't answer, I continued. "Have you received any threats?"

He gave a dubious snort and gestured around him, indicating his current environment. "You mean, other than the ones I get daily?"

He had a good point. Jail was nothing if not stressful. "To be totally honest," I said honestly, "I don't think these people would waste their time making threats. Based on the last twenty-four hours, they seem more proactive than that."

"No kidding. Who kills three lawyers?"

"Just keep a weather eye, Mr. Weir. We're working it from this end."

"I'll try. I'm real sorry to hear about those lawyers," he said, scraping his fingers over scraggly stubble then up over his eyes.

He was tired, exhausted from the stress of being convicted for something he didn't do. My heart ached for him more than I'd wanted it to.

"I really liked them," he said. "Especially that Ellery girl." He put his hand down and tried to shake off his emotions. "She was sure something to look at."

"Yes, she was very beautiful."

"You were friends?"

"No, no, but I've seen pictures." I never quite knew how to explain my connection to the departed. One slip could haunt me for years to come. Literally.

"And you came here to tell me to watch my back?"

"I'm a private investigator working with APD on this case." He seemed to bristle at the mention of APD. I could hardly blame him. Though I couldn't blame APD either. All the evidence did point straight toward him. "Did you know about the informant? The one who'd asked to speak with Barber the same day they were all killed?"

"Informant?" he asked, shaking his head. "What did he want?"

I breathed in and watched Mr. Weir closely before answering, trying to discern how much I should tell him. This was his case. If anyone deserved to know the truth, it was him. Still, a sign that read PROCEED WITH CAUTION kept flashing in my head. Either I needed to proceed with caution or that fifth cup of coffee was just now kicking in.

"Mr. Weir, the last thing I want to do is to give you unfounded hope. Odds are this is nothing. And even if it is something, odds are we can't prove it. Do you understand?"

He nodded, but just barely.

"In a nutshell, this man told Barber you were innocent."

His lids widened a fraction of an inch before he caught himself.

"He said the courts had put the wrong man behind bars and that he had proof."

Despite my warning, a spark of hope shimmered in Mr. Weir's eyes. I could see it. I could also tell he didn't want it to be there any more than I did. He'd probably been disappointed countless times. I couldn't imagine the heartbreak of going to prison for something I hadn't done. He had every right to be disillusioned with the system.

"Then what are you waiting for? Bring him in."

I rubbed my forehead. "He's dead, too. They killed him yesterday as well."

After a full minute of tense silence, he let out a long hiss of air and slumped back in his seat, stretching the phone cord to its limit. I could see the disappointment wash over him. "So what does this mean?" he asked, his tone embittered.

"I don't know exactly. We're just finding all this out ourselves. But I'll do everything I can to help you. How beneficial my efforts will be is the question. It's damned hard to get a conviction overturned, no matter the evidence."

He seemed to slip away, to lose himself in his thoughts.

"Mr. Weir? Can you tell me about the case?"

It took him a while to find his way back to me. When he did, he asked, "What do you want to know?"

"Well, I've got the court transcripts on the way, but I wanted to ask you about this woman, your neighbor who testified that she saw you hide the kid's body."

"I'd never seen that kid in my life. And the only time I'd ever seen that woman was when she was in her backyard yelling at her sunflowers. Crazy as a june bug on crack. But they listened to her. The jury listened to her. They lapped up everything she said like it was being served to them on a silver platter."

"Sometimes people hear what they want to hear."

"Sometimes?" he asked as if I'd grossly understated the fact. I had, but I was trying hard to stay positive.

"Any idea how the kid's blood got on your shoes?" This one stumped me. The man was clearly innocent, yet forensics confirmed he had the kid's blood on his shoes. That one piece of evidence alone was enough to turn a jury of twelve against him.

"It had to have been planted. I mean, how else would it get there?" he asked, just as stumped as I was.

"Okay, can you give me a quick rundown of what happened?"

Luckily, I'd stopped at Staples along the way. I pulled out my new notepad, the exact same kind Garrett and Uncle Bob used. Plain. Nondescript. Unassuming. I jotted down anything I thought could be pertinent.

"Wait a minute," I said, stopping him at one point. "The lady testified that the kid had been staying with you?"

"Yes, but she'd seen my nephew. He stayed with me for about a month before all of this happened. Now the cops think I killed him, too."

I blinked in surprise. "He's dead?"

"Not that I know of. But he *is* missing. And the cops have convinced my sister I had something to do with his disappearance."

This could be the connection I'd been looking for. I had no idea what that connection might be, but I'd worked with less.

"When did he disappear?"

He glanced down and to the right, which meant he was remembering instead of inventing. Another sign of his innocence, not that I needed it. "Teddy stayed with me about a month. His mom had kicked him out. They didn't get along."

"She's your sister?"

"Yes. Then she'd talked him into moving back home with her despite their constant bickering. That was the last time I saw him. I was arrested about two weeks later. No one told me he was missing until after the arrest."

"What did the prosecution say was your motive?" I asked.

His expression morphed into one of disgust. "Drugs."

"Ah," I said in understanding. "The one-size-fits-all motive."

"Ask him more about his sister."

I turned to see Barber standing behind me, arms crossed and head bowed in thought.

"I had to have missed something."

"Can you tell me more about your sister?" I asked Mr. Weir, who was busy looking past me to check out what I was looking at.

After a moment, he said, "She's not the best mom, but not the worst. She's been in trouble here and there. Drugs, and not just pot. Some shoplifting. You know, the usual."

The usual. Interesting defense.

"What about recently?" Barber asked. I passed the question along.

"I haven't seen her in a year. I have no idea how she's doing."

I wondered if she'd ever been questioned about the deceased kid. "What about—?"

"Could she have gotten involved in anything more serious?"

I slid an annoyed glance to Barber for interrupting me—lawyers— then relayed his question to Mr. Weir. Barber didn't notice my glare. Mr. Weir did.

"With Janie," he said, becoming more leery of me, "anything is possible."

"Would you say—?"

"I mean, could she have become indebted to someone? Someone with enough malevolence to kidnap—"

"That's it," I whispered through my teeth. "No one asks questions but me." I was doing my best ventriloquist impersonation, as though Mr. Weir couldn't hear me because of my lack of facial movement. Or see me pretending not to talk to anyone.

Barber looked at me, bemused. "I'm sorry," he said, sobering. "I just keep thinking I missed something. Something that was right there in front of me the whole time."

Great, now I felt guilty. "No, I'm sorry," I said, feeling bad but having to keep the stupid grin on my face so I wouldn't move my lips. "I shouldn't have snapped at you."

"No, no, you're right. My fault entirely."

I turned back to Mr. Weir. "Sorry about that. It's a voices-in-my-head thing."

His expression changed, but not as I would've expected. He suddenly looked . . . hopeful again. "Can you really do what they say you can?"

Since I wasn't sure what he was talking about—who *they* were and what *they* said I could do—my brows raised in question. "And *they* would be . . ."

He leaned in, as if that would help me hear him better through the glass. "I heard the guards talking. They were surprised you'd come to see me."

"Why?" I asked, surprised myself.

"They said you solve crimes nobody else can solve. That you even solved a decades-old cold case."

I rolled my eyes. "That was one time, for heaven's sake. I got lucky."

A woman who'd been murdered in the fifties had come to me. I'd convinced Uncle Bob to help, and we closed her case together. I couldn't have done it without him. Or all the new technology law enforcement had on their side. Of course, it helped that she knew exactly who murdered her and exactly where to find the murder weapon. That poor woman'd had one mean stepson.

"That's not what they said," Mr. Weir continued. "They said you knew things, things that no one could know."

Oh. "Um, who said that?"

"One of our guards is married to a cop."

"Well, then, that explains it. Cops don't really think—"

"I don't care what cops think, Ms. Davidson. I just want to know if you can do what they say."

A dismal sigh slipped through my lips. "I don't want to get your hopes up."

"Ms. Davidson, your mere presence is giving me hope. I'm sorry, but that's just the way it is."

"I'm sorry, too, Mr. Weir. The odds that this will lead to anything—"

"Are better odds than I had this morning."

"If you want to see it that way," I said, giving up, "I can't stop you."

"But you *can* do what they say."

Reluctant to offer any more hope than I already had, I felt tension crawl up my spine, hunch my shoulders. It was easy to believe in my abilities when it would benefit a cause. I just didn't know how advantageous my talents would be in this particular case. Maybe hope itself would benefit Mr. Weir. It was the least I could offer him.

"Yes, Mr. Weir, I can do what they say." I waited for that little jewel to sink in, for his mildly shocked expression to return to normal, then said, "They'll be taking you to the Reception and Diagnostic Center in Los Lunas for evaluation before sending you to prison. I can brave the hordes of Los Lunatics and visit you there if you'd like. Keep you up to date."

A reluctant smile appeared at last. "I'd like that."

I spoke to Barber through the side of my mouth. "You got any more questions?"

He was still buried in thought and simply shook his head.

"Okay," I said to Weir, "see ya soon."

After hanging up, I started to put my notepad and pen away when I had an epiphany. Of sorts. I turned and tapped on the window to get Mr. Weir's attention.

The guard allowed him to walk back and pick up his phone again.

"How old is he?" I asked as I balanced the phone on my shoulder and tore through my notepad, clicking my pen to the ready.

"Excuse me?"

"Your nephew. How old is your nephew?"

"Oh, he's fifteen. Or he was. I guess he'd be sixteen now."

"And they still haven't found him?"

"Not that I know of. What—?"

"How old was the kid? The one in your backyard?"

"I see where you're going with this," Barber said.

"He was fifteen. Do you think there's a connection?"

I winked at Barber, then leaned toward Mr. Weir with a touch more promise in my eyes. "There has to be, and I'll do my damnedest to find out what it is."

The last thing I wanted to do was jump to conclusions, but I couldn't shake the feeling that those two boys ran in the same circles. Two boys with similar backgrounds, one missing and one dead? My mind screamed *predator*.

Though I needed Barber's files, I didn't want to deal with Nora, the lawyers' administrative assistant. If she was anything like other administrative assistants I knew, she had only slightly less power than God at her fingertips, and she wouldn't take kindly to any nosing about. Breaking and entering was much safer. But breaking and entering would have to wait until nightfall.

In the meantime, Uncle Bob was rounding up everything APD had on the case, and Barber was headed to Mr. Weir's sister's house to see if there'd been any contact with Teddy, the missing nephew. I decided to send in Barber first to get the lay of the land before I talked to her, figuring I could use the time to mosey back to my office and glean as much information as possible off the Internet. As I headed out of the detention center, I opened my cell and called Cookie.

"Hey, boss," she said by way of a greeting. "Planning a jailbreak yet?"

"Nah. Believe it or not, they're letting me walk out of here."

"Crazy people. What are they thinking?"

"Probably that I'm more trouble than I'm worth."

She chuckled. "You have three messages, nothing too pressing. Mrs.

George still swears her husband is cheating and wants to meet with you this afternoon."

"No."

"That's what I told her, only I wasn't quite so wordy about it," she said teasingly. "Everything else can wait. So, what's up?"

"I'm glad you asked," I said, walking out the glass doors. I did a quick scan of the area for Billy, but he must've had better things to do. "The lawyers gave me some interesting news at lunch."

"Yeah? How interesting?"

"Pretty darned."

"Sounds promising."

"Can you pull up the prison registry and do a search for the name Reyes?"

"The *prison* registry?"

I cringed. She made it sound so . . . criminal. "Yeah, long story."

"Well, there are about two hundred inmates and/or parolees with the last name of Reyes."

"That was fast. Try it as a first name."

I heard clicking; then she said, "Better. There're only four."

"Okay, well, he'd be about thirty now."

"And then there was one."

I stopped with my key halfway in the door. "One? Really?"

"Reyes Farrow."

My heart thrummed nervously in my chest. Could this really be it? After all these years, could I finally have found him?

"Do they have a mug shot posted?" I asked. When Cookie didn't answer, I tried again. "Cookie? You there?"

"My god, Charley. He's . . . it's him."

My keys fell to the ground, and I braced my free hand against Misery. "How do you know? You've never seen him."

"He's gorgeous. He's exactly like you described."

I tried to control my breathing. I didn't have a paper bag around if it came to that.

"I've never seen anyone so, I don't know, so fierce, so stunningly beautiful."

"That would be him," I said, knowing without a doubt she had the right guy.

"I'm sending the mug shot now."

I held out my phone and waited for the text. After several long seconds, a picture popped onto the screen, and I was suddenly concentrating on staying vertical. My knees weakened regardless, and I slid down to sit on the running board, unable to take my eyes off the screen.

Cookie had nailed it. He was fierce, his expression wary and furious at once, as if he'd been warning the officers to keep their distance. For their own protection. Even in the poor lighting, his eyes sparkled with what seemed like barely controlled rage. He had not been a happy camper when they'd taken his picture.

"He's still listed as an inmate. I wonder how often they update these things. Charley?" Cookie was still on the line, but I couldn't tear my eyes off his picture. She seemed to realize I needed a moment and waited in silence for me to recover.

I did. With a new purpose, I put the phone to my ear and bent to pick up my keys. "I'm going to see Rocket."

Figuring I could kill two birds with one stone, I pulled around to a side street and parked beside a Dumpster, hoping the neighbors wouldn't realize I was planning to break into their abandoned mental asylum. The hospital, closed by the government in the fifties, had somehow ended up in the hands of a local biker gang, aka the neighbors. They called themselves the Bandits and were none too keen on trespassers. They had Rottweilers to prove it.

Just walking up to the asylum had my stomach clenching in knots, but not because of the Rottweilers and not in a bad way. Asylums fascinated me. When I was in college, my favorite weekend trips involved tours of abandoned psychiatric hospitals. The departed I found there were vibrant and passionate and full of life. Ironic, since they were dead.

This particular asylum was home to one of my favorite crazy people. Rocket's life—when he was actually alive—was more of a mystery than the Bermuda Triangle, but I did learn that he'd been a child during the Depression. His baby sister had died from dust pneumonia, and though I'd never met her, he told me she was still around, keeping him company.

Rocket was a lot like me. He'd been born with a purpose, a job. But no one had understood his gift. After the death of his sister, his parents handed him over to the care of the New Mexico Insane Asylum. Subsequent years of misunderstanding and mistreatment, including periodic doses of electroshock therapy, left Rocket a fraction of the person he'd most likely been.

In many ways, he was like a forty-year-old kid in a cookie jar, only his jar was a crumbling, condemned mental asylum, and his cookies were names, the names of those who'd passed that he carved, day in and day out, into the walls of the asylum. The ultimate record keeper. I couldn't imagine Saint Peter having anything on Rocket.

Except for maybe a pencil.

My adrenaline was flowing with the excitement. I could find out in one shot if Mark Weir's nephew Teddy was still alive—fingers crossed—and find out about Reyes as well. Rocket knew the moment someone passed, and he never forgot a name. The sheer volume of information that flooded his head at any given moment would drive a sane man to the brink, which could also explain Rocket's personality.

The doors and windows to the asylum had been boarded up long

ago. I sneaked around the back, listening for the pitter-pat of Rottwei-
ler paws, and slid on my stomach through a basement window I jim-
mied open each time I visited. I had yet to get caught at this particular
asylum—a good thing, since I'd probably lose a limb—but I did get
caught at one I'd *visited* outside Las Vegas, New Mexico. A sheriff arrested me. I could be mistaken, but I'm pretty sure my men-in-uniform
fetish began that day. That sheriff was hot. And he handcuffed me. I've
never been the same.

"Rocket?" I called after tumbling headfirst onto a table and
stumbling—rather impressively—to my feet. I dusted myself off, turned
on my LED flashlight, and headed toward the stairs. "Rocket, are you
here?"

The first floor was empty. I walked the halls, marveling at the thousands upon thousands of names carved into the plaster walls, then
started up the service stairs to the second level. Abandoned books and
furniture lay strewn in crumbled disarray. Graffiti covered most sur-
faces, attesting to the countless parties that'd been thrown over the
years, probably before the biker gang had acquired the property. Apparently the class of '83 had lived free, and Patty Jenkins put out.

The myriad of nationalities that Rocket carved into the walls awed
me. There were names in Hindi and Mandarin and Arapaho and Farsi.

"Miss Charlotte," Rocket said from behind me, a mischievous giggle exciting his voice.

I jumped and whirled around. "Rocket, you little devil!" He liked to
scare me, so I had to feign a near-death experience each time I visited.

He laughed aloud and pulled me into a suffocating hug. Rocket was
a cross between a fluffy grizzly and the Pillsbury Doughboy. He had a
baby face and a playful heart and saw only the good in people. I always
wished I'd known him when he was alive, before the government quite
literally fried his brain. Had he been a grim reaper like me? I did know
that he could see the departed before he died.

He set me down, then drew his brows together in a comical frown. "You never come to see me. Never."

"Never?" I asked, teasing him.

"Never."

"I'm here now, aren't I?"

He shrugged begrudgingly.

"And there is a small matter of Rottweilers I have to contend with each and every visit."

"I guess. I have so many names to give you. So many."

"I don't really have time—"

"They shouldn't be here. No, no, no. They need to leave." Rocket was also a consummate tattletale, always giving me names of those who had passed but had yet to cross.

"You're right, Rocket, but this time I have a name for you."

He paused and eyed me in confusion. "A name?"

I decided to toss out a name of someone I knew had already passed. "James Enrique Barilla," I said, quoting the name of the kid found murdered in Mark Weir's backyard.

"Oh," he said, jumping to attention.

It was a cheap trick, throwing out a name like that, but I had to keep Rocket focused. I didn't have much time. I had a date with one Mr. Illegal Activity. That breaking-and-entering gig wouldn't break and enter itself.

Rocket recognized the name immediately and began walking with a purpose, which unfortunately included taking shortcuts through walls. I struggled to keep up, jogging around corners and through doorways, hoping the dilapidated floor held beneath my weight.

"Rocket, wait. Don't lose me."

Then I heard him, down the stairwell and through the kitchen, repeating the name to himself over and over. I tripped on a broken chair and dropped my flashlight, sending it tumbling down the steps.

Then Rocket was in front of me. "Miss Charlotte, you never keep up."

"Never?" I asked, struggling to my feet.

"Never." He grabbed my arm and jerked me down the stairs. I just managed to scoop up the flashlight as we ran past.

He meant well.

Then he stopped. With an abruptness I hadn't expected, he skidded to a halt. I slammed into his backside, ever thankful of its plumpness, and bounced off him to land, once again, on my ass. Normally, Rocket would have laughed when I stood and dusted myself off, but he was on a mission. Based on past experience, nothing swayed Rocket from one of his missions.

"Here. Here it is," he said, pointing repeatedly to one of the thousands of names he'd scraped into the plaster. "James Enrique Barilla."

Finding James's name among those of the departed really wasn't surprising, since there was a man going to prison for his murder. But I had to check, just in case.

"Can you tell me how he died?" I asked, already knowing the answer.

"Not how," he said, suddenly annoyed. I fought back a grin. "Not why. Not when. Only is."

"How about where?" Now I was just being obstinate.

He glared at me. "Miss Charlotte, you know the rules. No breaking rules," he said with a warning shake of his pudgy finger. That'd teach me.

I sometimes wondered if he really did know more and was just following some cosmic set of rules I was unaware of. But his vocabulary, I had a feeling, stemmed from years of institutionalization. Nobody liked rules more than institutionalizationers.

I pulled out my notepad and thumbed through it. "Okay, Rocket Man, what about a Theodore Bradley Thomas?" If nothing else, I'd leave here today knowing if Mark Weir's missing nephew was dead or alive.

Rocket bent his head in thought for a moment. "No, no, no," he said at last. "Not his time yet."

Relief flooded every cell in my body. Now I just had to find him. I wondered how much danger the kid was in. "Do you know when his time will be?" I asked, already knowing the answer. Again.

"Not when. Only is," he repeated as he turned and started carving another name into the plaster.

I'd lost him. Keeping Rocket's attention was like serving spaghetti with a spoon. But I had another name to give him. An important one. I inched closer, almost afraid to say it aloud, then whispered, "Reyes Farrow."

Rocket stopped. He recognized the name; I could tell. That meant Reyes was dead after all. My heart dropped into my stomach. I'd hoped so hard he wouldn't be.

"Where is his name?" I asked, ignoring the sting in my eyes. I scanned the walls as if I could actually find his name among the mass of scribbled chaos that looked like an M. C. Escher on acid. But I wanted to see it. To touch it. I wanted to run my fingers along the rough grooves and lines that made up the letters of Reyes's name.

Then I realized Rocket was gazing at me, a wary expression on his boyish face.

I lifted a hand to his shoulder. "Rocket, what's wrong?"

"No," he said, stepping out of my reach. "He shouldn't be here. No, ma'am."

My eyes slammed shut, trying hard not to see the truth. "Where is his name, Rocket?"

"No, ma'am. He should never have been born."

They flew open again. I'd never heard such a thing from Rocket. "I can't believe you just said that."

"He should never have been a boy named Reyes. He should have stayed where he belonged. Martians can't become human just because they want to drink our water." His eyes locked on to mine, but he stared past me a long moment before refocusing on my face. "You stay away from him, Miss Charlotte," he said, taking a warning step toward me. "You just stay away."

I held my ground. "Rocket, you're not being very nice."

He leaned down to me then, his voice a raspy whisper as he said, "But, Miss Charlotte, he's not very nice either."

Something beyond my senses caught his attention. He turned, listened, then rushed toward me and clenched his meaty hands around my arms. I winced, but I wasn't scared. Rocket would never hurt me. Then his grip tightened, and I almost cried out, realizing I might have spoken too soon.

"Rocket," I said in a soothing voice, "sweetheart, you're hurting me."

He jerked back his hands and retreated in disbelief, as if astonished at what he'd done.

"It's okay," I said, refusing to rub my throbbing arms. It would only make him feel worse. "It's okay, Rocket. You didn't mean to."

A horrified expression flashed across his face as he disappeared. I heard three words as he left. "He won't care."

Chapter Eight

The sun nested on Nine Mile Hill for several heartbeats before losing interest and slipping down the other side. I sat in Misery—the Jeep, not the emotion—and waited for the skyline to swallow it completely so I could get on with my breaking-and-entering gig. But the more I waited, the more I thought about Reyes. And the more I thought about Reyes, the more confused I became.

Rocket knew Reyes's name, but did that necessarily mean he'd passed? Could it mean anything else? I'd never seen Rocket scared before, and that scared me. He seemed to be hiding something as well, but trying to differentiate between Rocket's lucid and less-than-lucid moments was nearly impossible.

On the plus side, I did learn that Martians should never try to become human just to drink our water. Since Martians didn't exist, I figured they were part of some bizarre Rocket Man analogy. So what

on Earth could be comparable to alien beings? Besides circus perform-
ers? It had to be someone living contrary to the norm. I could think of
a couple of groups, but I felt strangely secure in the knowledge that
Reyes was neither an IRS auditor nor a member of the Manson family.
Thank goodness, because swastikas aren't as easily accessorized as one
might think.

Perhaps the bigger piece to the puzzle was the water. What did it
represent? What would a person living outside the boundaries of society want for badly enough to conform? Money? Acceptance? Power?
Green chili enchiladas? I was clueless. It happened. In my own defense,
Rocket used a bad analogy. We lived way too close to Roswell to think
logically about alien invasions.

But I could think logically about the case. Mark Weir's nephew was
alive, and I had a very strong suspicion he'd known James Barilla, the
deceased kid in Weir's backyard. There had to be a connection. Mostly
because I wanted one. Whatever that connection might be, Teddy was
in trouble because of it.

Where the heck was Angel when I needed him? He rarely stayed
away this long. How could I do supernatural recon without a supernatural reconnaissance team? Namely, Team Angel, which was pretty
much a team of one. But by calling it a team, I could say things like,
"There's no *i* in *team,* mister!" I friggin' loved saying crap like that. As
it stood, I was having to do way more legwork than I'd planned when
I decided on these boots.

On the way over from the asylum, I'd called the lead detective on
Weir's case. He was a friend of Uncle Bob's, but not a big fan of mine.
I think I irked him. I could be irksome when I put my left ventricle
into it. I figured he was either jealous of Uncle Bob's success—and my
part in it—or he didn't like hot chicks with attitude. Probably a smid-
gen of both.

Our conversation didn't last long. Detective Anaya's answers were short and to the razor-sharp point. According to him, APD had tried to find Teddy in connection to the case as well, but they were looking for another body, another death to pin on Mark Weir. Such an investigation would lead them continually in the wrong direction. Since I knew Teddy was alive, I would have a slight advantage over APD, emphasis on the word *slight*. Advantage might be a bit overstated as well.

When they'd interviewed Teddy's mom, she told the police her son never moved back home from her brother's house. And yet she'd waited until Mark was arrested for murder to report him missing? That left two weeks of Teddy's whereabouts unaccounted for. I may not have been the state academic decathlon champ, but even I could tell the facts weren't adding up.

As I waited for the lingering light to stop lingering and let darkness blanket the area, I flipped open my phone to study Reyes's picture for the hundredth time that day. And just like each time before, my breath caught at the first glimpse of him. I couldn't get over it. After more than ten years, I'd found him. True, I'd found him in prison, but for the moment—as I was fairly adept at living in denial—I was ignoring that part. The one ray of hope I clung to lay in the fact that Reyes was pissed when they took his mug shot. Not just upset, not just angry, but wildly, ragingly furious. Guilty people aren't pissed. They're either relieved at having been caught or worried. Reyes was neither.

I closed my phone, resisting the inane urge to make out with the screen, and made my way up the walk to the front entrance of the Sussman, Ellery & Barber Law Offices. A wide oak door sat conveniently hidden by evergreens and Spanish daggers, making my breaking and entering all the more uncomplicated—though, really, it wasn't so much breaking as entering, since I had a key and all.

Barber's office was only slightly less organized than a postapocalyptic war zone. I thumbed through stacks of papers and found Weir's case files in a cardboard box marked WEIR, MARK L. Which was a totally logical place to find them. But the mysterious flash drive was another matter. Barber said it would be on top of his desk. It wasn't, and his pencil drawer had seven flash drives without so much as a label in sight. I couldn't loiter all evening. I had a stakeout to attend, which sadly involved neither steaks nor vampires.

I weighed the pros and cons of taking all the flash drives with me and checking them out later. The pros won. Mentally scheduling another B & E for tomorrow night to return them, I started stuffing flash drives into my pockets. That led to the realization that mocha lattes and cheeseburgers weren't doing me any favors. Which, in turn, led to an angry growl echoing against the walls of my empty stomach. I was starving.

As I hopped up and down, trying to cram the last two flash drives into my pockets, I ran a mental list of all the fast food joints I could hit between here and the warehouse we were staking out.

"You're about as inconspicuous as a monster truck at an exotic car show."

I started and whirled around to see Garrett standing in the doorway. "Holy crap, Swopes," I said, placing a hand over my heart. "What are you doing here?"

He strolled in, eyeing the moonlit surroundings before returning his attention to yours truly. "Your uncle sent me," he said, his voice flat. "Any evidence you obtain without that warrant will be useless in court."

Ah, we were back to being mortal enemies. Coolness wafted off him. I'd have to be on guard in his presence, ever wary of his traitorous tendencies. I'd have to eat, sleep, and potty with one eye open.

"Do the words *chain of custody* mean anything to you?" he asked.

"They would if I gave a crap." I picked up the box and headed for the door. "I just need to know what I'm up against, Swopes."

"Besides mental illness?"

Dang, we were even back to the volatile insults. It felt good to be home.

"I'm not out to prove my investigative prowess, Swopes, or how ginormous my dick is by making a name for myself. I'm helping my clients. It's what I do," I said as I edged past him. "It's what I've been doing for years now, long before you came along."

Garrett followed me out the front door. "What's the code?" he asked to reset the alarm.

I yelled the numbers over my shoulder—apparently so everyone in the neighborhood could hear—then put the box in the back of my Jeep. He walked up behind me.

"I have to stop for sustenance along the way. I'll meet you at the warehouse," I said.

After closing the back door for me and making sure it was locked, he said, "We're not far from your place. Why don't we drop off your car, and you can ride over with me."

I put the key in to unlock my door. "I'm hungry."

"You can eat on the way."

An annoyed sigh slipped through my lips as my hand hovered over the door handle. "Is Uncle Bob paying you to babysit me now?"

"We have four dead bodies, Davidson. He's . . . concerned."

"Ubie?" I asked with a snort.

"I'll follow you to your place."

"Whatever makes your balloon red, Swopes," I said, climbing into Misery and slamming the door. He didn't seem any happier about Charley-sitting than Charley did herself. Somewhere deep inside, she felt bad about that. Not.

"Mmm. Tacos are good." I looked over at Swopes as we pulled in beside Uncle Bob's unmarked police car, a bland, dark blue sedan. "I just hope I don't spill any more salsa on your nice vinyl seats."

Garrett's jaw flexed as he gritted his teeth. It was funny. "They're leather," he said, his voice tightly controlled.

"Oops. Well, they're real nice."

He threw the truck into park, and I hopped out before the tension could escalate into random acts of violence, ducked back in for my monster cup of diet soda, then dashed over to Uncle Bob's car. Aka the Safety Zone.

We were parked a fair distance away from the warehouse; a wide field of ragweed and mesquite lay between us and the rusting metal building. It looked like a cross between an airplane hangar and a mechanic's shop and sat perched smack-dab in the middle of nowhere. Not a single neighbor for miles. A fact I found most interesting.

Uncle Bob sat in his car, staring out of a nifty pair of binoculars from behind his steering wheel. I leaned over his windshield, peered into the binocular lenses, and smiled. He pulled the specs away from his eyes and frowned at me.

"What?" I mouthed before bouncing around to the passenger's side and climbing inside the warm interior. Death by starvation had been staved off another day, thanks to Macho Taco. Life was good.

"Who's that?" I asked, pointing to a second unmarked police car strategically parked a few yards away. Totally camouflaged by darkness. Except for one small, teensy-tiny, minuscule blunder. His parking lights were on. I took a shot and guessed the guy hadn't graduated at the top of his class.

"That's Officer Taft," Uncle Bob said.

"No," I breathed.

"He volunteered."

"No."

"He's a good egg, that one."

I rolled my eyes and eased lower into the seat as Garrett opened the back door to get in, shining the minisearchlight directly on me.

"Close the door," I whispered with a furtive urgency.

Uncle Bob frowned. Again. I didn't know why. It wasn't like he needed the practice.

"Taft has a fan," I explained. "An adorable little girl has been stalking him. I think her name is Hell Spawn of Satan."

Uncle Bob chuckled. "What the Hell Spawn of Satan are you wearing?"

What Ubie was so indelicately referring to was the outfit I'd changed into, carefully picking out my most comfortable black-on-black attire and meticulously applying black greasepaint to my face to complement a desert-at-midnight look. Naturally, I had to struggle through several costume changes as Garrett sat out in his leather-seated truck waiting for me. I sure hoped my time-consuming endeavor didn't annoy him.

"I'm blending," I said.

"With what? Evil?"

"Laugh it up, Uncle Bob," I said before pausing to take a noisy slurp of my soda. "Just wait until someone has to go traipsing through the desert for a closer look. You'll appreciate my forethought."

Garrett chose that moment to join the conversation. "I appreciate your forethought," he said, his tone distant, as if his mind were elsewhere. "Not as much as your fore-*parts,* but still . . ."

I twisted around in my seat to face him. "My fore-parts, as you so ineloquently put it, have names." I pointed to my right breast. "This is Danger." Then my left. "And this is Will Robinson. I would appreciate it if you addressed them accordingly."

After a long pause in which he took the time to blink several times, he asked, "You named your breasts?"

I turned my back to him with a shrug. "I named my ovaries, too, but they don't get out as much. Did you ever think that this whole operation was blown when they tortured Carlos Rivera?" I asked Uncle

Bob. "If these guys are anywhere near intelligent, they would have cleared out any incriminating evidence the moment they figured out what Rivera did."

"True," Uncle Bob said. "But there's only one way to be certain."

"Why don't you just get a warrant, gather a small army, and storm the place?"

"Based on what probable cause? Anonymous tips aren't enough to obtain a search warrant, pumpkin. We need that flash drive."

He had a point. Not a particularly pointy one, but a point nonetheless. And he called me pumpkin. I slurped as loud as kinesthetically possible in response. It would help if we knew what we were looking for. I sighed to emphasize my impatience-slash-boredom. Stakeouts were nothing if not boring. I felt it my civic duty as a certified connoisseur of sarcasm to liven it up a bit, so I slurped some more.

"Why don't you go keep Taft company?" Uncle Bob suggested from behind his binoculars.

"Can't."

He lowered them. "Why not?"

"Don't like him."

"Perfect. I don't think he likes you either."

"Also," I said, ignoring my unappreciative uncle for the moment, "he has the Hell Spawn of Satan following his every move. Remember?" Then I realized what Uncle Bob had said. "He doesn't like me?"

Ubie shrugged with his brows.

"What have I ever done to him?" I glared at Taft's stupid car. "Little punk. See if I help him when demon child starts making her presence known."

An electric hum sounded behind me as Garrett rolled down his window. "Movement."

We all looked toward the warehouse, where a vertical shaft of light appeared. The massive doors slid open, spilling light over a waiting van. It rolled inside before the doors closed again.

"At this rate, we'll never solve the case and Mark Weir will grow old in prison. This stakeout sucks," I said, whining into my calorie-free beverage. "We can't see a thing. We need to get closer."

"Send in your people," Uncle Bob said.

"I don't have any people with me."

"What?" he asked, suddenly panicked. "What about Angel?"

I shrugged. "Haven't seen that little shit in days. Why do you think I'm dressed like this? Greasepaint wreaks havoc on my complexion."

"I am not sending you over there, Charlotte Jean Davidson."

Uh-oh. Ubie seemed *über*serious. I gave it two minutes. Sixty-seven seconds and three long slurps later, he changed his mind.

"Fine," he said with a heavy sigh.

Finally.

"Go do your thing."

I knew he'd cave.

"But for God's sake, be careful. Your dad'll shank me if anything happens to you."

He handed me a radio, and I traded him my soda. "No backwash," I warned.

"No getting caught." He turned to Garrett. "Watch her close."

"What?" I squeaked into the radio, having been surprised in the middle of my sound check. Uncle Bob scowled. "I am so not taking Swopes. He's in a bad mood."

Garrett eyed me, his expression expressionless.

"Either Swopes goes with you, or you don't go at all."

I snatched back my diet soda and slumped down in my seat. "Then I guess I'm not going."

"Be careful."

I scowled at Garrett through the chain-link fence as I dropped to the other side. Well, not *the* other side. The other side of the fence. "Yeah, I got that much from Uncle Bob," I said, my voice acidic. I'd lost the argument. Despite the fact that I'd had lots of practice, losing wasn't my forte.

Garrett followed suit, climbing the eight-foot chain-link fence with way more upper-body strength than I had and dropping beside me. But could he tie a knot in a cherry stem with his tongue?

We started out across the open field toward the warehouse. It took most of my concentration to keep from falling, and even more of my concentration to keep from clutching on to Garrett's jacket for balance.

"I read that grim reapers collect souls," he said, jogging beside me.

I tripped on a cactus and just barely managed to catch myself. Night was so dark. Probably because of the time. The moonlight helped, but traversing the uneven ground still proved challenging.

"Swopes," I said, breathing slowly so he wouldn't realize I was getting winded, "there are oodles of souls running around, wreaking havoc upon my life. Why would I collect the darned things? And even if I did, where would I keep all the jars?"

He didn't answer. We sprinted across the parking lot to the back of the windowless building. Luckily, it had no security cameras. But I could tell from the soft glow illuminating the roofline that it did have skylights. If I could get to the roof, I might be able to see what they were up to. No good, surely, but I did need some kind of evidence to back that up.

When Garrett pulled me behind a grouping of garbage bins, I bumped into a metal pipe that led all the way up and over the roofline with brackets every few feet for stability. Perfect footholds.

"Hey, give me a boost," I whispered.

"What? No," Garrett argued, eyeing the post faithlessly. He shoved me aside nonetheless. "I'll go up."

"I'm lighter," I argued back. "This pipe won't hold you." Even though I was pretty much arguing for argument's sake, the pipe did look a tad flimsy. And it had more rust than a New Mexico sunset. "I'll go up and check out the skylights. Odds are I won't be able to see in, but maybe I can find a hole. Maybe I can make a hole," I said, thinking aloud.

"Then the guys inside will make a hole as well. In your obstinate head. Probably two if history is any indication."

I studied the pipe while Garrett ranted something incoherent about holes and history. I'd chosen that particular moment not to understand a word he said. When he was finished, I turned to him. "Do you even know English? Give me a boost," I added when his brows furrowed in confusion.

Shouldering past him, I gripped the pipe with both hands. He let an annoyed breath slip through his lips before stepping forward and grabbing my ass.

Thrilling? Yes. Appropriate? Not on your life.

I slapped his hands away. "What the hell are you doing?"

"You said to give you a boost."

"Yes. A boost. Not a cheap thrill."

He paused, looked down at me a long, uncomfortable moment.

What'd I say? "Cup your hands," I ordered before he got all mushy. "If you can get me to the first bracket, I can take it from there."

Reluctantly, he put one hand in the other and bent forward. I'd brought my gloves to go with my black-on-black ensemble, so I slipped them on, placed one foot in Garrett's cupped hands, then hoisted myself up to the first brace. Easy enough with his upper body strength and all, but the second was a tad trickier. The sharp metal of the brackets tried to cut its way through my gloves, making my fingers ache instantly. I struggled to hold on to the pipe, struggled to keep my footing, and struggled to lift my own weight to the next bracket. Surprisingly, the worst pain centered in my knees and elbows as I used them for leverage against the metal building, slipping and squirming far more often than was likely appropriate.

A decade later, I pulled myself up and over the roofline. The metal cap scraped agonizingly into my rib cage as if mocking me, as if saying, *You're kind of dumb, huh?* I collapsed on the roof and lay completely still a full minute, marveling at how much harder that had been than I thought it would be. I'd have hell to pay in the morning. If Garrett had been half a gentleman, he would have offered to climb the pipe in my stead.

"You okay?" he whispered into the radio.

I tried to respond, but my fingers were locked in a clawlike position from clinging on to the brackets for dear life, and they couldn't push the little button on the side of the radio.

"Davidson," he hissed.

Oh, for heaven's sake. I pried my fingers apart and pulled the radio out of my jacket pocket. "I'm fine, Swopes. I'm trying to wallow in self-pity. Would you give me a minute?"

"We don't have a minute," he said. "The doors are opening again."

I didn't waste time with a response. After rolling to my feet, I hunkered down and crept to the skylights. They were actually greenhouse panels, but they were old and cracked and had more than one peephole I could see through. To do so, however, to be able to see down into the warehouse, I'd have to almost lie across a panel. A thin beam of light shot up through one of the cracks and I leaned into a push-up, my wobbly arms braced on either side. As long as the metal frame held, I figured I wouldn't fall through the roof. Which would be a plus.

The van was driving out of the warehouse when I peeked down. Two men were boxing up papers and files from an old desk. Other than the desk, the warehouse itself, at least fifty thousand square feet of space, was completely and startlingly empty. Not a candy wrapper or cigarette butt in sight. My concerns had been well founded. Whoever owned this warehouse cleaned it out the moment Carlos Rivera met with Barber.

My arms still shook from the climb, and I was deeply regretting the tacos and forty-four-ounce soda I'd inhaled. Forty-four ounces was forty-four ounces. Calorie-free or not, it weighed the same. Time to make like a sheep.

As I inched back on the metal frame, I rehearsed my told-you-so speech to Uncle Bob. *The warehouse was empty. Yes, just like I said it would be. I know I was right, but— Really, Uncle Bob, stop, you're embarrassing me. No really, stop it. I'm not kidding.*

It was about the time I was imagining my reluctant appearance and off-the-cuff speech at the Really, Really Right Awards Ceremony that my mind processed movement. Something flashed in my periphery, a fist possibly, and was quickly followed by a burst of pain in my jaw. Then all I could think as I fell through the skylight was, *Holy crap!*

Chapter Nine

I first saw him the day I was born. His hooded cloak undulated in majestic waves like the shadows cast by leaves in a soft breeze. He'd looked down at me while the doctor cut the cord. I knew he was looking down at me, even though I couldn't see his face. He'd touched me as the nurses cleaned my skin, though I couldn't feel his fingertips. And he'd whispered my name, husky and deep and soft, though I couldn't hear his voice. Probably because I was screaming at the top of my lungs, having recently been evicted.

Since that day, I'd seen him only on the rarest of occasions, all dire. So it made sense that I would see him now. The occasion being dire and all.

As I fell through the skylight, the cement floor rushing toward me at the speed of light, he was there, looking up at me from below—though I couldn't see his face. I tried to stop in midair, tried to pause my descent, to hover for a better look. But gravity insisted that I continue my downward journey. Then somewhere in the dark and scary—and some would say psychotic—recesses of my mind, I remembered. I remembered what he'd whispered to me the day I was born. My mind instantly rejected the idea, because the name he'd whispered wasn't mine. He'd called me Dutch. On the very day I was born. How did he know?

While I was busy reminiscing about my first day on earth, I'd forgotten that I was falling to my death. Damned ADD. I was reminded quite effectively, however, when I stopped. I hit hard, and the air rushed out of my lungs. Yet he was still looking up at me. That meant I hadn't made it to the ground. I hit something else, something metal, before flipping back and crashing onto steel grating.

An excruciating pain exploded in my midsection and ripped through me like a nuclear blast, so severe, so startlingly intense, it stole my breath and darkened my vision until I felt myself liquefy and slip through the grates. And as darkness crept around the edges of my consciousness, I saw him again, leaning over me, studying me.

I tried so hard to focus, to block out the pain watering my eyes and blurring my vision. But I ran out of time before I could manage it, and everything went black. An inhuman growl—angry and full of pain—echoed off the walls of the empty warehouse, shook the metal of the building until it hummed like a tuning fork in my ears.

Though I couldn't hear his voice.

It seemed like the moment I lost consciousness, I found it again. It certainly wasn't where I'd left it. Still, I was breathing and coherent. Amazingly, the old saying was right: It isn't the fall that will kill you, but the sudden stop.

I tried to pry open my lids. I failed. Either I wasn't really conscious or Garrett had found a tube of Super Glue and was getting even for the salsa incident. While I waited for my eyelids to realize they were supposed to be in the upright position, I listened to him babble into the radio, something about my having a pulse. Always a welcome observation. His fingertips rested on my neck.

"I'm here," Uncle Bob blurted breathlessly through the radio. Then I heard footsteps on metal steps and sirens in the background.

Garrett must have sensed I was awake. "Hey, Detective," he said to Uncle Bob, who was now trudging across the grating toward us. "I think we're losing her. I have no choice but to perform mouth-to-mouth."

"Don't you dare," I said, my lids still in lockdown.

He laughed under his breath.

"Bloody hell, Charley," Uncle Bob said in a wheezy voice that sounded more concerned than angry. Maybe the rubber band at his wrist was working after all. "What happened?"

"I fell."

"No shit."

"Someone hit me."

"Again? I didn't realize it was National Kill Charley Davidson Week."

"Do we get a vacation day with that?" Garrett asked. Uncle Bob must have flashed him his famous glower because Garrett jumped up and said, "Right. I'm on it." He took off, supposedly in search of the assailant.

The sirens were getting closer, and I heard men shuffling about below me.

"Is anything broken?" Uncle Bob's voice had softened.

"My eyelids, I think. I can't open them."

I heard a soft chuckle. "If it were anyone else, I'd say eyelids can't be broken. But considering the source . . ."

A weak grin spread across my face. "So I'm, like, special?"

He snorted as he pressed gingerly here and there, testing for broken bones and the like. "Special wouldn't even begin to cover it, my dear."

Miracles happen. I figured I was living proof. To walk away—well, to limp away with lots of help—from a fall like that without a single broken bone was nothing short of miraculous. With a capital *M*.

"We really should get some X-rays," the EMT said to Uncle Bob as I lounged on the stretcher.

Ambulances were cool. "You just want to fondle my extraneous body parts," I said to the EMT as I picked up a silver gadget that looked disturbingly like an alien orifice probe, broke it, then promptly put it back, hoping it wouldn't leave someone's life hanging in the balance because the EMT couldn't alien-probe his orifices.

EMT Guy chuckled and checked my blood pressure for the gazillionth time.

"Really, Uncle Bob, I'm fine. Who owns this warehouse?"

Uncle Bob closed his phone and looked at me through the open doors of the ambulance. "Well, if you're hoping for a neon sign above his head that flashes *Bad Guy,* you're going to be very disappointed."

"Don't tell me. The guy's a canonized saint?"

"Close. His name is Father Federico Díaz."

Wow. Why would a Catholic priest own a warehouse in the middle of nowhere? Why would a Catholic priest own a warehouse, period? This case was getting more bizarre by the minute.

"No one," Garrett said, jogging up to us. "I don't understand it. If there were two guys inside and one on the roof, where'd they go?"

"The van was the only vehicle on the premises. They had to leave on foot," Uncle Bob said, scanning the area with a quizzical look on his face.

"Or not leave at all," I added. "Where are the boxes?"

They both turned around and surveyed the empty warehouse.

"What boxes?" Uncle Bob asked.

"Exactly." I eased off the stretcher, picked up and handed the broken probe to the EMT, who reattached the alien part and put it back with a grin, then stepped to the ground with far more wincing than was socially acceptable.

"I have three words for you," EMT Guy said. "Possible internal bleeding."

I turned back to him. "Don't you think if I was bleeding internally, I'd know somewhere deep inside? Like, internally?"

"One X-ray," he bargained. When I winced again, he added, "Maybe two."

Uncle Bob wrapped a beefy arm around me. I was a nanosecond away from arguing with EMT Guy when he said, "Charley, we have men all over the place. I promise we'll look for your missing boxes."

"But—"

"You're going to the hospital if I have to handcuff you to that stretcher," Garrett said, stepping in front of me as if to block my only escape route.

With an annoyed sigh, I folded my arms and glared at him. "Stop trying to get me into your handcuffs. I want to be there when you talk to Father Federico," I said to Uncle Bob, ignoring Garrett's surprised expression. Would he never learn?

"Deal," Uncle Bob agreed before I could change my mind. "I'll call you tomorrow with a time."

"You'll need a ride home from the hospital," Garrett reminded me.

"You just want to try out those handcuffs. I'll call Cookie. Go figure out where those boxes went."

"Do you want to look at mug shots tomorrow, as well?" Uncle Bob asked. "Can you ID the guy who hit you?"

"Well . . ." My nose scrunched as I considered the possibility of positively identifying my assailant based on the knuckle sandwich he gave me. "I got an almost clear peripheral look at the guy's left fist. I might could recognize his pinkie."

For some bizarre reason that baffled the heck out of me, Cookie seemed none too happy about being called out at one in the morning to extract me from the hospital.

"What did you do now?" she asked, walking into the examining room. Still in her pajama bottoms with a massive robelike sweater thrown over a tee, she looked a tad postapocalyptic. And she had a wicked case of bedhead. It was funny.

I eased off the examining table, moving as if there were a bomb in the room set to go off with a motion-detecting sensor. She rushed to my side to help. Had there actually been a bomb set to go off with a motion-detecting sensor, we'd have been blown to bits.

"Why are you assuming it was my fault?" I asked when my feet were firmly planted.

Her lips thinned into a grim reprimand. "Do you have any idea what it's like to get a call from the hospital in the middle of the night? I jump into panic mode. I can barely put two words together."

"I'm sorry." After limping to my jacket, I shrugged into it, amazed at how much effort it took not to pass out. "You probably thought something happened to Amber."

"Are you kidding? Amber's an angel compared to you. Having you around makes me appreciate her pubescent, hormone-induced ways. Honestly, I don't know how your stepmother did it."

A lightbulb went off in my head when she said that. Not a particularly bright one—maybe a 12-watter—but it did make me reassess my

stepmother's lack of interest in my well-being. Perhaps our rocky relationship was partially my fault.

Not.

Cookie lectured me all the way home. Thankfully, I'd had the ambulance take me to Pres, so it was a short drive. Her concern was sweet
and, at the same time, oddly annoying. *My* concern, however, was leaning toward homicidal. Hard as I tried, I couldn't help but get a little hot
under my seven-dollar thrift-store Gucci collar. Someone hit me. Someone tried to kill me. Had he succeeded, I could have died.

Then, as if my perpetual state of sunshine couldn't allow such a
negative thought to infect my mind—I'm pretty sure I was a flower
child in a past life—I just *had* to see the cup half full. Hopefully of Jack
Daniel's. I'd learned something tonight, besides the legitimacy of the
sudden-stop thing. I'd learned that somehow, in some bizarre coinci-
dence of fate, Reyes and the Big Bad were connected. But how? Reyes
couldn't have been more than three when I was born. How did Bad
know he would call me Dutch fifteen years later?

I couldn't have been imagining it. I remembered it so clearly. Dutch.
Whispery and soft, deep and mesmerizing. Rather like Reyes himself.
And the similarities didn't stop there. My mind started registering all
kinds of likenesses between the two. The heat and energy that radiated
off them both. The way they moved—a blur—very unlike the departed. The paralyzing power of their touches, their stares. The way
my knees almost gave beneath my weight with the appearance of either one.

Maybe I was losing it. Either that or Reyes and Bad were the same
kind of being. But how was that even possible? I needed a second opinion. As Cookie pulled her Taurus into the parking lot, I said, "I saw
him again."

She braked short and looked at me.

"When I fell through the skylight," I added.

"Reyes?" she asked in disbelief.

"No. I don't know." Fatigue seeped into my voice. "I'm beginning to wonder. I'm beginning to wonder about a lot of things."

She nodded her head in understanding, eased up to the curb, and turned off the engine. "I've been doing some research. It's late, but I have a feeling you won't be able to sleep until some of your questions are answered."

After Cookie more or less carried me into my apartment, she went to check on Amber. I shouted out a hey to Mr. Wong then put on a pot of coffee in my brand-new coffeepot that, according to the card and bow attached, had been provided by the good people at AAA Electric for the investigation I did on the missing switchgears—whatever the heck a switchgear was and why ever the heck anyone would steal one. It was red. The coffeepot, not the switchgear. I had no idea what color switchgears were, as I'd discovered the thief long before it came to that. Still, I doubted they were red.

I poured a small glass of milk and downed it so I could take four ibuprofen at once without tearing up the lining of my stomach. I'd refused the prescription painkillers the doctor in the ER had offered. Scripts and I didn't generally get along. But the soreness was already infiltrating my muscles, stiffening them until I thought they would break with each move I made. That fall may not have done any permanent damage, but the temporary crap was going to suck. I could barely breathe.

Still, even a slight ability to breathe was better than a nonexistent one.

Between visiting Mark Weir in jail, chasing Rocket around the asylum, breaking into the law offices, and falling through the skylight at the warehouse, I had yet to get my hands on a computer long enough to search the prison database for more information on Reyes. As I eased into the chair at my computer, Cookie strode in with an armful of notes and printouts. Knowing her, she'd already researched Reyes's life down to his shoe size and blood type. I logged on to the New Mexico Department of Corrections Web site while she poured us some coffee. Ten seconds later, thanks to fiber optics, Reyes's mug shot shone brightly on the screen.

"My god," Cookie said from behind me, apparently experiencing the same visceral reaction to Reyes that I did every time I looked at him.

She set a cup beside me.

"Thank you," I said, "and I'm sorry I had to call you out in the middle of the night."

She pulled up a chair, sat down, and put a hand over mine. "Charley, do you honestly think it bothers me one iota that you called me?"

Was that a trick question? "Well, yes, with a sprinkle of *duh* on top. Who wouldn't be upset?"

"I wouldn't," she said, taken aback, as if I'd hurt her feelings for even suggesting such a thing. "I would have been furious had you *not* called me. I know you're special and you have an extraordinary gift that I'll never fully understand, but you're still human, and you're still my best friend." Her face transformed into a map of worry lines. "I wasn't upset that you called me. I was upset because you think you're indestructible. You're not." She paused to let her gaze bore into mine, to drive her point home. It was sweet. "And because of this false sense of security, you get yourself into the most . . . bizarre situations."

"Bizarre?" I asked, pretending to be offended.

"Three words. *Sewage plant disaster.*"

"That totally wasn't my fault," I argued, balking at the very idea of it. As if.

She pursed her lips and waited for me to come to my senses.

"Okay, it was my fault." She knew me too well. "But only a little. And those rats had it coming. So, what did you find out?" I asked, looking back at Reyes's picture.

Cookie thumbed through the printouts and slid one out. "Are you ready for this?"

"As long it doesn't contain nude pictures of elderly women, I'm good." I kept my eyes locked on to Reyes's, fierce and intense as they were.

She handed me the printout. "Murder."

"No," I whispered, as if the wind had been forced out of my lungs. It was a news article dated ten years earlier. No, no, no, no, no. Anything but murder. Or rape. Or kidnapping. Or armed robbery. Or indecent exposure, 'cause that's just creepy. I scanned the article with a reluctant eye, like when you pass by an accident and can't help but look.

ALBUQUERQUE MAN FOUND GUILTY.

Short. To the point.

A man with a past more mysterious than the circumstances surrounding his father's death was found guilty Monday after three days of jury deliberation. The prosecution faced several unusual problems during the trial, such as the fact that Reyes Alexander Farrow, 20, doesn't exist.

Reyes Alexander Farrow. I stopped a moment, tried to catch my breath, to slow my pulse. Even Reyes's name gave me heart palpitations. And he didn't exist? Heck, I could have told them that.

"Farrow has no birth certificate," the prosecution stated after the two-week trial ended. *"He has no medical records, no social security number, no school records beyond a three-month stint at Yucca High. On paper, this man is a ghost."*

A ghost. As Morpheus would say, fate is not without a sense of irony.

Farrow's father, Earl Walker, was found dead in his car after a group of hikers discovered it at the bottom of a canyon five miles east of Albuquerque. Though his

*body had been burned beyond recognition, the autopsy concluded that he'd died
from blunt force trauma to the head. Several witnesses saw Farrow fighting with
his father the day before Walker was reported missing by his fiancée.*

*"Our hands were tied," Stan Eichmann, the lead defense attorney for Far-
row, stated after the verdict was handed down. "There is much more to this case
than meets the eye. I guess we'll never know how it could have turned out."*

*Eichmann's statement was only one of dozens of mysteries surrounding this
case. For example, Walker has no social security number either and has never
filed a single tax return.*

*"He had nothing that would establish him as a law-abiding citizen," Eich-
mann said. "He seemed to be living under several aliases. It took weeks to track
down what we believe was his real name."*

*"This is actually more common than you might think," the prosecution stated.
"But it's a choice career criminals make as adults. Farrow, on the other hand, has
never existed. According to our records, he was never born, and DNA results
conclude that Walker was not his biological father. Based on what we know about
him, if I had to guess, I'd say Reyes Farrow was quite possibly abducted as a
child."*

My breath caught in my chest. Could he really have been abducted?
I quickly scanned the rest of the article.

*Farrow never took the stand in his own defense, leaving jurors hard-pressed to
see past the circumstantial evidence despite the defense's success at debunking several key theories pertinent to the prosecution's strategy.*

The article went on to talk about Walker's fiancée, Sarah Hadley.
She'd testified that Reyes had threatened Walker on several occasions—
right—and that they were both in fear for their lives. Yet another witness, an associate of Ms. Hadley's, refuted the statement, swearing
under oath that Walker's fiancée was secretly in love with Farrow and
would have left Walker in a heartbeat to be with him. The witness
stated that if Ms. Hadley was afraid of anyone, it was of Walker
himself.

"This is a case about a broken heart and a broken mind," Eichmann told the jury minutes before they broke for deliberation. "Walker's criminal record alone casts numerous doubts as to the legitimacy of anything even remotely resembling a motive by his only child."

His only child? But Reyes had a sister.

"The circumstances surrounding his death are about as transparent as I am," Eichmann continued.

Farrow, who had been taking night classes with a stolen social security number before his arrest, ironically, toward a law degree, stood impassively, his head bowed slightly, as the verdict was read.

My heart sank in my chest with the image of Reyes standing in a courtroom, waiting for his peers to judge him, to find him guilty or innocent. I wondered what he felt, how he coped with their decision.

"The mystery that is Reyes Farrow deepens by the minute," I said. Walker's fiancée was, for lack of a better phrase, full of shit. Abused children rarely attack their abusers, much less torment them. And women were never secretly in love with someone who they believed might kill them at any moment.

"But murder, Charley."

"Do you know how many people are in prison for crimes they didn't commit?"

"You think Reyes is innocent?"

In my dreams. "I'd have to see him in person to know for certain."

Her brows slid together. "Is that part of your ability?"

Though I'd never really thought of it that way, I said, "Yeah, I guess it is. I forget that not everyone can see what I see."

"Speaking of which, you said you saw him again tonight? Were you talking about Reyes?"

"Oh, right." I straightened then winced with the action and burrowed back into my seat, wondering where to begin. Better just to get it all out in the open, air my dirty laundry, so to speak. "You know

how I've never told you certain things, because I didn't want you to
have to seek therapy?"

Cookie laughed. "Yes, but you know you can tell me anything."

"Yeah, well, that's a good thing, because you're about to get a crash
course in all things grim. I'm lost."

"Aren't you usually?" she said, mischief glittering in her eyes.

"Funny. I'm not talking about my usual state of confusion. This is
different."

"Different from utter chaos?" When I scowled, feigning annoyance,
she shifted in her chair, and said, "Okay, you have my complete attention."

But I was still stuck on the utter-chaos thing. Cookie was right. My
life tended to be in either park or overdrive, careening through traffic
with little thought to the cars around me or the destination. "I do just
sort of stumble through life, don't I?"

"Well, yeah, but that's okay," she said with a one-shouldered shrug.

"Ya think?"

"Sure. We're all just sort of stumbling through life, if you ask me."

"Still, this whole grim reaper thing should have come with a man-
ual. Or a diagram of some kind. A flowchart would have been nice."

"Oh, you're right," Cookie said with her supportive, I've-got-your-
back head nod. "One with colored arrows, huh?"

"And simple, easy-to-read yes/no questions. Like, 'Did death incarnate visit you today? If no, skip to step ten. If yes, stop now, 'cause you
are so screwed, girlfriend. You may as well call it a day. Take a deep
breath, because this is going to hurt. You might want to phone a friend
about now, tell her to kiss your ass good-bye. . . .' "

I realized Cookie wasn't doing her supportive, I've-got-your-back
head-nod thing anymore. I glanced at her suddenly pale face. It was
kind of pretty. Sure made the blue in her eyes stand out.

"Cookie?"

Just as I was about to check for a pulse, she whispered, "Death incarnate?"

Oops. "Oh, that," I said with a dismissive wave of my hand. "He's not really death incarnate. He just *looks* like death incarnate. Come to think of it, he looks like death." I glanced up in thought and decided to ignore the cobwebs on the light fixture for the time being. "He kind of looks like, well, a grim reaper. Except I'm a grim reaper and he looks nothing like me. But if I didn't know what grim reapers really looked like, not that I've ever met one besides myself, I'd say that's exactly what he resembles." I glanced back at her. "Yep. Death incarnate should just about cover it."

"Death incarnate? There really is such a thing?"

Perhaps I was going about this the wrong way. "He's not really death. He's kind of cool, I guess, in a terrifying way." She whitened further. Darn it. "When you eventually have to seek therapy, will I have to pay for it?"

"No," she said, straightening her shoulders, pretending to have everything under control. "I'm good. You just took me by surprise, that's all." She waved me on with a wiggle of her fingers. "Go ahead. I can handle this."

"Swear?" I asked, suspicious of the blue around her lips.

"Pinkie swear. Crash course. I am *so* ready."

When she gripped the arms of the chair as if preparing for an aerial assault, my doubts reemerged. What the bloody heck was I doing? Besides scarring her for life?

"I can't do this," I said, reevaluating my telling her everything just so I could tell her about Bad in the warehouse to get her opinion on the whole thing. I couldn't do that to Cookie. "I'm sorry. I should never have mentioned any of this."

She peeled her hands off the arms of her chair and looked at me, purpose glimmering in her eyes. "Charley, you can tell me anything. I promise not to freak out on you again." When my gaze turned to one of utter doubt, she clarified, "I promise to *try* not to freak out on you again."

"It's not your fault," I said, bowing my head. "There are some things people are better off not knowing. I can't believe what I almost did to you. I apologize."

One of the consequences of my being honest with those close to me was the effect it had on their psyche. I'd learned long ago that, yes, it hurt when people didn't believe me, but when they did, their lives were changed forever. They never saw the world the same again. And such a perspective could be devastating. I chose very carefully who I let in. And I'd told only one other person on Earth about Bad, a decision I've regretted ever since.

Cookie edged back into her chair, picked up her cup, and gazed into it. "Do you remember the first time you told me what you are?"

I thought back a moment. "Just barely. If you'll recall, I was into my third margarita."

"Do you remember what you said?"

"Um . . . third margarita."

"You said, and I quote, 'Cookie, I'm the grim reaper.' "

"And you believed me?" I asked, incredulity raising my brows.

"Yes," she said, coming to animated life. "Without a shadow of a doubt. By that point, I'd seen too much not to believe you. So what on Earth could you tell me now that would sound worse?"

"You might be surprised," I hedged.

She frowned. "Is it really that bad?"

"It's not that it's bad," I explained, trying to allow her to keep a little of her innocence and possibly her sanity, "just maybe a little less believable."

"Oh, right, because there's a grim reaper on every street corner these days."

She had a point. More often than not, however, my abilities got me into trouble and took away people whom I'd believed I could trust. Those facts alone made me hesitant now, no matter how much I thought of Cookie. Honestly, what had I been thinking? Sometimes my selfishness astounded me.

"When I was in high school," I said, angling for the old it's-for-your-own-good spiel, "I told my best friend too much. Our friendship ended badly because of it. I just don't want that to happen to us."

Not that I could place all the blame on Jessica. Past experience and my mad skill at reading people should have stopped me from telling my ex–best friend more than she could handle. Still, her sudden and complete hatred of all things Charley Davidson struck hard. I simply couldn't comprehend where her hostilities were coming from. We were best friends one minute, then mortal enemies the next. It was such a shock. I still thought about it often, even though I realized years later she'd just been scared. Of what I could do. Of what was out there. Of what my abilities meant in the grand scheme of things. But at the time, I was devastated. Betrayed, once again, by someone I'd loved. By someone I'd thought loved me.

Between Jessica's hostilities and my stepmother's indifference, I sank into a very deep depression. One that I hid well with sarcasm and sass, but the incident sparked a cycle of self-destructive behavior that took me years to crawl out of.

Oddly enough, Reyes was the one who knocked me out of the depression itself. His situation made me appreciate what I had, namely a father who didn't kick my ass for the sheer joy of it. I had a dad who loved me, a commodity Reyes lacked. Yet he wasn't wallowing in a cesspool of self-pity. His life was a hundred times worse than mine, but he didn't feel the least bit sorry for himself. Not from what I'd seen, anyway. So I'd put my little pity party on hold.

Trust, however, was another issue. Trusting the living had never been my strong suit to begin with. But this was Cookie. The best friend I'd ever had. She'd accepted everything I ever told her without doubt or contempt or instantaneous musings of monetary gain.

"And you think I won't be able to handle what you tell me?"

"No. That's just it. If anyone can handle it, you can. I just don't know if I want to do that to you." I put a hand on her arm and leaned forward, willing her to understand. "It's not always better knowing."

After a long pause, she gathered the files with a weak smile on her face. "Your abilities are a part of you, Charley, a part of who you are. I don't think there's a thing you could tell me that would change my perception of you."

"It's not your perception of *me* I'm worried about."

"It's late," she said, slipping papers into a file folder. "And you need to get to bed."

Had I hurt her feelings? Did she think I didn't want her to know? Sharing every part of my life with a very best friend whom I could confide in would be like finding the pot of green chili stew at the end of the rainbow. Did I dare? Could I risk one of the best things that had ever happened to me?

It *was* late, but as wonderful as slipping into unconsciousness sounded, the thought of telling Cookie everything—of her knowing the truth, the whole truth, and nothing but the truth—had my adrenaline pumping. It would be nice to have someone to trust in, a confidante, a comrade in arms and hair gel, despite the fact that it was almost two in the morning and I was exhausted and sore and near comatose. I just prayed neither of us was biting off more than we could chew. I did that once with bubble gum. It wasn't pleasant.

Maybe I could take a chance. Just this once. Maybe she'd come out of it unscathed and as sane as she was going in. Not that that was saying much, but still.

I ran a finger along the edge of my coffee mug, unable to meet her gaze. I was about to change her life forever. And not necessarily in a good way. "He's like smoke," I said, and I felt her still beside me. "And he's powerful. I can feel it pulse off him in waves. It makes me weak when he's near, like he absorbs a part of me."

She sat quiet for a few stunned moments, then placed the files back on the desk. She'd crossed a schism, a gap between two worlds that few people even knew about. As of this point in time, Cookie Kowalski would never be the same again.

"And that's who you saw today?" she asked.

"In the warehouse, yes. But this morning as well, when Reyes appeared in the office."

"This being was there?"

"No. I'm beginning to think he and Reyes are the same kind of being. But Reyes is real, a human, and then I keep seeing these blurs lately and having unimaginable sex in my sleep, and then he shows up in my shower—"

"Shower?"

"—and he called me Dutch the day I was born, just like Reyes, only Reyes was too young to be there when I was born, duh, so how did he know? How did the Big Bad know what Reyes would call me fifteen years later?"

The coffee mug slipped from my fingers, as Cookie placed it on the desk. "No more caffeine."

"Sorry," I said, trying to suppress a sheepish grin.

"We should start at the beginning." She patted my arm in support. "Unless you want to start with the shower scene."

"There's just so much I've never told you, Cookie. It's a lot to handle."

"Charley, *you're* a lot to handle."

I chuckled, snatched my cup back, and downed the last of my coffee.

"When did you first have contact with this being?"

"The day I was born." Wasn't she listening? "That was the first time I saw 'the Big Bad,'" I said, adding air quotes for effect.

"The Big—"

"He's the smoke. He's this creature-slash-monster-type thing that shows up at the most bizarre times. Mostly when my life is in danger. We should make popcorn."

She scooted to the edge of her seat. "And he was there the day you were born?"

"Yep. I just call him the Big Bad because Humongous Slithering Creature that Scares the Ever-Lovin' Piss Outta Me is too long."

Cookie nodded, enthralled with where my story might lead, aware by now that my accounts were a bit more engrossing than the average my-aunt-had-a-ghost-living-in-her-attic tale. Mine were not the stuff of campfires or slumber parties. Which could explain the lack of invitations growing up.

"Anywho, like I said, he was there the day I was born."

She held her cup in limbo between the table and her mouth, trying very hard not to drool. I hadn't realized until that moment how much she'd been craving to know more. How much my silence had affected her.

With brow knitting, she asked, "So, how do you know that? Did someone tell you?"

"Tell me what?" My coffee mug was pretty. It had a tiger lily on it, my favorite flower. I was studying it in an attempt to keep my eyes off Reyes.

"That this big, bad creature was there when you were born."

"Um, what?" What the heck was she talking about? Maybe I was unconsciously slipping into unconsciousness after all.

"How did you know it was there the day you were born?"

Oh, right. She didn't know that part yet either. "I pretty much remember everything from day one."

"Day one?"

I nodded, noticing for the first time that one petal of the tiger lily brushed the rim of the mug just so.

"Day one of what? The first grade? Desert Storm? Your menstrual cycle?" She hissed in a breath of realization. "That's it! It all happened when you had your first period. A hormone thing, right? That's when you figured it all out?"

I grinned. She was funny. "Day one of my life. My existence. My presence on Earth."

"I'm not following."

"The day I was born," I said with a roll of my eyes. Cookie wasn't usually this slow on the uptake.

She sat in stunned silence after that. It was weird.

"I know. That throws everyone." After running my finger along the brightest orange petal, I added, "Apparently it's rather rare for people to remember the day they were born." The petals opened in an explosion of color, darkest at the center, at its most vulnerable point.

"Rare?" she asked, finding her voice at last. "Seriously? Try nonexistent."

"Well, that's just odd." I traced the next petal. "I remember it like it was yesterday. Not that yesterday isn't fuzzy." Then I ran out of petals and my gaze drifted up and locked on to Reyes's again. The pain and anger in his expression were almost palpable. And the color of his eyes, the rich, deep brown, grew darker as it neared the centers, their most vulnerable points.

"My god, Charley, you remember being born?"

"I remember *him*."

"This big, bad guy?"

"*The* Big Bad. And I remember other things, too, like the doctor cutting the cord and the nurses cleaning me off."

Cookie sat back in astonishment.

"He said my name. Or what I thought was my name."

She inhaled a breath of realization. "He called you Dutch."

"Yes, but how? How could he possibly have known?"

"Hon, I'm still working on the day-you-were-born thing."

"Right, sorry. But could you hurry up and get over it? I have questions."

Her expression turned dubious. "Got any other astonishing tidbits to impart?"

With a shrug, I said, "Not really. Unless you count the fact that I've known every language ever spoken since that whole day-I-was-born thing. That's probably worthy of note."

I was tired, so I couldn't be completely positive, but I had the distinct feeling Cookie seized.

Chapter Ten

Don't fear the reaper. Just be very, very aware of her.

—CHARLOTTE JEAN DAVIDSON

"So, I look up and there he is."

Cookie held a piece of popcorn at her lips as she listened to my tale, her eyes wide with astonishment. Or possibly primal, bone-chilling fear. It was hard to tell at that point. "The Big Bad," she said.

"Right, but you can call him Bad for short. Anywho, he's standing there just watching and I'm all naked and covered in afterbirth—though that didn't really register at the time. I just remember being mesmerized by him. He seemed to be in a constant state of fluid motion."

"Like smoke."

"Like smoke," I said as I snatched the buttery morsel out of her hand and popped it into my mouth. "You snooze, you lose, *chica*."

"Do you remember anything before him?" she asked as she reached for another piece, only to hold it in limbo at her mouth as well. I was trying not to crack up and break the spell.

"Not so much. I mean, I don't remember being born or anything—thank the gods, 'cause that would just be gross. Just the stuff that came after. And it's all very peach fuzzy. Except for him. And my mom."

"Wait," she said, holding up a finger, "your mom? But, your mom died the day you were born. You remember her?"

A slow smile slid across my face. "She was so beautiful, Cookie. She was my first . . . um, customer."

"You mean—"

"Yes. She passed through me. She was light and warmth and unconditional love. I didn't understand it at the time, but she told me she was happy to give up her life so that I could live. She made me feel calm and cherished, which was a good thing, 'cause Bad was kind of freaking me out."

Her gaze slid past me as she processed what I'd said. "That's . . . that's . . ."

"Impossible to believe, I know."

"Amazing." She looked at me then.

The relief that flooded my body couldn't be helped. I should have known she'd believe me. But people I'd grown up with, people I was closest to, never believed the being-born thing.

"So, you kind of got to know your mom in a way, right?"

"I did." And as I grew older, I realized it was more than a lot of kids got. I would be forever grateful for those few moments we had together.

"And you know every language that's ever been spoken on Earth?"

Thankful for the change in subject, I replied, "Every single one."

"Even Farsi?"

"Even Farsi," I said with a grin.

"Oh, my goodness!" she almost shouted. A thought must've popped into her brain. Then her features changed, darkened, and she pointed an accusative finger at me. "I knew it. I knew you understood what that Vietnamese man said to me that day in the market. I could see it in your eyes."

I smiled and looked back at Reyes's image, fell into him. "He said he liked your ass."

She gasped. "Why, that little perv."

"Told you he had the hots for you."

"Too bad he was small enough to fit into my cleavage."

"I think that's why he liked you," I said, a bubble of laughter slipping out.

Cookie sat silent a long while after that. I gave her some time to absorb everything I was telling her. After a moment, she asked, "How is it even possible?"

"Well," I said, deciding to tease her, "I don't think he could've actually fit in your cleavage. Though I'm sure he would have enjoyed the challenge."

"No, I mean the language thing. It's just so—"

"Freakishly cool?" I asked, my voice hopeful.

"—mind-boggling."

"Oh. Yeah, I guess it is."

"And you understood what people were saying to you on the day you were born?"

With my nose crinkling in thought, I said, "Kind of. Not literally, however. I had no schema, no past to relate the words to, no meaning to process it with. When people spoke to me, I understood them on a visceral level. Oddly enough, I talked and walked and did everything else at a normal rate. But when anyone talks to me, I understand them. No matter what language they're speaking. I just know what they're saying."

I nudged my mouse when the screen saver popped up, forced the image back to Reyes. "I understood the first words my father ever said to me, too," I continued, trying to disguise the sadness in my voice. "For the most part anyway. He told me my mother had died."

Cookie shook her head. "I'm so sorry."

"I think my dad knew. I think he knew I understood him. It was like our little secret." I grabbed a handful of popcorn and tossed a piece into my mouth. "Then he married my stepmother, and everything changed. She figured out pretty quick I was a freak. It all started when I got hooked on Mexican soap operas."

"Charley, you're not a freak."

"It's okay. I can't blame her."

"Yes, you can," she said, her voice suddenly honed to a razor's edge. "I'm a mother, too. Mothers don't do that, step or otherwise."

"Yeah, but Amber wasn't born a grim reaper."

"It doesn't matter. She's your stepmother. Period. It's not like you became a serial killer."

God, I loved having someone on my side. My dad had always loved me without reservation, but he never really had my back like that. I think Cookie would have taken on the Mafia single-handedly for me. And won.

"So, the day you were born, that's when he called you Dutch?"

"Yes."

"Now, was this before or after your mother crossed through you?"

"After, but I just don't get it. How did he know? I'd never realized until tonight that Bad didn't say my actual name that day. He didn't call me Charlotte. He'd called me Dutch, Cookie, just like Reyes did when I was in high school. How could he have known?" My mind started spinning, trying desperately to put the pieces together.

"Okay, let me ask you this," she said, her forehead crinkling in thought. "The first time you saw Reyes, did you notice anything unusual about him?"

"Besides the fact that he was getting his ass kicked by psycho-dad?"

"Yes."

I pulled in a long, deep breath and thought about it. "You know, I may have but didn't realize it at the time. I mean, maybe there was something different, something supernatural, but all the adrenaline flooding my body had me thinking it was just the direness of the moment. He was so magnificent. So beautiful and agile and perfect."

"From the way you've described it, maybe Reyes is some kind of supernatural being. The fact that he took a beating like that and just walked away like you seem to do every other week has me wondering."

"I'd never looked at it that way." As I thought back to that night, the memory both unsettling and fascinating, I could see Reyes in my mind. "You know what?" I asked in realization. "He *was* different. He was, I don't know, dark. Unreadable."

"Well, he sounds suspiciously supernatural to me."

If I hadn't been so tired, I would have laughed. "You're suddenly the expert?"

"If it's hot and dark, yeah, pretty much."

That time, I did laugh.

"So how many times have you seen Bad?" she asked, seeming to come to terms with everything I'd told her. This was good. Productive. Cheaper than therapy.

"Not many."

"Well, when you saw him, what happened?"

I picked up my cup and took a sip of the hot chocolate Cookie'd insisted I switch to.

She placed a hand on my shoulder, a knowing look on her face. "In the park. With the Johnson girl."

When I placed the cup down, I tried to do so with as much nonchalance as I could muster. Thinking of the incident with the Johnson girl was like running a finger over a raw nerve. I had been trying to help a mother out of the grieving hole she had withdrawn into when her daughter went missing. Instead, I caused a town scandal that ended up being the final straw for my stepmother. She turned against me that day and never looked back.

So, yes, the incident was a sore spot on my psyche, but I had worse. I had gaping wounds that refused to heal, and Cookie knew only a minute amount about them.

"Yes," I said, raising my chin. "In the park. That was the third time I saw him."

"But your life wasn't in danger. Or was it?"

"Not at all, but maybe he thought it was. He was so mad, I think because my stepmom was yelling at me in front of all these people." My head lowered at the memory. "And she slapped me. It was quite a shock." I locked eyes with Cookie, suddenly wanting her to understand how afraid I was of him. "I thought he was going to kill her. He was shaking with anger. I felt it, like electricity prickling over my skin. I whispered to him as my stepmother berated me in front of half the town and begged him not to hurt her."

Cookie's mouth thinned in sympathy. "Charley, I'm so very sorry."

"It's okay. I'm just not sure why he scares me so much. I can't believe what a wuss I can be at times."

"I'm sorry that he scares you, too, but I meant the part about your stepmother."

"Oh, no, don't be," I said, shaking my head. "That was totally my fault."

"You were five."

After a hard swallow, I bowed my head and said, "You don't know what I did."

"Unless you doused the woman in gasoline and set her on fire, I'm not sure her reaction was appropriate."

A half smile crept across my face. "I can assure you, no petroleum products were harmed in the making of that memory."

"What happened then? With Bad?"

"I guess he heard me. He left, but he was not a happy camper."

Cookie nodded in understanding, then said, "And I would be willing to bet one of the times he showed up was when you were in college."

"Wow, you're good."

"You know, you've told me about how you were attacked when you were walking home after a class one night, but you didn't tell me he was there."

"Yep, he was. He saved me, just like he did when I was four."

Surprise washed over her face. "Four? What happened when you were four? Wait, he saved you when you were attacked in college? How?" she asked, stumbling over the questions that were surely tumbling through her head. I realized my description and taxonomy of the Big Bad may have led Cookie to believe that he was, well, big and bad. And he was. Kind of.

But I still couldn't tell her *how* he saved me. I couldn't do that to her, not until I knew she'd be okay with the knowledge.

"He . . . got the guy off me."

"Oh, my goodness, Charley. I guess I didn't realize. . . . I mean, you made it sound so minuscule. And your life had been in danger?"

With a shrug, I said, "Maybe a little. There was a switchblade involved. I didn't even know they still made those things. Aren't they illegal?"

"He shows up when your life is in danger," she repeated, deep in thought, "and he saved you when you were four? So, what happened when you were four again?"

I shifted in my chair, so sore I could barely manage it. "Well, I was kind of kidnapped, though not really kidnapped so much as led away."

A hand shot to her mouth to squelch a gasp.

"God, all this sounds so awful when I say it out loud," I complained. "I whine more than a Goth with a blogging fetish. It's really not that bad. I actually grew up rather happy. I had lots of friends. They were mostly dead, but still."

"Charley Jean Davidson," she said in warning. "You cannot use the word *kidnapped* in a sentence, then not elaborate."

"Fine, if you really want to know. But you're not going to like it."

"I really want to know."

After a long, breathy sigh, I said, "It happened here."

"Here? In Albuquerque?"

"Here in this building. When I was four."

"You've lived in this building before?"

I suddenly felt like I was in therapy and all the things that had happened to me in the past, both good and bad, were gushing from a festering wound. But what happened in this building was the worst of the worst. The knife in my flesh, buried so deep inside me, I doubted it could ever be extracted fully. At least not without some serious anesthesia.

"No," I said, drawing another sip, testing the rich, warm chocolate on my tongue before swallowing. "I've never lived here. But even before my dad bought the bar, it'd been a cop hangout. And he'd taken me to it on several occasions, quite innocently, mostly for birthday parties and such. And a few times he had to chat with his partner, as those were the eighties BC." When Cookie's brows slanted in question, I added, "Before cells."

"Ah, of course."

"But on one particular occasion, I'd upset my stepmother when I told her, in a rather matter-of-fact way, that her father had died and had crossed through me because he wanted me to give her a message. She hadn't known yet that he'd passed away and she was furious, refused to listen. She never even let me give her the message. I didn't understand it anyway. Something about blue towels."

"She wouldn't listen even after she found out he'd actually passed away?"

"Absolutely not. By that time, Denise was anti-anything-death-related."

Cookie took a deep breath as if to calm her nerves. "The woman never ceases to amaze me."

"You should try her meat loaf. It'll put some pretty coarse hair on your chest."

She chuckled. "I have enough hair to deal with, thank you very much. I'll pass on family night at the Davidsons'."

I shrugged. "Your loss."

"So, you were four."

Geez, she was so pushy. "Right. Four. So, my feelings were hurt as usual, and when we drove to the bar where my dad was having a beer, Denise left me on the bench by the kitchen to go tell on me to Dad. I loved it in the kitchen, but I was all mad and hurt, so I decided to run away. When Mr. Dunlop, the cook, wasn't looking, I snuck out the back."

"A four-year-old, alone at night, on Central? A parent's worst nightmare."

"Yeah, well. I figured I'd show her," I said. "I wasn't the brightest four-year-old on Central. Of course, the minute I stepped outside, I changed my mind. Not that I was scared. I don't get scared like most people. I was just . . . aware. But before I could dash back inside, a super nice man in a trench coat offered to help me find my stepmother. Oddly, instead of going into the bar where I knew she was, we came into this building."

"Oh, honey," she whispered, despair in her voice.

"But nothing much happened," I said with a lift of my shoulders. "Like I said, Bad saved me." Trying to make light of a dark situation, I added, "Looking back, I don't think that man ever planned to help me find my stepmother."

Cookie reached toward me and wrapped me into a huge, long hug.

It made me think of warm fires on winter nights. And, for some reason, roasting marshmallows.

After, like, an hour and twenty-seven minutes, I mumbled, "Can't . . . breathe. . . ."

She leaned back with her brows creased in thought. "Is it just me, or does the fact that you live in the same building you were abducted into seem a bit morbid?"

"Pffft. It's just you," I said, discounting the entire bizarre, ghoulish thing.

I was so happy she didn't push for more details. The devil was in the details, and I wasn't feeling particularly satanic at that moment. "Oh," I said remembering another incident. "This guy in high school tried to run me over with his dad's SUV. Bad shoved the vehicle through a store window." The memory brought a smile to my face.

"Someone tried to run you over in high school?" she asked, appalled.

"Only that one time," I answered.

She pinched the bridge of her nose, then asked, "So, those are the only times you've seen Bad?"

I counted off silently with my fingers. "Yep, that just about covers it."

"And our job is to figure out how Reyes plays into all of this?"

"Yep again. We should roast marshmallows."

"Then I feel it my duty," she continued, unfazed, "as friend and confidante, to analyze in panoramic detail the shower scene."

I held back a giggle. "I'm not really sure the shower scene plays into this on a salient level. It seems more, I don't know, nonsalient."

"Charley," she said in warning, "spill or die a slow and painful death. Who was in the shower with you? Reyes? The Big Bad? Work with me here."

"Okay," I said, acquiescing, "you know that Reyes called me Dutch that night when I was fifteen, right?"

"Right," she said, clearly impatient to jump to the shower scene.

"And you know about the beautiful man showing up in my dreams every night for the past month, right?"

"Right," she said, a sigh softening her voice.

"Well, today, Dream Guy wrote *Dutch* in the condensation on my mirror, and he called me Dutch in the shower."

"Now we're talking." She scooted to the edge of her seat, then stopped abruptly in realization. "So, Dream Guy is Reyes?"

"That's what I mean. I realized tonight Bad called me Dutch the day I was born."

She frowned in confusion. "So, who was in the shower?"

I grinned and gazed at her, suddenly in awe of the woman sitting beside me. "You know, I just told you that this big, scary creature follows me around and saves my life every so often and that I remember the day I was born and that I know every language ever spoken, and you have yet to run out of the room screaming. How can you just accept what I say?"

After a long, thoughtful pause, she asked, "Are you purposely trying to change the subject?"

A deep chuckle almost doubled me over. I grabbed my aching ribs and cried out, "Stop! Don't make me laugh. It hurts."

"Sorry."

She wasn't. I could tell.

"What did you find out from the prison?" I asked, my tearful gaze returning to the screen. "Is Reyes still there? Is he . . . alive?"

"All the officer could tell me was that Reyes was still listed as an inmate in the prison registry, housed in D Unit. But I have to say, I got the feeling she wasn't telling me everything."

"I'm going tomorrow."

"To the prison?"

"Yes." I clicked on the personnel files that listed the administrators of the prison and highlighted the picture of Neil Gossett. "I went to school with the deputy warden."

"Really? Friend or foe?"

I wondered the same thing myself. "That's a tough call. Had I suddenly burst into flames in the school lunchroom, I doubt he would have sacrificed his vitamin D to save me, but I'm pretty sure he would have felt guilty about it later."

"Oh, my goodness," Cookie said, gazing wide eyed at another article in her hands. I leaned over, winced at the pain the movement caused, then stopped when I read the last paragraph of the article.

Uncle Bob had been the lead detective in the case against Reyes. Well, crap.

Chapter Eleven

I'd have a longer attention span if there weren't so many shiny things.

—T-SHIRT

I awoke at the butt crack of dawn with the call of nature urging me out of bed. After my fall, however, I felt like I'd just downed a fifth of Jack.

After tripping on a planter, stubbing my pinkie toe on a step stool, and running face-first into the doorjamb, I eased onto the toilet and reviewed my agenda for the day with a tinkling melody playing in the background. Thank goodness I had a minimalist attitude toward home decor. If anything else had stood between me and the porcelain throne, I might not have lived to see my next birthday.

I glanced down at the football jersey I was wearing, stolen from a boyfriend in high school, a blond-haired, blue-eyed devil with sin in his blood. Even on our first date, he'd been more interested in the color of my underwear than the color of my eyes. Had I known that before-hand, I would totally have worn the teal ones. Odd thing was, I didn't remember donning the jersey last night. I didn't even remember going to bed.

Maybe Cookie slipped a roofie into my hot chocolate. We'd have to talk later, but for now I needed to figure out what to do with my day. Should I ditch my APD responsibilities and go to the prison to check on Reyes? Or should I dump all my APD responsibilities on Cookie and then go to the prison to check on Reyes?

My heart raced in anticipation with the thought of seeing him, though admittedly I was nervous. What if I didn't like what I found? What if he was actually guilty? I couldn't help but hold out hope that his conviction was all some big misunderstanding. That Reyes had been wrongfully accused. That the evidence had been mishandled or even fabricated. Denial was not just a river in Egypt.

From what I'd been able to garner last night, reading article after article on the case—not that any of them were in a particularly pretty font—and even part of the court transcripts Cookie had unearthed of Reyes's trial, the evidence was nowhere near enough for a conviction. Yet twelve people found him guilty. And even more disturbing was the fact that there wasn't a single mention of the abuse he'd endured. Wouldn't being almost beaten to death by your father count for something?

As badly as I wanted to go back to sleep, I knew it wouldn't happen. My mind was racing too hard, too fast, even though I had a very good reason for wanting to go back to sleep, to fall into oblivion, come what may. For the first night in a month, Reyes didn't visit me. He didn't slip into my dreams with his dark eyes and warm touch. He didn't trail kisses down my spine or slide his fingers between my legs. And I couldn't help but wonder why. Did I do something wrong?

My heart felt hollow. I'd become quite addicted to his nightly visits. I looked more forward to them than to my next breath. Maybe my trip to the big house would shed some fluorescents on the situation.

As I was brushing my teeth, I heard shuffling in the kitchen. While most women who live alone would be alarmed by such an occurrence, I just chalked it up to job security.

I stepped out of the bathroom and squinted against the harsh light. "Aunt Lillian?" I asked, limping to the snack bar and scooting onto a stool. Aunt Lillian's small frame was being swallowed by a floral muu-muu, which she had accessorized with a leather vest and love beads straight out of the sixties. I'd tried over the years to figure out what she'd been doing when she died. I just couldn't make anything click that would require muumuus and love beads. Other than playing a wicked game of Twister on LSD.

"Hey, pumpkin head," she said, her ancient smile bright, albeit tooth-less. "I heard you stumble your way to the bathroom, so I figured I'd earn my keep and make us some coffee. Sure looks like you could use some."

I grimaced. "Really? How sweet." Damn. Aunt Lillian couldn't re-ally make coffee. I sat at the counter and pretended to drink a cup.

"Is it too strong?" she asked.

"No way, Aunt Lil, you make the best."

Pretending to drink coffee was similar to faking an orgasm. Where in the supernatural afterlife was the fun in that? But caffeine withdrawal was the least of my problems. I still couldn't get Reyes's no-show out of my head. Maybe I did do something wrong. Or didn't do something I should have. Maybe I needed to be more proactive in bed. Of course, that would imply that I actually had anything tantamount to control during our *sessions. Controlled* would not be my first adjective, were I to describe them in panoramic detail to Cookie.

"You seem . . . distracted, honey pot."

Well, I wasn't voted Most Likely to Become Distracted for nothing.

"Do you have a temperature?"

I glanced back. "I'm sure my temperature's fine, Aunt Lil. Thanks for asking."

I neglected to mention that, yes, I did indeed have a temperature. Every being on Earth has a temperature. Even dead people have a temperature. It's not a good one, but it's there.

"And thanks so much for the coffee."

"Oh, anytime, sweetness. Would you like some breakfast?"

Not if I planned to make it through the day. "Oh, no, I couldn't ask you to do that. I need to get in the shower, anyway. Big day ahead."

She leaned in and grinned conspiratorially. I often wondered if her hair had been that blue in real life, or if it was an effect of her being incorporeal. "You goin' after some bad guys?"

I chuckled. "You know it. The baddest."

She sucked in a dreamy breath. "Ah, to be young and reckless. But really, pumpkin," she said, sobering and leveling a very serious stare on me, "you need to stop getting your ass kicked. You look like hell."

"Thanks, Aunt Lil," I said, easing off the stool with a grimace, "I'll keep that in mind."

She smiled, revealing an empty cavern where her dentures had been. Apparently, they didn't make it to the other side. I'd never been sure if Aunt Lillian knew she was dead or not, and I never had the heart to tell her. I really should, though. I finally had a coffeepot that worked, and my departed great-great-aunt decided to make herself useful.

"By the way, how was Nepal?" I asked.

"Ugh," she said, raising her hands in helplessness, "humid and hotter than a june bug in August."

Since the departed weren't affected by the weather, I had to hold back a grin.

Just then, Cookie crashed into the apartment, took one look at me, and rushed forward, her sky blue pajamas skewed and crinkled. "I fell asleep," she said in a breathless rush.

"Isn't that what you're supposed to do at night?"

"No," she said, looking me over with a mother's eye, "well, yes, but I meant to check on you hours ago." She leaned forward and peered into my eyes. Why, I had no idea. "Are you okay?"

"I'm alive," I said. And I meant every word.

Only half convinced, she smoothed her pajama top and looked around. "Maybe I should make us some coffee."

"Why?" I asked, my tone accusatory. "So you can slip me another roofie?"

"What?"

"Besides," I said, indicating Aunt Lillian with a nonchalant nod of my head. "Aunt Lil already made coffee."

I watched—and tried really hard not to giggle—as Cookie's hopes for a caffeine high were dashed on the mocking rocks of irony. She hung her head and took the cup I handed her. "Thanks, Aunt Lillian. You're the best."

She's a trouper, that one.

I set Cookie on the arduous task of going through Mark Weir's court transcripts—which Uncle Bob had left on my desk—and checking Barber's flash drives. Hopefully Barber wasn't into fetishes. And if he was, hopefully he wasn't into leaving evidence of such a thing on a flash drive where anyone could find it. Those things were much better off in a password-protected file buried deep in the underbelly of one's hard drive with an inconspicuous file name. Something like Hot Firefighters in Love. For example.

My cell broke out into a chorus of Beethoven's Fifth, and I did the find-the-needle-in-the-haystack thing while cruising at ninety in a seventy-five, marveling at how a cell phone could make itself so obscure in one tiny handbag.

"Hey, Ubie," I said after a three-hour search.

"Must you call me that?" he asked in a groggy voice. He seemed almost as caffeine deprived as I was.

"Yep. I got the files you put on my desk. Cookie's going through everything now."

"And what are you doing?"

"My job," I said, pretending to be offended. As badly as I wanted to ask him about Reyes's conviction, I wanted to be face-to-face, where I could read his every expression. Or read things into his every expression, whichever worked best to my advantage. I still couldn't believe he was lead detective on Reyes's case. What were the odds?

"Oh, okay," he said. "They found a partial on the shell casing from the Ellery site."

"Really?" I asked, suddenly hopeful. "Did you get a hit?"

"This isn't *CSI,* sweetheart. Things don't happen quite that fast 'round these parts. We should know by this afternoon if it'll get us any-where." He yawned loudly, then asked, "Are you in your Jeep?"

"Sure am. I'm headed to the prison in Santa Fe to check out some intel."

"What intel?" he asked, suspicion altering his voice.

"It's . . . another case I'm working on," I hedged.

"Oh."

That was easy.

"Hey, what does *bombázó* mean?"

"Uncle Bob," I said reproachfully, "have you been in that Hungar-ian chat room again?" I tried really hard not to giggle, but the thought of some Hungarian chick calling Ubie "the bomb" was just too much. I cracked up regardless.

"Never mind," he said, annoyed.

I laughed harder.

"Call me when you get back to town."

After he slammed down the phone, I closed mine and tried to focus on the road through my tears. My reaction was insensitive and uncalled for. I thought this as I doubled over the steering wheel in laughter, holding my aching ribs.

It took me a few moments to sober, but at least laughing at Ubie's expense was better than pining over Reyes like I'd been doing all morning. Unfortunately, my hour-long shower—while revealing exactly how black and blue I was becoming—didn't lend any insight as to why he wouldn't have shown up last night. But the closer I got to the Penitentiary of New Mexico, the more optimistic I became. Surely this place would have some answers. Then I drove up to the gates of the maximum-security prison, and my optimism morphed into a crackly kind of sweat-induced pessimism.

I glanced down at my clothes one more time. Loose pants, long sleeves, high collar. Covered neck to kneecaps. I wondered if looking masculine in a maximum-security prison, however, would actually be of benefit. Considering.

Thirty minutes and two elderly Italian women later—they had crossed through me, arguing all the way, as I sat in the waiting room—I was led to the office of Deputy Warden Neil Gossett. It was small but bright, with dark office furniture and mountains of paperwork nesting on every available surface. Neil had been a more-than-decent football player in high school, and he'd kept the bulk of his youth, though not in exactly the same proportions. He looked good, despite the tragic emergence of male-pattern baldness.

He stood and circled his desk. "Charlotte Davidson," he said, more than a little surprised.

His height had me looking up as I took his hand. "Neil. You look great," I said, wondering if it was okay to say such things to persons with whom you weren't exactly friends.

"You look . . ." He spread his hands in a helpless gesture.

I wondered if I should be insulted. It couldn't have been the bruises. I'd worked really hard on covering them. Was it my hair? It was probably my hair.

"You look spectacular," he said at last.

Oh. That would do nicely. "Thank you."

"Please." He gestured toward a chair with a sweep of his hand and took his own seat behind the desk. "I have to admit," he admitted, "I'm a little surprised to see you."

A coy grin spread across my face as I angled for "light and flirty." "Well, I had some questions about one of your inmates, and I figured I'd just start at the top and work my way down." The sexual innuendo in that statement was not lost on me.

He almost blushed. "I'm not exactly the top, but I'm glad you think so highly of me."

I chuckled appropriately and brought out my notebook.

"Luann tells me you're a private investigator now."

Luann, meaning his secretary. "Yes, I am. I'm currently working with APD on a DOA resulting in an FTA." I purposely threw around a few acronyms to make myself sound savvy.

He arched his brows. At least he seemed impressed. That would help in the long run. "And this is about that case?"

"It's all related," I said, lying my ass off. "I'm actually here about a man who was convicted of murder about ten years ago. Can you tell me anything about a—" I looked down at my notepad, feigning tedium. "—a Reyes Farrow? I was hoping to question him regarding a case, you know, about this case thing I'm working on with . . ."

I lost my train of thought when Neil paled before my eyes. He picked up his phone and stabbed a button. "Luann, can you come in here?"

Damn, was I in trouble already? Was he kicking me out? I just got here. I knew I should have thrown around more acronyms, but I just couldn't think of any. The NAACP! Why didn't I think of the NAACP? That scares the crap out of everyone.

"Yes, sir?" Luann asked as she opened the door.

"Can you get me the file on Reyes Farrow?"

Phew.

But Luann hesitated. "Sir?"

"It's okay, Luann. Just get me Farrow's file."

She glanced at me, then back at him. "Immediately, sir."

She was good. Cookie never said, *Immediately, ma'am.* We'd have to talk. And Luann's reaction was just as interesting as Neil's. She had a very feminine demeanor. Very bubble baths and wine beneath her business suit. But in a heartbeat, she had become protective. Almost angry. Though her anger didn't seem directed at me.

"Is this about the incident?" Neil asked. "I didn't think Farrow had any relatives."

"The incident?" I asked as Luann brought in the file and handed it to him. She left without giving me a second glance. Had something happened to Reyes? Maybe he really was dead. Maybe that's why he suddenly started showing up out of the blue.

Neil flipped open the file and studied it. "Right. This shows no living relatives. Who hired you?" He locked his gaze with mine, and the rebel in me took over.

"That information is privileged, Neil. I would hate to have to bring the DA into this."

"The DA? He's already aware of the situation, I assure you."

Oops. Well, that didn't help. Oh, for heaven's sake. I pulled in a deep breath. "Look, Neil, this is more of a personal quest, okay. I am working on a case, but it's not related. I just . . ." I just what? Want to rape your prisoner? Want to see if he can become incorporeal? "I just want to talk to him."

My lashes lowered with my admission. I probably looked like an idiot. One of those prison groupies who wrote love letters to inmates and got hitched for the conjugal visits.

"So, you don't know?" he asked. A hint of relief laced his voice. But something else, too. Regret maybe?

"Apparently not." He was going to say it. Reyes was dead. Died, what, a month ago? I waited with bated breath for the news.

"Farrow's in a coma. Has been for almost a month."

It took me a few moments to pick my jaw up off the floor and find my voice again. When I did, I asked, "A coma? What? Why? What happened?"

Neil rose from his desk and handed me the file. "How about some coffee?"

As if it were encrusted with precious jewels, I took the thick folder from him, then said absently, "I'd kill for some." Oops. "No, I wouldn't," I assured him, glancing around the *maximum-security prison.* "I've never killed anyone. Except that one guy, but he had it coming."

My feeble attempt at humor seemed to relax Neil. An echo of a smile thinned his mouth. "You haven't changed at all."

I bit my lower lip. "That's probably bad, huh?"

"Not in the least."

He left me wondering about his statement and went for coffee as I examined Reyes's file, also known as the Holy Grail.

Chapter Twelve

*Reyes Farrow.
Because perfection is a dirty job,
but someone has to do it.*
—CHARLOTTE JEAN DAVIDSON

"You knew him?" Neil asked me over an hour later. I'd been reading. We'd been chatting. Garrett called. I ignored.

And I learned. Approximately one month earlier, a fight broke out in the yard, and the prison immediately went into lockdown. Everyone was supposed to get on the ground. When one of the inmates, a large childlike man Reyes had befriended, got confused and didn't go down, a guard in one of the towers prepared to fire a warning shot. Reyes saw this and tackled his friend to get him down, thinking the guard was going to shoot him. Instead of burrowing harmlessly in the dirt as intended, the bullet found Reyes's skull and pierced his frontal lobe. He'd been in a coma since.

I glanced up and refocused on Neil's question. "Just from that one incident when I was in high school," I said. I'd told him about the night I first saw Reyes, the physical abuse he'd suffered at the hands of the man he supposedly killed. Neil didn't seem surprised. I closed the file and looked into his gray eyes. "Just between us," I said, leaning forward to make the statement more intimate, "between old friends," I elaborated, "what did you know about him? What did you think of him?" I tapped the file with my fingertips. "What's not here?"

Neil sat back in his chair, adjusted his collar, and dragged in a long, deep breath. "If I told you, you wouldn't believe me."

That was promising. "Bet I would," I said with a wink.

He stared at me a good minute before he spoke. And when he did speak, it was with a reluctance I understood all too well. He truly doubted I would believe him. If he only knew . . .

"Something strange happened when Farrow first got here, about a week after he'd been released into gen-pop," he said, glancing down to study the clasp on his watch. "South Side sent three of their soldiers to kill him. Why, I don't know, but when South Side attacks, people die. Period."

My chest tightened and I ground my teeth together, trying hard not to react, not to show what the thought of Reyes in that position did to me.

"It ended almost the minute it began," he continued, his face growing dark as he reconstructed his memories, pieced together what he knew. "I was just a guard then, fresh out of training, positive I was hot shit. I almost pissed my pants when I saw those men heading toward Farrow, not that I knew who he was at the time. I called for backup, but before I even finished the request, three South Side members lay on the ground in pools of their own blood with this twenty-year-old kid . . . I don't know . . . crouched on a table, ready to spring at anyone else who came near him, eyeing the inmates with absolutely no emotion, no fear whatsoever."

I sat stone still, barely breathing as I watched the events unfold in my mind.

Neil shook his head and looked up at me, his expression a mixture of relief and reverence. "He wasn't any more winded than I am now. I just barely caught a glimpse of what happened, but . . ."

"But?" I nudged, barely able to contain my curiosity.

"But . . . he didn't move like a normal man moves, Charley. He was a blur, so fast it was impossible for my eyes to follow him. Then he was crouched on the table like an animal, powerful, dangerous." Neil shook his head again, as if still not believing his own eyes. "That's how he got his name."

"His name?" I asked, even more intrigued.

"No one ever touched him again," he continued. "In all the years I've been here, I've never seen anything like it. He's a legend to these men, almost godlike."

I scooted closer to his desk, almost drooling. "You mentioned a name?"

"Right," he said, snapping to attention. "They call him El Aliento del Diablo."

"The devil's breath," I echoed in English.

"Told you it'd be hard to believe," he said with a heavy sigh, clearly expecting me to balk at his story.

"Neil, I don't doubt a single word you've said." When his expression turned to one of surprise, I added, "I saw something similar the night I met him as well. The way he moved. The way he walked."

"Exactly," Neil said, pointing at me repeatedly. "Not quite . . . not quite . . ."

". . . human," I finished for him.

He glanced at the file in my hands. "I guess he's human enough, though."

I couldn't help but hug the file to me, to hold on to every nuance that was Reyes Alexander Farrow. "I guess." He was such an enigma, surreal and mystical.

"You know, I never really liked you in high school," Neil said, pulling me back to the present.

Um, okay. Least he was being honest. "I know," I said apologetically. "I didn't really like you either."

"You didn't?" He seemed shocked.

"No, I'm sorry."

"Yeah, me, too. I used to think you were such a nutcase."

"And I thought you were an arrogant bastard."

"I was an arrogant bastard."

"Oh, right," I said, suppressing a sad giggle.

"But you weren't a nutcase, were you?"

I shook my head, grateful for the validation.

"I can let you see him, if you'd like."

My heart skipped a beat and seemed to rise physically in my chest.

"But I have to tell you, Charley, he won't pull through. He's brain-dead."

Just as quickly, it plummeted to my toes and the floor seemed to slip out from under me. Brain-dead? How could that be?

"He has been since it happened," he added. He stood and walked around the desk to put a hand on my shoulder. "I'm sorry to have to tell you this, but the state plans to terminate care in three days."

"You mean pull the plug?" I asked. A wave of panic washed over me. I tried to swallow, but my throat was suddenly parched and raw.

Neil's lips thinned in regret. "I'm sorry, Charlotte. With no relatives to contest it—"

"But what about his sister?"

"Sister? Farrow has no living relatives. And according to his file, he's never had any siblings."

"No, that's not right," I said, reopening the file and tearing through the pages. "He had a sister that night."

"You saw her?" Neil's voice was filled with hope. He didn't want Reyes to die any more than I did.

Knowing there would be nothing about his sister in the file, I stopped and closed it again. "No," I said, trying not to let disappointment swallow me whole. "The landlady told me."

With a disappointed sigh, Neil collapsed into the chair beside me. "She must have been mistaken."

As I drove to the Guardian Long-Term Care Facility in Santa Fe, where they were keeping Reyes, my head swam in a sea of information, trying to fit each piece into neat little folders, to organize what I'd learned. Reyes had continued his education, and one year after his conviction, he'd received a degree in criminology. Then, surprisingly, he'd switched to computers. He had a master's in computer information systems. He'd bettered himself. He would have been a productive, taxpaying member of society when he got out.

Yet now they were going to kill him. Neil had explained that the only way to stop the state would be to get an injunction, but I'd have to have a damned good reason. If I could just find his sister . . .

As I picked up my phone to call Cookie, it rang with her personal ringtone, Rod Stewart's "Do Ya Think I'm Sexy?"

I flipped it open, and Cookie asked, "Well?"

"He's in a coma."

"No stinkin' way."

"Stinkin' way. And they're going to take him off life support in three days, Cook. What am I going to do?" The emotions I'd held at bay in Neil's office threatened to break free. I fought hard to tamp them down with the deep-breathing techniques I'd learned on my *Yoga Boogie* DVD.

"What *can* we do? Did Mr. Gossett tell you?"

"I need to find Reyes's sister. She's really the only one who can stop this. Not that I'm giving up. I'll blackmail Uncle Bob. Maybe he can do something." I was not going to lose Reyes without a fight. Finding him after all these years . . . there had to be a reason.

"Blackmail is good," she said.

The world turned green as I pulled my car into a parking lot that resembled an English garden. Before hanging up, I gave Cookie yet another job. According to the article I'd read the night before, Reyes had spent three months at Yucca High. Maybe his sister did, too. I needed those transcripts.

Cookie went to work on the transcripts as I headed inside the gorgeous health-care facility. This was certainly better than the prison infirmary. I figured they couldn't have cared for a comatose patient in prison, so they moved him here. Neil had called ahead and told the corrections officer watching Reyes that I would be paying him a visit.

When I walked down the hall to the nurses' station, the officer stood in an alcove off the main hallway, flirting with an RN. I couldn't blame him. Watching a comatose prisoner could hardly be exciting. And flirting was fun.

He straightened when I approached, and the RN hastened off to see to her duties. "Ma'am," he said, tipping an invisible hat. "You must be Ms. Davidson."

"I am. I guess Mr. Gossett got ahold of you."

"He did, indeed. Our boy's in there," he said, gesturing to a sliding-glass door across the hall with a pale blue curtain covering the opening.

A little surprised the officer didn't ask for an ID, I headed toward the door. Well, most of me headed for the door. My boots were cemented to the floor. What would I find when I went in? Would he look the same? Would he have changed much in the ten years since the mug shot had been taken? In the twelve years since I'd seen him? Would he have the look of prison about him? The hardness that seemed to saturate people who'd done such a substantial amount of time behind bars?

The officer seemed to recognize my distress. "It's not bad," he said, sympathy softening his voice. "He has a breathing tube. That's probably the worst of it."

"Do you know him personally?"

"Yes, ma'am. I asked for this duty. Farrow saved my life once during a prison riot. I wouldn't be standing here today if not for him. Felt like the least I could do, you know?"

My throat tightened and I wanted to ask him more, but something was suddenly pulling me toward Reyes's room, like the gravity in that one spot had just increased exponentially. I finally took a step, and the officer tipped his invisible hat again and strolled away toward the coffee machine.

When I crossed the threshold, I scanned the area, just in case he was in the room incorporeally. I was a little disappointed when he wasn't. He did incorporeal well.

Then I glanced at the bed. He lay there, Reyes Farrow, solid and real, his dark hair and skin a bronze shadow against the white sheets. Gravity took hold again; only this time, it was centered on him as I stepped closer, walked to the edge of the bed, and saw utter perfection for the second time in my life.

A breathing tube had been inserted into his trachea, and he had a bandage wrapped around his head. His mussed hair, thick and dark, swept over the bandage and brushed his brow. Three days' worth of stubble framed his strong jaw, and his lashes, long and thick, cast shadows across his cheeks. And then my gaze landed on his mouth, sensual and sculpted and impossible to forget.

The ventilation machine made the only sound in the room. No beeps of a heart monitor, though one had been hooked up, its lines and numbers in a constant state of flux. I stepped closer, brushed a hip against his arm that lay beside him. The sleeves of the pale blue hospital gown were short and afforded a generous view of sinewy muscles, hard and lean even in slumber. He had a tattoo that flowed along his tanned biceps, lending to its beauty and fluidity. A tribal work of art with graceful lines and sensual curves, lines and curves that had meaning. I'd seen them before. They were ancient, as old as time. And important. But why?

My heart and mind were having difficulty grasping the fact that it was truly Reyes Farrow in the bed, lying there, vulnerable and powerful at once. My knees had liquefied, and I wondered how long I'd be able to stand in his presence without falling. After all this time, he seemed even more surreal than in my dreams. More beautiful than in my fantasies.

His wide chest rose and fell to the rhythm of the machine. I ran my fingertips along a shoulder that scalded. A quick glance at the chart hanging from the end of his bed confirmed his temp to be a perfect 98.6, yet his heat was as real as if I were standing in front of a furnace.

Even at rest he looked wild and untamed, something impossible to domesticate, to restrain for very long. Enduring the heat of his touch, I placed a hand in his and leaned over him.

"Reyes Farrow," I said, my voice cracking with emotion, "please wake up." I didn't care what the state said; Reyes was no more dead than I was. How could they even consider taking him off life support? "They are going to turn this machine off if you don't. Do you understand? Can you hear me? We have three days."

I glanced around the room, hoping he'd show up in another form. I still didn't know exactly what he was, but he was something more than human. I knew that now beyond a shadow of a doubt. I had to find his sister. I had to put a stop to this.

"I'll be back," I whispered. But before I could leave, I lowered my head and put my mouth on his. The kiss scalded my lips, but I stayed for several miraculous heartbeats, relishing the feel of his mouth beneath mine.

I tried to rise, to end the kiss, but images started coming at me in a rush. I began to remember our nights over the past month. His hands gripping my hips, my legs wrapped around him as if holding on for dear life as he pushed inside, sending waves of unimaginable pleasure crashing into me. I remembered the kiss in Cookie's office, how he guided my hand, how he held me when my knees gave beneath my weight. Then I remembered that night so long ago. When his father hit him, when he lost consciousness for that split second. I remembered the look in his eyes when he snapped back. The anger. Directed not at his father but at me! He had looked at me. For a split second, he saw me and anger washed over him.

Then I remembered a cup at my mouth, a warm towel at my head, an arm holding me in place as I swam back to reality, wondering where my bones had run off to.

"Are you okay? Ms. Davidson?"

"Here," a female said, "drink this, sweetheart. You had quite a fall."

I sipped on cold water and opened my eyes to see the corrections officer and the RN standing over me. The officer held a wet towel at my head while the nurse tried to coax me into drinking more water. They'd dragged me to a chair outside the room and were trying to keep me in it despite my limp body's insistence on eating floor tile.

"Oops," the nurse said. "Got her?"

"I had her the first time. She just keeps slipping out of my grip. She's like really heavy spaghetti."

"What?" I shrieked, jerking to my senses. "How heavy? What happened?"

Glancing up into the grinning eyes of the officer, I took another sip as he explained.

"You either fainted or you wanted a much closer look at the cracks in the tile. Either way, you hit hard."

"Seriously?"

He nodded. "Maybe you shouldn't have been trying to make out with him," he suggested.

How did he know that? "I was kissing him good-bye."

He snorted and exchanged glances with the nurse. "That's not what it looked like to me."

Probably not. But what happened? Could Reyes Farrow take control over me even from a freaking coma? I was doomed.

"Oh my gosh!" I said, jumping out of the chair. After a woozy moment that reminded me way too much of the night I celebrated my high school graduation—in a pool of my own vomit—I stumbled back into Reyes's room, marveled at his beauty a few seconds more, gave him a quick kiss good-bye—on the cheek—then hurried out of the hospital with a thank-you and a wave to the officer and the nurse. I had to find Reyes's sister, and time was running out.

"You fainted?"

I sighed into the phone and waited for Cookie to get over her surprise. Why anything should surprise her at this point was beyond me. "Did you get a hit on Reyes's high school transcripts?"

"Not yet. You passed out? Kissing him?"

"Is there anything else I should know?"

"Well, I've scoured these flash drives. They're all Mr. Barber's. There's nothing on them but his case files."

"Damn. I'll have to talk to Barber about that." Where were my lawyers, anyway? "And I'll have to get those flash drives back before the secretary finds out they're missing."

Before we hung up, I asked Cookie to find out if the lawyers' secretary, Nora, went into the office that day. Hopefully not. She wouldn't have missed the flash drives if she hadn't been there.

Just as I pulled Misery into the parking lot of the Causeway, aka home sweet home, Beethoven's Fifth rang out on my cell. Uncle Bob told me they had an ID and an address on our shooter. Or the guy they believed was our shooter. I just wished at least one of the lawyers had seen the assailant so we could be sure we had the right guy. Apparently he worked for Noni Bachicha, a local body shop owner. I knew Noni personally, and he'd never be involved in something like this, so there had to be another angle. But we wouldn't know anything until we brought in the alleged shooter. Uncle Bob was on his way to do that very thing. With half the force acting as backup.

Naturally, I couldn't miss out on all the fun. I would be able to tell if the guy was guilty or not in a heartbeat. Part of my being a grim reaper, I figured. The problem came when whomever I was assessing was guilty of a myriad of other crimes. Guilt was guilt. Sometimes it was hard to distinguish between two crimes. Still, I had to try.

I got the address, pulled a U-ey, and flew to an apartment complex in the middle of the Southern War Zone, where one Mr. Julio Ontiveros resided.

The teams were still a block away, prepping for the extraction. Apparently they had fairly solid intel that Julio was asleep inside his apartment. He must have had a late night. I pulled in between Uncle Bob's SUV and a patrol car, put my phone on silent—because there's nothing worse than a cell phone going off in the middle of an extraction; everyone glares at you really mean—then went in search of Ubie.

Ninety-nine percent of the time I don't carry a sidearm—hence the motivation to perfect my death stare. But today all the cool kids were packing. I felt like the girl who showed up at a formal dinner party in jeans and a Pink Floyd T-shirt. Probably 'cause I did that once.

Spotting Ubie beside another patrol car also brought me within screaming distance of Garrett Swopes. I tamped down the angry hornetlike sting of jealousy when I realized Ubie must have called him first. I'd been solving cases for the man since I was five, and he calls Swopes first? Aggravation coursed through me, ruffled my feathers, got my hackles up, whatever hackles were. Was a little appreciation too much to ask? A little nepotistic favoritism?

Uncle Bob was on the phone as usual when Garrett looked up at me from behind the patrol car's open trunk, concern flashing in his eyes. With a curse, I realized the ache in my ribs and hip had me limping. I gritted my teeth, straightened my spine, and walked as normally as possible. Then I had to force myself to relax a little, fearing my walk resembled the robot dance from the eighties.

"I can't believe you don't have twenty-seven broken ribs," Garrett said as I robot-walked forward.

"I don't have twenty-seven ribs."

"Are you sure?" he asked, eyeing my rib cage. "Maybe I should count them."

Ridiculously ticklish, I wrapped my arms protectively around my stomach in reflex. "Only if you want to lose a hand," I warned, though he did look rather hot in jeans and a white T-shirt with a dark blue bulletproof vest strapped around his torso. Very machismo. "But don't worry," I continued. "Surely that whole learning-to-count thing will pay off someday."

He grinned, unscathed, as he checked his clip. "Surely."

"'Kay, I'm going around back."

"Why?"

"'Cause I can. And you're not there."

"Oh. Don't get shot."

I snorted—*as if*—and hobbled away.

"And don't fall off anything," he half whispered, half yelled.

He was funny.

I had scarcely taken up a position behind the complex with a cute cop named Rupert when we heard what sounded like a gunshot coming from inside. Rupert sprang into action. He scaled six feet of chainlink and rushed toward the back entrance, crashing to a halt against the redbrick building with gun at the ready. Rupert was young.

Being older and wiser, I chose to enter through the opening where a gate once stood several feet back. Taking Garrett's warning about not getting shot to heart . . . considering . . . I scrunched down and eased inside the yard. Twelve seconds later, I lay sprawled in the dirt, gasping for air. Apparently, the suspect had spotted the opening in the fence as well. And for some reason, when surrounded by cops with nickel-slick badges and chambered rounds, the path of least resistance is most often through the unarmed chick, despite her attitude. I had just enough time to check out Rupert's nicely shaped ass before a large hoodie-clad gangbanger determined to make a hole in the universe tore through me.

We hit the ground hard, and the pain in my ribs had me seeing white-hot stars . . . and fear. His fear. And his innocence. He didn't shoot anyone. Damn.

Chapter Thirteen

Well-behaved women rarely make history..
—LAUREL THATCHER ULRICH

My PI techniques would never be the stuff of legend. They would never make it into criminology textbooks or university lecture halls. But I did feel that, with some focus, I could have a strong presence in chat rooms.

If I couldn't be a good example, I'd just have to be a horrible warning.

Cookie's attempts to get her hands on the transcripts and class rosters from Reyes's high school failed. It was rare, but it happened. Something about laws and confidentiality. With this in mind, I strode into the police station, a singular objective guiding me. Carrying what was perhaps too big a chip on my bruised and swollen shoulder, I ignored the wary glances and suspicious looks directed my way and walked straight back toward the interrogation room.

That's when I heard the "Pssst."

I slowed and looked around the station. Nothing but desks and uniforms from my vantage point. Then I looked toward the restrooms. An elderly Latina in a light floral dress beckoned me forward with a crooked finger. She had a black lace mantilla wrapped around her head and shoulders, and I would've bet my last nickel she made tortillas like nobody's business. When she had been alive, anyway.

I didn't really have time to counsel a departed, but I couldn't say no. I could never say no. I glanced around the station and ducked into the women's room all cool and nonchalant, not really sure why. Answering the call of nature was hardly illegal. But five minutes later, I exited the same way. Only this time I was armed to the teeth—metaphorically—and ready to make a deal.

I spotted Uncle Bob standing at the door to observation. He was talking intently with Sergeant Dwight when I strode up.

"I want to negotiate a deal," I said, interrupting.

Dwight glared at me.

Ubie raised his brows in interest. "What kind of deal?"

"Julio Ontiveros didn't shoot our lawyers." Guilt poured off a person. I could sense it a mile away. And Julio Ontiveros was not a guilty man. Not of murder, anyway. And what had sounded like a gunshot coming from inside the apartment was actually his motorcycle misfiring. Apparently, he took it in at night so no one would steal it. Smart kid.

"Great," Sergeant Dwight said, rolling his eyes. "Glad we have you to tell us these things."

But Uncle Bob slanted his brows, lowered his chin, and eased closer. "Are you sure?"

"Are you serious?" the sergeant asked in disbelief.

Uncle Bob, in a rare moment of hostility, cast a razor-sharp scowl in Dwight's direction that would wither a stout winter rose. Dwight clamped his jaw shut and turned his back to us to study the suspect through the two-way mirror.

"This is pretty big-time, Charley. I need you to be certain. There's a lot of pressure on this one from the guys up top."

"It's always big-time. I want you to think back to the last time I was wrong."

Ubie thought, then shook his head. "I can't remember the last time you were wrong."

"Exactly."

"Ah. Right. And your deal?"

Ubie was going to love this. "If I can get him to confess his part in all of this today, right now, and turn state's evidence on the real shooter, I need you to do two things for me."

"This should be good," he said.

"I need you to get an injunction to stop the state from pulling the plug on a convicted felon who's in a coma."

His brows shot up. "On what grounds?"

"That's part of number one," I said with a one-shouldered shrug. "You gotta come up with something. Anything, Uncle Bob."

"I'll do what I can, but—"

"No *buts*," I said, interrupting him with an index finger in the air. "Just promise me you'll try."

"You have my word. And two?"

"I need you to go back to high school with me. And bring your badge."

After a second jolt of surprise widened his eyes, he said, "I take it you'll explain all this later?"

"Cross my heart," I said, doing that very thing with my extended index finger. "For now, let's get this guy to tell us what he knows."

Sergeant Dwight, hearing our conversation, snorted at what seemed like arrogance on my part.

An annoyed sigh slipped through my lips. "This shouldn't take long," I told Uncle Bob.

Unable to stand by and do nothing, Sergeant Dwight turned around to us. "You're not seriously going to jeopardize this entire investigation by allowing her to go in there, are you?" When Ubie just stood in thought, quite effectively ignoring the irate man, Dwight ground his teeth and stepped in Ubie's face. "Davidson," he said, expecting an answer.

I didn't have time for this. While Uncle Bob dealt with Dwight the dipstick, I walked into the observation room and studied Mr. Ontiveros through the two-way mirror. The other officer in the room turned to me in surprise. Naturally, I ignored him. Julio sat in a small sparse area across from the observation room, fidgeting in his chair and glaring into the mirror. He had the basic gangbanger do—shaved on the sides, a little longer up top—and wore attitude like it was the latest thing. But fear leached from every pore in his body.

He wasn't exactly innocent, but he didn't shoot anyone. His fear stemmed from the thought of going to prison for something he didn't do. There seemed to be a lot of that going around lately.

I turned and winked at Yesenia, the Latina I'd just conversed with in the women's room who also happened to be Julio Ontiveros's aunt. She stood waiting in the corner and flashed me a wicked grin as I walked out.

"I'm ready," I tossed to Uncle Bob before entering the interrogation room itself. As I shut the door, I heard him and Dwight scramble to get inside the observation area to watch. Then I heard more footsteps doing the same. Apparently we were going to have an audience. They might be disappointed. This wouldn't take long.

Julio sat handcuffed to a small metal table. He looked up at me, a wary surprise widening his eyes and lowering his brows for a split second before he took control over his features again.

He leaned back in his chair, lowrider style. "Who the fu—?"

"Shut up," I said, walking purposely toward him. I leaned on the

desk in front of him, brushing his cuffed wrist with my hip and blocking his view of the two-way, but more important, blocking the men in
the observation room from listening in. I was close enough to give Ontiveros a lap dance. A necessary evil because what I had to say could
not be overheard. Not without me being sent to a very special place
with padded rooms and medication in little white cups.

I could just feel Uncle Bob coming unglued with my proximity to
what he still thought of as a cold-blooded killer. But I knew better.

I'd taken Julio by surprise. Using to my advantage the seconds it
would take for him to recover, I leaned forward and whispered into his
ear. I didn't have much time before Uncle Bob stormed into the room,
afraid for my safety. Just a few words, two or three short sentences, and
Julio Ontiveros would spill like wine on silk.

I prayed for ten seconds. I got them.

"We don't have much time, so be quiet and listen."

He took advantage of the situation, playing the tough guy all the
way. He turned into me and inhaled the scent of my neck and hair.

"Your *tía* Yesenia sent me—"

He stilled.

"—and told me the exact location of the three things you desire
most in the world."

I could hear the doorknob turning. I could also feel doubt wafting
off Ontiveros, his admiration for my neck and hair evaporating. That
always happened when I talked about dead people. I leaned back a little
and peered into his wary eyes.

"You are five minutes away from going down for three murders you
and I both know you didn't commit. Tell your part in this, without
holding anything back, and I'll tell you where the medal is. For starters."

He sucked in a soft breath of surprise. That was desire number one.
Desire number two was pretty solid as well, but number three would
be a bit trickier, mostly because Ontiveros's aunt didn't know the *exact*

exact location of the number three so much as its general proximity. I figured that's what I had Cookie for.

Just as I finished my spiel, Uncle Bob rushed through the door, a warning glare on his face. I winked at him, turned back to Julio, pulled a business card from my back pocket, and slid it beneath his cuffed hand.

"You have my word," I said before leaving.

After strolling back to the observation room, I waited to see if he'd cave. Not that I could see much. The tiny room was now full. Half the men were looking at me—including an enraged Garrett Swopes, who could kiss my smoking-hot ass—and half were staring into the interrogation room. Then I heard it.

"I'll talk," Julio said through the speakers. "I'll tell you what I know, but I want immunity from prosecution. I didn't kill no one, and I ain't going down for this."

With a twinkle in my eye, I turned, high-fived Julio's *tía* Yesenia, the woman who'd raised him and wouldn't leave the earthly plane until he straightened his shit out—her words—then strode out of the station with a relieved smile plastered on my face. Uncle Bob would call me later with the details, and I could explain the terms of our deal then. At the moment, I was tired and sore and in dire need of a long, hot bath. Had I known what awaited me at home, my needs may have shifted in a more sensual direction.

With thoughts of bubble baths and candlelight swimming through my head, I unlocked my door and sneaked into my apartment, trying not to disturb Cookie and Amber across the hall. It was late. The sun had drifted to the other side of the world hours ago, and I hated to keep Cookie up two nights in a row. Before coming home, I'd stopped by the office and found that Neil, in a surprising act of kindness, had couriered a copy of Reyes's file to me. I wasn't sure how legal it was, but I couldn't have been more grateful if he'd handed me the winning Powerball ticket. The file had a note attached to it that simply read, *You didn't get this from me.*

I checked with Dad for any messages, just in case Rosie, the woman I'd helped escape from her abusive husband, needed anything, sneaked a quick bite of green chili stew, then humped it back across the parking lot to the Causeway. Though the lack of messages from Rosie was a good thing, I couldn't help the concern that prickled down my spine, wishing she would call despite my strict orders.

Flipping on the living room light, I was in the middle of a quick hello to Mr. Wong when Reyes turned toward me. Reyes, standing regal and godlike in front of my living room window. Reyes Farrow. The same Reyes Farrow who was lying in a coma in Santa Fe an hour away. He turned back to stare out the window, giving me a chance to put my stuff on the snack bar.

I stepped forward then, eased closer to him. He shifted, cast his powerful gaze downward, and examined me through his periphery. Though he was clearly incorporeal, he seemed to be made of a matter denser than human flesh, more solid and unyielding.

I scrambled for something to say. Somehow, *You're really hot in bed* didn't quite have the ring I was looking for. In an act of desperation, I blurted out the first thing that came to mind.

"They're going to take you off life support in three days."

He looked toward me then, starting at my feet and traveling slowly up. A tingling warmth followed in its wake, suffusing every molecule in my body with an irradiating energy that pooled in my abdomen, swirled, and percolated low in my belly, branding my flesh and deboning my limbs. I struggled to stay focused.

"You have to wake up," I explained, but he remained silent. "Can you at least give me your sister's name?"

His gaze lingered on my hips before continuing its journey north.

"She's the only one who can stop the state."

Still nothing. Then I remembered Rocket's reaction to him at the asylum. His fear. I stepped closer, careful to stay out of arm's reach. Despite the fact that my body was shaking with his nearness, begging for his touch in a Pavlovian-style response that would've made any behaviorist proud, we needed to talk.

"Rocket's afraid of you," I said, my voice suddenly hoarse. When he paused at Danger and Will Robinson, I asked, "You wouldn't hurt him, would you?" Then his gaze, piercing and turbulent, locked on to mine.

Though we stood several feet apart, his heat radiated toward me. Hard as I tried not to, I took a step closer. I had so many questions, so many doubts.

More than anything else at that moment in time, I wanted to know—pathetic as it sounded—why he hadn't visited me the night before. He'd come every night for a month, then nothing, and my insecurities were getting the better of me. Reyes frowned, his brows inching together over deep mahogany eyes, and tilted his head to the side as if wondering what I was thinking.

As badly as I wanted to ask my own self-indulgent questions, I had to make sure Rocket was in no danger from him, though I couldn't imagine why he would be.

"If I asked, real nice with a cherry on top, would you please not hurt Rocket?"

His gaze dropped to my mouth, making it difficult to breathe, to concentrate, to resist jumping him right then and there. I had to focus.

"Blink once for yes," I said before losing all sense of self-respect and attacking. He was obviously a very dangerous being, and I was beginning to wonder more and more just what kind of being that might be. Maybe he was like me and Rocket. Maybe he'd been born with a purpose, a job, but then his life turned out bad like Rocket's and he'd never been able to fulfill his duties. The fragile hold I had on my self-control was thinning. I was getting lost in the sparkling gold flecks of his eyes. I felt like a child, mesmerized by a magician, lured to his side by sheer force of will.

He turned suddenly, breaking the spell he had me under, as if something had demanded his attention. Then he was in front of me, his sensual mouth barely inches from mine.

"You were tired," he said, disappearing in a swirl of dark mass before he'd even finished his statement.

I stood in the aftereffects of his presence, the rich tones of his voice flowing down my spine like molten gold, as Cookie rushed through the door.

"Garrett called, said you got hurt," she said, rushing to my side. "Again. But you're upright." She tilted her head slightly to the left. "Sort of. Have you ever considered that maybe your ability to heal so quickly is part of your being a grim reaper?"

Reyes was here, in my living room, standing before me as solid and ethereal as the statue of *David*.

"Charley?"

The heat of his mouth, so close to mine, lingered still. Wait. I was tired? What did he mean by . . . Oh, my god. He was answering my question about why he hadn't shown up last night. The question I didn't ask aloud, but thought. That was disturbing.

"I could slap you. If you think that would help."

Blinking to attention, I focused on Cookie at last. "He was here."

She scanned the room, her eyes wide, uncertain. "That big, bad thing?"

"Reyes."

She stilled, chewed her bottom lip a moment, then looked back and asked, "Did you say hey for me?"

The next morning, I was still sore. But again, I was still breathing. The cup half full and all. I'd made it to the bathroom without one mishap. Surely that was a sign my day was going to go well. I figured I was due because my night hadn't. Reyes was a no-show. Again. I tossed and turned, and the next thing I knew, Uncle Bob sent me a text.

After getting over the shock of that little jewel—Ubie didn't text—I tried to read it. Something about FECAL DABL and HIKE SCHOOP. It was enough to make me look forward to the day. We were going to Reyes's high school.

I'd stayed up half the night reading Reyes's prison jacket, the file thick with priceless tidbits of information about him. It was truly one of the most interesting things I'd ever seen in print. He had the highest IQ of any prisoner in New Mexico history. What did they call it? Immeasurable? He'd kept pretty much to himself in prison, though he did have a few friends, including a cellmate who'd been paroled six months earlier. And that corrections officer at the hospital had been telling the truth. Reyes had saved his life during a prison riot. The officer had been locked inside when the riot began and a group of prisoners surrounded him. He had been knocked nearly unconscious by the time Reyes showed up, so he didn't have any concrete details of what went down. He just stated that Reyes saved his life, then dragged him to safety, hiding him until the riot was over.

I was so proud of Reyes. I knew he was one of the good guys. While all the information in his file would lend itself nicely to countless fantasies to come, none of it led me to his sister. In fact, there was no mention of her at all.

I'd considered bringing Garrett into this whole thing. If anyone could find Reyes's sister, he could. But that would take some explaining. Putting that idea on the back burner, I stepped out of the shower to find Angel Garza, my thirteen-year-old attitude-infested investigator, leaning a hip against the sink.

"Need me, boss?" he asked, running his fingers along the faucet.

"Where have you been?" I reached for my robe while he wasn't looking. "I was worried. You never stay gone this long."

"Sorry. I was hanging with my mom."

"Oh." Keeping my suspicions in check, I wrapped a towel around my hair. I had been buck naked only seconds earlier, and the consummate flirt, Angel Garza, didn't even notice. Something was wrong. Angel lived—metaphorically—to see me naked. Especially buck naked. He'd told me so on several occasions. But instead of ogling me, he was fondling the faucet. Something was definitely off in Angel land.

Dead thirteen-year-old gangbangers were so moody.

Angel and I had hooked up soon after I met him on the Night of God Reyes, as I liked to call it. He'd followed me through high school, college, and eventually into the Peace Corps. When I finally opened my own investigations business, we negotiated a deal where I sent his mother the money he would have made working for me—anonymously, of course—and he became my top, number one, and only investigator.

But eventually Angel started seeing the benefits of our arrangement from another angle. He did his darnedest to convince me to take money from people using our unique situations.

"Dude, we could have such a racket," he'd say.

"*Racket* being the optimal word."

"Think about it. We could go to these people's relatives that died and score like maniacs."

"That's extortion."

"That's capitalism."

"That's punishable with one to four in the state pen and a substantial fine."

He'd eventually get frustrated and accusatory. "You're just using me for my body."

The day I use a thirteen-year-old dead guy for his body is the day I have myself committed. "You don't have a body," I'd remind him.

"Throw that in my face."

"Technically, you don't have a face either. And even if we did make money with our abilities, it's not like you can go buy a new skateboard."

"Man, extra money for my mom."

"Well, there is that."

"And I like the light-up."

"The what?"

"The light-up," he'd say. "You know, that look people get when they finally realize you're for real. It's like electricity. It makes me tingle all over. Like a blanket full of static."

Ew. "Really? I've never heard that."

"Yeah, and I like it when people realize we're out here."

I leaned in close once and asked him, "Do you want your mom to realize you're out here? Do you want her to know?"

"Nah. It took her too long to get over me."

All in all, he was a good kid. But his behavior today was very out of character.

I scooted him out of the way and started digging through my makeup bag. "Is everything okay?" I asked as nonchalantly as possible.

"Sure," he said with a shrug. "You look like hell, though. I can't leave you alone for two seconds."

"I've had an interesting week. I got Rosie off," I said, referring to our assisted-disappearing case. It was Angel's idea for her to go back to Mexico, and he'd done a lot of the legwork locating the small hotel on the beach for sale. We had to do some creative fund-raising, but it all worked out in the end.

He touched a bottle of perfume I had on the counter. "You know, it's not all bad here," he said cryptically.

After marveling at all the new shades of green on my face, I put my foundation down and looked at him.

"On this side, I mean. It's not like we get hungry or cold or anything."

Okay, this was just weird. "Is there something you're not telling me?"

"No. I just wanted you to know that. For future reference and all."

When I realized he might have been alluding to Reyes, I sucked in a soft breath. "Angel, do you know something about Reyes Farrow?"

He flinched and looked up at me in surprise. "No. I don't know anything about him. You got a job for me or what?" he asked, changing the subject.

Damn. Nobody knew anything about Reyes, but everyone sure seemed to stand at attention when I mentioned his name. I'd kill to know what was going on.

I filled Angel in on our case with the lawyers and the wrongly convicted Mark Weir. He couldn't wait to meet Elizabeth, naturally. Then I sent him to see if he could come up with a connection between the kid who'd died in Mark's backyard and the missing nephew.

"Oh," Angel said before he left, "Aunt Lillian's here. I like her."

I tried not to look disappointed. "I like her, too, but her coffee sucks. Mostly 'cause it's nonexistent."

He snickered and went on recon. In the meantime, Aunt Lillian took off with Mr. Habersham, the dead guy in 2B. I didn't even want to know what that was about. A knock on the door had me rushing to zip up my boots. I was meeting Uncle Bob in twenty, and I couldn't imagine who would be at my door this early in the morning.

Smoothing my brown sweater over my jeans, I glanced through the peephole and came to a screeching halt, metaphorically, when I saw Officer Taft. No way was this happening. Not now.

I opened the door slowly, mostly because it hurt. My entire body hummed in a dull, continuous ache. "Yeah?" I asked, peeking through the slit.

"Hey," he said, looking at me like I was half crazy, "I was just wondering if I could have a word with you."

"What kind of word?" I couldn't open my door farther. I knew she was there. I could feel the heat of her laser glare trying to sear my gray matter. And singe my hair.

"Is this a bad time?" he asked, shifting uncomfortably. "I'm sorry to bother you—"

"Yeah, yeah. Got it. It's okay. What do you need?"

"I just think that, well, strange things have been happening."

Damn. My shoulders slumped against the door, and I eased it wider to reveal the blond-haired, blue-eyed spawn of Satan. Plastering my hands over my eyes, I cried, only a little melodramatically, "No! You did not do this to me! You did not bring her to my home, my sanctuary."

"I'm sorry," he said, his gaze darting around in fear. "It's true, huh? I'm being haunted."

Demon Child sighed in annoyance. "Not haunted. Just watched."

I freeze-framed my tantrum and eyed her. "That's called stalking, dear, and is in fact frowned upon in most cultures."

"Can you . . . can you see someone?" Taft asked, leaning in to whisper.

"Dude, she can hear you. Just come in before the neighbors start talking." That was an excuse. The neighbors had started talking the moment I moved in. But may as well move the circus inside, let them burrow in my humble abode, take root on my furniture, raid my refrigerator.

I gestured for Taft to sit on the sofa while I took the opposite chair. "I'd offer you coffee, but my Aunt Lillian made it."

"Um, okay."

"So, what do you want to know?"

"Well, it's just that strange things have been happening lately."

"Mm-hmm." I was trying really hard not to yawn.

"You know, like I keep hearing this bell that sits on my mantel, but no one's there."

"I'm there," she said, looking up at him. "I'll always be there. I love you so much."

I glared at Demon Child. "Seriously? This early?"

She stuck out her tongue at me.

"I've heard stuff around the station about you. You know, *blah, blah, blah.*"

I kind of lost my train of thought and left Taft to his own devices as my gaze drifted to the spot where Reyes had stood only hours earlier. I'd never encountered anything like him. In fact, I'd never encountered anything supernatural besides the departed. No poltergeists or vampires or demons.

"Why are you so bright?" Demon Child asked. "You look kind of dumb."

Well, maybe demons.

After tossing her my best sardonic scowl, I decided to piss her off. I was pissed for having to put up with her ass. It seemed only fair.

"Officer Taft is talking, dear. Shut up."

The anger that sprang into her eyes was a little funny. I was seriously going to have to convince her to cross. Angel and I could play exorcism again. He hated playing exorcism. Mostly because he looked silly, writhing around on the floor, pretending to burn from the holy tap water I was throwing on him.

"Look," I said, interrupting Taft. "I get it. And yes, you have a little girl following your every move, probably the one from that accident you told me about. She has long blond hair, silvery blue eyes—but that could be 'cause she's dead—and pink pajamas with Strawberry Short-cake on them." I glanced over at Taft. "Oh, and she's evil."

Taft was a cop through and through. He'd learned how to keep a poker face, so it took me a moment to see the anger simmering inside him. The energy that was building encircled him in a mirage, like when you see water on the road where there is none.

Was it something I said?

He bolted to his feet, and I followed suit. "How the fuck do you know that?" he asked through gritted teeth.

What? "Um, because she's standing right beside you."

"Where I'll always be," she said. "Forever and ever."

Not if I had anything to say about it. Strawberry Shortcake was becoming a nuisance.

Taft nearly came unglued. His anger arced out like a Tesla coil. He stepped toe to toe with me, and I steeled myself against whatever he might bring. But I swore on all things holy, if I got hit, tackled, or pushed through a skylight one more time this week, I was going on a killing spree. Starting with him.

He stood in my face a solid minute, whispered a hoarse, "Fuck you," then stalked out the door.

Okey dokey. As interesting as that was, I had a date with Uncle Bob. And destiny.

After stuffing Reyes's file in my shoulder bag, I locked up and headed to the office. Strawberry Shortcake followed, and it hit me that her initials were SS. Appropriate, but seriously, could this day get any worse?

"He doesn't want me around, huh?" she asked, swinging her little arms at her sides. I barricaded my heart.

"Nope," I said, checking my phone for messages. "Neither do I."

She stomped her foot in a fit and stalked off. That was way easier than I thought it would be. When I had more time, I'd deal with the SS. For now, I had people to see and places to be.

Dad wasn't in yet, so I took the outside staircase, slowly 'cause it hurt. The sun shone bright, making the day seem deceptively warm.

On my long and arduous journey to the second floor, I went over what I had to do for the day. Number one, Yucca High. Ubie could flash his badge and get all kinds of cooperation. I needed transcripts and class rosters. Surely someone would remember Reyes. How could they forget him? I could cross-reference the students in each of his classes and find out who shared more than one class with him. The more exposure, the more likely they'd remember him. And his sister.

In one smooth move, I dumped my coat and bag on a chair, turned up the heat, then sashayed—somewhat rigidly—to the coffeepot for my morning fix. That's when the world fell out from under me. Was it karma? Was my less-than-caring attitude toward Taft coming back to bite me on the ass, hot as it was? I checked and double-checked, searched and prayed, only to be left utterly and completely without a single coffee ground.

How was this possible? How could the universe be so cruel?

A knock on my door raised my hopes. It was the inside door to my office that Dad always used. He'd have coffee. If he knew what was good for him.

I opened the door wide, only to be met by a tense Garrett Swopes. My lungs released a long breath as I scowled at him. "What do you want?"

His expression softened. "I have coffee."

I eyed the coffee in his hands, tried to keep from drooling, wondered if the gods were toying with me, then gave in. Fine, I'd play along.

Plastering a bright smile on my face, I began again. "Oh, hey there, Garrett. What's up?" Good enough. I snatched the coffee from his hands and started back for the slippery comfort of my plastic wood-grained office furniture and faux-leather chair. "What do you want?" I asked over my shoulder.

"I just want to talk."

"I'm busy."

"You don't look busy. What are you doing?"

"Whatever the little voices tell me to do."

"Will you just give me a minute?"

As if a delayed reaction had suddenly hit, Taft's outburst was starting to gnaw. Another person angry with me for no reason. Eating
away at me as well were the hostile, wary glances at the police station
yesterday. In fact, men in general were pretty low on my list of priori-
ties at the moment. Garrett could bite my ass.

"I don't feel particularly inclined to give you anything, Swopes.
Not even a minute."

"How did you do it? Yesterday at the station. What did you say to
him?"

"Please. Like you'd believe me if I told you."

"Look," he said, stalking forward, "you gotta admit, it's all a little
hard to swallow, but I'm trying."

I jumped out of my seat, suddenly angry at the world, and faced
Garrett head-on. "You know what I'm tired of?"

He thought a moment. "Unsightly cellulite?"

"People like those assholes at the station yesterday. People like Taft
with their sideways glances and hushed whispers who turn their backs
on me every time I walk into a room. People like you who treat me
like shit until they figure out I really can do what I say I can do. And
then suddenly I'm their best friend."

"Taft? That cop?"

"And, and them!"

"Them?"

"All of them! Wanting me to tie up all the loose ends they left hanging when they bit it."

"I would think your lawyers—"

"Not the lawyers," I said with a dismissive wave of my hand. "They have every reason to want their loose ends tied up. It's these people who come to me with, 'I didn't tell Stella I loved her before I got sucked into that jet engine.'"

"Okay, slowly, and without making any sudden movements, hand over the coffee. I'll go get you another cup, and we can start over."

"What's wrong with this cup?" I asked, eyeing it suspiciously.

"You need decaf."

I pulled in a long deep breath and sat back behind my desk. Tantrums never got me anywhere fast. "Sorry. I'm working on a deadline."

"This case?"

"No," I said, thinking about Reyes in that hospital bed, connected to machines just to keep him alive. After several soothing sips of java, I calmed down. Well, kind of. My insides were still seething a bit. Taft was a freak. "So, that's why you're here? To find out what I said?"

"Pretty much. And to chew your ass out for being at the wrong place at the wrong time again."

"Pffft. Stand in line."

"That guy tackled you pretty hard. Do you *look* for ways to be maimed?"

"Not daily. Have you heard anything about the warehouse?"

"I've gotten just enough on it to make me think it's not what we think it is."

"Oh, well, good thing I wasn't married to my beliefs."

"I've heard talk that the good Father who owns it really is a good Father. He runs a mission for runaway kids downtown."

"Kids?" I asked.

"You're not going to tell me, are you?" he asked, referring back to my deal with Julio Ontiveros.

"Nope. Since we have two kids involved in Mark Weir's case, I'd say there's a connection somewhere."

"It's possible. Can you give me a hint?"

A knock at the door saved me from once again having to say no. What was it with men and the word *no* anyway?

It was the side door Garrett came through. "Come on in, Dad," I called. Then I turned to Garrett. "You know, we do have a front door."

He lifted one shoulder in a careless shrug.

When Dad didn't come in, I stood and walked to the door. "Dad, you can come in," I said as I opened it. A split second later, my life flashed before my eyes, and I came to one important conclusion about it.

It was fun while it lasted.

Chapter Fourteen

Well, this is awkward.

—T-SHIRT

Apparently, this really was Kill Charley Davidson Week. Or at least Horribly Maim Her. I considered the slick gun pointed at me from across the threshold confirmation. It would probably never get government recognition, though, destined to be underappreciated like Halloween or Thesaurus Day.

When I opened the door, Zeke Herschel, Rosie's abusive husband, stood across from me with vengeance in his eyes. I glanced at the nickel-plated pistol clenched in his hand and felt my heartbeat falter, hesitate, then stumble awkwardly forward, tripping on the next beat, then the next, faster and faster until each one tumbled into the other like the drumroll of dominoes crashing together. Funny how time stands still when death is imminent. While I watched Herschel's muscles contract through my periphery, his finger squeeze the trigger, I focused on his face. A cocky arrogance glittered in his colorless eyes.

I glanced down at the gun again, watched as the firing pin snapped forward; then my gaze traveled up and to my right . . . to him. Bad stood beside Zeke Herschel, glaring down at him, his hooded cloak mere inches from the man's head, his silver blade glinting in the low light. Then he turned the full heat of his gaze on me. The effect was similar to the flash of a nuclear explosion. His anger, thick and palpable, hot and unforgiving, washed over me, stole my breath.

In the time it took to split an atom, Bad severed Herschel's spinal cord. I knew this because he'd done it before. But at the same time, the tip of his silver blade sliced into my side. The moment I realized I had been nicked by Bad's blade, Herschel flew back and crashed against the gate of the elevator so hard it rattled the building.

Then Bad turned to me, his robe and aura fusing together as one undulating mass, his blade tucked safely into the folds of the thick black matter. I realized then that I was falling. The world rushed to meet me at the exact moment arms locked around my waist, and I saw him for the first time beneath the hooded robe.

Reyes Alexander Farrow.

Dad handed me a cup of hot chocolate as we stood together outside the bar, leaning against his SUV. He had wrapped his jacket around me, as mine was still part of a crime-scene investigation. The jacket swallowed me. I was surprised, considering how thin my dad was. The arms hung to my knees. With infinite care, Dad rolled up the sleeves one at a time, relocating the cup in the opposite hand when he switched.

The elevator came to a creaking halt inside the bar, and I knew the EMTs were bringing Herschel out. I waited, my breaths shallow, as they wheeled him inside the ambulance and closed the doors. This was the same man who hit me in the bar. The same man who beat his wife into submission on a regular basis. The same man who pulled a gun on me with pure hatred in his eyes and violence in his heart. He must have figured out his wife had left his sorry ass, put two and two together, and came after me wanting revenge. Possibly even information.

And now he would be paralyzed for the rest of his life. I should've felt bad about that. What kind of person wouldn't? What kind of monster relishes in the pain and suffering of others? Was I any different from Bad? From Reyes?

My heart stopped a moment when I realized, once again, that Bad and Reyes were the same being. The same creature of destruction. In fact, he must have been the blur I'd been seeing as well, swooshing around like an evil Superman. So, blurry guy equaled Bad equaled Reyes. The unholy trinity. Why did he have to be so freaking hot?

Placing a hand on my ribs where I'd felt the blade slice clean through, I marveled at the unmarred skin, the lack of blood staining my sweater. Bad had a way of slicing from the inside out. I'd been cut, but only slightly, and only an MRI could reveal the true extent of the damage.

Since I didn't feel like I was bleeding internally, I decided to postpone the emergency room visit that would more likely end in a trip to the nuthouse than a meeting with a surgeon.

"Here's the bullet," a uniformed officer said to Uncle Bob. He held up a sealed plastic evidence bag for Ubie's inspection. "It was in the west wall."

How did it end up there? The gun was directly in front of me.

Cookie blew her nose again, unable to wrap her head around the fact that I'd almost been shot. I patted her shoulder. Her emotions drifted toward me like a tangible entity. She wanted to scold me, to tell me to be more careful, to hug me until my next birthday, but to her credit, she kept them controlled in the face of so many uniforms. Uncle Bob was talking to Garrett, who seemed in a state of shock if his pallor was any indication.

He'd laid me on the ground. Reyes. When he caught me, he'd laid me back on the ground, looked me over, paying special attention to where the tip of his blade sliced, then dissolved into nothing before my eyes with a growl. My lashes fluttered; then Garrett was over me, speaking loudly, asking me questions I couldn't comprehend. Reyes had left palpable traces of himself. His desperation settled in every molecule in my body and began flowing through my veins. I could smell him and taste him, and I craved him now more than ever.

"This isn't the first time this has happened, you know."

I glanced up at Dad. Earlier, I'd begged him not to call my step-mom. He acquiesced reluctantly, swearing he'd have hell to pay when he got home. Somehow I doubted it.

"In the apartment building where you live now," he said, standing beside me, "this exact same thing happened. You were little."

Dad was fishing for information. He'd long suspected something had happened to me that night. He was lead detective on the case of the paroled child molester's bizarre attack. After more than twenty years, he was putting it all together. He was right. This wasn't the first time, or the second. It would seem Reyes Farrow had been my guardian angel for quite some time.

Unable to piece together the whys and wherefores, I decided not to think about it and focused on two things that were not Reyes related: drinking my hot chocolate and steadying my shaking hands.

"A man's spinal cord was severed in two with absolutely no external injury to the surrounding area. No extraneous bruising. No trauma whatsoever. And you were there both times."

He was fishing again, waiting for me to give up what I knew, what he suspected. I guess I'd changed that day, become a little withdrawn, even for a four-year-old. But why should I tell him now? It would only cause him pain. He didn't need to know every detail of my life. And there were some things that, even at twenty-seven, were impossible to tell your father. I don't think I could have gotten the words out if I'd tried.

I placed a hand in his and squeezed. "I wasn't there, Dad. Not that day," I said, lying through my teeth.

He turned away from me and closed his eyes. He wanted to know, but like I'd told Cookie, it wasn't always better knowing.

"That was the same guy from the other night? The one who hit you?" Uncle Bob asked.

After lowering my cup, I answered, "Yes. He was trying to pick me up, I said no, he got hostile, and the rest is history." I wasn't about to tell them the truth. Doing so would risk Rosie's freedom.

"I say we all go to the station and talk about this," Uncle Bob said.

Dad flashed him a warning glare, and my muscles tensed. When those two fought, it wasn't pretty. A little humorous, perhaps, but I doubted anyone was in the mood to laugh. Besides me. Laughing was like Jell-O. There was always room for Jell-O.

"Great, I'd like to get out of the cold, anyway," I said, narrowly averting World War III.

"You can ride with me," Uncle Bob said after a moment. What did Dad expect him to do? He knew the rules. We'd have to go to the station eventually anyway. May as well get it over with.

Then Uncle Bob looked over at Garrett. "You can ride with me as well."

Dad looked at him in surprise then gratitude when Uncle Bob winked at him. As Dad walked me to Uncle Bob's SUV, he leaned down and whispered, "You two have to get your stories straight on the way. In your statement, just say that when you opened the door, there were two men there. They were fighting, the gun went off, and the other guy fled down the fire escape."

He patted my back and offered me a reassuring smile before closing the door. A haze of worry surrounded him, and I suddenly felt guilty for all the things I'd put him through growing up. He'd carried a lot for me. Made up excuses, found ways to put men behind bars without involving me directly, and now he had to trust in Uncle Bob to do the same thing.

"How did you do that?" Garrett asked before Ubie got into the car. "That guy must have weighed over two hundred pounds."

We were both sitting in the backseat. "I didn't."

He stared at me hard, trying to understand. "One of your dead guys?"

"No," I said, watching Dad and Uncle Bob talk. They seemed okay. "No, this was something else."

I heard Garrett lean back in his seat, scrub his face with his fingers. "So, there's more than just dead people walking around? Like what? Demons? Poltergeists?"

"Poltergeists are just pissed-off dead people. It's really not that mysterious," I said. But I was lying. Reyes was about as mysterious as it got.

It didn't matter what I did, I could not stop thinking about him. I wondered about his tattoos, trying to unearth their meaning from the jumble of chaos in my mind. If only I didn't have so many useless facts floating around in there. Damn my pursuit of trivia.

I wondered other things as well. Was he carbon based? Was he really thirty years old or thirty billion? Was he an innie or an outie? I knew enough not to question his planetary origins. He wasn't extraterrestrial. The fourth dimension, the other side, didn't work that way. There were no planets or countries or landmarks to distinguish its borders. It spanned the universe and beyond. It simply was. Everywhere at once. Like God, I figured.

"Okay," Uncle Bob said after buckling his seat belt. "I have to think really hard on the way to the station. I probably won't hear a thing you guys say to each other." He glanced at me from the rearview mirror and winked again.

By the time we arrived at the station, there had miraculously been two men in the hallway when I opened the door. The other man had dirty blond hair and a beard, nondescript dark clothes, and no distinguishing marks, making him almost impossible to identify. Darn it. Frankly, I was a little surprised Garrett was going along with it.

"Like I want to be locked in a padded cell," he said as we strolled inside the station. He was beginning to see my side of it, why I never told people what I was.

The first pair of eyes I met in the station belonged to a still-seething Officer Taft. He stood reading an open file at his desk and glared at me as we walked past. So did Strawberry Shortcake. At least she didn't attack me. That was a plus.

Still, I couldn't stop myself. I whipped out my best smirk for Taft, and said while barely slowing my stride, "When you figure out what's really going on and you need help, don't come to me."

"I'm not the one who needs help," he shot back.

Uncle Bob quickened his step to catch up with me. "What was that about?" he asked, clearly intrigued.

"The Hell Spawn of Satan, remember? She's making her presence known, and he can't deal—so he's mad at me."

He turned back with a thoughtful expression. "I could send him on a doughnut run to cool his jets."

Sounded like a plan. After we finished giving our statements, which were remarkably similarly worded, we all grabbed a bite; then Uncle Bob and I dropped off Garrett and headed to Yucca High. Like a kid being left at home on a Saturday night, Garrett begged to go. Even whined a little.

"Please," he'd said.

"No means no." He had to learn that sometime.

Yucca High sat deep in the southern heart of Albuquerque, an old school with a sordid past and an excellent reputation. We drove up during a late-afternoon class change. Kids were taking advantage of the five minutes they had by talking and flirting and roughhousing the freshmen. Before we arrived, I hadn't particularly missed high school. When we got there, I still didn't particularly miss it.

The aftereffects of the morning still weighted down my limbs. Things weren't moving at a normal speed. Everything felt slow, lethargic as I swam through the reality that the world did not come to a screeching halt after a near-death experience. It remained in motion, a never-ending cycle of those episodic adventures called life. The minutes pressed forward. The sun slid across the sky. The heel of my boot had a tack in it.

We walked into the Yucca High School office and found a frazzled administrative assistant. There were no fewer than seven people vying for her attention. Two wanted tardy passes. One had a note from his dad saying that if the school didn't let his child take his medicine to school, he was going to sue the fancy new uniforms off their athletes' backs. Another was a teacher who'd had her keys stolen off her desk during lunch. Two were office aides waiting for instructions. And the last was a beautiful young girl with a dark ponytail, cat-eye glasses, and bobby socks, who looked to have passed away in the fifties.

She sat in a corner with her books clutched to her breast and her ankles crossed. I sat down beside her and waited for the chaos to filter down. Uncle Bob took the opportunity to step out and make a call. As always. Bobby Socks kept staring at me, so I did my cell phone trick and looked directly at her as I talked.

"Hi," I said.

Her eyes widened before she batted her lashes in surprise, wondering if I was talking to her.

"Come here often?" I asked, chuckling at my astounding sense of humor.

"Me?" she asked at last.

"You," I said.

"You can see me?"

I never figured out why they always asked me that when I was looking directly at them. "Sure can." Her mouth slid open a notch, so I explained. "I'm a grim reaper, but in a good, nongrouchy kind of way. You can cross through me if you'd like."

"You're beautiful," she said, gazing at me in awe. I did that to people. "You're like a swimming pool on a sunny day."

Wow, that was different. A quick glance told me the crowd was thinning. "How long have you been here?"

"About two years, I think." When my brows creased in doubt, she said, "Oh, my clothes. Homecoming week. Fifties Day."

"Oh," I said. "Well you certainly look the part."

She bowed her head bashfully. "Thanks."

Only one tardy kid to go. Apparently the principal was dealing with the lawsuit threat, and maintenance was dealing with the stolen keys.

"Why haven't you crossed?" I asked.

Another kid walking down the hall called out to his friend. "Hey, Westfield, you gonna get spanked again?"

The boy waiting for the tardy pass, clearly a jock, flipped him off behind his back, incognito style. I tried really hard not to giggle.

The girl next to me shrugged, then indicated the administrative assistant with a nod of her head. "That's my grandma. She got really upset when I died."

I looked up at the woman. He name tag read MS. TARPLEY. She had stylishly messy hair, dark with red highlights, and a killer pair of green eyes. "Wow, she looks great for a grandma."

Bobby Socks giggled. "I just have to tell her something."

Was it not mere moments ago I went on a stark-raving rant in front of Garrett about this very thing? How'd I put it? Tired of tying up loose ends? I could be such a bitch.

"Would you like me to help?"

The girl's face brightened. "You can do that?"

"Sure can."

After chewing on her bottom lip a moment, she said, "Can you tell her that I didn't use all her mousse?"

"Seriously?" I asked with a smile. "That's why you're still here?"

"Well, I mean, I did use all her mousse, but I don't want her to think badly of me."

A Vise-Grip clamped around my heart at her confession. The thoughts that ran through people's heads before they died never ceased to amaze me. "Honey, I doubt your grandmother thinks anything but wonderful things about you right now. In fact, I'd bet my soul the mousse thing has never even crossed her mind."

With her chin lowered and her feet swinging under the chair, she said, "I guess I can go, then."

"If you'd like me to tell her something, even the mousse thing, I can make sure she gets the message."

A grin slowly spread across her face. "Can you tell her my lily pad is bigger than hers?"

I chuckled and shook my head. As much as I'd have loved to hear the story behind that one, the office was now empty of kids and teachers. "I promise."

And Bobby Socks was gone. She smelled like grapefruit and baby lotion and had a pink elephant named Chubs when she was little.

"Can I help you?" Grandma asked.

Uncle Bob, aka knight in shining armor, strode in and flashed his badge in true five-oh fashion. Man, he was good. We couldn't get the records without some kind of warrant. There were apparently laws against their giving out student information to just any Joe off the street. I was hoping Ubie's badge would be enough and we wouldn't need an actual warrant, 'cause I had no idea on what grounds we would get one.

"We need all the transcripts and class rosters on a student who went here about . . ."

Uncle Bob turned to me. I closed my phone and jumped up. "Oh, right, about twelve years ago."

The woman eyed Ubie a moment before grabbing a pen and writing down the dates I had. Ubie eyed her back. Sparks flew.

"And the name?" she asked.

Right. The name. Hopefully Uncle Bob wouldn't remember the man he put away for twenty-five to life. "Um," I leaned closer, trying to exclude him from the conversation, "Farrow. Reyes Farrow."

I didn't have to look at Uncle Bob to know that he stilled beside me. I could feel the tension thicken the air to a tangible mass. Well, crap.

Chapter Fifteen

Life isn't about finding yourself.
It's mostly about chocolate.

—T-SHIRT

"Uncle Bob," I said, "would you just give me a chance to explain?"

We were standing in the hall outside Ms. Tarpley's office, where Uncle Bob had dragged me by the arm.

"Reyes Farrow?" he asked, his teeth clamped together. "Do you know who Reyes Farrow is?"

"Do you?" I countered, trying to control the worry in my voice.

"I do."

"So you two are tight?" I asked hopefully.

He cast me a dubious scowl. "I don't usually hang with murderers."

Snob. "I just need to get some information on him."

"He beat his father to death with a baseball bat then threw him in the trunk of his Chevy and set it on fire. What more do you need to know about a person, Charley?"

I let out a huff of air, stalling for time to come up with a good argument. Where the heck were my lawyers when I needed them? Nobody was better at arguing than a lawyer. When nothing jumped out at me, I decided to let Ubie in a little further. Desperate times called for desperate measures.

"He wouldn't have done that," I said in a hushed whisper.

"You weren't there. You didn't see——"

"He wouldn't have had to." Leaning closer, I said, "He's . . . different."

"Most murderers are." Ubie wasn't budging without some earth-shattering bit of evidence.

After taking a deep, deep breath, I said, "It was him. Today. The spinal cord thing? He did it."

"What?"

Uncle Bob didn't want to hear me, to listen, but he couldn't help it. His curiosity always got the better of him. And I knew one surefire way of getting his complete and undivided attention.

I curled my fingers into his blazer and said, "You have to promise not to tell Dad."

Uncle Bob was suddenly salivating to know more. I explained as quickly as possible how Reyes was more than human. How he looked and moved. How he had been there on the day I was born—at which point, I was sure Ubie went into some bizarre kind of trance brought on by the stress of it all.

I left out the other two spinal taps and, well, the whole nightly seduction thing. He didn't need to know how deep my feelings for Reyes ran.

"What is he?" he asked at last.

With a shake of my head, I said, "I wish I knew. But he's going to die in two days if we don't stop it. And the only way to do that for sure is to find his sister."

"But, if he's this . . . powerful being—"

"In human form," I corrected. "I don't know what will happen to him if his body dies." I knew what would happen to me, though. I didn't want to live without him. I didn't know if I could. Not at this point.

Fifteen minutes later, we had printouts of Reyes's class schedule along with a roster for each course.

"Do you remember him?" I asked Ms. Tarpley.

She ripped her gaze off Uncle Bob to settle it on me. "I've only been here ten years," she said.

"And there are no other Farrows in the system?"

"No. I'm sorry. Perhaps his sister wasn't in high school yet."

"That could be. And he only came here three months." I looked back at the file I had on Reyes. "But this says he graduated from here."

"Not from this high school," she said. "Wait." Her fingernails clicked on the computer keys. "We do have a record of him receiving a diploma, but that's impossible."

I leaned over to Uncle Bob. "Not for an expert hacker." I was beginning to piece together how Reyes put his intelligence and computer skills to work.

"Thank you so much for this, Ms. Tarpley," Ubie said, taking her hand in his.

She made googly eyes. He made googly eyes. It was all quite romantic, but I had a missing person to find. I elbowed Uncle Bob. "Shall we hit the road?"

After a soft protest, he turned back to her and said his good-byes. Just as we started out the door, I skidded to a halt. "Oh," I said, bringing forward a note, "I found this in the corner over there. It looked . . . important."

"Thank you," she said, opening it.

As we passed by the front of the building, I looked in her window.

She was clutching the note to her breast and crying. It must have been the lily pad thing.

We swung by my office to give the class rosters to Cookie. She'd cross-reference the students Reyes'd had classes with and try to contact a few of them, fishing for a hit on the mysterious sister. Now that I could get into my office again, I grabbed my Glock out of the safe, slid into a shoulder holster, and snapped it in. With my leather jacket, it was hardly noticeable. I'd never actually had to pull it on anyone. I just wanted the feel of it against my body, to know it was there, if only for a little while.

On the drive back to the station, two of my lawyers popped into Uncle Bob's SUV. I'd been driving earlier, but after a little mishap, Ubie insisted on taking over.

The blond-haired, ruby-lipped Elizabeth Ellery sat behind him. "Hey, Charlotte."

"Hey, there." I turned to them. "How are you two doing?"

Jason Barber shrugged his brows. "My mom's upset."

"Are you surprised?" I asked, watching Uncle Bob shift uncomfortably in his seat. He never really got used to having them around. It was a situation in which he had zero control. He didn't like zero control. He didn't even like zero-calorie soft drinks.

"Well, yeah, kind of."

"Is your uncle okay?" Elizabeth asked, concern in her blue eyes.

With a dubious grin, I said, "He's mad at me."

Uncle Bob straightened. "Are you talking about me?"

"Elizabeth and Barber are here with us. She just asked if you were okay."

His knuckles turned white as he gripped the steering wheel just a tad tighter than was probably necessary. "You are never driving this vehicle again."

I did my signature rolling of the eyes. "Puh-lease. That sign was totally superfluous. Honestly, Uncle Bob, how many times do we need to
be reminded of the speed limit? No one's gonna miss it."

He pulled in a deep, soothing breath. "I'm getting too old for this
crap."

"Ah, yes. Impotence, decrepitude. Still, you'll always have Werther's
Originals." I watched as Uncle Bob's face went from a pale, post-fender-
bender white to a flushed shade of rosy pink. I had to laugh. On the inside, because he really was mad at me. "Where's Sussman?" I asked the
lawyers.

Elizabeth lowered her eyes. "He's still with his wife. She's having a
very difficult time."

"I'm sorry." I didn't just hate the people-left-behind part. I hated
talking about the people-left-behind part. Unfortunately, it was often
necessary. "How is your family?"

"My sister is doing remarkably well. I think she's on drugs. My
parents . . . not so much."

"Your sister isn't sharing?"

Elizabeth shook her head.

"I can't imagine how hard this must be for them."

"They'll need closure, Charlotte."

"I agree."

"We have to find who did this. I just think it will help."

She was right. Knowing the whys and hows of any crime often helped
the victims cope with what was done to them. And putting those respon-
sible behind bars was like the icing on the cake. Justice may be blind, but
she was an awesome elixir.

I looked back at Barber. "Oh, I took seven flash drives out of your
office, but they were all yours. Do you remember what you did with
the one Carlos Rivera gave you?"

He patted his jacket. "Damn, what did I do with that thing?"

"Maybe they took it? Maybe they knew he gave it to you?"

"I guess that's possible." He pinched the bridge of his nose. "I'm sorry, I just can't remember."

That happened often. Especially when the subject had two bullets in his head. Since we couldn't rely on the flash drive, we'd have to rely on our mad skill.

"Well, our former suspect and current informant, Julio Ontiveros, stated that he'd given a friend a box of ammunition after he sold his own nine millimeter. That's the only way he could see his fingerprints showing up on casings at a crime scene."

"Who was the friend?"

"Chaco Lin. And guess who Chaco Lin works for?"

"Satan?" Elizabeth asked.

"Close. Benny Price."

Elizabeth and Barber glanced at each other knowingly.

"Normally we couldn't mention this," Barber said, "but since we're not really here, I think the rules no longer apply. Benny Price has been accused of human trafficking."

"Tell them about the human trafficking investigation," Uncle Bob said.

"Apparently they already know." I looked back at Barber. "And we have one murdered teen and one missing one. Did you get anything on Mark Weir's missing nephew?" He was supposed to check out Weir's sister, see if she'd had any contact with her son.

"Not exactly, but I have to admit, it seemed like something was going on with the boy's mother."

"Going on?" My insides were suddenly tingling. "Could you be more specific?"

Uncle Bob perked up as well.

"She got a call a few days ago from a Father Federico. Sure put her in a tizzy."

I sucked in a sharp breath at the mention of the man who owned the warehouse.

"What?" Uncle Bob asked.

Barber continued. "From what I got out of a one-sided phone conversation, she was supposed to meet him, but he never showed up."

Ubie flashed me a look of desperation.

"Janie Weir was supposed to meet Father Federico, but he never showed," I explained.

We pulled up to the station. "Seems like no one has seen him lately."

"Are you thinking foul play?"

"It's possible. Has he, you know, shown up see-through style?"

"Nope. But that doesn't necessarily mean—"

"Right," he said, opening his phone and speed-dialing one of his detectives. That man spent more time on the phone than most thirteen-year-olds.

I turned back to the lawyers. "Do either of you know how much a bumper for a Dodge Durango costs?"

Barber shook his head. Elizabeth chuckled.

As we strolled into the station to go over operation Bring Benny Price to His Knees, Garrett stood in the hall, checking over his notes for the day.

"You know what's disturbing?" Garrett asked, closing his notebook as we walked up.

"Your addiction to little people porn?"

"Nobody has seen Father Federico in days," he said without missing a beat. Apparently, it was a rhetorical question. I wished he'd stated that before I wasted one of my best lines on an answer. I hated being wrong.

"Mark Weir's sister was supposed to meet him a few days ago, and he never showed up," Uncle Bob said.

Things were starting to come together. If Benny Price was trafficking children out of the country, maybe he'd gotten ahold of Mark
Weir's nephew Teddy. And maybe he'd gotten ahold of James Barilla,
the kid found murdered in Weir's backyard. Maybe James put up a struggle, tried to escape, and they killed him. But why on former planet Pluto
would they put the body in Weir's backyard and frame him for the murder? Did he pose a threat somehow? I needed caffeine.

I stepped past the meeting of the minds and headed for the coffee-
maker. The minds followed, made their coffee, then led the way to a
small conference room.

"Why can't I smell it?" Barber asked.

"Excuse me?" I set my coffee on the table and pulled out chairs for
them.

"The coffee. I can't even smell it."

"I tried to smell my niece's hair," Elizabeth said, a sadness permeating her voice.

"I'm not sure," I said. "Can you smell anything?"

"Yeah." Elizabeth tested the air. "But not stuff that's right in front
of me."

"You're picking up scents from the plane you're on, which technically isn't this one."

"Really?" Barber said. "Because I could have sworn I smelled bar-
becue a while ago. Do they have barbecues on this side?"

I chuckled and sat down next to Uncle Bob.

After twenty minutes of arguing on how to go about taking down
Benny Price, I came up with a plan. Benny owned a series of strip clubs
called the Patty Cakes Clubs. The name alone was all kinds of disturbing. And according to the file the investigative task force had on him,
Benny liked those strippers, though not half so much as he liked himself.

"I have a plan," I said, thinking aloud.

"We already have a task force investigating him," Ubie said. "If anything, we need to coordinate our efforts with them, take our cues from their investigation."

"They're taking forever. In the meantime, Mark Weir is sitting in jail, Teddy Weir is missing, and we have families who want answers."

"What do you want me to do, Charley?"

"Set up a sting," I said.

"A sting?" Garrett asked, his expression incredulous.

"Just give me a chance. I can get evidence on the man before the sun goes down today."

While Garrett practically bucked in his seat, Uncle Bob leaned toward me, interest sparkling in his eyes. "You got something cooking?"

"Detective," Garrett said in a scolding tone, "you can't be serious."

Ubie shook himself as if coming out of a trance. "Right. It was just a thought."

"But, Uncle Bob," I said, whining like a child who'd just been told she couldn't have a pony for her birthday. Or a Porsche.

"No, he's right. Besides, your dad will put a contract out on me."

"Psh," I *psh*ed, raking my gaze over him in disappointment. "Can you say wuss?"

That had to sting. I didn't *psh* him often.

"Charley, you were almost killed today." Garrett's silvery gaze glittered with anger. He was so moody. "And yesterday. Oh, right, and the day before. Maybe you should give it a rest?"

"Maybe you should bite my ass." I turned back to Uncle Bob. "I can do this, and you know it. I do have a slight advantage over the average Joe."

"What did you say?" Garrett asked. "You have a slight advantage over the average psycho? I doubt it."

Well, that was just mean.

"What are you thinking?" Ubie asked, unable to help himself, and my smile shone bright with superiority. Would Garrett never learn?

"You said that you haven't been able to get wiretaps in his office, right?" I asked.

"Right. Not enough evidence."

"I can't believe you're listening to her," Garrett said.

"We're listening, too," Barber said. Elizabeth nodded her head in agreement.

"Thanks, guys. As I was saying," I continued, glaring at the traitor before turning back to Ubie, "he videotapes all his interviews with the new girls."

"Yeah." Uncle Bob's brows knitted in thought.

"And he does all his *interviews* in his office, right there on a couch he has for just such occasions."

"Okay."

As I explained my plan to Uncle Bob, Garrett sat boiling under his hot collar. Honestly, the man was going to have a heart attack.

"That's a pretty good plan," Uncle Bob said when I'd finished my spiel, "but can't you just walk up and whisper something in his ear like you did with Julio Ontiveros? You're like the horse whisperer, only with bad guys."

"That worked for one reason and one reason only."

"And that would be?"

"Julio was not the bad guy."

"Oh. Right."

"My powers of persuasion are only as strong as the bullshit I have to back it up."

"Well, I like it," Elizabeth said. "And watching Mr. Swopes get spitting mad is entertaining."

Barber and I agreed with a snicker.

"I'm glad you can laugh about all of this, Charley," Garrett said with a nasty scowl lining his face. "You have no idea what kind of man Price is."

"And you do?"

"I know what kind of man it takes to get involved with something as barbarous as human trafficking."

"I get it, Swopes. He's not the kind of man you take home to meet your stepmom." I rethought that. "Wait a minute. Maybe my stepmom *would* like to meet him. Do you think he ships to Istanbul?"

"Charley," Uncle Bob said in a warning tone. He knew only too well the stones that made up the foundation of the rocky relationship between my stepmother and I, even telling me once he'd never understood why my dad didn't do something about it. That one stumped me, too.

"It was just a thought," I said defensively.

While Uncle Bob started negotiations with the investigation task force already assigned to Benny Price, I decided to hunt down Sussman, who'd been MIA for some time now. Garrett stormed off in true Garrett fashion as I checked my phone outside the conference room. He could storm off all he wanted. While he'd retrieved his truck earlier, I had yet to fetch Misery, so he was giving me a ride. The faster he stormed to his truck, the longer he'd have to wait. Which worked for me on several levels.

I had two texts, both from Cookie, both saying, CALL ME WHEN YOU GET THIS. Must be important.

"I got ahold of one of the women at Reyes's high school," Cookie said when I called her. "She and a friend of hers remember our boy very well."

"Nice work." I loved that woman.

"They can meet you at Dave's tonight, if you'd like."

"I'd like. What time?"

"Whenever you can be there. I'm supposed to call them back."

"Purrrrrfect," I purred into the phone, doing my best Catwoman impersonation. "I have to go check on Sussman. He's MIA. How about an hour from now?"

"I'll call them. How are you, by the way? We haven't had time to talk since your latest near-death experience."

"I'm alive," I said. "Guess I can't ask for much more than that."

"Yes, Charley, you can."

After a long pause, I said, "Can I ask for a million dollars, then?"

"You can ask," she said before hanging up with a snort. She knew me well enough to figure out I wasn't going to talk about my latest drama at that time. I'd vent later. And she'd get the brunt of it all. Poor woman.

Chapter Sixteen

Sarcasm. Only one of the services offered.
—T-SHIRT

Thirty minutes and one eerie ride later—Garrett stewed in his ire over my plan the whole way to my Jeep—I sat outside Sussman's house, watching him through a second-story window. His back was to me, and I realized he was probably watching his wife.

Several cars lined the curb in front of his gorgeously decorated three-story abode. People came and went, talking softly. Unlike the movies, however, they were not all dressed in black and they weren't all crying. Well, some were. But several were laughing at this or that, making animated conversation with their hands, greeting visitors with arms open wide.

I strode awkwardly to the front door and walked in. Nobody stopped me as I meandered through the crowd to the stairs. Taking them slow, I climbed to the second floor on thick beige carpet and found what looked like the master bedroom.

The door was slightly ajar, and I could hear sobbing coming from inside. I knocked hesitantly. "Mrs. Sussman?" I said, easing inside.

Patrick's gaze landed on me in surprise. He was leaning on a windowsill, watching his wife. Another woman, large and dressed in true mourning attire, sat beside her, an arm wrapped firmly around Mrs. Sussman's shoulders.

She raised a viperous glare on me. *Uh-oh.* Turf war.

"I'd like to talk to Mrs. Sussman, if it's okay with her," I said.

The woman shook her head. "Now is not a good time."

"No, it's okay, Harriet," Mrs. Sussman said. She looked up at me, her large brown eyes reddened with sorrow, her blond hair haphazardly brushed back. She was the kind of beautiful that men didn't notice at first. A soft, honest attractiveness. I had a feeling her smiles were genuine and her laughs were sincere.

"Mrs. Sussman," I said, leaning forward to take her hand. "My name is Charlotte Davidson. I'm terribly sorry for your loss."

"Thank you." She sniffed into a tissue. "Did you know my husband?"

"We'd met only recently, but he was a great person." I had to explain my presence somehow.

"Yes, he was."

Ignoring the caustic stare of the other woman, I continued, "I'm a private investigator. We were working on a case together, and now I'm working with APD, helping to find out who did this."

"I see," she said in surprise.

"I hardly think now is the time for this, Ms. Davidson."

"Not at all," Mrs. Sussman said. "This is precisely the time. Do the police know anything yet?"

"We have some promising leads," I said evasively. "I just wanted to let you know that we are working very hard to solve this case and that—" I turned back to Sussman. "—you're all he talked about."

The sobs began again, and Harriet went to work consoling her friend. A weak, appreciative smile spread across Sussman's face.

After handing her my card and saying good-bye, I gestured for Sussman to meet me outside.

"That was awkward."

We were in front of his house, leaning against Misery, watching the occasional car slide past. The wind had picked up. Its crisp chill gave me goose bumps, and I hugged myself, thankful for the sweater underneath my leather jacket.

"Sorry," he said. "I meant to go back with the others. I just . . ."

"Don't worry about it. You have a lot on your plate. I understand."

"What have you found out?"

After I filled him in, he seemed to perk up a little. "You think this is about human trafficking?"

"We have a semi-solid plan of action if you want in."

"Sure do." Good. He seemed to be doing better. He turned thoughtful a moment, then asked, "In the meantime, can I jump in your body and make out with my wife through you?"

I fought a grin. "It doesn't really work that way."

"Then can you just make out with my wife and pretend I'm in your body?"

"No."

"I can pay. I have money."

"How much we talking?"

I sneaked back into the law offices of Sussman, Ellery & Barber, dumped the flash drives into Barber's desk, then did another quick search, just in case I missed one. Nora hadn't been in, which was good. She couldn't have realized the flash drives were missing and made a mess for me.

Now on to Reyes's classmates. Dave's Diner was a fifties flashback, complete with tin signs and chocolate egg cream sodas, which surprisingly contain neither eggs nor cream. When I walked in, two women sitting in a corner booth waved me over. Wondering how they knew what I'd look like, I strolled to their table.

"Charley?" one asked. She was big and startlingly pretty with a dark brown bob and wide smile.

"That's me. How did you know?"

The other one smiled, a Latina with curly hair pulled back into a frizzy ponytail and skin to die for. "Your assistant told us that you'd probably be the only girl walking through the door who looked like she could do the name Charley Davidson proud. I'm Louise."

I shook Louise's hand, then the other one's.

"I'm Chrystal," she said. "We just ordered food, if you're hungry."

After sliding into the circular booth, I ordered a burger and a diet soda. "I can't tell you how thrilled I am that you agreed to meet me."

They laughed at some private joke, then took pity on me and explained. "We jump at any chance to talk about Reyes Farrow."

"Wow," I said in surprise, "I do, too. You knew him well?"

After another sideways glance at Chrystal, Louise said, "Nobody knew Reyes Farrow well."

"I don't know," Chrystal said, "Amador."

"Right. I'd forgotten that he hung out with Amador Sanchez."

"Amador Sanchez?" I opened my bag and pulled out the file I had on Reyes. "Amador Sanchez was in prison with him. They were cellmates, in fact. Are you telling me they were friends before they met in prison?"

"Amador went to prison?" Chrystal asked, surprised.

"That surprises you?" Louise arched a delicate brow at her friend.

"Kind of. He was a good guy." She looked at me then. "Reyes mostly kept to himself until he met Amador. They became friends pretty quick."

"Can you tell me about Reyes?" My heart raced with wanting and anticipation. I'd searched for him for so long, only to have him find me instead, to have him turn out to be the Big Bad. How could I not have known?

Louise studied a napkin she'd folded into a swan. "Every girl on campus was in love with him, but he was so quiet, so . . . withdrawn."

"He was really smart, you know?" Chrystal added. "I'd always taken him for a slacker. He wore a lot of layers."

"Hoodies," Louise said in agreement. "Always had hoodies on with the hood up. He got in trouble for that constantly. But he kept doing it."

"Every day in class," Chrystal said, taking her turn, "he would try to get away with his hood up, and every day in class, the teacher would tell him to put it down."

Louise leaned into me, a sparkle in her dark brown eyes. "Now, what you have to understand is that even in the short amount of time that he was there, this became a ritual. Not for him, not for the teachers, but for the girls."

"The girls?" I asked.

"Oh, yeah," Chrystal said, nodding her head in dreamy remembrance. "There was a moment every day when you could have heard a pin drop. He would raise his hands and push the hood back, and it was like watching heaven reveal itself."

I could see it in my head. His beautiful face revealed in such a way as to cause hearts to flutter, blood to rush, and young girls to sigh in choreographed unison.

After a bit of reminiscent thought, Louise said, "And he was so smart. He was in the same calculus class as our friend Holly, and he always blew the curve. Aced every test."

"We had him for English and science. One day, Mr. Stone gave us this assessment," Chrystal chimed in excitedly, "and Reyes got a hundred, and Mr. Stone accused him of cheating because some of the concepts weren't even presented until college."

"Oh, I remember that. Mr. Stone said there's no way Reyes got a hundred on it. And Reyes was like, 'Screw you, I didn't cheat,' and Mr. Stone was like, 'Yes, you did,' and he took Reyes to the principal."

"Suzy worked as an aide that hour, remember?" Chrystal asked Louise. Louise nodded. "Said they went into the office and Mr. Stone got in trouble because the principal said Reyes gets hundreds on everything, and he had no right to accuse him of cheating."

"Was he ever given an IQ test?" I asked.

"Yes," Louise said. "The principal had him tested, and then these men showed up from some educational board wanting to talk to him, but Reyes's family had moved away."

Yeah, I was sure they did. Reyes's father kept them on the move constantly. Dodging the authorities at every turn.

"I still can't believe he killed his dad," Chrystal said.

"He didn't," I said, wondering if my convictions were more wishful thinking than evidence based.

They looked up at me in surprise. I probably shouldn't have done it, but I wanted them on my side. On Reyes's side. I told them about the first night I saw him, about his father beating him senseless, and about the sister he'd left inside.

I paused when our food arrived, waiting for the server to leave before I continued. "That's why we're here. I need to find his sister." I also explained what happened in prison and the fact that he was in a coma, but neither of them could remember very much about the girl. "She's really the only one who can stop the state from terminating care. Do you know anyone who might have hung out with her?"

"Let me make some calls," Louise said.

"Me, too. Maybe we can come up with something. How much time do you have?"

I looked at my watch. "Thirty-seven hours."

On the way home, I called Cookie and told her to find me one Mr. Amador Sanchez. He seemed to be the only person who might know anything substantial about Reyes. It was late, but there were few things Cookie loved more than hunting down a warm-blooded American for me. Give her a name, and she was like a pit bull with a bone.

Right after I hung up, my cell rang. It was Chrystal. She and Louise remembered that her cousin, an eighth grader at the time, used to hang out with a girl who hung out with Reyes's sister on occasion during lunch. Thin, but more than I had five minutes ago. They'd tried to call the cousin but couldn't get through, so they left a message with my name and phone number.

After I took down her information and thanked them several thousand times, I ran into a supermarket for the basic essentials of life. Coffee, tortilla chips, and avocados for guacamole. One can never have too much guacamole.

When I stepped out of my Jeep, I heard my name and spun around to see Julio Ontiveros behind me. He was bigger than I remembered from the station.

I closed my door and went around to collect my bags. "You look better without your cuffs," I said over my shoulder.

He followed me. "You look better without my cuffs, too."

Uh-oh. Time to fend off amorous advances. I stopped to face him. May as well get this over with.

"Your brother's medal from Desert Storm is in your aunt's jewelry box."

Disappointment flooded him. "Bullshit. I looked there." He stepped closer, anger and worry that he'd been duped sparkling in his eyes.

"She said you'd say that," I replied as I opened the back for my bags. "It's not in that jewelry box. It's in the one hidden in her basement. Behind the old freezer that doesn't work."

He paused and thought a moment. "I didn't know she had another jewelry box."

"No one does. She kept it hidden." I hefted the two bags in one hand and went for the third. "And the diamonds are there, too."

That bit of info stunned him even more. "She really had diamonds?" he asked.

"Yes, only a few, but she saved them for you." I stopped and looked him up and down. "Apparently, she thinks there's hope for you yet."

He breathed out an astonished breath, like his new knowledge had punched him in the gut, and leaned against Misery. "How do you . . . how can you possibly . . ."

"Long story," I said as I locked up Misery and headed for the front door of my apartment building.

"Wait," he said, trudging after me. "You said you knew where to find the three things I desired most in life. That's only two."

He still had his doubts. His mind was like a hamster on one of those wheels, spinning and spinning, trying to figure out how I knew these things. If I knew these things.

"Oh, right." I transferred all the bags to one arm and rummaged around the purse hanging from my shoulder with the other. "Oh, no, please," I said, sarcasm dripping from each word, "don't help me with the bags or anything." He folded his arms over his chest and grinned. Why did I even bother? My hand emerged at last with a pen. "Give me your hand."

He held it out, inching nearer as I wrote a phone number on his palm. And nearer.

His smile turned decidedly wicked after he studied the number with slanted brows, and he stepped even closer. "That's not what I want most."

Without missing a beat, I closed the distance between us and looked up into his eyes, throwing him off but widening his grin. "José Ontiveros."

He paused, his grin fading completely as he reassessed his palm.

"He's in Corpus Christi, staying at a shelter. But he moves around a lot. It took two hours for my assistant to track him down, even with the information your aunt gave us."

He stood in stunned disbelief, studying the number on his palm. "Two hours?" he asked at last. "I've been looking for my brother for—"

"Two years. I know. Your aunt told me." I shifted the bags again, their weight making my arm shake. "And just in case there is any doubt whatsoever in your head, yes, your *tía* Yesenia is watching. She told me to tell you to get your shit together, quit getting into ridiculous situations—I'm paraphrasing here—and go find your brother. You're all he's got."

Having kept up my end of the bargain, I turned and walked into the building before lover boy could reemerge. He had a lot to think about.

When I stepped off the elevator onto my floor, I noticed immediately the darkness of the hall. The manager had been having trouble with the wiring to the light fixtures on this floor since I'd moved in, so my awareness heightened only a notch or two.

Fumbling for my keys, I heard a voice from the darkened corner past my door.

"Ms. Davidson."

Again? Seriously?

At about eight thirty that morning, my tolerance level for National Kill or Horribly Maim Charley Davidson Week had reached its peak.

I'd armed myself soon afterwards. I pulled my Glock and pointed it into the darkness. Whoever stood in the shadows wasn't dead. I'd have been able to see him despite the dim lighting. Then a kid stepped forward, and my breath caught. Teddy Weir. It was impossible not to recognize him. He looked exactly like his uncle.

Holding up his hands in surrender, he tried to make himself seem as innocuous as possible.

I lowered my gun.

"Ms. Davidson, I didn't mean to hit you."

I raised it again and arched my brows in question. I thought about throwing my grocery bags at him and making a run for it, but those avocados were expensive. Damn my love of guacamole.

He paused midstride, lifting his hands higher. Even at sixteen, he topped my best height by at least three inches.

"I thought . . . I thought you were one of Price's boys. We were clearing out of there, but I thought he'd found us before we could manage it."

"You were the one who hit me on the roof?"

He grinned. He had sandy blond hair and light blue eyes. The stuff of movie stars and lifeguards. "I hit you on the jaw. We just happened to be on a roof at the time."

I leveled a death stare on him and muttered, "Smart-ass."

He chuckled, then grew serious again. "When you fell through that skylight, I thought my life was over. I figured I'd go to prison forever."

After holstering my gun, I unlocked my apartment. "You mean like your uncle?"

He gaze darted to the floor. "Carlos was supposed to fix that."

"Carlos Rivera?" I asked in surprise.

"Yeah. I haven't seen him in days."

Teddy strolled in after me, then closed and locked the door. Normally, that would have worried me, especially with the new holiday and all, but I could tell he'd been through a lot. Something had happened to him, and he wasn't taking any chances.

Also, Reyes was in the room. I almost stumbled when I saw the dark haze of fog by the front window. Then I felt him. His heat, his electricity. The room smelled like a desert storm at midnight.

"Have a seat," I said to Teddy, gesturing to a stool at my snack bar, pretending nothing was amiss. To disguise the fact that my body was shaking with Reyes's nearness, I kept moving. First, I put on a pot of coffee, then stuck my perishables in the fridge. After noticing that Teddy's hands were shaking as well, I took out some ham, turkey, lettuce, and tomatoes. "I'm starved," I lied. "I was just going to make a sandwich. Want one?"

He shook his head politely.

I hit him with my best scowl. "Clearly, you've never had one of my sandwiches."

The desperate gleam in his eyes testified to his current state of hunger.

"Ham, turkey, or both?" I asked, making him feel like he had a choice in the matter of my feeding him.

"Both, I guess," he said with a hesitant shrug.

"That sounds good. I think I'll have the same. Now for the hard part."

His brows drew together in concern.

"Soda, iced tea, or milk?"

His mouth slid into a grin as his eyes wandered to the coffeepot.

"How about milk with the sandwich. Then you can have coffee."

Another shrug of confirmation lifted his shoulders.

"We've already figured out Benny Price is the bad guy here," I said while piling a third slice of ham onto his sandwich. "Can you tell me about the night your friend died?"

He lowered his head, reluctant to talk about it.

"Teddy, we have to get your uncle out of prison and get Price into it."

"I didn't even know Uncle Mark had been arrested. The thought of him killing anyone is laughable," he added with a snort. "He's the calmest person I've ever met. Not like my mom, I can tell you that."

"Have you seen your mom since you've been back?"

"No. Father Federico said he would set up a meeting when we got back where she'd be safe, but we haven't seen him either. I think maybe Price figured out what was going on and got to him, too."

"What is going on?" I asked after pouring him a tall glass of milk.

He took a huge bite, then washed it down with the ice-cold milk. "Price sends out scouts. You know, people who look for homeless kids and the like. Kids that won't be missed."

"Gotcha. But you weren't homeless."

"James was, kind of. His mom had kicked him out when she remarried. He didn't have anywhere to go, so he was staying in Uncle Mark's shed."

"And when he got hurt, that's where he went."

"Yeah. James got suspicious of this one scout who kept asking questions, wanted to know if James had any family, if he'd go stay with him. So James and I did our own little investigation." He put his sandwich down. "We figured out who the scout worked for and snuck into one of Price's warehouses. It was all very James Bond, you know? We had no idea what was really going on."

"So they caught you, but you got away?"

"Yeah, but James got hurt pretty bad. We were running and just kind of got split up. I had two guys on my ass. Big guys. I'd never been so scared."

I sat beside Teddy and put an arm on his shoulder.

He took another bite. "I heard about what Father Federico was doing—"

"Doing?"

"Helping runaways and stuff."

"Right," I said. "And you went to him?"

"Yeah. Funny thing was, he knew all about Benny Price. He hid me in his warehouse."

"Wait, the same warehouse—"

"The same one. Sorry about that again, by the way."

Ah, finally my chance to find out where everyone disappeared to that night. "Okay, there were two guys in the warehouse packing boxes, but when I reached the ground, everyone was gone. Any thoughts?"

Teddy smiled. "That warehouse has a basement with an entrance that's almost impossible to find. We hid in there till everyone left."

Smart. "So Father Federico was trying to hide the kids Price wanted?"

"Yeah."

"Why didn't he just go to the cops?"

"He did. They said they were building a case against him. In the meantime, kids were still disappearing. You've seen the posters."

I had.

"They said Father Federico didn't have enough hard evidence to prove Price was behind any of the kidnappings."

"So, you've been in this warehouse for two years?"

He choked on a bite and took a gulp of milk. "No. You have to understand, Father Federico is a take-charge kind of guy. When the cops couldn't help, he took matters into his own hands. He started a watch, a search-and-rescue team, and an underground railroad of sorts."

I bit back my surprise and waited for Teddy to continue.

After popping the last piece into his mouth, he said, "We have all kinds of guys working this thing. Me? My end is Panama."

"Panama?" I asked, taken completely by surprise. *This thing* was way bigger than I thought. Than anybody thought.

"Yeah. We got shipping records, invoices, and even buyers' addresses.

They're freaking everywhere. But Price was constantly on the lookout for me, so Father Federico made sure I stayed hidden."

"So Carlos Rivera worked for Father Federico?"

"Not at first. He was a scout. *The* scout. The one who tried to pick up James. I guess when James got killed, Carlos decided he'd had enough. He went to the Father, and they worked out a deal. Father Federico can be very persuasive when he wants to be. How 'bout that coffee?"

Right. I couldn't help but wonder why Carlos didn't just go to the police. Of course, the big fat target he would have become might have had something to do with his decision. Some people think the police are worse than the criminals. Going to them would be like committing suicide.

"So, you've been in Panama?"

"Yes. I've saved seven kids, in case you're wondering," he said proudly. "Well, I helped save seven kids."

"And you didn't know what was going on with your uncle?"

"Yeah, I knew. Father Federico kept me informed, but we just kept thinking they'd drop the charges on Uncle Mark. I mean, he didn't do anything. I couldn't imagine he'd actually get convicted. We didn't want to risk our operation to save Uncle Mark, but when he got convicted, we didn't have a choice. I still can't believe it. I mean, how did James's blood get on Uncle Mark's shoes?"

"I've already got that one covered," I said. "It had been raining. Your uncle took out the trash that evening and must have stepped in a puddle James's blood had run into. He didn't see him behind the shed, but someone must have seen James stumble over the fence and called the police."

"Of course," he said, taking a long sip of the piping-hot black coffee.

"Are you old enough to take your coffee black?"

He smiled. In that moment, he looked old enough to drink coffee any color he wanted. His eyes had seen too much. His heart had experienced too much fear and grief. He'd probably aged ten years in the last two.

"Why did you come back?" I asked.

"I had to. I couldn't let Uncle Mark go to jail for something he didn't do."

"Even if it meant risking your life?" I asked, pride nudging my heart.

With a shrug, he said, "That's all I've done for two years. I'm tired of running. If Price wants me, he can come and get me."

My chest tightened. No way was I letting that happen. "We have to call the police, you know."

"I know. That's partly why I'm here. Father Federico has disappeared, and we need to hire you."

Chapter Seventeen

Do not disturb. Already there.

Throughout the evening, Reyes nudged me, brushed up against my arm, slid his fingers over my mouth, causing little earthquakes to shimmy through my body. But at the moment, I had a house full of badges. Literally. I'd bet my last nickel even Mr. Wong was feeling claustrophobic, hovering in his corner, his back to the world. Heck, even the police chief and the DA were in my apartment. I totally should have spruced up the place. Put out some candles. Made a cheese ball. Cookie was busy filling cups of coffee, and Amber was busy flirting with a rookie named Dead Meat if he didn't stop flirting back. She was eleven, for heaven's sake! Of course, he may have just been humoring her. And it was a little cute. In a gross, Chester-the-molester kind of way.

Around midchaos, I got a call from Chrystal's cousin.

"Hi, is this Ms. Davidson?" she'd said, her voice iffy.

"That's me. Is this Debra?" I asked, glancing over at Teddy. I was sure he'd freak with all the cops around, but he seemed calm, almost relieved.

"Yeah," the caller said. "Chrystal told me you're looking for Reyes Farrow's sister. I called my friend Emily, and she could only remember his sister's first name as well. It was Kim. She and Reyes had different last names."

Interesting. I wondered if it was Walker, as in Earl Walker.

"That's all we remember about her," she continued. "Except she was really nice."

"Well, that's more than I had yesterday."

"Sorry I can't be of more help. You know, they were really good friends with Amador Sanchez."

"Yes, I keep hearing that." Perhaps this Amador Sanchez was the way to go. He clearly knew them both well. "Hey, what school did you guys go to?"

"Oh, we were at Eisenhower Middle School."

"Okay, I got a Kim at Eisenhower Middle School about twelve years ago, right?"

"Exactly. I hope you find her."

"Thanks so much for calling, Debra."

"Not at all."

Well, that didn't get me anywhere fast. But I had a Kim and an Eisenhower Middle School. Looks like I'd be hanging with Uncle Bob again tomorrow if he'd have me. I wondered if he'd let me drive.

"Oh," Cookie said, sashaying up to me. She'd been flirting as well. "I got an address and a number for your Amador Sanchez."

"Suh-weet." Before going to the school, I'd pay Mr. Sanchez a visit. He could probably tell me the sister's last name and where to find her. Cell mates shared everything. Especially cell mates who'd been friends in their previous lives.

We high-fived, and she went to warm another cup. It was almost eleven, and all the late nights were taking their toll, as were the beatings. While my body throbbed with fatigue, my mind refused to be subdued.

I sat down beside Teddy to make sure he was doing okay. Surprisingly, he took my hand into his. I squeezed. The kid had stolen my heart the moment he walked out of the shadows. I hated when that happened. The DA sat across from us, questioning Teddy, his expression a mixture of interest and worry.

"Can I talk to you?"

Officer Taft stood over me, looking down. I looked past him toward Demon Child. She was doing her best to lure Mr. Wong into a game of hopscotch.

"Not really in the mood, Taft," I said, dismissing him with a frosty shoulder.

"I'm sorry about this morning. You just took me by surprise."

With a glare of distrust, I turned back to him. "If you're going to throw another tantrum, there's really no need to talk."

He set his coffee cup down and squatted beside me. "I promise. No tantrums. Would you just give me a chance to explain?"

He wasn't in uniform, and I was sure he'd come over just to talk to me, having no idea he'd be met by a room full of uniforms. After giving Teddy's hand another quick squeeze, I led Taft into the bedroom, where we could talk in private. Reyes followed. That worried me. I didn't want to have to explain why Taft's spinal cord was severed if he did anything stupid. It would be awkward. I'd probably have to make a statement, and I wasn't good at statements. I was much better at icy glares and smart-ass comebacks.

I plopped onto my bed, leaving Taft no choice but to stand. The only chair in the room was home to several pairs of jeans, a lace camisole, and a pristine pair of government-issue handcuffs. Oh, and pepper spray. A girl's gotta have her some pepper spray. He leaned against my dresser, bracing his hands on either side of his hips.

But Reyes . . . Reyes was another story. He must have been growing impatient. He hovered beside me, brushed against my arm, feathered a breath over my ear, ruffling the hair at the nape of my neck. His nearness kick-started my libido. Knowing what the man was capable of, I started to shake. My lack of control where he was concerned was getting ridiculous.

Demon Child strolled in then and stopped short at the door, her eyes as wide as flying saucers as she took note of Reyes. While I couldn't really see him—he was all dark fog and mist—she must have been getting an eyeful. Her jaw dropped, and she stood there, staring at him.

As if suddenly uncomfortable with the audience, Reyes moved to the window, and a chill settled over me with his absence. Demon Child stood stock-still, as if afraid to move. It was funny.

"This morning," Taft said, luring me back to the task at hand, "the girl you described wasn't from the accident scene."

"Duh. Figured that." My attitude didn't seem to faze him.

He lowered his chin, clenched his hands on the dresser. "It was my sister."

Damn. I should have known this went deeper than just some kid he knew from elementary school.

"She drowned in a lake by my parents' house," he added, his voice strained with sadness.

"He tried to save me," Demon Child said, her eyes still locked on Reyes. "He almost died trying to save me."

Steeling my heart against the daughter of Satan, refusing to notice her tiny arms locked at her sides, her large blue eyes glowing in wonder, her doll-like mouth slightly agape, I leveled my best scowl of disgust on her.

"Gross," I said.

"What?" She finally tore her eyes off Reyes, but only for a split second before relocking onto him as if she had a radar tracking system in her corneas.

"You love him so much?" I asked her, quoting her earlier sentiment. "He's your brother."

"Is she here?" Taft asked.

"Not now, Taft. We have more serious issues to deal with at the moment."

Strawberry's expression morphed into bemusement as she finally focused on me. "But I do love him. He tried to save me. He was in the hospital for a week with pneumonia from all the water that got into his lungs."

"I get that," I said, raising a hand as if giving witness in church. I keep forgetting that there are siblings out there who actually love each other. "But he's still your brother. You can't be stalking him like this. It's just wrong."

Her bottom lip quivered. "He doesn't want me around anymore, anyway."

Double damn. Concentrating on anything besides the tears gathering between her lashes—taxes, nuclear war, poodles—I asked, "What do *you* want to do?"

"I want to stay with him." She wiped her cheeks with the sleeve of her pajamas, then sat on the floor with her legs crossed. She started drawing circles in the carpet and allowed her eyes to stray to Reyes for only brief moments at a time. "But if he doesn't want me . . ."

Pulling in a long, tired breath, I said to Taft, "She tells me you tried to save her."

He looked at me in surprise.

"That you spent a week in the hospital afterwards."

"How does she know that?"

"I was there," she said. "The whole time."

I relayed what she was saying to Taft and watched as his expression became more and more astounded with every word.

"She said you hate green Jell-O now, which you've refused to eat since your stay in the hospital."

"She's right," he said.

"Do you want her to go?"

My question threw him. He stumbled over one answer after another before finally saying, "No. I don't want her to go. But I think she'd be happier somewhere else."

"No, I wouldn't!" she yelled, jumping to her feet and scrambling beside him. She grabbed his pant leg as if holding on for dear life.

"She wants to stay, but only if you want her to."

After a moment, I realized Taft was visibly shaking. "I can't believe this is happening."

"Me neither. I wasn't kidding when I said she was evil."

Ignoring me, Taft said, "If she wants to stay, I'd love to have her. But I don't know how to talk to her. How to communicate."

Uh-oh. I could see where this was headed. "Look. I don't do the whole interpreting gig, savvy? Don't even consider coming to me every time you want to know what she's up to."

"I could pay you," he said, sounding a lot like Sussman. "I have money."

"How much we talking?"

After a soft knock on the door, Uncle Bob poked his big head with his burly mustache into the room. "We're heading out," he said.

"What are you doing with Teddy?" I asked, concern leaping into my voice.

"He's going to a safe house with a couple of uniforms. We'll make more permanent arrangements tomorrow."

Taft and I stepped out of my bedroom to a near-empty apartment.

The DA took my hand, pumping it hard in enthusiasm. "Ms. Davidson, you have done an outstanding job here today. Outstanding."

"Thank you, sir," I said, choosing not to mention that my outstanding work involved falling through a skylight and making a ham-and-turkey sandwich. "Uncle Bob helped. A little."

The man snorted and headed out the door. After Teddy pulled me into a big bear hug, he followed. The hug felt nice. He would be okay. Well, if Price didn't get to him.

"Are we on for the sting tomorrow night?" I asked Ubie as the last of the officers shuffled out.

"The task force wants to meet with us first thing tomorrow morning. We'll see. This could be enough to bring him down."

"Wait, no," I said in protest. "Uncle Bob, we can't risk Teddy's life. We have to get more evidence on Price without resorting to Teddy's testimony. And we still have to find Father Federico. What if Benny Price has him?"

Uncle Bob lowered his brows, frustrated himself. "Right now, Teddy's testimony is all we've got. We need to bring this guy to his knees, Charley, and we need to do it soon. We have to put a stop to his whole operation."

I stood my ground, refused to budge, stomped my foot . . . metaphorically. "Just give me one chance. You know what I can do. We have to at least try."

With what looked like the weight of a sumo wrestler on his shoulders, Uncle Bob thought about my offer. "Let's see what the task force has to say tomorrow."

"What are you cooking up now?" Cookie asked after Ubie left.

"Oh, you know me," I said, pointing at Amber with a grin. "Nothing I can't handle."

Amber had fallen asleep on the couch, her hair a perfect arc framing her delicate features. That girl was going to be such a heartbreaker.

Cookie pursed her mouth against a smile and shook her head. "Flirting's exhausting work."

"Damn straight, it is," I said, rounding the sofa to open the door.

Cookie nudged Amber awake, then led her across the hall to their apartment. After a couple of near misses with a doorjamb and a potted plant, Cookie turned to me and said, "Don't think we're not going to talk about what happened today."

Oh, right, the near-death experience. "Well, don't think we're not going to talk about your attitude," I said, angling for a distraction.

She winked at me and closed her door.

And then we were alone. I stood grasping the doorknob as if it were a life raft, shaking with anticipation. In a whispery rush of air, he materialized behind me. The earthy smell of elements, rich and potent, surrounded me. Then his arm encircled my waist while the other reached up and closed the door.

He pulled me back against his chest, and I melted against him. It was like falling into fire, his heat blazing against my skin, everywhere at once.

"You're him," I said, my voice shakier than I'd hoped. "You were there when I was born. How is that possible?"

His mouth was on my neck, searing my flesh as his hand reached under my sweater and trailed flames over my stomach. Cautiously, he tested the area where the tip of his blade had sliced. Somewhere in the back of my mind, I was grateful for his concern.

Then his mouth was at my ear. "Dutch," he said, his breath fanning across my cheek. "At last." I turned into him, but he pulled back, studied my face, and I finally had a clear, undiluted view of the magnificent being known as Reyes Farrow.

He did not disappoint. He was the most glorious man I'd ever seen, solid and fluid at once, his lean muscles sculpted from a stone that could liquefy between heartbeats. Coffee-colored hair tumbled over a strong brow and curled behind an ear. The deep mahogany of his eyes, laced with spikes of gold and emerald green, shimmered with barely controlled lust. And his mouth, full and masculine, parted sensually. I now recognized his attire; a prison uniform, as Elizabeth had said. The sleeves had been rolled up to expose his forearms, long and corded with sleek muscles.

With infinite care, he slid his fingertips over my bottom lip, his expression severe, like a child who'd just discovered fireflies and wanted to know what lay behind the magic that illuminated them.

When his finger brushed along my lower teeth, I bit down softly, enclosed my lips over the tip, and suckled the taste, earthy and exotic, off his skin. He hissed in a sharp breath, rested his forehead on mine with eyes closed, and seemed to struggle for control as I drew more of him into my mouth. I wasn't sure if it was for me or for him, but he braced an arm on the door and pushed me back against it with a groan, his other hand suddenly around my throat, holding me captive as he fought for control over his body.

It was the sexiest thing that had ever happened to me. My body responded to his every touch with a jolt of arousal. A hunger—so hot, it ached—pooled in my abdomen, swirled and expanded with the white heat of desire. I wanted him forever, and in the back of my mind, I couldn't help but wonder what would happen if he died. Would I still get to have him? Would he come to me after he passed, or would he cross over and leave me to navigate the earthly plane alone? I was so afraid I'd lose him if his physical body expired. I wanted him to wake up, to be mine in flesh as well as in spirit. I was selfish that way.

"Reyes," I said, my voice breathy with need as his mouth found an especially sensitive spot behind my ear, "please wake up."

He leaned back with brows furrowed as if he didn't understand; then his head descended and his mouth covered mine, and I lost all sense of reason. The kiss started soft, his tongue drifting across mine, tasting and teasing with infinite care. It grew quickly like a wildfire, intensified, became savagely fierce and demanding as he plundered my mouth, explored and invaded with a driving primal need. The kiss siphoned every last bit of uncertainty I'd tucked away. He tasted like rain and sunshine and flammable substances.

He stepped closer, pushed into me, and a spark ignited between my legs. Just as my hands dipped in search of the hardness pressed against my abdomen, he stopped.

In a movement so quick it made me dizzy, he broke the kiss and spun around. His robe materialized instantly, a liquid entity that encased us both, and I heard the sing of metal coming to life, of a blade being drawn. A sinister growl, deep and guttural, thundered from his chest, and I blinked to awareness—so weak, I could barely stand. Was someone in the room with us? Something?

I couldn't see what lurked beyond Reyes's wide shoulders, but I could feel tension solidify every muscle in his body. Whatever lingered near, it was very real and very dangerous.

Then he turned back to me, wrapped his free hand around my waist, and pulled me against him, his mahogany eyes glowing as they searched mine, begging for understanding. "If I wake up," he said, his voice an agonized whisper, "they'll find me."

"What? Who?" I asked, alarm seizing my heart.

"If they find me," he continued, his gaze lingering on my mouth, "they find you."

Then he was gone.

About three seconds later, I hit the floor.

Chapter Eighteen

When fighting clowns, always go for the juggler.
—BUMPER STICKER

Had I been asleep for the last twenty-seven years? Were there beings and entities I'd never seen? Beings so dangerous and savage that only something supernatural could fight them?

I sat in the conference room with Uncle Bob, unable to fully focus after last night. Garrett was there, too, as well as the DA, the lead detective on the Price task force, the lawyers, and a very fidgety Angel. We were finalizing the plans for the evening. It was tricky making plans when not everyone in the room was in the loop, but Uncle Bob sold it. I knew he would.

Garrett and Angel had been surprisingly quiet. Garrett, I could understand. He was against the whole thing. But Angel had a prime opportunity to flirt with a hot, departed lawyer in a miniskirt, and he didn't take it. In fact, he hardly looked at her. I couldn't imagine what ate at him. Was it Reyes? Did he know I had fantasies about him that bordered on criminal?

After the detective and the DA left, Uncle Bob turned to me. "Okay, what's the real plan?"

Back to reality. A weak grin slid across my face. "I go in with my ridiculous video and fabricated evidence and get Price to confess everything."

"You can do that?"

"I can do that."

"Damn," he said, impressed already, "you really are a whisperer."

Garrett shifted in his seat but refused to say anything.

"What if we can't find him?" Barber asked in reference to their search for Father Federico. "What if the task force doesn't know about all of Price's holdings? Maybe they're keeping him somewhere else?"

"Or they've already killed him," Sussman said.

"That's always a possibility," I said, "but Price is Catholic, through and through. I just think he'd have a hard time offing an ordained priest."

"So, Barber and I are searching his holdings," Elizabeth said, "while Sussman and Angel assist you?"

"That's the plan."

"What's the plan?" Uncle Bob asked. I summarized our ideas, and he gave us a thumbs-up. Good thing, 'cause we really didn't have a Plan B.

"Angel," I said as everyone was taking off, "are you going to spill, or do I have to resort to the torture techniques I learned last year during Mardi Gras?"

He smiled and added a bounce to his step for my benefit. "I'm good, boss. I can do this with my eyes closed."

"Only 'cause you can see through your lids."

"True," he said with a shrug.

I checked my phone. Cookie'd left me a message. "You just seem so sad," I said, dialing voice mail. "Like someone stole your favorite nine millimeter."

"I'm not sad." He started down the hall, then turned back. "Least not when I look at you."

Aw. That was sweet. He was totally up to something; I just couldn't put my finger on what it might be.

"Guess what? Guess what?" Cookie chimed happily into the phone. "I got her name. I called that cell mate of Reyes's, that Amador Sanchez, and threatened to have him picked up on a parole violation if he didn't spill. I got her name and address. She's—" The voice mail beeped; then another message started. "Sorry. Damn phones. She's still in Albuquerque. Her name is Kim Millar, and she's still here."

My knees weakened beneath my weight. I grabbed a pen and paper off a uniform's desk as I walked past, earning a hostile glare for my efforts, and wrote down the address.

"He didn't have a number, but he said she works from home, so she should be there when you get this."

I could have kissed that woman.

"I know. You could kiss me. Just find Reyes's sister, and we'll make out later."

With a mad chuckle, I jumped into Misery and headed downtown. The anticipation growing inside me had my heart and stomach switching places. I glanced at my watch. Twenty-four hours. We had twenty-four hours to stop this.

The ride gave me time to contemplate what Reyes had said the night before. What did he mean when he said they would find him? Who would find him? Was he being hunted? I chose not to think about what Reyes had been growling at. Clearly there were things out there that even I couldn't see. Which brought up an important conundrum:

What was the point of my being a grim reaper if I couldn't see every-thing out there? Shouldn't I be kept in the know? Seriously, how could I be expected to do my job?

After pulling up to a gated apartment complex, I padded across the walk to the door of 1B and knocked. A woman about my age answered with a towel in her hands, as if she'd been drying dishes.

Stepping forward with my own hand outstretched, I said, "Hi, Ms. Millar, I'm Charlotte Davidson."

She took it warily, her paper-thin fingers cold to the touch. With dark auburn hair and light green eyes, she looked nothing at all like Reyes. A tad Irish and then some.

"What can I do for you?" she asked.

"I'm a private investigator." I fumbled for a card and handed it to her. "May I speak with you?"

After studying the card a long moment, she opened the door wider and gestured me inside. When I stepped into the sunlit room, I scanned the area for photos of Reyes. There were no pictures at all, of Reyes or otherwise.

"You're a private investigator?" she asked, leading me to a seat. "What can I do for you?"

She sat across from me in the front room. The morning sun filtered in through gauze curtains and bathed it in warmth. Though her fur-nishings were sparse, they were clean and in perfect shape.

Wondering if she had a touch of OCD, I cleared my throat and con-templated how to begin. This was harder than I'd thought it would be. How did you tell someone her brother was about to die? I decided to save that part for later.

"I'm here about Reyes," I began.

But before I could elaborate, she said, "Excuse me?"

I blinked. Had she not heard me? "I'm here about your brother," I repeated.

Because I had mad skill at reading people, I could tell instantly she was lying when she said, "I'm sorry. I have no idea who you're talking about. I don't have a brother."

Wow. Why would she lie? My mind started running scenario after scenario, trying to solve this newest mystery. But I didn't have time to play games. Even one so intriguing. I decided to fight fire with fire and lie right back.

"Reyes told me you'd say that," I said, a pleased smile on my face. "He gave me the password so you'd know it was okay to talk to me."

Her brows slid together. "What password?" She leaned forward. "Did he tell you about me?"

That was too easy. I almost felt guilty. "No," I said in regret, "he didn't. But you just did."

Anger flared in her Irish eyes, but it wasn't directed at me. She was mad at herself. The concave angle to her shoulders, the disappointment thinning her lips and pinching her brows told me everything I needed to know. Reyes wasn't the only one in the family who'd been abused.

"Please don't be angry with yourself," I said, still not feeling guilty so much as empathetic. "I do this stuff for a living because I'm good at it." She eyed the rag in her hands as I continued, her grip tightening. "Why would Reyes want your identity to remain a secret? There's nothing about you in his prison jacket. He's never listed you as a relative or a contact of any sort. There's not a word about you in any of the court transcripts."

After a long pause, she spoke with a sadness that seemed almost palpable. "There wouldn't be. He made me promise not to tell anyone who I was. We have different last names. It was easy to fade into the shadows at the trial. No one suspected a thing."

Why on Earth would Reyes want her to remain anonymous during his trial? If anything, she should have been a key witness. "Do you know what's happened to him?" I asked.

Her chin dropped farther, her hair shielding her eyes. "I know he was shot. Amador told me."

"Ah. Does Amador keep you informed?"

"Yes."

"So you know the state is going to take him off life support tomorrow."

"Yes," she said, her voice catching.

Finally, we were getting somewhere. This might just work after all. "You have to fight it, Kim. No one else can. You seem to be his only living relative."

"I can't," she said, shaking her head vehemently. "I can't get involved."

Astonishment sucked the air out of my lungs, and I stared at her, shocked and bemused.

She twisted the rag between white-knuckled fists. "Please don't look at me like that. You don't understand."

"Obviously not."

A soft sob escaped from her chest. "He made me swear I would never contact him again. He said when he got out, he would find me. That's why I've stayed here in Albuquerque. But I don't go visit him, I don't write him or call him or send him gifts on his birthday. He made me swear," she said, her eyes pleading with me to understand. "I can't get involved."

Though I couldn't imagine why Reyes made her swear to such a thing, the situation had clearly changed. I decided to go for the jugular. Desperate times and all. "Kim, he protected you all those years," I said, my voice acidic with accusation. "How can you do nothing?"

"*Protected* is not the right word," she said, sniffing behind the dish towel.

"I don't get it. Was there . . . sexual abuse?" I couldn't believe how presumptuous I was becoming, how much nerve I'd suddenly garnered in the face of adversity. To just blurt out something so sensitive like that bordered on brutality.

Tears pushed past her lashes and flowed in rivulets down her cheeks, answering for her.

"And he protected you the best he could. How can you turn your back on him now?"

"I told you, *protected* is not the right word."

The end of my patience was rocketing toward me. Why would she not want to help him? I saw how much he'd worried about her, how he'd risked his life that night just to stay with her. He could have run away, gone to the police, turned his psychotic father in to the authorities and been free. But he stayed. For her.

"What is the right word, then?" I asked, a caustic edge to my voice.

After a long moment of thought, she looked up at me, her green eyes shimmering in the afternoon sun. "Endured."

Okay. That threw me. "I don't understand. What—?"

"My father"—she interrupted, her voice cracking under the weight of her words—"my father never touched me. I was simply the weapon he wielded to control Reyes."

"But you just . . . implied there was sexual abuse."

Her gaze lifted to mine, her green eyes almost hostile at what I was forcing her to say. "He never touched me. *Me.* I didn't say there wasn't sexual abuse."

I sat blindsided, stunned into silence a full minute, absorbing what Kim told me, turning it over and analyzing it in my mind. It was painful even to contemplate, like the thought itself was a physical entity, a box covered in razor sharp shards of glass, slicing through my fingertips every time I tried to open it.

"At first, he used animals to control him."

Refocusing on her fragile face, I stumbled back to her.

"When Reyes was little, he used animals. If Reyes misbehaved, the animals paid the price, suffered because of him. Our father learned early on he couldn't control him otherwise."

I blinked, allowed the words to sink in despite my sudden reluctance to hear them.

"Then my mother, a drug addict who ended up dying from complications due to hepatitis, gave him the ultimate weapon. Me. She dropped me on his doorstep and never looked back. She gave my father power over Reyes. If he did not obey the man's every command, I went without dinner. Breakfast. Lunch. And eventually water. On and on, until Reyes gave in. Our father had no interest in me whatsoever except as a tool. Leverage over my brother's every move."

I sat speechless, unable to comprehend such an existence. To even imagine Reyes so helpless, a veritable slave to a monster. My chest tightened and my stomach knotted and I felt my breakfast edging back toward my mouth. I swallowed hard and took several deep breaths, disgusted with myself for making Kim relive horrors I could barely imagine.

"But you have to understand how Reyes is," she continued, unaware of my predicament, "how he thinks. What I've just told you is the truth, but the way he sees it, our father hurt me because of him. He took the burden onto his own shoulders all those years, carried the weight of my well-being like a king shoulders the welfare of his people."

I fastened my jaw shut to keep my chin from quivering.

"He told me that no one would ever hurt me because of him again. How can he think that? It was just the opposite. My father hurt him because of me." After she wiped at a tear, she leveled a hapless gaze on me. "Do you know why I'm telling you this?"

Her question surprised me, and I shook my head. I hadn't thought of it.

"Because it's you."

I did my best to focus, to get past everything she was telling me and listen.

"From the time Reyes was little, he's had seizures. Sometimes they would last for over an hour. When he came out of them, he would have the most bizarre memories. Memories of a girl with dark hair and sparkling gold eyes. I knew the minute I opened the door, it was you."

He had memories? Of me? My pulse quickened.

"He said he saved your life once. Said a man had taken you into an apartment." She leaned forward. "In case you've ever wondered, you weren't going to make it out of that apartment alive. The man was going to do what he wanted and then smother you. He'd done it before."

A jolt of anxiety rushed through me. "Reyes knew I was in danger?" I asked, finding my voice at last.

"Yes. Another time, he only *thought* you were in danger, but he said your stepmother was yelling at you in front of dozens of onlookers. You were scared and mortified. Those strong emotions are what caused him to seize. He was so outraged when he got there, so worried about you, he said he almost cut your stepmother in two just to teach her a lesson. But you begged him in soft whispers to let her be."

With the images of that day swimming in my head, I said, "I remember. He was so angry."

"Later, he learned how to find you without the seizures. He would go into a trancelike state just to see you, just to watch you." She smiled, remembering happier times. "He called you Dutch."

Shaking visibly, I released a long, labored breath. Every word she spoke only evoked more questions, an even deeper lack of understanding.

"If Reyes learned to control what he is, to harness the power he had and to use it, why didn't he . . . stop your father?"

She shrugged. "I don't think he believed it."

My brows slid together. "I don't understand."

"In Reyes's mind, it was all a fantasy. None of it was real at that time. Even you were a fabrication of his imagination, the girl of his dreams. But I knew what he did was real. When we got older, I started to research some of what he had imagined, what he'd done. Everything he told me actually happened."

The intelligence sparkling behind Kim's eyes belied the soft-spoken, meek woman I'd met earlier. She'd learned to hide what she was. What she was capable of. Admiration welled inside me. I would've loved to be friends with her in a different life. Under different circumstances. Then again, anything was possible.

"Do you know . . . do you know what he is?"

The question didn't surprise her. "No. Not at all," she said, shaking her head. "I just know he's special. He's not like us. I'm not even sure he's human."

I couldn't have agreed more. "What about his tattoos?" I asked. "Did he ever tell you what they mean?"

"No." Her posture relaxed minutely. "He just told me he'd always had them. Ever since he could remember."

"I know they mean something—I just can't put my finger on it." I pressed a palm to my forehead as if to stop my thoughts from racing so fast.

"Are you like him?" she asked, her voice completely matter-of-fact.

I took a deep breath and refocused. "No. I'm a grim reaper." Which always sounded so bad when said aloud. But she just smiled, wide and pretty. It took me by surprise.

"That's what he told me. You ferry souls to the other side. He said you sparkle like a newborn galaxy and have more attitude than a rich kid with his daddy's Porsche."

I couldn't keep a hiccup of laughter from escaping. "Yeah, well, he's got a little attitude himself."

She chuckled and folded the towel in her lap. "I think that's what kept him going. His attitude. If he hadn't been so strong, I don't think he would have made it."

My heart ached with everything Kim had told me. I wanted him to be okay. I wanted everything bad that had ever happened to him to be erased. But how could it if he didn't wake up? "Can't you please try to stop this?" I asked, my voice desperate.

Her fingers ironed out the creases of the towel. She'd made her decision. "Charlotte, he's suffered enough because of me. I made him a promise. I can't break it now, not after everything he's done for me."

As badly as I wanted to argue, I understood her position. I could see the love on her face and hear it in her voice. What I had originally taken for disregard was, in fact, a deep and ardent loyalty. I'd just have to put all my hopes in Uncle Bob. He knew people who knew people. If anyone could get it done, he could.

I left in the same state of surreality I'd been swimming in for days. With the passing of each hour, I learned something new, something amazing about Reyes. After searching for him for so long to no avail, the avalanche of information coming at me from all directions was a little overwhelming. Not that I was complaining. People dying of thirst don't denounce a flood. The enigma that was Reyes Farrow became more mysterious at every turn. And I planned to find out exactly how many turns the mystery held. The question remained, however: Could I do it in twenty-four hours?

Chapter Nineteen

I may not look like much,
but I'm an expert at pretending to be a ninja.
—BUMPER STICKER

"Where are you?"

I'd just left the courthouse when Uncle Bob called. Sussman suggested I file a preliminary injunction against the state on the basis of the fabricated possibility that Reyes might be the only man alive with information on a serial killer in Kansas. I hated to pull the Hannibal card, but it was all we could come up with on such short notice. If granted, it would restrain the state from taking Reyes off life support only temporarily, but it would buy me more time. I needed another chance to talk to him, preferably without him getting too close. Without him touching me. Or looking at me. Maybe then I could get some solid intel. I wondered if I could restrain him somehow, tie him to the kitchen sink or something. I needed supernatural rope. Or handcuffs sprinkled with fairy dust.

"Where are *you*?" I asked back. Uncle Bob was so nosy.

"We need to get you prepped."

"Prepped? For what? Did I agree to get prepped?" I didn't remember agreeing to get prepped. I'd never even been to preparatory school.

Ubie exhaled loudly. It was funny. "The sting," he said, his voice exasperated.

"Oh, right!" Forgot about that. "I just filed an injunction against the state. Can you get it pushed through ASAP? We don't have much time."

"Sure. I'll call a judge I used to date."

"Uncle Bob, we want the person you call to actually like you and want to do you a favor."

"Oh, she liked me. Every inch."

I paused midstride while a quiver of denial shuddered through me, then continued my walk to Misery. "Thanks, Uncle B, I owe you one."

"One? Are you serious?"

"Um, are we keeping score? 'Cause if we're keeping score—"

"Never mind. Just get your ass over here."

After reviewing the plan ad nauseam with our two teams, one on the tech stuff and one on the exterior of the premises, I ran back to my apartment to get dressed for the part. I worked mostly on covering the bluish bruises I was still sporting from my most recent adventures. By the time I strolled on-scene, I looked like an oppressed librarian with sex kitten eyes and a pout that could make grown men cry.

Garrett stopped what he was doing and ogled me. I took it as a good sign, until he spoke. "You're supposed to seduce him, not audit his taxes."

Taking my cues from Elizabeth Ellery, I was wearing a red skirt suit with three-inch stilettos. Unlike Elizabeth, however, I had my hair pulled into a tight bun and wore glasses with thick plastic frames that screamed *anal retentive*.

"Swopes, are you even male?" When he frowned in confusion, I asked, "Have you never had a wet dream about a secretary or a librarian or a German schoolmistress?"

He glanced around guiltily, making sure no one was listening.

"Bingo," I said in triumph, then strolled over to the surveillance van. Garrett followed, so I continued to rant. "Like Benny Price wouldn't suspect a setup if some hooch off the street dressed to entice him and get him to confess to murdering four people. Hmmm. That's a terrific idea. And if I were feeling slightly more suicidal today, we might have gone that direction. Look around you." I waited for Garrett to notice the two women down the block, clearly strippers, strolling into the club. "Those chicks are more available to him than tap water. I, on the other hand," I said, indicating my businesslike attire, "am not."

We walked to the van parked half a block away from the club and knocked.

I turned to Garrett and whacked him on the head just as Uncle Bob opened the back doors. "Major in sociology, remember?"

He shrugged, semi-agreeing, when Uncle Bob took my hand and lifted me inside. Skirt suit and stilettos. Probably not the best clothes to wear to a stakeout. I was a little worried Garrett would try to give me a boost again by grabbing my ass. Then a little disappointed when he didn't. A girl had to get her thrills somehow.

The van dipped when Garrett stepped inside.

"We still don't have any news from Team Father Federico," I said to Uncle Bob. "If they can't find him, I don't know what we'll do."

"We'll have to worry about that later," Ubie said. "For now, let's get this on you." He lifted a tiny mic from a padded box. "We got the smallest wire we could find."

"Are you for real?" I asked, appalled. "A wire? The plan is for Angel to turn on that spiffy, high-dollar camera Price has set up behind his desk. We'll get him on tape without him even knowing it. And more important, I'll live through this."

"Right, but we've got to have some kind of surveillance," he argued. "How will we know if you're in trouble?"

"If I'm in trouble, I'll get you a message." I looked over at Angel, who'd just stepped in. He was getting excited about the plan, I could tell. And he knew exactly what to do. "Do you honestly think Price won't have his men frisk me once he finds out why I'm there?" I leaned into Uncle Bob. "Just because I see dead people doesn't mean I want to be dead people."

Twenty minutes later, I was stepping out of a room full of half-naked chicks and fairly decent music and into the surprisingly quiet office of Benny Price. Businessman. Father of two. Murderer.

"She's not wired, boss," one of his bouncers said, a tall and muscled blond at whom the strippers had batted their lashes as we walked past. He'd brought me into a shadowy hall that led to Price's office before searching me, simultaneously providing me with a rush of indignation and a rather inappropriate thrill. "She does have a video camera, though."

Benny Price, who was sitting behind a massive teak desk, turned out to be much more striking in person than his surveillance photos had led me to believe. But in all fairness, he hadn't been prepared for those shots and didn't know to pose. He had short black hair and a neatly trimmed mustache and goatee. Where I lost complete respect for him was with his tie and kerchief. The tie was magenta against a sleek black shirt and pin-striped vest, and the handkerchief peeking from the vest pocket was much closer to violet. That settled it. He had to go down.

"You wanted to see me, Ms.—?"

"Mrs. . . . Magenta. Violet Magenta," I said. While keeping a straight face.

The bodyguard stepped forward and placed the video camera he'd found in my handbag on Price's desk. "She told me her name was Lois Lane."

Sadly, I think he believed me.

Price stood and picked up the camera. His very stance was meant as a threat, meant to belittle and intimidate. I knew plenty of women his tactics would work on. I was not one of them.

I sat down opposite him as he opened the LCD monitor and played the video on the camera.

"My name is Donna Wilson," I heard myself say from the other side. Well, not *the* other side . . .

"I have sent this video to ten people, including my lawyer, a co-worker, and my pedicurist." Pedicurist. I tried not to giggle. "If I do not call each and every one of these people by nine P.M. today, they will take the tape directly to the police. I have irrefutable proof locked in a safety deposit box that Benny Price, owner and operator of the Patty Cakes Strip Clubs, is trafficking children and selling them as slaves in foreign countries. One of the ten persons mentioned has the key to the box and will give it to the police if I do not return unharmed within the allotted time."

Benny stood stunned for a moment before closing the monitor and handing my camera back to me. Since I seemed to have his complete attention, I started the act. Breathing heavy, I curled my fingers into my handbag—a gorgeous silk clutch Cookie let me borrow—and leveled a determined, and slightly naïve, stare on him.

Clearly, I would not win the Patty Cakes Club's fave person of the year award. Though he hid it well, Price was angry. He forced himself to stay calm as he sat back behind his desk. "And what kind of proof do you have?" he asked, his voice like ice water.

I let my gaze dart to my purse then back up, hoping I wasn't overdoing the nervous damsel-in-distress bit. I had to sell it, not cram it down his throat.

"I have a USB flash drive I obtained from my employer, a lawyer who was shot a couple of days ago. He said it had everything we would need to put Benny Price—you—behind bars."

Price calmed then. The corners of his mouth twitched, and I knew he had the flash drive. Maybe he would be just stupid enough to . . .

He opened his desk drawer and withdrew a flash drive. "You mean this one?"

Yep. He was precisely stupid enough. While my insides were doing a Snoopy dance, my outsides were starting to panic. Angel and Sussman had stepped from the room behind Price with a thumbs-up. The camera was recording.

"Can I go watch the strippers now?" Angel asked.

With teeth gritted, I shot him a quick glare, then continued to hyperventilate. Price smiled one of those superior smiles of Mafia bosses and nursing home directors. Sussman stood back, glared at him.

"Oh, I almost forgot," Angel said. Hopping over to me, he popped open the top button on my too-tight blouse, giving Price, and hopefully the camera, a nice shot of my cleavage. Price's gaze landed instantly on the erotic zone. Danger and Will Robinson. Distractions extraordinaire. When he looked back up, a few strands of my hair had magically fallen to frame my face just so.

I pushed up my glasses in a nervous gesture. "I can assure you, that's not the same one." After licking my lips slowly in thought, I said, "He handed me a flash drive. . . . I know it has . . . he said it had evidence. It was encrypted, but—"

"Perhaps he handed you the wrong one?" Price offered politely.

"No, that's not possible. He has . . . I mean, he has several thousand flash drives on his desk at any given moment, but . . ."

"I promise you, little beauty, my man took this directly off your lawyer. Seconds after he died."

Little beauty? What was I? A racehorse? You'd think a man who hung around beautiful women all day could come up with something a little less corny.

While I was doing my best to hyperventilate without actually hyperventilating, Price stood, walked around his desk, and leaned against it in front of me. Partly, I was certain, so he could look down his nose while watching his newest victim squirm, like watching an ant burn through a magnifying glass. But a bigger part of the partly was so he could check out the girls.

Taking advantage of the situation, Angel went for another button, an evil smirk glittering on his face. I pretended to close my blouse and slapped his hand away in the process—the little perv. Angel frowned in disappointment.

"Were you after money?" Price asked, so cool an inferno wouldn't have melted his bravado. He gestured for blondie to leave.

I gulped, unable to meet his stare any longer—in theory—and nodded.

He reached down and pulled off my glasses. Guilt, utterly remorseless guilt, oozed off him and pooled at his feet. "And you just decided to waltz in here and demand some from me?"

"Yes. I'm . . . in trouble. With the deaths of the lawyers at my firm, there'll be an audit."

"Ah," he said, folding the glasses and placing them on his desk. "And you've been a naughty girl."

"You . . . killed them? It was you?" Without raising my chin, I looked up at him through my lashes. He seemed to enjoy it.

"Of course not. I have men for that."

Damn. Could he be any more evasive? I needed a confession, not a paltry assertion any lawyer worth his weight could weasel him out of.

I struggled to get to my feet, but he was ridiculously close. I brushed against him, making sure my shoulder grazed over his erection. "You sent men to kill my bosses? Why would you do that?"

As with most criminals, his arrogance was his downfall. He wrapped a hand around my arm and helped me up. "Because I can."

After sucking in an appalled breath, I tried to wrench free of his grip. I pretended to pretend like I was pretending to be confident when I said, "I'm leaving." He had just confessed to conspiracy. No way on Earth was I getting out of that office alive.

"What's your hurry?"

"If I don't show up by nine o'clock tonight, you *will* go to prison."

Price glanced at his watch, then pulled me closer, encircled my waist with his arms. "That gives us almost three exquisite hours to find out who your friends are."

Oddly, I was finding it easier and easier to act afraid. With a toss of my head, I gave Angel the signal. He nodded and took off, but Sussman stood there, cemented to the spot, a peculiar hatred seething in his eyes.

"So, in answer to your question, yes, I did kill those three lawyers." He ran a finger along my collarbone, dipped it into my cleavage. "But you don't have to be next."

Yeah, right. I pushed against his chest all helpless-like. Seriously, how long can it take to storm into a room? All Angel had to do was tug on Uncle Bob's tie, thus giving the signal for Ubie to send his men in with guns blazing. It wasn't brain surgery.

"You mean we could work something out?" I asked, my voice breathy with fear.

A sleazy smile widened across his once-handsome face. The face of a killer and a kidnapper who sold children as slaves. Or worse. He wrapped a confident hand around my throat, dipped his head to access one corner of my mouth. I was beginning to wonder if I'd underestimated him.

Suddenly a red light on Price's desk started flashing. He straightened in surprise as his bodyguard rushed into the room.

"Cops," the guard said, and Price turned an astonished gaze on me.

I could have been a smart-ass and said something like, *Don't drop the soap.* But the look on Price's face convinced me to bite my tongue. For once. He seemed, I don't know, annoyed. His face reddened within the span of a heartbeat.

Before I could warn him about the dangers of sudden acute spikes in blood pressure, he wrapped a hand around my arm with enough force to break it and pushed me back against the wall. Only it wasn't a wall. It opened to a dark hallway lined on one side with two-way mirrors. We could see directly into his office.

As I struggled with Price, the tactical team smashed into the room and tackled the bodyguard to the ground before scanning the area for me. I took a deep breath, readying myself to scream as Price dragged me down the hall, but his large hand clamped down on my face none too gently. It cut off my scream and my air supply. Which sucked. Blue was not my best color.

Then I felt Reyes. I felt him even before I saw him. A heat wave rushed over me, and I watched as he materialized in front of us. A swirling dark mass of smoke, thick and palpable. The air was suddenly drenched in his anger, bringing the water molecules to a boiling point that prickled hotly over my skin. Panic clutched my throat. How would I explain another severed spine?

Since I could hardly scream what I was thinking—which was basically, *Down boy!*—I formed the command in my mind. He had read my thoughts before. Maybe he would again.

Don't you dare, I thought. Really hard. Trying to project my sentiments past the wall of his anger and into his head.

The high-pitched ring of his blade being drawn halted, and Reyes paused. Though I couldn't see his face, I felt him staring at me from behind the hood.

Don't even think about it, Reyes Farrow.

He leaned over us and grumbled at me, but I held my ground. With legs flailing and lungs burning, I thought, *Do it and I will kick your ass.*

The mass stepped back, seemingly surprised that I would threaten him. But I didn't have time to worry about that. Or contemplate how exactly I would go about carrying out such a threat.

Clawing at Price's hands was getting me nowhere. Time to tap into my inner ninja. The first move of what I'd hoped would be many was to kick my assailant in the shins. Well-placed kicks could bring down the stoutest of opponents. And with heels? Forget about it.

As my mind raced to prepare for the kick and figure out my next move, I felt a sharp pain shoot from my neck down my spinal cord, saw a burst of white-hot light, and heard a loud crack echo against the walls. I turned to jelly in the blink of an eye. In the seconds before I felt consciousness slip completely away, I realized Price had broken my neck. Asshole.

I semi-expected to hear trumpets blaring, or angels singing, or even the sound of my mother's voice welcoming me to the other side. I mean, I was a fairly good person. All things considered. Surely I would head in the general direction of up.

Instead, I heard water dripping, slow and steady like the beat of a heart that barely had the endurance to continue. I smelled dirt under my face, cement, and chemicals. And I tasted blood.

It took only seconds for me to realize Reyes was near. I could feel him. His strength. His biting anger.

I blinked my eyes open and glanced around without moving, just in case Benny Price was nearby. I didn't want him to see that I was awake and have him try to finish what he'd started. We were in a small storage room. Shelves with equipment and cleaning supplies lined the cinder block walls. Reyes was perched on one of them, balancing himself on the balls of his feet like a bird of prey, not so much gazing out the open door as refusing to look down at me.

Yep, he was angry. Still enshrouded in the dark mass of his cloak, he had laid the hood back, his face and hair now visible. The cloak had settled around him. It was calm, waiting, as was his blade. The lethal weapon was drawn, and he held the shaft in his powerful grip as the tip rested on the cement floor. It was the first time I'd really seen it. It had a straight blade like other swords, only much longer, and its edges were curved, with vicious-looking spikes. It reminded me of two things: a medieval torture device and his tattoo.

"I'm alive," I croaked when I realized Price wasn't in the room with us.

"Barely," he said, still refusing to look at me.

But how? I brought up a hand and rubbed it over my throat. "He broke my neck."

"He tried to break your neck."

"He felt pretty successful to me."

Reyes finally turned toward me. The force of his gaze took my breath away. "You're not like other humans, Dutch. It's not that simple."

And you're not like anything I've ever met. Our eyes stayed locked a long moment as I tried unsuccessfully to fill my lungs with air. Then we were interrupted by a male voice.

"Who's there?"

I struggled to a partially sitting, partially wobbling position and turned to see a bound man with a cloth tied over his eyes huddled in a corner of the room. He had a graying beard and thick dark hair. He also had the Roman collar of a Catholic priest.

"Father Federico?" I asked.

He stilled, then nodded his head.

Score!

He was alive. I was alive. This day was just getting better and better. Till I felt the gun at my temple.

Before I could even turn toward Price, I heard the swing of a blade slice through the air. The gun fell harmlessly to the ground, and Price doubled over with a sharp cry of pain.

Well, crap. Dad was going to kill me.

I scrambled out of Price's reach, dived back for the gun, then re-scrambled out of his reach again. But he was writhing in pain, holding his wrist, and rocking on his knees. Most men with severed spinal cords couldn't rock on their knees. I glanced up, but Reyes went all dark and smoky and disappeared before I could say a thing. And I could have sworn he was wearing a grin when he did it.

"What . . . what did you do to me?"

That was a good question. What had Reyes done? As usual, there wasn't a drop of blood.

Sussman popped in, assessed Price's condition, nodded toward me in approval, then popped back out again.

"I can't move my fingers." Price was crying and slobbering. It was fairly grotesque. Reyes must have severed the tendons in his wrist or something. Cool.

I kept the gun aimed at his head as I scooted back toward Father Federico. Just as I started to untie him, Angel rushed into the room, followed by a disheveled Uncle Bob, and I had to wonder how Angel managed to lead him here.

After two other uniforms stormed in and took Price down, Uncle Bob knelt beside me. "Charley," he said, worry lining his face. He brushed at my mouth with his thumb. It probably had blood where Price's grip had been. "Are you okay?"

"Are you kidding?" I asked, struggling with Father Federico's blind-fold. "I totally had this."

Then there was this odd moment. Like a reality check or some-thing. Uncle Bob took the gun from me, then helped me with the

Father's blindfold, lifting it off him—and the look on the man's face, the gratitude and relief, overwhelmed me. Uncle Bob looked back at me, his expression so soft, so concerned, that I jumped into his arms and held on as long as I dared. He wrapped me in a hug that was like heaven, only less glitzy.

It must have been the relief. Of being alive. Of finding Father Federico. Of bringing Price down. While I let myself wallow in the warmth of Ubie's hug, I fought the tears that threatened to surface with every ounce of my being. This was no time for tears. I could be such a girl.

Then I felt a hand on my shoulder, and I knew it was Garrett's.

"So, can I go watch the strippers now?"

I peeked over Ubie's shoulder at a grinning, wingless Angel. I would have hugged him, too, but it looked odd when I hugged the dead in public.

"He pulled my tie," Uncle Bob said when I asked him how he found us.

"Angel pulled your tie?"

"Led me right to you."

We sat in the conference room at the station, watching the tape of Benny Price's confession. It was ridiculously late, and we'd replayed the video about seven thousand times already. I think Garrett was watching it for the shots of the girls. They seemed to get along well.

"I gotta tell you, Davidson, I'm impressed," he said, his eyes glued to the screen. "That took balls."

"Please," I said with a snort, "that took ovaries. Of which I have two."

He turned to me, a new appreciation lighting his face. "Have I mentioned that I'm a licensed gynecologist? If your ovaries ever need anything . . ."

With a roll of my eyes, I rose from the table and hobbled barefoot to the door. While I was hiding the fact that I'd pretty much had my neck broken during Price's attempted getaway, I couldn't hide the fact that I'd twisted my ankle walking back to the van. Damned stilettos. So now my neck and my ankle were killing me.

In the meantime, Barber and Elizabeth popped in to say they'd found Father Federico. He was at the hospital. They were only a little disappointed when I told them he was there because we took him there. He wasn't in the best condition, but he'd live.

All in all, it had been a very good day. We had the flash drive, the video, and Father Federico's testimony. Benny Price would likely spend the rest of his life in prison. Or at least a healthy chunk of it. Of course, he'd have to learn to use his left hand, I thought with a chuckle.

And Uncle Bob would take all the credit, but that was simply how it had to be. Still, my becoming a private investigator really helped in the cover department. We no longer had to make up excuses to explain why I was at a crime scene or what kind of *consultant* I was, exactly. I was a PI. People pretty much stopped asking questions after that.

"You never told me their names," Garrett called to me.

I turned back and raised my brows in question.

An evil grin spread across Garrett's face. "You introduced me to Danger and Will Robinson, but you neglected to acquaint me with the other two." His gaze strayed down to my abdomen.

"Fine," I said with an impatient sigh. "But you can't make fun of their names. They're very sensitive."

He showed his palms. "I would never."

After I subjected him to a warning scowl, I pointed in the general vicinity of my left ovary, "This is Beam Me Up." Then to my right. "And this is Scotty."

Garrett chuckled and buried his face in his hands. He asked.

"Wait for me," Uncle Bob said. He'd offered to drive me home, since my foot was wrapped and packed in ice.

"Good job, Davidson," one of the officers said as I walked out. The skeleton crew that was manning the station stood and offered smiles and nods of approval. Their way of saying congratulations. After years of living on the receiving end of hostile looks and snide remarks, it was a little disturbing.

"We'll get your Jeep to you tomorrow," Garrett said, following us out. He helped me into Ubie's SUV and made sure I buckled my seat belt before closing the door. "Good job," he mouthed as we drove out of the lot. It was all getting a little creepy.

Once back in my apartment, I felt a thousand times better. I hadn't realized how tired I was. Uncle Bob helped me in and waited while I changed into my pj's so he could check my ankle one more time.

The lawyers met me in my bedroom after I'd changed.

"We did it," Elizabeth said, an excited glow lighting her face.

"Yes, we did." I stepped into her arms for a frosty hug.

"So, what now?" Barber asked.

I looked at him almost sadly. "Now you cross."

Elizabeth turned, stepped toward him. "Well, if you ever get by that way, I'm in the first grave on the right of that new addition."

He chuckled. "I'm way on the other side. My funeral was . . . nice."

"Mine, too."

"I might be wrong," I said, trying not to laugh, "so don't come back and haunt me or anything, but I'm pretty sure you guys will see each other where you're going. I have a strong suspicion friends and loved ones are very close over there."

"It's so strange," Elizabeth said. "I feel like I want to go now. Almost like I don't have a choice."

"I feel the same way," Barber said. He took her hand as if to anchor himself to the spot.

"The pull is strong," I explained. "Why do you think there aren't more of you on Earth? It's warm and it's alluring, and it's where you need to be."

They looked at each other and smiled. Without another word, they were gone.

Crossings from my perspective were a little like watching people disappear before my eyes. I felt them as they drifted through me. Their emotions. Their fears. Their hopes and dreams. But I had yet to feel hatred, animosity, or jealousy. Mostly, I felt an overwhelming sense of love. Every time someone crossed, my faith in humanity grew.

Elizabeth had left everything she had to her nieces and nephew, and a few years ago, Barber had taken out an enormous life insurance policy. His mother was going to be a very rich woman. Though I was certain she would rather have had her son, I hoped it would offer her a little comfort. He'd ended up writing his mother a letter after all, like Elizabeth and Sussman, and while his was a little less . . . poignant, I felt certain his mother would appreciate it.

I turned to Sussman. "What about you?"

He'd been staring out my window. He lowered his head. "I can't leave."

"Patrick, they'll be fine."

"I know. I'll go, just not yet."

He disappeared before I could say anything else.

"Hey, pumpkin head."

Turning to Aunt Lillian, I almost screamed aloud when I saw who she was with. Instead, I forced a smile and said, "Hey, Aunt Lil, Mr. Habersham." Mr. Habersham was the dead guy from 2B for whom I'd invented the transcendental pest repellent.

They were all googly and giggly, and I threw up a little in my mouth.

But Aunt Lillian had the sweetest look on her soft, wrinkly face. "We're going down to the Margarita Grill to smell the lobster, then we're going to watch the sunrise, and in between we'll probably have hot, unsafe animal sex."

Wh-what? Even my internal dialogue stuttered. I couldn't believe what she'd just said. Does the Margarita Grill even serve lobster? "'Kay, Aunt Lil, have fun!"

All right, I'll admit it, the thought of those two having hot, unsafe animal sex was a bit creepy, especially since my aunt didn't have any teeth, but honestly, their body temperatures were just below freezing. How hot could it get?

I hobbled back into the living room, wondering if I should tell Ubie what his great-aunt was up to, then decided against it.

"I still can't believe you did this," he said, shaking his head as he unwrapped my ankle. "You make it through a drunken bully hell-bent on rearranging your face, a ten-foot fall through a skylight, and not one, but two attempted murders, only to be brought down by a stiletto. I knew those things were dangerous."

"A genetic tendency toward mental illness is dangerous, too, but you don't see me complaining."

He chuckled and tossed the bandage onto my thrift-store sofa. "The swelling has gone down. A lot. That's amazing."

The swelling had gone down. I guess Reyes was right. I did tend to heal PDQ compared to those around me. And it took a lot to bring me down. Obviously. "You can just leave off the wrap. It feels tons better now."

"Okay, guess I'll go, then. But I had something to tell you," he said as he rose and headed for the door. "Oh, I got ahold of my judge friend. She's checking into your injunction."

Relief flooded every cell in my body. Now to figure it out from there, how to stop the state permanently, in case Reyes didn't come out of it.

"And dispatch called. Father Federico is resting well at the hospital and sends over a huge thanks. Teddy's with him now. The father would like to see you when you can stop by." He turned and headed for the door again, then stopped and scratched his head. "And the DA will start the paperwork for Mark Weir's release first thing in the morning." He started for the door again and stopped . . . again. I tried not to laugh. He was never going to make it home at this rate.

"Oh," he said. Taking out his notepad, he thumbed through it. "And it seems that assailant who tried to put you in the ground yesterday, that Zeke Herschel, was well on his way to becoming a mass murderer. You weren't the first person he went after. Thank God you put a stop to it."

My breaths stilled in my chest, my lungs seized, suddenly paralyzed, and a prickly sensation cut down my spine. "What . . . what are you talking about?"

"PD got called to his house this afternoon. We found his wife in their bedroom, marinating in a pool of her own blood."

The room dimmed and the world fell out from beneath me.

"One of the worst domestic cases I've ever seen."

I fought gravity and shock and a pathetic, panicky kind of denial. But reality swept in and kicked my ass, hands down. "That's impossible."

"What?" Uncle Bob looked up, took a step toward me.

"Herschel's wife. It couldn't have been her."

"Did you know her?"

"I . . . sort of." She couldn't be dead. I dropped her off at the airport myself. I met Herschel at the bar immediately afterwards. There was just no way it was her.

"Charley." The sternness in Uncle Bob's voice jerked me to attention. "Did you know her? Is there something else I need to know about this case?"

"You're wrong. It wasn't his wife. It must be someone else."

Uncle Bob sighed. Recognizing and dealing with denial was a daily part of his job. "It's Mrs. Herschel, hon. Worried because she hadn't heard from her, Mrs. Herschel's aunt flew in from Mexico. She ID'd the body this afternoon."

I sank onto my sofa then into myself and let oblivion take hold. I wasn't sure when Uncle Bob left. I wasn't sure if I was awake or asleep. I wasn't sure when I crawled onto the floor and curled into a blanket I had stashed in the corner. And I wasn't sure when—not the precise moment, anyway—I became the monumental fuckup I was infamous for today.

Chapter Twenty

Do not meddle in the affairs of dragons,
for you are crunchy and taste good with ketchup.
—BUMPER STICKER

No, that was a lie. I did know the precise moment I began my long and illustrious career as an utter and complete fuckup who should never have been allowed to walk and chew gum at the same time, much less be set loose on the streets of Albuquerque. I'd been in the habit of leaving death and destruction in my wake since the day I was born. Even my own mother wasn't immune to my poison. I was the very reason she died. Every life I touched, I tainted in some irreversible way.

My stepmother knew. She tried to warn me. I just didn't listen.

We were at the park—my stepmom, Denise, Gemma, and I. Mrs. Johnson was there, like she'd been every day for two months, staring into the tree line, hoping for a glimpse of her missing daughter. She wore her signature gray sweater, kept it wrapped tightly about her shoulders, as though afraid if it opened, her soul would fly out and she'd never be able to catch it. Her dingy brown hair was pulled back in a

messy bun with strays flying out of her head in every direction. Denise, in one of her more unselfish moments, sat beside her, tried to
strike up a conversation, to little accord.

Denise had warned me not to talk about the departed in public. She
said my *imagination* upset people, and on several occasions, she'd tried
to talk Dad into putting me in therapy. But by that time, Dad was beginning to believe in my abilities.

So, it wasn't like I didn't know not to talk about it. But Mrs. Johnson was so sad. Her eyes were glazed over with it, and she was turning
almost as gray as her sweater. I just thought she'd want to know, was
all.

I ran up to her with a wide smile on my face. After all, I was about
to give her the best news she'd had in a long time. After a quick tug on
her sweater, I pointed to the field where her daughter was playing, and
said, "There she is, Mrs. Johnson. Bianca's right there. She's waving at
you. Hey, Bianca!"

As I waved back, Mrs. Johnson gasped and jumped to her feet. Her
hands shot to her throat as she searched frantically for her daughter.

"Bianca!" she screamed, running forward and stumbling through
the park. I was going to lead her to where Bianca was playing, but Denise grabbed me, her face frozen in mortification as she watched Mrs.
Johnson run through the field, howling her daughter's name. She
screamed to a little boy to call the police and rushed into the forest.

Denise was in a state of shock when the police arrived. My dad had
answered the call as well. They found Mrs. Johnson and brought her
back to see what was going on. But my dad already knew. His head
was bowed in something disturbingly similar to shame. And then everyone was yelling at me. All I could see were legs and fingers and
teeth screaming my name. How could I? What was I thinking? Didn't
I understand what Mrs. Johnson was going through?

And Denise stood on the front line, crying and shaking and cursing the day she became my stepmother. Her fingernails dug into my arms as she shook me to attention, the disappointment on her face palpable.

I was so confused, so hurt and betrayed, that I withdrew into myself. "But, Mom," I whispered through my pathetic tears that meant nothing to anyone there, least of all my stepmother, "she's right there."

She slapped me before my eyes even registered movement. There was no sting at first, just a baffling force and then a moment of blackness when my mind processed the sharp crack as my stepmother's hand clapping against my face. Then I was back, nose to nose with Denise, her mouth moving in an exaggerated, angry fashion. I could barely focus on her through the flood of tears distorting my vision. I glanced through the blur at the faces of fury, the outraged expressions on each and every person surrounding me.

Then Bad was there, Reyes, his anger even more distinct than those around me. But he wasn't angry at me. If I had let him, he would have sliced my stepmother in two. I knew this like I knew the sun would continue to rise. I begged him underneath my breath not to hurt her. I tried to make him understand that what was happening was my fault. That I deserved the wrath of the people around me. Denise had warned me not to talk about the others. But I hadn't listened. He hesitated. Then, with an earth-shattering roar, he disappeared, leaving in his wake his essence, his earthy smell and rich, exotic taste.

My dad stepped forward then and took Denise by the shoulders. She shook with sobs as he led her away to his squad car. The cops questioned me for what seemed like hours, but I refused to speak about it any longer. Not really understanding what I'd done wrong, I closed my mouth and said no more. And I never called Denise Mom again.

It was a hard lesson, but one I'd never forgotten.

Two weeks later, I'd sneaked off to the park alone. I sat on the bench, watching Bianca play. She motioned for me to join her, but I was still too sad.

"Please, tell me," Mrs. Johnson said from behind me, "is Bianca still there?"

She'd scared me, and I jumped off the bench, watching her with wary concern. She looked over to where Bianca was playing in her homemade sandbox near the tree line.

"No, Mrs. Johnson," I said, edging back. "I didn't see anything."

"Please," she begged. "Please tell me." Tears streamed down her face.

"I can't." My voice was nothing more than a frightened whisper. "I'll get in trouble."

"Charlotte, sweetheart, I just want to know if she's happy." She stepped forward and knelt beside me, her breath catching in her throat.

I whirled and ran away, hiding behind a trash bin as Mrs. Johnson crawled onto the park bench and cried. Bianca appeared beside her and ran a tiny hand over her hair.

I knew better. I knew not to say anything, knew the consequences, but I did it anyway. I sneaked up and hid in the bushes behind the bench. "She's happy, Mrs. Johnson."

The woman turned to me, bobbed and weaved her head, trying to see me through the leaves. "Charley?"

"Um, no. My name is Captain Kirk." I wasn't the most imaginative being on the worldly plane. "Bianca asked me to tell you not to forget to feed Rodney and that she is sorry for breaking your grandmother's china cup. She had assumed Rodney would have had better table manners."

Mrs. Johnson's hands flew to her mouth. She stood and circled the bench, but I was not about to be slapped again. I tore out of there and headed for home, swearing never again to talk about the departed. But she chased me! She ran me down and jerked me off the ground like an eagle snatching his dinner from a lake.

I'd thought about screaming, but Mrs. Johnson hugged me to her. For, like, a really long time. Uncontrollable sobs racked her body as we sank to the ground. Bianca stood beside us, smiling and petting her mother's hair again before she drifted into me. I figured she'd told her mom what she needed her to know—apparently it had been a really important cup—and she felt she could leave. She smelled like grape Kool-Aid and corn chips as she passed.

Mrs. Johnson continued to rock me for some time before my father came in his patrol car. She stopped and looked at me. "Where is she, darling? Did she tell you?"

I lowered my head. I didn't want to say, but she seemed to need to know. "She's by the windmill past the trees. The search party was looking in the wrong place."

She cried some more, then discussed what'd happened with my dad as I watched Bad in the distance, his black robe undulating like a sail in the wind, spanning the width of three massive trees. He was magnificent, and he was the only thing I'd ever truly been afraid of my whole life. He dissipated before my eyes when Mrs. Johnson came to give me another hug, and Bianca's body was found that afternoon. The next day, I received a huge bouquet of balloons and a new bike, which Denise wouldn't let me keep. But every year on Bianca's birthday, I got a bright bouquet of balloons with a card that simply read, *Thank you*.

I learned two things from that experience: that most people would never believe in my abilities, even those closest to me. And that most people would never understand the devastating need of those left behind, the need to know the truth.

Regardless of how things had turned out, I'd caused a lot of pain that day. And a lot since. I should have made sure Rosie Herschel boarded that plane. I should have escorted her to the security checkpoint and then slipped one of the personnel a twenty to make sure she stayed put. Zeke couldn't have found her before the plane boarded. He was with me. Had she changed her mind? Surely not. She was like a kid in a candy shop, ridiculously excited about the new life awaiting her. The enormous burden of living under the constant threat of violence had already been lifted from her shoulders. No, she hadn't changed her mind. And instead of protecting my client, I was playing dodge-the-right-hook with her scum-of-the-underworld husband.

But therein lay the rub: She'd trusted me. With her life. And once again, I had let someone down in the most severe way possible.

I felt Angel standing across the room and glanced up through my lashes. His head was down, his eyes darting occasionally to my right, where Reyes sat. In the dark, I realized he was there as well, sitting patiently beside me. Not touching or demanding. Heat drifted off him like sand off a dune.

Angel wouldn't come closer. Not with Reyes so near. He was afraid of him. I was beginning to understand that Reyes wasn't the average everyday entity. He even freaked out the dead people.

I curled back into my blanket, buried my face. "You could have told me," I said to Angel, my voice muffled through the thick material.

"I knew it would upset you."

"That's why you took off for two days."

I could almost feel him shrug. "I just figured you'd keep thinking she got away. You know, that nobody would ever find her."

"On the bedroom floor in a pool of her own blood?"

"Yeah, I hadn't figured that part out yet."

"I wanted her to be happy," I said by way of explanation. "I had it all planned. She was going to open a hotel, get to know her aunt all over again, and be happier than she's ever been in her whole life."

"She is happier than she's ever been in her whole life. Just not in the way you wanted. If you could know what it's like here, really like, you wouldn't be so sad."

I sighed. For some reason, that knowledge didn't really help. "What happened?"

"She did everything right, just like you told her," he said. "She left dinner simmering on the stove. She left her purse with her wallet in it on her nightstand. She left her shoes and coat in the entryway. He would never have suspected she'd just run away. He would have thought something had happened to her."

"Then what? What went wrong?"

"Her baby's blanket."

My head whipped up. Angel was peeling paint off the side of the snack bar, doing his best not to look in Reyes's direction.

"She went back for her baby's blanket," he explained.

"She didn't have a baby," I said, confused.

"She would have, if he hadn't sucker punched her in the gut."

I buried my head again, fought the sting of tears.

"She'd knitted it. Yellow because she didn't know if it would be a boy or a girl yet. She lost the baby the night she mustered the courage to tell him she was pregnant."

My lids squeezed shut, forcing the most useless tears I'd ever cried past my lashes. The blanket absorbed them, and I wished with all my heart it would absorb me as well. Just swallow me whole then spit out the bitter bones. Why was I even on Earth? To make a fool of myself and my family? To hurt people I'd never met?

"But Zeke Herschel was in jail," I said, unable to fully accept what had happened.

"He made bail almost the minute they booked him; his cousin is a bail bondsman."

I knew that, but I never expected her to go back.

"Herschel caught her as she was leaving the house a second time. And he knew from the look in her eyes what she was doing." Angel chewed on his bottom lip a moment before continuing. "After he . . . did what he did, he found your card in her pocket and put two and two together."

A long silence ensued as I tried desperately to figure out my role on this Earth. Clearly, I was going about the whole grim reaper thing wrong. Maybe that was the problem. Maybe there was no going about it. Maybe I was just supposed to live my life without trying to help people, without trying to fix their problems, living or otherwise.

"It wasn't your fault, you know," Angel said after a while.

"Yeah," I said, my voice spent as fatigue and depression set in, "right. It was probably Rosie's fault. We can blame her."

"That's not what I meant. I just know how you are. You take everything onto your shoulders like that guy who holds up the world, and you shouldn't. You're not nearly as muscular."

"Why do you suppose I'm here?" I asked him. Angel. A thirteen-year-old departed gangbanger.

"Just 'cause you're supposed to be, I guess."

"Oh, right, I hadn't thought of it that way."

"Why do you think you're here?"

"To wreak havoc and misery upon the masses," I answered. "Duh."

"Well, if you knew . . ." A glimmer of a smile lifted the corners of his mouth.

Reyes stirred beside me, and Angel's gaze darted to him.

"Why do you suppose he's here?" I asked Angel, indicating Reyes with a nod of my head.

Angel thought about it, then said, "To wreak havoc and misery upon the masses." He left out the *duh,* and I realized he was serious.

I glanced at Reyes. His gaze was locked on to Angel, as if in warning.

"I'm outta here," Angel said. "My mom has a hair appointment in the morning. I like to watch her get her hair done."

It wasn't the lamest excuse he'd ever used, but it was pretty darned close.

"Will you just tell me next time?" I asked.

He winked at me, the flirt. "We'll see." Then he was gone.

"Why do *you* suppose I'm here?" I asked Reyes as he sat beside me. He didn't answer. Naturally. "You saved my life. Again. Are you planning on waking up anytime soon? I don't know how long I can hold the state off."

My pulse had quickened the moment I realized he was beside me. Now that we were alone, it charged headlong into warp drive, heedless of any stars lurking nearby. Reyes's energy was like a tangible thing, electric and arousing as it encapsulated my body. He hadn't moved, but I could feel him everywhere.

Trying to keep my wits about me, or at least nearby, I asked him, "What *are* you, Reyes Farrow?"

Without saying a word, he reached over and took hold of the blanket, tugged it off me, exposing my skin to his heat. I leaned toward him, ran my fingertips along the silky lines and curves that made up his tattoo. It was futuristic and primitive at once, a combination of intertwining lattice that ended in sharp tips like those on his sword and smooth curves that wound around his biceps to disappear under his shirtsleeve. The tattoo was one solid work of art that spanned his shoulder blades and spiraled over both shoulders and down both arms. And it meant something. Something big. Something . . . important.

Then suddenly I was lost. I fell in like Alice in Wonderland, stumbled along the curves, feared I would never escape. It was a map of an entrance. I had seen it before in another life, and I didn't associate it with fond memories. It felt like a warning of some kind. An omen.

And then it hit me. It was the tumbling, mazelike mechanisms of a lock that opened a realm of devastating darkness.

It was the key to the entrance of hell.

A jolt of shock snapped me back to the present. As if I'd been drowning, I broke through the surface with a gasp, filling my lungs with air. I turned to Reyes, looked at him in horror, and slowly, very slowly, started edging out of his reach.

But he knew. I'd figured out what he was, and he knew. Comprehension dawned in his eyes and he grabbed for me, the movement like a cobra strike. I tried to scramble out of his grasp, but he'd caught my ankle, pulled, and was on top of me at once, pinning me to the floor, holding me there as I thrashed about, fought for my freedom with nails scraping and teeth gnashing. He was simply too strong and too fast. He moved like the wind and thwarted my every attempt at escape.

After a moment, I forced myself to calm down, to slow my racing heart. He'd locked my hands above my head, his body, lean and hard, acting as a blockade if I should change my mind. I lay there winded, eyeing him warily, my mind racing in a hundred different directions as I panted beneath his weight. And a strange, unsettling emotion skimmed across his face. Was it . . . shame?

"I'm not him," he said through gritted teeth, unable to meet my eyes.

He was lying. There was no other explanation. "Who else bears that mark?" I asked, trying with all my being to sound disgusted instead of hurt and betrayed and more than a little dumbfounded. I lifted my head until our faces were inches apart. He smelled like a lightning storm with the promise of rain. And he was hot, as usual, almost scorching against my skin. He was also out of breath. That should have given me some consolation, but it didn't. "Who else in this world or the next?"

When he didn't answer, I tried to squirm out from under him again. "Stop," he said, his voice raw, husky, as if filled with pain. He gripped my wrists tighter. "I'm not him."

Laying my head back, I closed my eyes. He shifted on top of me, angled for a better hold.

"Who else in this world or the next bears that mark?" I asked again. I looked at him, accused him with my glare. "The mark of the beast. Who else has the key to hell branded on his body? If not him, then who?"

He rested his head against his shoulder, as if trying to hide his face. A deep sigh whispered across my cheek. When he spoke, his voice was filled with such shame, such indignation, I had to steel myself to keep from flinching. But what he said left me breathless.

"His son." He looked at me then, scrutinized my expression, tried to decide if I believed him. "I am his son."

A shock wave jolted through me. What he was saying was impossible.

"I've been in hiding from him for centuries," he said, "waiting for you to be sent, to be born upon the Earth. The God of Heaven does not send a reaper often, and each time before you, I'd felt such disappointment, such utter loss."

My lashes fluttered in confusion. How could he know such things? But perhaps the more important question was, "Why were you disappointed?"

He turned his face away before he answered, as if ashamed. "Why does the Earth seek the warmth of the sun?"

My brows slid together, trying to understand.

"Or the forest seek the embrace of the rain?"

I shook my head, but he continued.

"When I knew he was going to send you, I chose a family and was born upon the Earth as well. To wait. To watch."

After a moment, I asked, more than a little appalled, "And you chose Earl Walker?"

A corner of his mouth lifted in a half smile as his gaze traveled over my face. He released one hand, slid his fingertips over my arm to rest on my neck. "No," he said, staring at me with a feverish intensity, as if mesmerized. "A man took me from my birth family, kept me a while, then traded me to Earl Walker. Knowing I would have no memory of my past while I was human, I gave up everything to be with you. I didn't find out who I was . . . what I was, until I'd been in prison for years. My origins came to me in pieces, in fractured dreams and broken memories, like a puzzle that took decades to assemble."

"You didn't remember who you were when you were born?"

His grip on my wrists eased, but just barely. "No. But I'd done my research well. I should have grown up happy, gone to the same schools as you, the same college. I knew I would have no control over my own destiny once I became human, but it was a chance I was willing to take."

"But, you're his son," I said, trying really hard to hate him. "You're the son of Satan. Literally."

"And you are the stepdaughter of Denise Davidson."

Wow. That was a bit harsh, but, "Okay, point taken."

"Are we not all products of the world we were born into just as much as, if not more than, the parents we were given to?"

I'd heard the nature-versus-nurture argument all through college, but this was a little hard to justify. "Satan is just so . . . I don't know, evil."

"And you think I am evil as well."

"Like father, like son?" I said by way of explanation.

He shifted his body weight to the side. The movement stirred the swirling pool still growing inside me, and I fought the desire to padlock my legs around his waist and throw away the key.

"Do I seem evil to you?" he asked, his deep voice like a caress of velvet. He was busy eyeing the pulse at my neck, testing it with his fingertips, as if human life fascinated him.

"You do have a tendency to sever spinal cords."

"Only for you."

Disturbing but oddly romantic. "And you're in prison for killing Earl Walker."

His hand sank lower, skimmed over Will Robinson until it found the bottom of my sweater. Then it worked its way back up, palm skimming over bare skin, sending ripples of pleasure shooting to the most delicate nether regions of my anatomy. "That is a problem," he said.

"Did you do it?"

"You can ask Earl Walker when I find him."

No doubt he went straight to hell. "Can you go back? Can you go into hell and find him? I mean, aren't you in hiding?"

His hand eased farther up, cupped Will, teased her hardened center with his fingertips. I bit back a gasp of pleasure.

"He's not in hell."

Surprised, I said, "Surely he didn't go the other direction."

"No," he said before his head dipped and his mouth found that same racing pulse, christened it with tiny, hot kisses.

"So, is he still on Earth?" I was trying really hard to concentrate, but Reyes seemed dead set against it.

I felt him smile against my skin. "Yes."

"Oh. So, why are you hiding from your father?" I asked, breathless.

"Earl Walker?"

"No, the other one." I had so many questions. I wanted to know everything about him. About his life. About his . . . pre-life.

"Was," he said, nipping at my earlobe. The action sent shivers scampering down my spine.

"Was?" I whispered, trying to think of a distraction, something other than the waves of delight washing over my body.

"Yes. Was."

"Can you elaborate?"

"If you'd like me to. But I'd rather do this."

"Oh . . . my . . . g—"

His hand had tunneled down my pajama bottoms, slipped into my panties, and found a delicious spot to play with. I quaked visibly when his fingers brushed over the silken folds below. When he sank them deeper, I shuddered, the sensation so exquisitely intense.

Son of Satan. Son of Satan.

While his fingers continued to stroke the sensitive flesh between my thighs, his mouth—his glorious, perfect mouth—traveled south and was now nibbling on Danger. In the deepest recesses of my mind, I realized I was suddenly half naked and exposed to one of the most powerful beings on Earth. I just couldn't remember him disrobing any part of me. Did he have super-stripper powers as well as the spinal cord thing?

I wrested my hands from his grip and dug my fingers into his hair. Pulling him back to me, I kissed him with all the longing and desire I'd harbored for years. This was his kiss, the special one I'd saved for just such an occasion. I savored the smooth taste of him on my tongue as he tilted his head and delved deeper inside me, drawing on my essence, my life force.

This was the first time I'd really felt him without swimming in a sea of lust so strong, I could barely stay conscious. Not that I wasn't having a difficult time of it—I just felt a bit more in control, a bit more lucid. He was so real, so solid. This wasn't a dream. This wasn't an out-of-body experience. This was Reyes Farrow, as close to in-the-flesh as it got, considering he was in a coma an hour away.

The air undulated around us like heat radiating off a furnace. He grumbled and I helped him remove my bottoms, kicking and manipulating them down my legs. After a few moments, he broke the kiss, jerked them past my feet, and threw them at Mr. Wong.

Then he was on top of me again, like a blanket of fire, flames licking over all my girl parts, stoking and stirring my body into a frenzy of heat and desire. My hands fought off his clothes and he rose over me, his eyes drunken with sin. His wide shoulders, a wall of solid muscle, were covered in smooth, razor-sharp tattoos. Fluid and alive, they marked the boundaries between heaven and hell, so at one with his form, so natural and ethereal, they seemed to breathe when he did. I ran my palms over his chest, rigid and tempered like ancient steel, then down to his rock-hard stomach that contracted with the brush of my palms.

Finally, my hand sank farther, wrapped around his erection, my fingers barely able to encircle him. He hissed in a breath and clutched my wrist, holding it still as he fought for control. Shaking with need, he leaned back onto his knees. "I wanted this to last."

I wanted him inside me. With sore ankle forgotten, I rolled onto the balls of my feet, climbed onto him, and impaled myself, inhaling sharply, clenching my jaw with the desire that burst in my abdomen. He tensed to the density of fine marble when I slid him inside, his arms locking around me, immobilizing me when I tried to move. I gave him a minute, relishing the feel of him, the hardness that filled me to exquisite capacity. Even completely still, I hovered on the verge of orgasm, the distant sensation drawing nearer with each breath. I struggled against his hold, wanting to move, to come. Tangling my fingers in his hair, I anchored myself and pushed up with my legs, to no avail. He growled, secured me against him with his unshakable embrace.

Then, with a throaty groan, he laid me back and buried himself deeper inside me in one long thrust. I sucked in a lungful of air, held it as he eased out then back in again, his movements agonizingly slow, insanely meticulous. He tortured me for several long minutes, stopping when I came too close to the edge, pulling back when I clawed at his steely buttocks, wanting more. Slowly, he increased the rhythm, quickened the pace, lured me closer and closer to the inferno blazing in my abdomen until an orgasm exploded inside me. In one continuous rush of adrenaline, the sweet sting of orgasm washed over me, pulsing and coursing through every molecule in my body. I threw my head back, bit down, and steeled myself to ride out the wave, shuddering beneath him with the power of it.

He came moments after I did, sending a second climax bursting and spilling through my veins. But this one was different. This one was even more intense. More . . . important.

Stars exploded into white-hot supernovas in my head. Galaxies formed in my mind as I saw the universe being born. Planets were forged from raw material as gravity reached out and took what it could, manipulating and bending the elements to its will. Gases and sheets of ice became orbiting spheres, bright and incandescent against the black of eternity, while others shot through the sky at impossible speeds.

Then I saw the Earth form and its magnetosphere take shape, giving the brilliant blue orb the ability to sustain life like a shield from heaven. I saw one mass of land part and become many, and I saw the rise of the angels then the fall of the few. Led by a beautiful being, the fallen hid in stones and crevasses scattered throughout the universe, where the hottest molten rock flowed and ebbed like the seas of the Earth.

It was then, after the brief war of the angels, that Reyes was born. Nearly identical to his father, he was created from the heat of a supernova and forged from Earth's elements. He rose through the ranks quickly, becoming a great and respected leader. Second only to his father, he commanded millions of soldiers, a general among thieves, even more beautiful and powerful than his father, with the key to the gates of hell scored into his body.

But his father's pride would not be subdued. He wanted the heavens. He wanted complete control over every living thing in the universe. He wanted God's throne.

Reyes followed his father's every command, waited and watched for a portal to be born upon the Earth, a direct passage to heaven, a way out of hell. A tracker of flawless stealth and skill, he forged through the gates of the underworld and found the portals in the farthest reaches of the universe.

And then he saw me. As hard as I tried, I couldn't see myself through his eyes. All I saw was a thousand lights, identical in shape and form. But Reyes looked harder and saw one made of spun gold, a daughter of the sun, shimmering and glistening. She turned and saw him and smiled. And Reyes was lost.

Plummeting back to the present, I felt Reyes lean up on his arms, alarm evident in his expression. "I didn't mean for you to see that," he said, his voice spent, his breathing labored.

I was still quivering, shaking weakly from the climaxes that were just now waning. "That was me?" I whispered, astonished.

He lay beside me to catch his breath, rested his head on an arm, and watched. For the first time, I realized his eyes looked like small galaxies with a billion sparkling stars. "You're not going to try to run away from me again, are you?"

Too shocked to smile, I asked, "Would it do me any good?"

He lifted a solid shoulder. "If you knew what you were capable of, it might."

That was an interesting thing to say. I rolled onto my side to face him. His eyes sparkled, sated and relaxed. "And just what exactly am I capable of?"

He grinned, his handsome face—too handsome to be human—softening under my gaze. "If I told you, I would lose my advantage."

"Ah," I said, a piece of the puzzle falling into place. "The consummate general, with more tricks up his sleeve than a seasoned magician."

He lowered his chin as if ashamed. "That was a long time ago."

His body glistened beside mine, and I couldn't help but let my eyes stray to the hills and valleys that made up his exquisitely molded form. I suddenly realized he was covered in scars, some tiny and some . . . not so much. I wondered if they were a product of his life with Earl Walker or his life as a general in hell. "What did you mean earlier when you said that Satan *was* looking for you?"

He swirled a lazy finger around my belly button, creating tiny quakes that riveted straight to my core. "I mean that he is no longer looking."

"He gave up?" I asked hopefully.

"No. He found me."

My jaw dropped open in alarm. "But, isn't that bad?"

"Very."

I sat up so I could see his face better. "Then you need to hide again. Wherever you were before, you need to go there again and hide."

But I'd lost him. Something beyond my range of perception had stolen his attention. He was on his feet at once, covered in the black hooded robe. I scanned the area but could perceive none of what he was seeing. This disturbed me, especially after what I'd just witnessed. There was so much I couldn't see, so much going on around me every minute of every day that I had no access to.

"Reyes," I whispered, but almost before I'd gotten his name out, he was in front of me, covering my mouth with his hand.

His robe tingled along my skin, sparked along my nerve endings like static electricity. With eyes blazing, he shifted, liquefied, straddled two planes at once. After a moment, he let his hand drop and replaced it with his mouth in a kiss that had me shivering despite the heat that surrounded me.

"Remember," he said before he vanished, "if they find you, they will have access to all that is holy. The portals must be kept hidden at all costs."

I swallowed hard, because an urgent sadness had filtered into his voice. "What costs are all costs?" I asked, almost knowing the answer before he said it.

"If they find you, I will have to terminate your life force, to close the portal."

A jolt of shock rocketed through me. "Meaning?"

He pressed his forehead against mine, closed his eyes as he spoke. "I will have to kill you."

He dissipated around me, his essence ribboning over my skin, through my hair until only the frailest elements lingered, falling softly to the Earth. For the first time in my life, I knew what was at stake. I had answers I no longer wanted. Still, I couldn't help but feel a little betrayed, though I had no one to blame but myself.

I knew dating the son of Satan would turn out badly.

Chapter Twenty-one

*A clear conscience is usually
the sign of a bad memory.*
—STEVEN WRIGHT

"You obviously had waaaaay too much fun last night."

I tried to pry open my lids and orient myself to the environment at the same time, but I couldn't quite manage either. "Am I still naked on my living room floor?"

Cookie whistled. "Wow, you had more fun than I thought." She sat on the edge of the bed, bounced a little to irk me, then said, "I made coffee."

Ah, the three magic words. My lashes fluttered open to the blessed image of a coffee cup hovering in front of my face. I squirmed and shimmied into an upright position, then took the cup from her.

"And I brought you a breakfast burrito," she added.

"Sweet." After a long, rich draw, I asked, "What time is it?"

"That's how I know you had fun last night," she said with a chuckle. "You rarely sleep this late. Well, that and your pajamas were all over the living room floor. I picked up most of your things, but your bottoms are in Mr. Wong's corner. No way am I venturing into Mr. Wong's corner. So, are you going to spill now or later?"

With a shrug, I said, "Now, I guess, but I'll have to give you the *Reader's Digest* version."

"Deal," she said, sipping her own coffee and gazing over the rim expectantly.

"Well, I found out it takes a lot more to kill me than it does the average human."

An astonished frown commandeered her features.

"I found out Rosie Herschel never made it out of the country. Her husband killed her before he came after me."

Her frown turned to alarm.

"I found out that Reyes is a god of sex and all things orgasmic."

Now confusion.

"And I found out that he is, in fact, the son of Satan and that if they, meaning the beings from the underworld, find me, he will be forced to kill me."

Back to alarm.

"Yep," I said, thinking back, "that's pretty much last night in a nutshell. Do you think I'm psychotic?"

She blinked, worry lining her face.

"Because at this point, my sanity is all that I have. Well, that and a breakfast burrito."

She blinked some more.

"Holy smokes, is that the time?" I asked, looking at the clock.

She just glanced at it, apparently unable to talk. I couldn't imagine why. She was holding her coffee cup.

But it was almost nine. I jumped out of bed, heedless of my lack of clothing but heedful of the soreness that seemed to be fusing the vertebrae at my neck together, and rushed into the bathroom to get dressed. At ten o'clock, the state was scheduled to take Reyes off life support. If that injunction didn't go through . . .

I couldn't think about that now. Uncle Bob had a judge on it. Surely it went through.

After dressing in a dark sweater and jeans, brushing my hair into a ponytail, and downing four ibuprofen at once, I rushed to the office, where I had all the numbers on the case listed on an array of colorful sticky notes. I snatched them up, then booked out the door.

Cookie met me on the stairs, and I told her where I was headed. She mumbled something about needing a raise, but I hurried past her and rushed to the parking lot.

On the way to Santa Fe, I tried Neil Gossett at the prison, but he was out. I tried the Guardian Long-Term Care Facility, but a flustered receptionist said she couldn't give out patient information over the phone. I tried Uncle Bob, but he didn't answer. I tried the judge's clerk, where I'd filed the injunction, but she said the request had gone to the courthouse in Santa Fe.

Panic was setting in. What if the injunction didn't go through? What if the judge in Santa Fe denied the request?

At two minutes to ten, I pulled into the care facility to an array of flashing lights and bustling activity. My heart palpitated with anxiety. Maybe something happened at the facility and the state didn't get to do their thing. If that were the case, surely they would have to postpone the killing of Reyes Farrow to another day.

Then I saw Uncle Bob's SUV with the crunched-in bumper. What in the world was he doing here? The moment I threw Misery into park, my door opened.

"Your cell is dead again," Uncle Bob said, holding out a hand for me.

"Seriously?" I took it with one of mine and dug my cell out of my purse with the other. "I just called you." Sure enough. Dead as a doornail. I totally needed a new battery. Preferably one that was nuclear charged and lasted twelve years without giving me a brain tumor.

"I tried you at the office earlier," he said as I stumbled out of Misery. He sounded weird, distracted.

"I tried calling you on my way up here. You didn't pick up. What's going on?" A prickly kind of awareness laced up my spine. Ubie was acting strange. Not that strange was out of character for him, but he was acting stranger than his normal, everyday strange.

He closed my door and led the way through the melee of cops and health-care professionals.

"Uncle Bob," I said at his back, fighting to keep up with him, "did something happen to Reyes?"

"The injunction didn't go through," he said over his shoulder.

I skidded to a halt. A combination of disbelief and downright denial stole my breath as I stood there running a thousand scenarios in my head. If they took him off life support and he died, would he cross? Would he stay? Could we even have a relationship if he was departed? Maybe they would take him off life support and he would just wake up. He would be okay. I angled for a Hollywood ending with each hypothesis, hoping for what was most likely impossible.

"Charley," Uncle Bob said as he stopped and turned toward me, a hint of warning in his voice that shot my nerves to attention. "Are you telling me everything you know about Farrow?"

Something was up. That whole woman's intuition thing was tingling, among other womanly things. "What do you mean?"

"I mean, well, you told me—" He leaned in and softened his voice. "—that he's supernatural. But I thought you meant like you. Not like, you know, super-supernatural."

All I could think was, *Oh, my god*! Why was Uncle Bob asking me
such a thing? Surely Reyes was okay if Ubie suspected super-supernatural
phenomena. "So, um, why do you ask?"

"Charley," he said, his voice a warning, and my heart rate skyrocketed. He gripped my arm and began winding us through the crowd
again.

"What happened?" I asked at his back, hope evident in every syllable.
Reyes had to be alive. Something miraculous had to have happened.
Why else would Ubie ask such a question? Why else would all these
people be here?

"I don't know, Charley," he replied, his voice drenched in sarcasm.
"Nobody knows, Charley. Perhaps you can explain how a man can just
disappear off the face of the Earth."

"What?" That brought things to a second standstill. "What are you
talking about?"

Uncle Bob stopped again and turned back to me. "I knew how important this was to you, so I came up here to talk to the judge myself.
Not that it helped. She couldn't justify keeping your friend on life support when he was obviously brain-dead and it was costing the state a
fortune to keep him alive."

"You drove up yourself? For me?"

"Yeah, yeah," he said, pulling at his collar in discomfort. "So, I figured the least I could do was be here when they took him off life support. But when I arrived, the place was in an uproar. He was gone."

"Gone?" I squealed. I cleared my throat. "Gone where?"

He leaned in again, his voice a harsh, desperate whisper. "Not just
gone, Charley, disappeared."

"I don't understand. He escaped?"

"You'll have to see this for yourself."

We hastened through the front doors and into a small security room.

"Show her," he told the security officer, who obeyed immediately.

After he typed a couple of commands into his computer, I asked, "What is this?"

"Just watch it," he said.

The monitor showed footage from a security camera. I recognized the area. "Is this outside Reyes's room?"

"Just watch," he repeated, all mysterious and annoying-like.

Then I saw movement. I leaned in closer. Reyes's door was open, and the black-and-white footage centered directly into his room. He moved, raised an arm to his head, then shot up and looked around. The resolution was so low, it was hard to see anything definitive, but it was most assuredly Reyes. And he was awake. As if gaining his bearings, he calmed, took a deep breath, then turned toward the camera and smiled. He smiled! A wicked, lopsided kind of grin that had me melting into my boots.

A glitch in the footage caused the screen to go static, then black a fraction of a second, and when the picture returned, he was gone. In a heartbeat. He was literally there one moment then gone the next, his bed rumpled and empty.

"Where'd he go?" I asked the bemused security guard, who shrugged.

"I was hoping you could tell us," Uncle Bob said.

Reyes was certainly otherworldly, but the ability to dematerialize a human body simply didn't exist. At least not that I knew of. Course, I didn't figure Satan had a son until a few hours ago either. "Uncle Bob," I said, hedging away from the truth, "I didn't really tell you everything."

"Ya think?" Uncle Bob motioned for the security guard to leave.

After he was gone, I said, "It's just . . . well . . . I've *never* really told you everything."

"What do you mean?" he asked, even more perplexed than before.

"I mean, I'm different. You know that. But I've never told you exactly how different I am."

"Okay," he said, his tone wary, "how different are you?"

I couldn't imagine how telling Uncle Bob I was the grim reaper or that Reyes was the son of Satan would benefit the situation. Some things were better left unsaid.

"Let's just say that I'm more different than you know and that, yes, a part of Reyes is super-supernatural."

"Which part?"

"Um, the super-supernatural part?"

"I want more than that, Charley," he warned, stepping closer. "You have to explain this."

I eased down onto the edge of the security guard's chair, my back stiff, my jaw clenched shut. One word came to mind repeatedly. *Crapola*. How on Earth could I explain the dematerialization of a human body? If that's really what happened.

Just then, Neil Gossett walked in. His gaze landed on me instantly, then darted to Uncle Bob in a gesture of guilt, like we shared a secret. Which, in a way, we did. He just didn't have all the details.

"Mr. Gossett," Uncle Bob said, holding out his hand.

"Detective," Neil said as they shook hands. "Anything new?"

Uncle Bob looked back at me then. "Nothing substantial."

Both Ubie and Neil knew just enough to be dangerous. And neither knew the whole story. I wondered how long I could keep their questions at bay. I'd already revealed more about myself in the last week than I had in my entire life. While it was freeing in a way, it was also risky to invite so many people into my world. I'd done it before. And I'd paid the price.

"Who's Dutch?" Uncle Bob asked, gesturing toward the monitor, and my breath caught in my throat.

Though I hadn't touched it, the screen was now black. In the center sat that one solitary word followed by a blinking cursor, and relief flooded me so completely, I thought I would slide off the chair. Reyes.

Reyes Alexander Farrow was alive. I stared a long time at the nick-name he'd given me the day I was born, wondering if he could still come to me, if we could still be together. Then I felt him brush across my mouth, and I knew my life would never be the same again.

Turn the page for a sneak peek at
Darynda Jones's new novel

Second Grave
on the Left

Available August 2011

Chapter One

GRIM REAPERS ARE TO DIE FOR.
—T-SHIRT SEEN OFTEN ON CHARLOTTE JEAN DAVIDSON,
GRIM REAPER EXTRAORDINAIRE

"Charley, hurry, wake up."

Fingers with pointy nails bit into my shoulders, doing their darnedest to vanquish the fog of sleep I'd been marinating in. They shook me hard enough to cause a small earthquake in Oklahoma. Since I lived in New Mexico, this was a problem.

Judging by the quality and pitch of the intruder's voice, I was fairly certain the person accosting me was my best friend, Cookie. I let an annoyed sigh slip through my lips, resigning myself to the fact that my life was a series of interruptions and demands. Mostly demands. Probably because I was the only grim reaper this side of Mars, the only portal to the other side the departed could cross through. At least, those who hadn't crossed right after they died and were stuck on Earth. Which was a freaking lot. Having been born the grim reaper, I couldn't remember a time when dead people weren't knocking on my door—metaphorically, as dead people rarely knocked—asking for my assistance with some unfinished business. It amazed me how many of the dearly departed forgot to turn off the stove.

For the most part, those who cross through me simply feel they've been on Earth long enough. Enter the reaper. Aka, *moi*. The departed can see me from anywhere in the world and can cross to the other side through me. I've been told I'm like a beacon as bright as a thousand suns, which would suck for a departed with a martini hangover.

I'm Charlotte Davidson: private investigator, police consultant, all-around badass. Or I could've been a badass, had I stuck with those lessons in mixed martial arts. I was only in that class to learn how to kill people with paper. And—oh, yes—let us not forget grim reaper. Admittedly, being the reaper wasn't all bad. I had a handful of friends I'd kill for—some alive, some not so much—a family of which I was quite grateful some were alive, some not so much, and an *in* with one of the most powerful beings in the universe, Reyes Alexander Farrow, the part-human, part-supermodel son of Satan.

Thus, as the grim reaper, I understood dead people. Their sense of timing pretty much sucked. Not a problem. But this being woken up in the middle of the night by a living, breathing being who had her nails sharpened regularly at World of Knives was just wrong.

I slapped at the hands like a boy in a girl fight, then continued to slap air when my intruder rushed away to invade my closet. Apparently, in high school, Cookie had been voted Person Most Likely to Die Any Second Now. Despite an overwhelming desire to scowl at her, I couldn't quite muster the courage to pry open my eyes. Harsh light filtered through my lids anyway. I had such a serious wattage issue.

"Charley . . ."

Then again, maybe *I'd* died. Maybe I'd bit it and was floating haplessly toward the light like in the movies.

". . . I'm not kidding. . . ."

I didn't feel particularly floaty, but experience had taught me never to underestimate the inconvenience of death's timing.

". . . for real, get up."

I ground my teeth together and used all my energy to anchor myself to Earth. Mustn't . . . go into . . . the light.

"Are you even listening to me?"

Cookie's voice was muffled now as she rummaged through my personal effects. She was so lucky my killer instincts hadn't kicked in and pummeled her ass to the ground. Left her a bruised and broken woman. Groaning in agony. Twitching occasionally.

"Charley, for heaven's sake!"

Darkness suddenly enveloped me as an article of clothing smacked me in the face. Which was completely uncalled for. "For heaven's sake back," I said in a groggy voice, wrestling the growing pile of clothes off my head. "What are you doing?"

"Getting you dressed."

"I'm already as dressed as I want to be at—" I glanced at the digits glowing atop my nightstand. "—two o'clock in the freaking morning. Seriously?"

"Seriously." She threw something else. Her aim being what it was, the lamp on my nightstand went flying. The lampshade landed at my feet. "Put that on."

"The lampshade?"

But she was gone. It was weird. She rushed out the door, leaving an eerie silence in her wake. The kind that makes one's lids grow heavy, one's breathing rhythmic, deep, and steady.

"Charley!"

I jumped out of my skin at the sound of Cookie's screeching and, having flailed, almost fell out of bed. Man, she had a set of lungs. She'd yelled from her apartment across the hall.

"You're going to wake the dead!" I yelled back. I didn't deal well with the dead at two in the morning. Who did?

"I'm going to do more than that if you don't get your ass out of bed."

For a best-friend-slash-neighbor-slash-dirt-cheap-receptionist, Cookie was getting pushy. We'd both moved into our respective apartments across the hall from each other three years ago. I was fresh out of the Peace Corps, and she was fresh out of divorce court with one kid in tow. We were like those people who meet and just seem to know each other. When I opened my PI business, she offered to answer the phone until I could find someone more permanent, and the rest is history. She's been my slave ever since.

I examined the articles of clothing strewn across my bedroom and lifted a couple in doubt. "Bunny slippers and a leather miniskirt?" I called out to her. "Together? Like an ensemble?"

She stormed back into the room, hands on hips, her cropped black hair sticking every direction but down, and then she glared at me, the same glare my stepmother used to give me when I gave her the Nazi salute. That woman was so touchy about her resemblance to Hitler.

I sighed in annoyance. "Are we going to one of those kinky parties where everyone dresses like stuffed animals? 'Cause those people freak me out."

She spotted a pair of sweats and hurled them at me along with a T-shirt that proclaimed GRIM REAPERS ARE TO DIE FOR. Then she rushed back out again.

"Is that a negatory?" I asked no one in particular.

Throwing back my Bugs Bunny comforter with a dramatic flair, I swung out of bed and struggled to get my feet into the sweats—as humans are wont to do when dressing at two o'clock in the morning—before donning one of those lacey push-up bras I'd grown fond of. My girls deserved all the support I could give them.

I realized Cookie had come back as I was shimmying into the bra and glanced up at her in question.

"Are your double-Ds secure?" she asked as she shook out the T-shirt and crammed it over my head. Then she shoved a jacket I hadn't worn since high school into my hands, scooped up a pair of house slippers, and dragged me out of the room by my arm.

Cookie was a lot like orange juice on white pants. She could be either grating or funny, depending on who was wearing the white pants. I hopped into the bunny slippers as she dragged me down the stairs and struggled into the jacket as she pushed me out the entryway. My protests of "Wait," "Ouch," and "Pinkie toe!" did little good. She just barely eased her grip when I asked, "Are you wearing razor blades on your fingertips?"

The crisp, black night enveloped us as we hurried to her car. It had been a week since we'd solved one of the highest-profile cases ever to hit Albuquerque—the murder of three lawyers in connection to a human trafficking ring—and I had been quite enjoying the calm after the storm. Apparently, that was all about to end.

Trying hard to find her erratic behavior humorous, I tolerated Cookie's manhandling until—for reasons I had yet to acquire—she tried to stuff me into the trunk of her Taurus. Two problems surfaced right off the bat: First, my hair caught in the locking mechanisms. Second, there was a departed guy already there, his ghostly image monochrome in the low light. I considered telling Cookie she had a dead guy in her trunk but thought better of it. Her behavior was erratic enough without throwing a dead stowaway into the mix. Thank goodness she couldn't see dead people. But no way was I climbing into the trunk with him.

"Stop," I said, holding up a hand in surrender while I fished long strands of chestnut hair out of the trunk latch with the other one. "Aren't you forgetting someone?"

She screeched to a halt, metaphorically, and leveled a puzzled expression on me. It was funny.

I had yet to be a mother, but I would have thought it difficult to forget something it took thirty-seven hours of excruciating pain to push out from between my legs. I decided to give her a hint. "She starts with an *A* and ends with an *mmm-ber*."

Cookie blinked and thought for a moment.

I tried again. "Um, the fruit of your loins?"

"Oh, Amber's with her dad. Get in the trunk."

I smoothed my abused hair and scanned the interior of the trunk. The dead guy looked as though he'd been homeless when he was alive. He lay huddled in an embryonic position, not paying attention to either of us as we stood over him. Which was odd, since I was supposed to be bright and sparkly. Light of a thousand suns and all. My presence, at the very least, should have elicited a nod of acknowledgment. But he was giving me nothing. Zero. Zip. Zilch. I sucked at the whole grim reaper thing. I totally needed a scythe.

"This is not going to work," I said as I tried to figure out where one bought farming equipment. "And where could we possibly be going at two o'clock in the morning that requires me to ride in the trunk of a car?"

She reached through the dead guy and snatched a blanket then slammed the lid closed. "Fine, get in the back, but keep your head down and cover up."

"Cookie," I said, taking a firm hold of her shoulders to slow her down, "what is going on?"

Then I saw them. Tears welling in her blue eyes. Only two things made Cookie cry: Humphrey Bogart movies and someone close to her getting hurt. Her breaths grew quick and panicked, and fear rolled off her like mist off a lake.

Now that I had her attention, I asked again. "What is going on?"

After a shaky sigh, she said, "My friend Mimi disappeared five days ago."

My jaw fell open before I caught it. "And you're just now telling me?"

"I just found out." Her bottom lip started to tremble, causing a tightness inside my chest. I didn't like seeing my best friend in pain.

"Get in," I ordered softly. I took the keys from her and slid into the driver's seat while she walked around and climbed into the passenger's side. "Now, tell me what happened."

She closed the door and wiped the wetness from her eyes before starting. "Mimi called me last week. She seemed terrified, and she asked me all kinds of questions about you."

"Me?" I asked in surprise.

"She wanted to know if you could . . . make her disappear."

This had *bad* written all over it. In bold font. All caps. I gritted my teeth. The last time I'd tried to help someone disappear, which was pretty much last week, it ended in the worst way possible.

"I told her whatever her problem was, you could help."

Sweet but sadly overstated. "Why didn't you tell me she'd called?" I asked.

"You were in the middle of a case with your uncle and people kept trying to kill you and you were just really busy."

Cookie had a point. People had been trying to kill me. Repeatedly. Thank goodness they didn't succeed. I could be sitting there dead.

"She said she would come in and talk to you herself, but she never showed. Then I got this text a little while ago." She handed me her phone.

> Cookie, please meet me at our coffee shop as soon as
> you get this message.
> Come alone. M

"I didn't even know she was missing."

"You own a coffee shop?" I asked.

"How could I not know?" Her breath hitched in her chest with emotion.

"Wait, how do you know she's missing now?"

"I tried calling her cell when I got the message, but she didn't pick up, so I called her house. Her husband answered."

"Well, I guess he would know."

"He freaked. He wanted to know what was going on, where his wife was, but the message said come alone. So, I told him I would call him as soon as I knew something." She bit her lower lip. "He was not a happy camper."

"I'll bet. There aren't many reasons a woman wants to disappear."

She blinked at me in thought before inhaling so sharply, she had to cough a few moments. When she recovered, she said, "Oh, no, you don't understand. She is very happily married. Warren worships the ground she walks on."

"Cookie, are you sure? I mean—"

"I'm positive. Trust me, if there was any abuse in that relationship, it was to Warren's bank account. He dotes on that woman like you wouldn't believe. And those kids."

"They have kids?"

"Yes, two," she said, her voice even more despondent.

I decided not to argue with her about the possibility of abuse until I knew more. "So, he has no idea where she is?"

"Not a single one."

"And she didn't tell you what was going on? Why she wanted to disappear?"

"No, but she was scared."

"Well, hopefully we'll have some answers soon." I started the car and drove to the Chocolate Coffee Café, which Cookie did not own, unfortunately. Because, really? Chocolate and coffee? Together? Who-ever came up with that combination should have won a Nobel Peace Prize. Or at least a subscription to *Reader's Digest.*

After pulling into the parking lot, we pulled into a darkened corner so we could observe for a few moments without being observed. I wasn't sure how Mimi would take to my presence, especially since she told Cookie to come alone. Making a mental list of who could be after her, based on what little I knew, her husband was at the top. Statistics were hard to dismiss.

"Why don't you wait here?" Cookie asked as she reached for her door handle.

"Because we have a lot of paperwork back at the office, and that paperwork's not going to file itself, missy. No way can I risk losing you now."

She glanced back at me. "Charley, it'll be okay. She's not going to attack me or anything. I mean, I'm not *you.* I don't get attacked and almost killed every other day."

"Well, I never," I said, trying to look offended. "But whoever's af-ter her might beg to differ. I'm going. Sorry, kiddo." I stepped out of the car and tossed her the keys when she got out. After scanning the near-empty lot once more, we strolled into the diner. I felt only slightly self-conscious in my bunny slippers.

"Do you see her?" I asked. I had no idea what the woman looked like.

Cookie looked around. There were exactly two people inside: one male and one female. I wasn't surprised it was so slow, considering the freaking time. The man wore a fedora and a trench coat and looked like a movie star from the forties, and the woman looked like a hooker after a rough night at work. But neither really counted, since they were both deceased. The man noticed me immediately. Damn my bright-ness. The woman never looked over.

"Of course I don't see her," Cookie said. "There's no one in here. Where could she be? Maybe I took too long. Maybe I shouldn't have called her husband or taken the time to drag your skinny ass out of bed."

"Excuse me?"

"Oh man, this is bad. I know it. I can feel it."

"Cookie, you have to calm down. Seriously. Let's do a little investigative work before we call in the National Guard, okay?"

"Right. Got it." She placed a hand over her chest and forced herself to relax.

"Are you good?" I asked, unable to resist teasing her just a little. "Do you need a Valium?"

"No, I'm good," she said, practicing the deep-breathing techniques we'd learned when we watched that documentary on babies being born underwater. "Smart-ass."

That was uncalled for. "Speaking of my ass, we need to have a long talk about your impression of it." We walked to the counter. "Skinny? Really?" The retro diner was decorated with round turquoise barstools and pink countertops. The server strolled toward us. Her uniform matched the light turquoise on the stools. "I'll have you know—"

"Hey, there."

I turned back to the server and smiled. Her name badge said NORMA.

"Would you girls like some coffee?"

Cookie and I glanced at each other. That was like asking the sun if it would like to shine. We each took a barstool at the counter and nodded like two bobbleheads on the dash of a VW van. And she called us *girls,* which was just cute.

"Then you're in luck," she said with a grin, "because I happen to make the best coffee this side of the Rio Grande."

At that point, I fell in love. Just a little. Trying not to drool as the rich aroma wafted toward me, I said, "We're actually looking for someone. Have you been on duty long?"

She finished pouring and sat the pot aside. "My goodness," she said, blinking in surprise. "Your eyes are the most beautiful color I've ever seen. They're—"

"Gold," I said with another smile. "I get that a lot." Apparently, gold eyes were a rarity. They certainly got a lot of comments. "So—"

"Oh, no, I haven't been on duty long. You're my first customers. But my cook has been here all night. He might be able help. Brad!" She called back to the cook as only a diner waitress could.

Brad leaned through the pass-out window behind her. I'd expected to see a scruffy older gentleman in desperate need of a shave. Instead, I was met with a kid who looked no older than nineteen with a mischievous gaze and the flirty grin of youth as he appraised the older waitress.

"You called?" he said, putting as much purr into his voice as he could muster.

She rolled her eyes and gave him a motherly glare. "These women are looking for someone."

His gaze wandered toward me, and the interest in his expression was nowhere near subtle. "Well, thank God they found me."

Oh, brother. I tried not to chuckle. It would only encourage him.

"Have you seen a woman," Cookie asked, her tone all business, "late thirties with short brown hair and light skin?"

He arched a brow in amusement. "Every night, lady. You gotta give me more than that."

"Do you have a picture?" I asked her.

Her shoulders fell in disappointment. "I didn't even think of that. I have one at my apartment, I'm sure. Why didn't I think to bring it?"

"Don't start flogging yourself just yet." I turned to the kid. "Can I get your name and number?" I asked him. "And that of the server on duty before you as well," I said, looking at Norma.

She tilted her head, hesitant. "I think I'd have to check with her before giving out that information, honey."

Normally I had a totally-for-real laminated private investigator's license that I could flash to help loosen people's tongues, but Cookie dragged me out of my apartment so fast, I hadn't thought to bring it. I hated it when I couldn't flash people.

"I can tell you the server's name," the kid said, an evil twinkle in his eyes. "It's Izzy. Her number's in the men's bathroom, second stall, right under a moving poem about the tragedy of man boobs."

That kid missed his calling. "Breasts on men are tragic. How 'bout I come back tomorrow night? Will you be on duty?"

He spread his arms, indicating his surroundings. "Just living the dream, baby. Wouldn't miss it for the world."

I took a few moments to scan the area. The diner sat on the corner of a busy intersection downtown. Or it would be busy during business hours. The dead silver screen star with the fedora kept staring at me, and I kept ignoring. Now was not the time to have a conversation with a guy nobody could see but me. After a few hefty gulps of some of the best coffee I'd ever had—Norma wasn't kidding—I turned to Cookie. "Let's look around a bit."

She almost choked on her java. "Of course. I didn't even think of that. Looking around. I knew I brought you for a reason." She jumped off her stool and, well, looked around. It took every ounce of strength I had not to giggle.

"How about we try the restroom, Magnum," I suggested before my willpower waned.

"Right," she said, making a beeline for the storeroom. Oh well, we could start there.

A few moments later, we entered the women's restroom. Thankfully, Norma had only raised her brows when we began searching the place. Some people might've gotten annoyed, especially when we checked out the men's room, it being primarily for men, but Norma was a trouper. She kept busy filling sugar jars and watching us out of the corner of her eye. But after a thorough check of the entire place, we realized Elvis just wasn't in the building. Nor was Cookie's friend Mimi.

"Why isn't she here?" Cookie asked. "What do you think happened?" She was starting to panic again.

"Look at the writing on the wall."

"I can't!" she yelled in full-blown panic mode.

"Use your inside voice."

"I'm not like you. I don't think like you or have your abilities," she said, her arms flailing. "I couldn't investigate publicly, much less privately. My friend is asking for my help, and I can't even follow her one simple direction, I can't . . . Blah, blah, blah."

I considered slapping her as I studied the crisp, fresh letters decorating one wall of the women's restroom, but she was on a roll. I hated to interrupt.

After a moment, she stopped on her own and glanced at the wall herself. "Oh," she said, her tone sheepish, "you meant that literally."

"Do you know who Janelle York is?" I asked.

That name was written in a hand much too nice to belong to a teen intent on defacing public property. Underneath it were the letters *HANA L2-S3-R27* written in the same crisp style. It was not graffiti. It was a message. I tore off a paper towel and borrowed a pen from Cookie to write down the info.

"No, I don't know a Janelle." she said. "Do you think Mimi wrote this?"

I looked in the trash can and brought out a recently opened permanent marker package. "I'd say there's a better-than-average chance."

"But why would she tell me to meet her here if she was just going to leave a message on a wall? Why not just text it to me?"

"I don't know, hon." I grabbed another paper towel to search the garbage again but found nothing of interest. "I suspect she had every intention of being here and something or someone changed her mind."

"Oh my gosh. So what should we do now?" Cookie asked, her panic rising again. "What should we do now?"

"First," I said, washing my hands, "we are going to stop repeating ourselves. We sound ridiculous."

"Right." She nodded her head in agreement. "Sorry."

"Next, you are going to find out as much as you can about the company Mimi works for. Owners. Board. CEOs. Blueprints of the building . . . just in case. And check out that name," I said, pointing over my shoulder to the name on the wall.

Her gaze darted along the floor in thought, and I could almost see the wheels spinning in her head, her mind going in a thousand different directions as she slid her purse onto her shoulder.

"I'll call Uncle Bob when he gets in and find out who has been assigned to Mimi's case." Uncle Bob was my dad's brother and a detective for the Albuquerque Police Department, just as my dad was, and my work with him as a consultant for APD accounted for a large part of my income. I'd solved many a case for that man, as I had for my dad before him. It was easier to solve crimes when you could ask the departed who did them in. "I'm not sure who does missing persons at the station. And we'll need to talk to the husband as well. What was his name?"

"Warren," she said, following me out.

I made a mental list as we exited the restroom. After we paid for our coffee, I tossed Brad a smile and headed out the door. Unfortunately, an irate man with a gun pushed us back inside. It was probably too much to hope he was just there to rob the place.

Cookie stopped short behind me then gasped. "Warren," she said in astonishment.

"Is she here?" he asked, anger and fear twisting his benign features.

Even the toughest cop alive grew weak in the knees when standing on the business end of a snub-nosed .38. Apparently, Cookie wasn't graced with the sense God gave a squirrel.

"Warren Jacobs," she said, slapping him upside the head.

"Ouch." He rubbed the spot where Cookie hit him as she took the gun and crammed it into her purse.

"Do you want to get someone killed?"

He lifted his shoulders like a child being scolded by his favorite aunt.

"What are you doing here?" she asked.

"I went to your apartment complex after you called then followed you here and waited to see if Mimi would come out. When she didn't, I decided to come in."

He looked ragged and a little starved from days of worry. And he was about as guilty of his wife's disappearance as I was. I could read people's emotions like nobody's business, and innocence wafted off him. He felt bad about something, but it had nothing to do with illegal activity. He probably felt guilty for some imagined offense that he believed made his wife leave. Whatever was going on, I had serious doubts any of it had to do with him.

"Come on," I said, ushering them both back into the diner. "Brad," I called out.

His head popped through the opening, an evil grin shimmering on his face. "Miss me already?"

"We're about to see what you're made of, handsome."

He raised his brows, clearly up to the challenge, and twirled a spatula like a drummer in a rock band. "You just sit back and watch," he said before ducking back and rolling up his sleeves. That kid was going to break more than his share of hearts. I shuddered to think of the carnage he would leave in his wake.

Three *mucho grande* breakfast burritos and seven cups of coffee later—only four of them mine—I sat with a man so sick with worry and doubt, my synapses were taking bets on how long he could keep his breakfast down. The odds were not in his favor.

He'd been telling me about the recent changes in Mimi's behavior. "When did you notice this drastic change?" I asked, the question approximately my 112th. Give or take.

"I don't know. I get so wrapped up. Sometimes I doubt I'd notice if my own children caught fire. I think about three weeks ago."

"Speaking of which," I said, looking up, "where are your kids?"

"What?" he asked, steering back to me. "Oh, they're at my sister's."

A definite plus. This guy was a mess. Thanks to Norma, I'd graduated from taking notes on napkins to taking notes on an order pad. "And your wife didn't say anything? Ask anything out of the ordinary? Tell you she was worried or felt like someone was following her?"

"She burned a rump roast," he said, brightening a little since he could answer one of my questions. "After that, everything went to hell."

"So, she takes her cooking very seriously."

He nodded then shook his head. "No, that's not what I meant. She never burns her roast. Especially her rumps."

Cookie pinched me under the table when she saw me contemplating whether I should giggle or not. I flashed a quick glare then returned to my expression of concern and understanding.

"You're a professional investigator, right?" Warren asked.

I squinted. "Define *professional*." When he only stared, still deep in thought, I said, "No, seriously, I'm not like the other PIs on the playground. I have no ethics, no code of conduct, no taste in gun cleansers."

"I want to hire you," he said, unfazed by my gun-cleanser admission.

I was already planning to do the gig for Cookie pro bono—especially since I barely paid her enough to eat people food—but money would come in downright handy when the bill collectors showed up. "I'm very expensive," I said, trying to sound a bit like a tavern wench.

He leaned in. "I'm very rich."

I glanced at Cookie for confirmation. She raised her brows and nodded her head.

"Oh. Well, then, I guess we can do business. Wait a minute," I said, my thoughts tumbling over themselves, "how rich?"

"Rich enough, I guess." If his answers got any more vague, they'd resemble the food in school cafeterias everywhere.

"I mean, has anyone asked you for money lately?"

"Just my cousin Harry. But he always asks me for money."

Maybe Cousin Harry was getting more desperate. Or more brazen. I took down Harry's info, then asked, "Can you think of anything else? Anything that might explain her behavior?"

"Not really," he said after handing his credit card to Norma. Neither Cookie nor I had enough to cover our extra coffees, much less our *mucho grandes,* and since I doubted they would take my bunny slippers in trade . . .

"Mr. Jacobs," I said, putting on my big-girl panties, "I have a confession to make. I'm very adept at reading people, and no offense, but you're holding out on me."

He worked his lower lip, a remorseful guilt oozing out of his pores. Not so much an I-killed-my-wife-and-buried-her-lifeless-body-in-the-backyard kind of guilt but more of an I-know-something-but-I-don't-want-to-tell kind of guilt.

With a loud sigh, he lowered his head into his palms. "I thought she was having an affair."

Bingo. "Well, that's something. Can you explain why you thought that?"

Too exhausted to put much effort into it, he lifted his shoulders into the slightest hint of a shrug. "Just her behavior. She'd grown so distant. I asked her about it, and she laughed, told me I was the only man in her life because she was not about to put up with another."

In the grand scheme of things, it was quite natural for him to suspect adultery, considering how much Mimi had apparently changed.

"Oh, and a friend of hers died recently," he said in afterthought. His brow crinkled as he tried to remember the details. "I'd completely forgotten. Mimi said she was murdered."

"Murdered? How?" I asked.

"I'm sorry, I just don't remember." Another wave of guilt wafted off him.

"They were close?"

"That's just it. They'd went to high school together, but they hadn't kept in touch. Mimi never even mentioned her name until she died, so I was surprised at how much it affected her. She was devastated, and yet . . ."

"And yet?" I asked when he lost himself in thought again. This was just getting interesting. He couldn't stop now.

"I don't know. She was torn up, but not really upset about losing her friend. It was different." His jaw worked as he rifled through his memories. "I really didn't think much about it at the time, but quite frankly, she didn't seem all that surprised that her friend was murdered. Then I asked her if she wanted to go to the funeral, and my god, the look on her face. You'd think I'd asked her to drown the neighbor's cat."

Admittedly, drowning the neighbor's cat didn't really clue me in as much as I'd liked. "So, she was angry?"

He blinked back to me and stared. Like a long time. Long enough to have me sliding my tongue over my teeth to make sure I didn't have anything in them.

"She was horrified," he said at last.

Damn, I wished he could've remembered the woman's name. And why Mimi wasn't surprised when the woman was murdered. Murder is usually quite the surprise to everyone involved.

Speaking of names, I decided to ask about the one on the bathroom wall. Having found no foreign objects in my teeth, I asked, "Did Mimi ever mention a Janelle York?"

"That's her," he said in surprise. "That's Mimi's friend who was murdered. How did you know?"

I didn't, but his thinking I did made me look good.